McCook Community College

WITHDRAWN

A novel of retribution and transcendence
KARMA

A novel of retribution and transcendence

KARMA

Arsen Darnay

ST. MARTIN'S PRESS
NEW YORK

Copyright © 1978 by Arsen Darnay
All rights reserved. For information, write:
St. Martin's Press, Inc.,
175 Fifth Ave., New York, N.Y. 10010.
Manufactured in the United States of America

Published by arrangement with Ace Books

Library of Congress Cataloging in Publication Data

Darnay, Arsen.
 Karma.

 I. Title.
PZ4.D223Kar   [PS3554.A725]   813'.5'4   78-4404
ISBN 0-312-45085-0

PHASE I

The Origins of A Technology

1.
The Priesthood Proposition

It was one of those hot days in Washington — so humid that even the eyeballs seemed to sweat. Men walked the streets with jackets slung over their shoulders, ties loose and dangling, collars open, and faces red. Tourists stood in long, damp lines and waited to get into the White House. Cameras hung from their necks, waiting children tugged their hands, and their faces mirrored annoyance and discomfort.

One man among these tourists and strollers seemed unaffected by the weather. He approached Pennsylvania Avenue from the direction of the Elipse — a sturdy figure, stockily built, and unremarkable. If anything distinguished John D. Clark, it was his square, ox-like face with eyes a little too far apart for good looks. Jack was a bureaucrat. Although he was just barely thirty, his face already proclaimed the fact; a kind of grim, sullen expression marked his stony features. He wore a blue suit of uncertain vintage, a black tie, and black shoes. And he walked with a calm, clipped stride which suggested something of the military man.

Jack was just concluding his customary noon-time walk. He always followed the same path — twice around the Elipse, ogling the White House from a distance; then past the White House passing the tourists waiting to see the public portions of the Executive Mansion; then a jog through Lafayette Park; then back to the Department of Commerce where he worked. This June day in 1974 was no exception.

Having left the head-bobbing pigeons of Lafayette Park behind, having checked the temperature and humidity on a flashing bank sign on Pennsylvania Avenue, he approached the Department from the 14th Street side. Other civil servants had also braved the weather to go out, and up ahead Jack glimpsed his boss, Karl Hansley. Hansley returned from lunch with a tall man.

Hansley was a tiny creature, almost a miniature of a man. He was new at Commerce. He headed the Office of Energy Analysis, where people called him "Babyface" behind his back. He had been "imposed" upon the OEA from above. He had had some obscure hatchet job at the Office of Management and Budget during the first Nixon administration. People said that Hansley had burned his fingers somehow, and "they" had found a nice quiet job for him in the bowels of Commerce.

Hansley walked with a tall thin man — a dark, elongated figure wearing an expensive pinstriped suit. The tall man talked with animation, his long frame bent down toward the diminutive Hansley. He gesticulated as he walked to give emphasis to his seemingly impassioned pleading. Jack didn't know the stranger, but he guessed that the tall man was one of Hansley's school mates (Harvard) and possibly a consultant. Now that Energy was all the rage, consultants crawled out of every nook and cranny, and Hansley had a soft spot for his friends.

By the time Jack entered the dark lobby of Commerce and reached the elevators, those two were already gone — probably to take the stairs in order to save energy. Jack frowned. He had no patience with energy conservation. His work was to help the American people get all the energy they could ever want. Jack was in atomics, and he was glad he was.

Although his office was on the third floor, he went up to the fourth. In his jacket pocket lay a pair of tickets to a dinner theater performance of *Jesus Christ Superstar*. He had bought the tickets on a last, desperate impulse. The object of his desperation was a certain female section chief in the office, OEA's consumer relations officer, Evelyn Bantry, who had joined the team recently. Evelyn had resisted Jack's invitations for nearly a month. Today Jack meant to give it yet another college try. Evelyn's office was up on the fourth floor.

She had not returned from lunch. Oddly relieved — actually he didn't especially like the girl — Jack went down to his own office where he began to munch some dietary cookies in lieu of lunch.

Jack headed OEA's Contingency Planning Section — his job to find solutions to nuclear waste problems. The job belonged more properly to the Atomic Energy Commission, but in Washington those days every agency had formed its own energy arm on one pretext or another. OEA had been established recently, and Jack had transferred there from Aerospace. Commerce had a role to play. The atomic energy industry needed safe disposal sites for hot and long-lived wastes. By helping the industry find disposal sites, Commerce helped the economy expand, and helping the economy expand was Commerce's mission. Thus Jack saw his role as vital to the future of the U.S. of A. He loved his job. He had always wanted to be in atomics, ever since he had been a boy. Now at last he was close to his objective.

Munching his cookies, feet on a corner of his neat desk, he stared at a large map of New Mexico hung next to a National Guard recruiting poster. The map had been overlaid by acetate, and several areas were marked in grease pencil. Jack studied one of these areas, musing about the New Mexico Plan. But a part of his mind was still on Evelyn Bantry. And yet other strands of thought clung to Karl Hansley. In other words, Jack sat at leisure surrounded by the mental pictures of his day-to-day environment.

The New Mexico Plan was his pride and joy — and presently the only project in the newly formed section. The National Guard — it was a part time avocation. Jack was the captain and commander of a military police detachment stationed where he lived — in Alexandria. He "played soldier," as he put it, every Wednesday night. He had enjoyed soldiering during his army stint; he still enjoyed it. Service was his motto. He liked to serve the people of this nation, although he made distinctions between simple, honest folk and the less than perfect beings who ran things, higher up.

As for Evelyn Bantry — Evelyn fell in the "problem zone," as Jack put it to himself. She had come out of nowhere, one of Hansley's proteges. She had charge of all the "crazies," the people who opposed atomic power. And although Uncle paid her salary, Jack suspected that Evelyn sided with the kooks rather than with industry — an obvious reason why he should stay well clear of her. But with "that Bantry bitch" he couldn't quite help himself.

In fact, Jack was committed to another. His college sweetheart and fiancee, a girl called Betty Ham, lived back home in Kansas City. They had been separated for five years now, meeting at most three, four times a year. They had pledged to build a nest egg before settling down. Meanwhile they meant to be true to one another no matter what. And Jack had been true to Betty both in deed and thought — until Evelyn Bantry had bounced into his life.

She stood one day — less than a month ago — studying a civil rights poster in the hall. Jack passed her by on his way to the coffee room. He felt an instant something — and it was more than Evelyn's obvious sex appeal. He diverted himself into the men's room. Standing before the mirror, he squirted an aerosol-propelled mouth freshener between his jaws using a little tube he always carried. Then he went back — she was still there — and introduced himself.

Betty was on his mind in that moment, and he couldn't understand himself. Evelyn was not his kind of girl. Everything about her spoke of money. She had a soft, pampered look. She didn't wear a bra. Her breasts moved when she moved, riveting Jack's eyes. She wore an "I Voted for McGovern" button over one of her bosoms. She came from a hoity-toity family in Connecticut.

And she didn't like him especially either. That much became evident soon. Nevertheless, since that initial meeting, Jack had pursued her with dogged if hopeless persistence. And he was still doing it. The tickets to *Superstar* burned in his pocket. Betty's face hung accusingly in his mind. Yet he knew that he would try again later in the afternoon, right after seeing Hansley about a meeting at Interior.

Hansley, unfortunately, didn't seem like the kind of chief Jack thought could do the job — the tough fight over jurisdiction that loomed ahead. Hansley had no background in energy. He was politics and influence peddling. It was just Jack's luck to get a boss who played footsie with his friends, using Uncle's dollars. But truth to tell, Babyface had not yet leaned on Jack, and if the SOB ever tried — look out!

Jack dropped his feet to the floor, brushed dietary cookie crumbs from his chest and lap, stood up, did five knee bends, and then he set to work. One of his boys was in New Mexico, doing site surveys. Jack called the Shashtuk Indian Reservation and left word for Dickson to call back. Then he took up a list — members of the Interagency Committee — and began to call them one by one to arrange a meeting for a week from Monday.

He was still engaged in this task when steps approached, the door opened, and Karl Hansley walked in. Right behind him, ducking to get through the door, came the tall stranger Jack had glimpsed earlier. The man carried a suitcase of the type that fits beneath an airline seat. He set it down. Then the two men stood and talked in low tones while Jack concluded his telephone converstion.

A sick feeling spread through Jack when he saw Hansley and the stranger. From close up the gangly man looked weirder even than from a distance, and Hansley's presence with the man signalled the worst. Jack rose after hanging up. He wiped his right hand on his pants leg in anticipation of a handshake.

"Ah, Jack," said Hansley. "Meet Teddy Aspic, an old friend of mine."

Old friend . . . Jack greeted the visitor. Aspic's hand, long and narrow, was unusually hot. Huge, dark, bulging and moist eyes — oddly froglike in the thin, emaciated face — gazed coolly and pensively at Jack. Jack didn't like Aspic's calculating eyes.

"Ted is president of a west coast consulting firm," Hansley explained. He handed Jack a card. Jack read the words "Future Now" and noted the corporate symbol: A white double helix superimposed on a pale-blue parallelogram.

"Ted has come up with a very innovative idea," Hansley continued. "We chatted about it over lunch. But as I said to Ted, you're our real expert on nuclear waste around here, Jack, so he should bend your ear rather than mine." Jack nodded; Hansley was avoiding his eyes. Hansley then stepped back and clapped his hands together. "Well," he said, "why don't I let you two talk this thing over. Jack, get back to me on this. Let me know what you think." Hansley turned to Aspic. "Hey — it was fun, Teddy. We should do this more often. Give my love to Helen — and bring her east one of these days. I've got to run. Check with me later, Okay? Jack, see you." With that, waving, Karl Hansley was gone.

Feeling ill at ease and on his guard, Jack turned to Aspic. He still held the card in his hand. He glanced at it. "So you're from California," he said, offering Aspic a seat with a gesture.

But Aspic was not ready to sit down. He nodded. His eyes were on the New Mexico map. "Yes," he said. "I'm from that general neighborhood." He pointed to the map. "Karl tells me that you've got a project going out our way — on the Shashtuk Indian Reservation."

Jack hesitated before responding. He didn't know what Aspic wanted and didn't want to open himself for attack. The last thing he needed now was interference in that project from a west coast kook.

"Not a project exactly," he said, "or at least not yet. We're trying to find a site — the ideal site — for a big nuclear waste disposal complex. The site that Hansley mentioned is out here." Jack pointed to an area outlined in red. "It's on the edge of the Shashtuk reservation, and everything looks good. No people to speak of. The groundwater is so far down it can be disregarded. And the geology is as close to perfect as we've seen anywhere. But there are problems."

"Institutional problems," Aspic said, and his moist, penetrating eyes gazed at Jack.

"I guess Hansley told you."

"No," Aspic said. "I was just guessing. The problems are always institutional these days. The Indians, I suppose, don't want the facility."

"No. It's the other way around. The Indians want it. It would mean jobs for them. But the Bureau of Indian Affairs is dead set against it. They've lined up with the AEC against us. AEC doesn't want Commerce meddling in the atomics business. Interior is neutral. It doesn't want to override the boys at Indian Affairs, not unless it can get a piece of the glory. So it's a deadlock situation."

"How do you plan to resolve it?"

"Oh," Jack said, "we're still just getting our ducks in a row." He gestured again, inviting Aspic to sit. He hoped he hadn't said too much.

Aspic settled his enormously tall frame into the narrow space between the wall, the desk, and the door. Jack sat down as well. He stared across his neat desk at the west coast consultant. The time had come to see just what the damage was.

"Well, Mr. Aspic, what can I do for you?"

"Let's make that 'Teddy,' shall we? — The question, Jack, is what Future Now can do for the OEA. Let me tell you a little bit about us. And then I'll lay an idea on you. Is that all right?"

Jack nodded. Then he leaned back in his chair and folded his arms across his chest.

Aspic began. Jack listened; he formed a picture of this character as Aspic explained himself. He was a physicist — Harvard and then MIT. He had worked for General Electric for a while, at the Schenectady R&D center. But life in the big corporate structure had not appealed to Aspic — it had been too confining, not enough scope for creativeness, no freedom to deal with the really important issues of the day. So Aspic had made a decision to go out and set up his own company — "where I can do what pleases me," he said, "rather than what pleases my boss." Future Now had caught on right away, Aspic said. The market was right for a really creative consulting service. Future Now specialized in the "far reconnaissance," he said. "Our bag is futurology but applied to present day problems. We reach out into the future, as it were, conceptualizing possibilities. Then we bring those concepts back into the present and integrate them into the day-to-day routines of our clients."

Which has nothing much to do with me, Jack thought. Aspic had come into proper focus — a rich boy with the right connections who played his own games with other people's money. Jack's cheek muscles stiffened. He stole a look at his watch. Aspic, meanwhile, went through a listing of Future Now's clients — blue chip companies and big federal agencies.

"As you can see," Aspic concluded, "we've been supported by the best. We're not as kooky as we sound." Saying this, Aspic smiled, and his eyes were filled with a peculiar knowing.

Jack squirmed uncomfortably. Aspic made him feel ill at ease, inadequate. No. Not inadequate — angry. Aspic had nerve coming in here off the street and squandering Jack's valuable time with far-out west coast speculations . . . because he knew Karl Hansley and had "access" to the bureaucracy.

"You said you had an idea you wanted to discuss." Jack's tone was flat and conveyed impatience. *Get on with it*, his voice implied; *get to the bottom line*.

Aspic nodded. "As I said a moment ago, we're interested in the longer range — the far-out reconnaissance. A little while back we made a list of long range issues we should be tackling, things with a good time horizon. And of all the things we came up with, one item really stood out."

"Nuclear waste disposal."

"Precisely. We started to do a little homework. And

we soon understood that we really had our hands on something."

"Why? Because of the long half-lives?"

"Yes. Just take Plutonium-239. You're dealing there with a material that stays atomically active for about 250,000 years. That's a hell of a long time — even for Future Now."

Aspic now bent down toward his suitcase. Jack heard the sound of a zipper, the sound of papers rustling. Then Aspic straightened up again holding a sheaf of Xeroxed pages fastened by a paper clip.

"I don't know if you believe in fortuitous coincidence, serendipity, what have you," Aspic said, "but just as we were toying with some solutions, one of our people came across this article." Aspic waved papers. "Article by Dennis Farney in the *Smithsonian Magazine.*"

Jack nodded curtly. He knew the article. It was entitled "Ominous problem: What to do with radioactive waste." Half of the congressional mail had dealt with that article lately — a surfacy but clever survey of the field. Jack wondered how on earth Aspic could get an idea from Farney's piece.

Aspic was leafing through the sheets, searching for a specific spot.

"You know how it is," he said. "The same ideas seem to come to different people at the same time. While we were toying with institutional solutions for long term care — call it perpetual care — Farney wrote this thing." Aspic paused, reading. "Ah, here it is. Page twenty-four. Farney writes here — let me read it to you: 'Some have seriously proposed that society create a new kind of "priesthood" to watch over the waste, much as medieval monks watched over mankind's written history in the Dark Ages. Presumably, this priesthood would have to be supranational in character and somehow insulated from the rise and fall of nations through the centuries.'"

Aspic looked up questioningly.

Jack stared right back. A tightness had formed in the pit of his stomach. Suddenly he felt a powerful revulsion. This guy, this rat, this conman! Jesus key-ryst! He wouldn't actually propose now, would he, that . . . Even Congress had overlooked that paragraph of Farney's piece . . .

"What conclusion do you draw from all that," he asked, his voice tight and almost quavering with repressed emotion.

The dark moist eyes looked away, at the wall. "We've been thinking about a feasibility study."

"The feasibility of what?"

"Of setting up such a priesthood."

"Are you serious?"

"It's not as crazy as it sounds at first," Aspic said. "Jack, I reacted much as you did when my people came up with this. But I mulled it over, did a bit of scratching on a pad, and the more I looked at it, the better I liked it."

Horseshit, Jack thought. Then emotions carried him away.

"The idea stinks," he said, eyes flashing. "You're wasting your time — and mine."

The statement was out, pronounced with vehemence, before Jack knew that he had spoken. He regretted it instantly and began to soften the statement. But at that point Aspic suddenly shuddered. His eyes seemed to go out of focus. And he covered his face with his hands.

"Are you all right?" Jack asked.

Aspic shook his head, face still covered, bent over, seemingly fighting for control. But his motion signified neither agreement nor denial. It was a way of telling Jack to wait.

Aspic remained in that peculiar posture for another second or two. Jack didn't know what to do. He made a motion, almost rose; but by that time Aspic freed his face, straightened his frame, and shook his head.

"Fine," he said, giving Jack a delayed answer. His eyes were still out of focus. "Damnable sinuses. I had a sudden pain here." Aspic touched the bridge of his nose. "It's something genetic. It runs in our family."

"It's the humidity around here," Jack said. He sounded mild now, almost solicitous. He wasn't sure that Aspic had a sinus colic. Sinus colics didn't strike like seizures. He suspected rather that his own words had somehow touched a nerve. Aspic could be an unbalanced character, some sort of unstable genius. More than ever Jack regretted what he had said. He uncrossed his arms, leaned forward, and proceeded to undo the damage as best he could, his mind on Karl Hansley. Babyface might not take kindly to uncouth treatment of his friends.

"The humidity," he said, "plus all the pollution and the pollen — I'm not surprised that your sinuses are acting up. But back to your idea, about that priesthood thing. I guess it's the kind of idea that shakes you up a little. I mean, you know, it's a little far out. What exactly would you study?"

Aspic had dug out a handkerchief. He made a good deal of to do about blowing his nose, wiping his nose, folding the handkerchief again, putting it away. Yet he had had no need to blow his nose, Jack was sure of that. The whole procedure was nothing but a cover-up. For what? Epilepsy?

Aspic sniffed. Then, seemingly recovered again, he gestured and said: "You're right, of course. It is a kind of shocking idea. And you're right — maybe I'm wasting my time. But Karl didn't think so. I guess that's the only reason I am down here talking to you." The moist eyes gazed.

Aspic's words cut — they really cut. The west coast conman knew how to hurt you. Karl this, Karl that!

Jack felt that tightness in his guts again, but this time he kept his cool.

"Maybe I don't understand what you're getting at," he said. "I guess you'd better tell me more."

Aspic bent down to put his papers away. "Mind you," he said, straightening again, "you might be right, Jack. I don't claim to have all the answers. You have very real problems to deal with. Now. Today." Aspic gestured toward the New Mexico map. "Like getting that site approved. All I ask is that you give this idea a little consideration. Nobody plans far enough ahead. It's time somebody did. And if you really think about it, a priesthood isn't such a terrible idea. Think about it this way: the most enduring human institutions are religious. They have staying power. They outlive national organizations — or at least they've done so in the past. Can you guarantee that there'll always be a United States? I don't want to suggest that anything drastic will happen, but face it — 250,000 years is one hell of a long time. Even the Buddhists don't go that far back. Future generations have to be protected. Cheap electric power today could mean genocide in some future time."

Jack was not inclined to argue. "You've got a point there," he said mildly.

"Exactly what Karl said. He said it was worth an exploration. If it flies, fine, if it doesn't, not much lost."

"How much would such an...exploration cost?"

Aspic scratched unruly, prematurely greying hair; he screwed up his face. "A hundred thousand? Say eighty to a hundred thousand."

And if I don't blink, Jack thought, *he'll tell me that that's for Phase I. Well, time enough to kill this little monster later.*

Jack rose, "Look," he said, "why don't we leave it like this. You put together something. Just a few pages. Flesh out the idea a little more. Tell me what you'd like to do. I'll take a look at it, talk to Hansley about it, and we'll take it from there."

Aspic also rose. "Fine," he said. "That's all I ask. A fair consideration."

2.
Evelyn

An atomic priesthood to watch the wastes —for crying out loud, Jack thought. The elevator doors slid shut, hiding Aspic from view. Jack shook his head and turned toward the men's room down the hall.

What'll they come up with next? I can see them —on their knees before an altar, and on the altar a glass bubble filled with Plutonium-239. How can a grown man even think such foolishness . . .

Walking, he shook his head again, his mind a conundrum of irritations — with the press for suggesting crazy notions; with consultants who studied anything at all; with big political cheese-niks who pandered to such consulting greeds; and with the ignorant public for letting it all happen and paying all the bills.

In the men's room he washed his hands with a little more vigor than usual — to get that man's smell off his skin. Then he squirted Mouthfresh into his oral cavity and went to see Evelyn Bantry.

At this time Evelyn was taking a break. Seated with her feet up on the corner of her desk, reclined in a swivel chair, head half turned toward her window, she was caught up in a conversation on the telephone. Richard was on the line, one of her intimate friends. Richard had just returned from a trip to Japan, and he amused her now with anecdotes about the Japanese, promising to tell her all the really juicy parts tonight. They planned to meet for early tennis to be followed later by what Richard had termed Ooh-la-la.

Evelyn was an ample female. Today she wore checkered and bell-bottomed slacks of pink and white, tan sandals without socks, a white silk blouse, and — because the blouse was rather on the translucent side — she also wore a brassiere.

Sunshine and a mass of leaves formed the backdrop to her reclining figure as seen from the door. The furniture in her office was standard grey stuff, but she had placed her own Persian carpet before the desk, her own vivid prints decorated the walls, and in the regulation bookcase reclined her own books separated by her own African carvings.

Evelyn laughed, sounding like a bell, head thrown back, and for a moment her golden hair, tossed by movement, caught a bit of sun. "Did they really?" she asked. "Oh, that's too much."

Then she heard steps approaching down the flagstoned hall outside; she recognized their sound, and her manner abruptly changed. The soft lines of her peachy cheeks took on a harsh and angular expression. Her eyes darted a glance of apprehension toward the door. She took her feet off the desk and tried twice to interrupt the flow of Richard's chatter on the other end of the line.

Now the door opened and Jack walked in. He stopped just inside the door and looked at Evelyn. She glanced at him and then down on the surface of her desk. "Richard . . . " she tried again, but Richard kept going.

Evelyn was much perturbed by seeing Jack stand inside her door staring at her "like a wooden Indian," as she put it to herself. He always caused a rage to rise in her, a rage tinged with a little fear — although she didn't let herself perceive the fear. When she had come to Commerce from a reporter's job at the *Washington Post*, she had expected challenges, but she had not expected anything like Jack. Nor could she understand why, after nearly a month of this . . . this persecution, she didn't take more vigorous steps to rid herself of Jack. A single call would do the trick. So why didn't she call Hansley? Because she had no need for help — not really. But was that really true?

"Richard," she said finally, "someone just came into my office. I've got to go. Let's continue this later. Okay?" She listened to Richard's parting comments, laughed without mirth, said good-bye, hung up, and then she looked up.

"Hi," she said flatly. "How are things in Contingency Planning." She saw annoyance on Jack's face. He wore a blue suit — it seemed he only had blue suits. He came forward stiffly and sat down on the edge of the single visitor's chair placed in the center of the Persian rug.

"You know why I'm here. Let's talk about Saturday night."

"Broken record time," Evelyn said. "I'll say this for you, Jack. You're persistent."

He reached into his jacket pocket and pulled out a pair of tickets. "I'd like to take you out to dinner, Evelyn. Just once. You can't possibly object to that. I took the liberty," he said, showing her the tickets. "*Superstar* is playing in Arlington again. I'd like you to come."

Evelyn looked at the tickets rather than at Jack. She

saw oblong yellow pieces of slick cardboard printed with shiny ink.

"Why can't you take no for an answer?"

"Just give me *one* chance."

"Jack, I've said this to you so goddamned often, I'm sure it sounds like a broken record — but we haven't got anything going for us, you and I. I haven't got anything against you. I might even like you if you weren't such a pest. But beyond that — it just won't work. Do yourself a favor. Give it up. People are noticing. You're becoming a laughing stock."

"I don't mind."

Evelyn picked up a pencil. She bent it between her hands. Then she threw it on the desk.

"I'll say it again," she said, sounding firm but resigned. "We come from different backgrounds; we have different interests. We look at things differently. Even the way you want me to 'give you a chance' is — hell, it's such an alien approach. Alien for me. I just don't think that way. I'm not some kind of prize that you can win. Don't you understand that? I'm not property. I am a person."

"So am I," he said. "That's why I'd like you to give me a chance. To get to know me. Afterwards, if you say go, I'll go. So help me God."

Evelyn's lips worked in exasperation. She began speaking once or twice with little intakes of breath but stopped again with an inward smile and a shake of her head. She tried to be mature, but it just wouldn't work. She couldn't silence him by silence.

"I know you, Jack," she said. "I've known you for a month. You forced yourself on me the day I arrived. And I've seen you every day since then, not counting your telephone calls. You've embarrassed me with your attention. People have told me all about you. I know you better than any other person in OEA — man or woman. And I know this — you're a fanatical, singleminded, pushy, aggressive — Look, I'm tired!

Okay? I'm tired of seeing you sit there like a wooden Indian, insisting. You might have gotten where you are by sheer staying power, Jack, but I'm not some kind of thing. If you really care for me at all, you'll leave me alone."

She realized that she was close to tears. Suddenly she really *was* tired, tired beyond all fatigue. His big, square face hung there in the air. His little eyes looked at her with a steady stare . . .

"You hate me, don't you?"

"No . . . I . . . don't!" she cried; her feelings were taking over; her command was slipping. "Goddammit, Jack, I don't. I should. You're really a vile person. You know that? You've got no sense of decency — that's right. You can't leave well enough alone. You're not a gentleman, far from it. I come to work — there you are, lurking by the elevator. I slip out to have lunch — guess who sits down on the stool next to mine. You're calling, calling, calling — my girl snickers when she tells me that you're on the line. And you can't even leave me in peace at home — flowers, little notes. You're boorish and insensitive and a great big bore! But I don't hate you, buddy. I don't feel that strongly about you. All I wish is that you'd leave me alone."

"I come from the wrong class — that's it, isn't it?" Jack asked, and Evelyn saw pin-points of hate in his eyes.

"What's class got to do with it?"

"Everything," he said. "My daddy was a Kansas farmer — so I'm not good enough for fancy Evelyn Bantry from the New England Establishment."

"See what I mean?" she cried. "You're vile."

"I'm just telling it like it is — you ought to like that. Let it all hang out. Right on! Let's have a 'dialogue.' Let's rap! How come you love the little people so and when a 'little people' asks you for a date, you've got a 'different background.' That's class prejudice, Evelyn."

She was speechless with rage.

"So I'm supposed to go out with you because your daddy was a farmer—and because I was born in Connecticut?"

"You went out with Jackson just because he's black."

Her eyes blazed fire. She could feel her heart thumping in her throat. Her hands were cold and clammy. "Freddy is a sensitive and gentle person."

"And makes you feel generous and liberated and God knows what else—'with it,' I suppose," he said. "But you don't even give me the time of day. I don't need coddling, do I? I'm just a regular guy, lily white and protestant and from the provinces. So I get the back of Evelyn's hand and I'm a boor for sending her flowers or happening to be at the elevator when she arrives. Once," Jack said, holding up an index finger. "It happened once. And you make it sound like I persecute you. But when Jackson comes jiving in here, snapping his fingers and rolling his black eyes, why, then Evelyn Bantry can hardly wait to toot off in that there snow-white Cadi-lac!"

"Get out," she hissed.

"All right," Jack said, rising. He still held the tickets in his hand and for a second he looked at them absently. "All right," he repeated. "But I'll be back. Maybe tomorrow you'll be in a better mood."

For a second only, Evelyn felt relief beneath the seething rage he had aroused in her. She watched him turn toward the door. He moved very slowly, expecting her to stop him. She wished that he would just go—just *go*! She wished that he would remove himself from her sight—and not just for this moment, either, but for all eternity.

Jack had almost reached the door when, like a shock, Evelyn understood—viscerally and not just in her intellect—that Jack's going now wouldn't end the persecution. He would be back. Indeed, he would! And again, and again, and again. She couldn't stand the thought of that. She had to do something, anything — even if it meant to yield.

"All right," she cried. Her face had turned into a mask of hatred. Then she pulled herself together. He stood at the door. He waited. "All right, Jack," she said. She looked down at her desk. Her voice was barely audible. "I'll go with you. You've won. It's done." She looked up at him. "I'll go with you because I'm sick and tired of your constant persecutions. Saturday evening is all yours. But remember this — you forced me into it. And I resent that, Jack. Understand? I resent it."

He stared at her for a moment. His eyes expressed doubt. "All I want is a chance."

"You'll have it," she said. "But that's all you'll have, buddy. One date — to show you that I haven't got any ... prejudice. And then you'll fish on your side of the lake and I'll fish on my side. You can bet on that."

"All right, Evelyn," Jack said. He didn't look at her. "All right," he repeated. Then, still holding the tickets in his hands, he left the room.

3.
The Creative Consultant

By the time Jack reached his own office again on the third floor of the Commerce building — feeling a little triumphant because of his success with Evelyn ... and also a little depressed by the way in which Evelyn had yielded — he had forgotten all about Theodore J. Aspic III.

But Aspic had not forgotten Jack. Quite the contrary.

After the two men parted at the elevator, Aspic found a bathroom on the first floor, but he didn't use it in any of the usual ways. He simply stood before the mirror and looked at his own face, searching his features, eyeing himself anxiously. At one point he leaned as close to the glass as possible and peered intently into his own large, moist, and slightly bulging eyes. Apparently he noted nothing unusual; he shrugged skinny shoulders covered by expensive pinstriped fabric, and then on an impulse, he also washed his hands and also with unusual vigor.

Thereafter he caught a cab and rode out to Dulles airport by way of scenic George Washington Parkway along the Potomac. At Dulles he found a bar, ordered a double gin over rocks and consumed the drink quickly. He drank a single after that, paid, and was just in time to catch one of the huge mobile vans that took passengers to the jumbo jet. He was booked to fly first class, and consequently before the plane had even taken off the stewardess already had his order for more gin on ice and a lemon twist. Only after take-off, having added the airline gin to his earlier intake, did Aspic feel reasonably comfortable.

He was not a heavy drinker, and his behaviour this afternoon was quite unusual. But he had had a harrowing experience in Jack's office, and it had called for drastic countermeasures.

Aspic was not so naive a man as to have imagined that the priesthood proposition would be an easy sell. And he was far too tough and experienced a person, despite his relative youth (like Jack, he was just thirty years of age) to be put off by a little hostility.

He was anything but naive. "Brilliant," "brainy," "innovative," and "seminal" were the adjectives usually applied to him. His business acumen also got high marks. An unsympathetic associate at General Electric had put it like this: "Imagine a brain like Einstein's inside the skull of a piranha, and you'll have some small idea of Aspic in tight corners."

Aspic had anticipated problems at Commerce. In point of fact, the very absurdity of the priesthood idea challenged his inventiveness. Future Now specialized in "far reconnaissance." Future Now did its best work on "synthetic" projects where hard and soft disciplines had to be artfully blended. Study of an "atomic priesthood" combined these features — and if the bureaucracy had to be bent a little before it coughed back some of Aspic's taxes for creative research, so much the better. Aspic enjoyed bending bureaucracies.

Aspic's problem that afternoon had little or nothing to do with the priesthood notion. It had some murky connection with Jack Clark, but Aspic could not discover exactly how. And in any event, he now reflected groggily, the problem went back to the past, to Bobby Bell and acid trips . . .

Bobby Bell had been a love affair — not the first nor even the most recent, but certainly the weirdest ever. Aspic had met Bobby in Los Angeles late in 1971 in the course of a joint UCLA-Future Now project. Bobby (for Rebecca) was a professor at the University. She specialized in urban studies. She was the perfect antidote to robust, athletic Helen at the time — a flakey creature marked by wilting, far-out sensuality. Cheeks a little saggy, eyes a little rayed, long mournful breasts, baggy buttocks. She wore copper bracelets on both of her wrists and had her fingers into everything occult.

She introduced Aspic to LSD at the peak of their romance. She believed in reincarnation and swore to him that he could retrace his past lives under the drug's influence. Aspic had laughed at her at first, but later he dropped acid, impelled by curiosity.

His recollections now turned around his experiences with LSD. His acid trips had been dreadful . . . wonderful — ecstatic, twisted, oozing, mind-blowing and, at the end, terrible. The last session was what jargon called a bum trip. It had sent Aspic screaming from wall to wall in the bare room they had used for these experiments. The vision showed a concentration camp. Aspic was confined there. He was a Jew, a prominent doctor. He cleared forest land to make room for a road. At the end he had been killed somehow, and in the vision he had experienced his own death.

The vision had been powerful and loathsome enough so that Aspic had immediately broken up with

Bobby Bell and had not touched LSD since. For a while after that, the concentration camp had played a role in his nightmares, but for better than two years now he had not even thought about it.

And therein lay the problem. This afternoon, seated across from Jack, that vision had recurred to him as sharply as during that final session in Bobby Bell's guest room. It had all come compressed into a span of four or five seconds, and implausible though it seemed, Jack's eyes seemed to have started it.

Aspic reclined his seat, settled into the cushions, and closed his eyes. The alcohol had hit him like a rubber hammer. He pursued his thoughts a little longer. LSD visions *did* recur sometimes. That concentration camp scene had been a scene of hatred. Clark's eyes had flashed with menace. The mind worked by associations . . . Aspic fell asleep.

He slept deeply. Stewardesses served a meal. Then the shades were pulled and a movie was shown. Still Aspic slept. He awoke when the movie ended and bright sunlight flooded the smokey cabin as the stewardesses opened the shades. Aspic's first thought upon awakening was about Cam Templar, and he guessed he had been dreaming about Templar beneath the level of awareness.

He looked out the window. From the 747's nearly stratospheric altitude, the Rocky Mountains, now flattening slowly toward the west, looked like the uneven scales of a giant brown lizard. Empty land . . .

What about Templar? he asked himself. *Why does he pop into my mind? What does he have to do with it?*

By "it" Aspic meant his Washington experience. Its residues still pressed upon his mind much as the alcohol still heated his blood.

A moment later he recovered the thought that he had had just before awakening. He would ask Templar about the experience. Templar might have some insight or explanation.

Aspic's relationship with Camilio Ezra Templar might be explained by his unusual, some said "crazy" approach to research, his penchant for "synthesis." It was the most unlikely of associations.

Templar was a mystic, astrologer, a palmist, and a "sensitive." He did not look the part. He lacked all presence and "magnetism." He was no cult leader, no personality. He was not even from the east. Templar was a short, pudgy, and nearly blind little man. His face had a pasty pallor Aspic associated with the diet of the lower middle class. Templar was nearly blind and consequently wore glasses the thickness of fruit jar bottoms. He had virtually no chin, and his short, stubby nose was so arranged that his nostrils seemed to look at you. He was a timid, diffident man and some years Aspic's senior.

Aspic had met Templar at a party, seemingly by chance. The time was December 1973, and the occasion a giant bash, one of those "once-a-year" Christmas receptions. Aspic bounced about, a drink in hand, among total strangers. He moved from place to place in search of congenial company. Helen huddled with the sporty crowd somewhere. Aspic heard her voice boom loudly about backhand swings. He drifted off toward a lower level and found, in a corner, a group seated in a circle.

The guests were oddly still. They sat in chairs or on the floor, their drinks forgotten, their eyes fixed on a fattish, sallow man. A woman sat on the floor before the man, her hand extended toward him, and Cam — for the man was Templar — read her palm.

Aspic stopped in the entry and leaned against the door post. He listened with a small smile on his lips, gently swirling the ice in his glass. The palm reader didn't fit into this fashionable crowd, and Aspic guessed that the man had been invited purely for his entertainment value. Harmless, in a way. The latest ... rationality was just a thin veneer. Beneath a skin of enlightened sophistication, all men were true believers. They feared black cats and shunned the Number 13.

Templar discussed the character of guest after guest while Aspic listened. But Aspic knew few of the guests. He couldn't tell whether the palmist had hit or missed the mark. But Templar seemed to be making the right statements. People nodded as they listened. "So right, so right," they murmured. "How *ever* did you know," giggled a woman. "Hey," cried a man, "I don't think I *want* my fortune told. This guy is weird."

Aspic was sufficiently drunk and curious so that, when an occasion presented itself, he advanced toward Templar, a self-consious grin on his face. He lowered his long frame to the floor and held out his long fingers.

"Well, my friend," he said, "What do you make of that?"

By tone and manner he tried to convey that he took this matter very lightly, as a kind of joke.

Templar's hands were cold and moist, unpleasant to the touch. From close up it was obvious that the man had trouble with his eyes. He leaned down over Aspic's hands and peered at the lines with concentration through thick lenses. Then he rolled up Aspic's fingers, unrolled them again, and felt the ball of Aspic's thumb with a cold index finger. Finally he resumed his perusal of the lines.

At long last he looked up. "I don't think I should read your hand at this time," he said a little stiffly. He had a soft but high-pitched voice.

The guests let out a protesting outcry.

"Now, wait a minute," Aspic said with a forced laugh. "It can't be all that bad!" He glanced about with a sporting grin.

"It isn't," Templar said. "No. No, it isn't. You have a very interesting hand. Very interesting. But . . . "

The guests waited for him to finish, but he said no more.

"But?" Aspic prompted.

Templar squirmed. He was visibly uncomfortable and on edge. He had let go of Aspic's hand, had taken off his glasses, and now he rubbed them with a paper napkin.

"I — some hands reveal a great deal about the future. It is . . . " Templar squirmed. Then, evidently he screwed up his courage. "I have a professional rule about such things. Some hands can't be read except in absolute privacy."

The man's discomfort and the naive, pompous sincerity of his tone sent a chill through Aspic. It seemed to him that Templar had seen glimpses of his private life he would as soon keep hidden — even from these strangers. He had a strong impulse to withdraw. But, of course, he couldn't do that. He was in a social situation and had to maintain a modicum of face. So he attacked.

"Hey," he cried. "What is this? Some sort of a sales pitch? What do you expect me to do? Come to your studio to find out the big secret? Come on," he concluded, holding out his hand again, "just give it a whirl, will you!" Then with a glance at the guests: "You've got all these people wondering."

"I'll be more than happy to give you a free reading. But not . . . not under these circumstances."

"Later? — Oh, I see. You want to do a bit of research about me. Ask around, eh? Listen to some conversation, things like that? So that's how you do it!"

"Not at all." Templar was visibly offended. "I am prepared to give you a reading immediately. But not in front of witnesses."

"All right, my friend," Aspic cried, rising. "I'll just take you up on that. Where do you want to do it? Out in my car?"

"Fine," Templar said. "If you insist."

The guests groaned.

Aspic turned to them. "Sorry, ladies and gentlemen," he said, half bowing. "But I just can't let this . . . gentleman . . . challenge me without, well rising to the challenge."

He led Templar to a silvery Mercedes, unlocked the door, got in, and waited until Templar too had settled. Then he turned on Templar with something approaching fury.

"You made an ass out of me in there," he said, a long finger shaking. "Don't you have any more diplomacy than that? If you saw something in my hand, whatever the hell it was, couldn't you have — well, really, there's always *something* you could've said. What do you think they'll be saying in there? If this is some kind of con, you picked yourself the wrong mark."

Templar held out his hand. "I am Cam Templar," he said, disregarding Aspic's outburst. "I am sorry to have embarrassed you. You see, you look at this as some sort of a parlor game. But for me it's serious business. I never falsify my observations. Believe me, it would've been a good deal more embarrassing had I spoken up.

The hand still hung in the air.

For a second more Aspic hesitated. Then he took the clammy hand and gave it a shake. "Aspic," he said. "Ted Aspic."

"Pleased to meet you, Mr. Aspic. I mean it," Templar added. "I've never met a man quite as talented as you."

"You saw *that?* In my hand. Is that what's supposed to have embarrassed me?"

"No, sir," Templar said. "I never falsify my observations, and that was just *one* observation. You are also promiscuous. You have strong criminal tendencies. You have a most pronounced vindictive strain. Your capacity for love is stunted, consequently your marital relationship must be a shambles. You are the most ambitious man I've ever met and you also seem to lack all scruples — the two go hand in hand, as it were. On the positive side, you have the hand of a genius. I don't think you are an artist, but you have some kind of creative gift. Perhaps in science, mathematics, or music. Either you have made some kind of fundamental discovery, or you'll soon make one. Your fate line is strong, the strongest I've ever seen. You also have a gift for business, but it seems to me that your ambition comes first, and you are likely to subordinate your acquisitive instincts to your drive for fame. You have a very good thumb. You're the type that achieves what it sets out to achieve. Your vital energies are flowing well, and you should live to a ripe old age. My overall assessment is very positive. But there are those other things. They color and flavor your entire profile, and I didn't want to bring those things out into the open — not in company."

Aspic stared at Templar for a moment. Then he turned and looked out through the windshield of the car. The street was empty, lit by a lamp ahead. A corona of luminosity surrounded the lamp, caused by unusually high humidity. From the house came the faint echoing of the party.

Aspic opened his hand and looked at his palm. He saw nothing but lines and curlicues. It was just a hand, nothing more. Yet this sallow creature had penetrated very deeply. Damned if he hadn't.

He turned to Templar. "Somebody briefed you about me."

Templar shook his head slowly. "I know. It comes as a shock. Especially for those who're predisposed to disbelieve."

Predisposed to disbelieve . . . For a brief moment Aspic examined the territories of his disbelief. He found entire continents of occult murk that he had habitually avoided. Then it occurred to him that the Occult was popular at the moment. Professor Rhine at Duke . . . ESP . . . Russian experimentation . . . telepathy as a military tool . . .

"Tell me," he said, "what else do you do? Are you psychic? Telepathy, things like that?"

Templar looked away, presenting Aspic with a side view of his chinless face. "I have a modest gift along those lines. I am what is called a 'sensitive.'"

"What do you do? Where do you work? Do you . . ."

"I'm a bank teller," Templar said.

"What do you earn? Nine, ten thousand?"

"Eleven five hundred," Templar said.

"Uh-huh," Aspic said, chewing his lips. Then he made a decision. "Cam," he said, "how would you like to earn sixteen thousand?"

Aspic nodded to himself. He would ask Templar about it. Not tomorrow, but soon. See what the little man had to say . . .

He reached up and pushed the hostess call button, and a stewardess appeared. Aspic held out his empty bottle of Fleishman's gin. "Is there another one where this one came from?"

The girl hesitated. Then she flashed him a professional smile. "I think we might find one for you," she chirped. "But you'll have to drink up fast. We're almost there."

Stirring his drink a little later, Aspic stared out the window at the brown emptiness below. He imagined a great monastic cluster down there, a foundation worthy of ancient Cluny — but devoted to the maintenance of boiling, eternal, atomic wastes. Would the monks chant? Would they evolve a totally new religion? The idea had a peculiar appeal . . .

Templar, of course, might not have anything useful to say, he thought, pursuing a parallel line of thought. *But you never know . . .*

Then the pitch of the engines changed. The long descent had begun.

4.
Lunch in the Whittler

Future Now's accounting department consisted of a single, spacious, wide-open room. Neither walls nor space dividers separated the three accountants and the accounting clerk. In other words, there was no privacy.

Camilio Ezra Templar, however, needed privacy almost as much as he needed air, and consequently he had managed to obtain for himself one of the desks in the corner. With the help of filing cabinets arranged before his desk, and piles of thick computer printouts on top of the cabinets, he had created for himself an area of chancy seclusion. But his privacy was always subject to invasion. Templar lived in his hide-away forever trembling, forever dreading this and that like — he imagined — some tiny rodent in a jungle full of predators.

But Templar had always felt like that, throughout his life. Walls didn't really matter in the final analysis.

Even inside the vault of the bank he had left to join Future Now, with the door closed, Templar had been subject to the world's threatening vibrations. Only at home in his two-room apartment, in the dead of night — and only on some nights — did he feel something approaching peace. And even then noises disturbed him. The more his eyesight failed, the more he feared all sorts of noises — the sudden roar of trucks, the scream of tires, the slither of steps, the crackling of walls and furniture heating up or cooling down . . .

Templar felt ambiguous about his psychic gifts. They were a grace, a distinction bestowed on him from Higher Up. But his powers sufficed, alas, only to disturb what little serenity life offered. His gifts did not suffice to give him certainty — either about the life below or the life above.

Today, for instance, Templar knew that Aspic would have a talk with him — but he couldn't guess the subject. Yet he knew with certainty that the meeting would be unpleasant. Something odd was going on. Strange vibrations had begun to spread through Future Now since Aspic's return from Washington. Aspic had been rattled by some event . . .

Whatever it was, Templar knew that he would learn a good deal more about it today. He had a strong premonition, and to reinforce that premonition, he had awakened that morning with flashing pains in the region of his solar plexus. Consequently Templar spent his morning in a state of tense expectancy. He could barely work on the internal audit of a major project that lay before him.

Then, at around eleven-thirty, his phone rang shrilly. Templar had expected it to ring. Nonetheless he jerked involuntarily in his seat. The caller was Aspic.

"Cam," he said, "are you free for lunch? I need to talk to you about a thing."

"I'm free."

"Good. Meet me downstairs in about ten minutes."

"I'll be there," Templar said.

Both men hung up. But while Templar sagged back in his chair, one floor above him Aspic continued working at a nervous pace. He pulled a stack of papers before him — items ready for signature — and he began signing letters, proposals, and final reports as he came to them in sequence. One of these, a slender folder bound with plastic at the back, the cover letter clipped to the front, was a concept paper addressed to the Department of Commerce. Aspic spent some time looking the package over. Then he signed the cover letter — it was addressed to Karl Hansley with a copy to Jack Clark — and tossed the item into his Out box. A little later, his desk clear, he rose and went to meet Templar in the downstairs lobby.

Ten minutes later the two men entered The Whittler, a bar not far from Stanford University. By night it was a student hang-out, but by day it catered to business lunchers. The place featured a massive bar made of rough wood. Drinkers were free to carve their initials into its surface, hence the name of the place.

Aspic led Templar to a corner booth. The waitress was a college girl with hair down to her shoulders and ink spots on her fingers. She lit the candle in the bell-shaped red glass. She brought Aspic a martini-on-the-rocks. Templar received a glass of tomato juice. Then they chatted for a while about general subjects, Aspic guiding the conversation. He wanted to have a drink in his stomach before he broached the subject.

Templar, for his part, was apprehensive. He had not been in Aspic's immediate company for several weeks now. On the way to the restaurant, he had scrutinized Aspic closely in the sunlight and had seen strain in Aspic's features. Aspic had had a dried-out, feverish appearance. His skin had seemed drawn tightly over his face. His big eyes had appeared to be on fire.

Now, close to Aspic in the booth, Templar sensed

Aspic's aura. Templar couldn't see the aura; he didn't have that talent. But Aspic's psychic emanations reached him as a feeling, an awareness. He sensed contradictory emotions in Aspic — residues of psychic pain and hints of fear.

They finished their drinks and ordered food. Only then, using a lull, did Aspic start.

"I need some advice," he said, "and my guess is that you're probably the best man on the staff to help me on a matter like this — because of your background and . . . talents, shall we say?" Aspic now raised an index finger. It gleamed like a candle in the candle's light. "All this is in strictest confidence, Cam. I'm consulting you on a personal matter, and obviously I don't want it spread about."

"Of course," Templar said. He had the urge to take off and to polish his glasses. For the moment he fought the urge. Suspense tightened his throat muscles. The sounds of the dark restaurant came to him with unnatural clarity — voices at the bar, the clink of glasses, the scrape of forks on plates, and frying sounds from the kitchen that went on and off as a swinging door swung. He waited while Aspic appeared to be collecting his thoughts.

"Some years ago," Aspic finally said, "I dropped some acid on a dare. In retrospect, it was a stupid thing to do, especially considering the circumstances — which are neither here nor there. Suffice it to say that a friend talked me into it. This person insisted that reincarnation was a fact and that you could retrace your past lives using the drug. This person — a woman — had read everything that Timothy Leary has ever written. Do you know who Leary is?"

Templar took off his glasses and began to rub them on a red napkin. "The professor. Leary tried to start an LSD religion."

"That's the one. I didn't fall for Leary's theories, but I

took LSD anyway. More than once. It was interesting — even fun in an odd, freakish way. But then, the last time, I had a terrible trip. I mean terrible. I imagined that I was an inmate in a concentration camp, and they were killing me. I say that I imagined it, but it wasn't really a fantasy. It felt very, very real." Aspic took a sip of water. "What do you make of it?"

Templar felt a chill. Something urged him dully to keep still, but he wanted to comment. He loved to speak on matters such as this. In this realm he had authority, lost his shyness, and felt a kind of potency. He ignored the dull inner warning.

"What were you? Do you recall that?"

"A Jew, of course."

"I don't mean that. What was your profession?"

"A doctor? Yes. I think I was a doctor. What difference does that make."

"It's a way to check on the authenticity of your recall," Templar said, sounding professorial. "You are a scientist in this life — you were a doctor in your LSD vision. There is a similarity of professions here. Some occult authorities claim that we continue to do the same sort of thing life after life until we have reached some goal we've set for ourselves. It could be that you've really experienced a portion of your last life. But LSD is a peculiar drug. You could just as easily have experienced a movie you once saw and have forgotten."

"I've considered that, " Aspic said. "But there is more to this." He went on to describe his odd encounter with Jack Clark.

"Odd, " Templar said when Aspic had finished. He wanted to say something else, but his anxieties were rising. He had a good idea now which way the conversation was drifting.

"Odd is right," Aspic said. "I was upset, of course. I don't exactly like to have little attacks of schizophrenia or whatever. But I didn't think too much about it until later. I had read somewhere that such things happen to people who take LSD — LSD visions recur spontaneously. But three days after my trip, it happened again. And then again the next day. And since then these states have been recurring, off and on. I don't mind telling you, Cam, I'm starting to worry. These states are acutely uncomfortable. They usually throw me into a depression for several hours."

"Have you seen a doctor?"

"In a round-about way, yes. I had a physical last week. I didn't say anything about this 'malaise.' The doctor said . . ." Aspic gestured.

"He told you that you were as good as new."

"That's right. Now, Cam, here is what I wanted to ask you. Is it possible that I might have met Jack Clark before, in a previous incarnation? And now that I've met him again, he triggered that LSD recall back into my memory? — I'm garbling this. Do you see what I mean?"

Templar knew exactly what Aspic had in mind, and he didn't like it in the least. Aspic's aura now exuded an emotion of vindictiveness mixed with pain, excitement, and expectation.

"I don't know," Templar said, feigning indifference and doubt. "That sounds a bit far-fetched to me."

Aspic began to smile. "You're not telling me what you really think. You rather think it's probable, don't you — but you don't want to encourage me in my folly. Is that it, Cam? Your face gives you away. You'd make a poor politician."

Templar squirmed uncomfortably. "All right. Suppose it's so? The past is past. You've got enough to do living this life. Why speculate about other lives?"

"Why not? Speculation is my business. Besides that, I am really interested in *this* life. If Jack Clark can incapacitate me, if he can trigger such memories in me, that's a problem of this life."

"You're jumping to conclusions," Templar protested. "How can you possibly blame a man you've seen once in your life?"

"Wait," Aspic said, holding up a hand. "I have more evidence. The fact is that I disliked Clark the moment I met him. And it's obvious to me in retrospect that he felt the same way about me. Hate at first sight, if you see what I mean. And since that time I've had the strongest feelings — intuitions, what have you — that Clark has some connection with that concentration camp. I'm not a nut on psychic phenomena, Cam, as you know, but I have a very open mind. Very open. Future Now is what it is because I accept all kind of loony hypotheses. And in this case I'm *driven* to a conclusion. I'm not jumping. What I want to know is how I could make sure — one way or the other. Are there signs? Are there symptoms? Is there a way that you can recognize people you've known before?"

Templar's thoughts raced. Aspic had to be diverted from his line of speculation, but Templar had no idea how to do it. He had heard about such cases in the past — cases of karmic bind. He hoped — and prayed — that he was not himself a part of one of these dreadful entanglements. He spoke at last, thinking he had found a way to scare Aspic off this dangerous path.

"Have you ever considered regressing further?" he asked.

"Regressing? What do you mean?"

"Have you considered taking LSD again — and going back to that concentration camp?"

Templar's words were having an effect. He felt a change in Aspic's aural emanations.

"No. Never." Aspic drank water greedily and shook his head with determination. "Never again. I never want to go through that again."

5.
The Eureka Moment

The luncheon continued, but Aspic changed the subject. He had no stomach for LSD trips, hypnotic journeys, or any other kind of regression to that dreadful past — if indeed it was his past. The food arrived. They discussed a proposal Aspic wanted to send to the Office of Education — a state-of-the-art survey on psychic research. He wanted Templar's ideas and "inputs." Templar was "plugged in" — he was the member of half a dozen occult societies and knew what was going on. Aspic made notes in a narrow little booklet he always carried.

They finished eating, at last, and the girl brought coffee for Aspic and tea for Templar. As an afterthought Aspic ordered a cognac. His lunch with Templar had turned out poorly, and he wanted to prolong it a little, he felt like probing a little more.

"How does it work?" he asked after a pause. "I mean life and death. The way you people see it, the way psychics see it. What are the theories. What are the mechanics of the thing."

Templar shivered inwardly. He had assumed that that subject was closed. He sighed. "There is a lot of evidence — much along the same lines we've just been discussing. But I'm afraid it's all very subjective. That's the very nature of psychic phenomena — their subjectivity. I don't think you can approach the subject in the same way as you would physical things. The very essence of those things is that they're *not* mechanical."

"Let me be the judge of that," Aspic said. "Just describe what's understood about it — from the psychic point of view."

Templar took off his glasses. At the bar a group of men, evidently bent on making an afternoon of it, roared at some joke.

"The masters all agree . . . " Templar began but he broke off. He recalled some derisive comments Aspic had once made about "authorities" who spoke from the "other side."

"There is the body — flesh and bones," Templar said, beginning again. "Then there is the soul, the psychic entity, the personality, emotions, mind, intellect: the things that make you Teddy Aspic. And then there is the spirit behind the phenomena — the real you, the individuated Godhead."

Aspic nodded.

"The first two die, body and soul. You die. Teddy Aspic dies, everything that you are now."

"But the spirit goes on?"

"The spirit goes on. It collects experience, evolves, strives. It strives toward the highest realms of being, the highest vibrational states."

"How can I remember other lives," Aspic asked, "if all that I really am — my personality and so forth — dies?"

"Nothing that has ever happened to you is ever really lost. The spirit carries all of your experiences. They are imprinted, as it were. Indelibly. But you don't remember them on this plane of experience — not unless you meddle, as with LSD. At the same time, the essence of your karmic acquisitions influences your life. Your past lives shine through, as it were. They leach into your current life. You have impulses, intuitions, notions, and hunches. Some of these come from earlier lives."

Silence. Then Aspic said, "How do you know it's so? No, wait. I wasn't going to ask that question. Tell me this instead. What is this 'spirit'? Is it some kind of substance, some kind of 'stuff'? A form of energy? A wave?"

"It's subtle. Not something you could record on a radar. It's much too fine for that, so fine it can penetrate matter. There is no way to hold it. Science will never get at it."

Sounds like a neutrino to me," Aspic said, thinking that Templar knew too little about physics. And he felt, at the same time, a stir of insight and excitement.

"What's a neutrino?" Templar asked. The word frightened him like a dark omen late at night.

"A subatomic particle. Very subtle, very enigmatic. Hundreds of thousands of them are passing through your head this very second. Then through the table, the floor, the foundations, the earth, out the other side, and on. Nothing can capture them. No ordinary electromagnetic force. Gravity has no effect. Very much like this 'spirit' of yours. We can record their presence. We know them by their effects."

"That's interesting," Templar said lamely.

"Isn't it? Aspic felt a tingling of excitement and recognized its nature immediately. A creative impulse was rising up from deep layers of unconsciousness, rising, rising — striving to surface. Even as this happened, even as he felt a rush of blood, he continued talking.

"You know — you're making me think. It surprises me that no one has ever made this analogy before. Look at it this way. We would never have found the neutrino if we hadn't looked for it. Theory predicted it. It was a necessary particle — necessary to balance the equations, to put it crudely. So we started looking for it and — presto."

Aspic slapped the table.

"God," he cried, "I'm getting excited. I can see it now: science has never postulated anything like 'spirit' before in a serious, physical way. But suppose that someone *did* so postulate?" He stared at Templar although he was really speaking to himself. "If we assumed that the soul really did exist, had to exist, and started looking for it — seriously, with instruments — why, by God, we might actually find it!"

Templar shrank back from Aspic's sudden intensity. It came like a hot, psychic wave across the table, a fog of excitement.

"Don't, Teddy. Don't meddle in such things. Please. Some things are beyond the reach of science."

Aspic laughed with unusual volume and force. "That's where you're wrong, my friend," he cried, elated. "Nothing is sacred. Science rejects all limits. She is the mistress of the Cosmos."

Then Aspic heard the echo of his own words and noted the inflated bombast of his statement, the product of excitement. As if they had heard him too, the men at the bar roared up in laughter.

6.
The Funding Decision

While Aspic lunched with Templar in The Whittler, Fritzie entered Aspic's office and carried off the priesthood proposal along with other items of mail. The proposal, now in an envelope, was later placed with other bulky mail next to the downstairs mailshaft in the building Future Now occupied. A mailman put it in a canvas sack; the sack went into a truck. Later yet men found the envelope while sorting mail. It flew through the air and landed in yet another sack. Then by truck, airplane, and by truck again, handled frequently on its way, it came at last into Lulu's hands. Lulu removed the envelope and placed the folder on Karl Hansley's desk. Hansley saw it, read the cover letter, glanced absently at the proposal itself, jotted a note, and flung the item into another basket. From there, by way of Lulu, the mailroom, and finally Tania, the package was conveyed to Jack.

Jack read the cover letter, his face lined with contempt. He sampled the proposal and found it ludicrous. He looked at Hansley's note, adjudged it mild, and on the force or lack of force of Hansley's note, Jack squirreled the proposal away into the lower left hand corner of his desk. It came to rest there with other items Jack expected just to "go away."

Then weeks passed. Other items covered the proposal. Jack's life raced along now, filled with two preoccupations — the New Mexico Plan and his stormy relationship with Evelyn Bantry — and Aspic's proposal was forgotten. Then came an August day . . .

Sunshine filtered through the foliage and gave Washington a cheerful, dappled look that afternoon. It was a Thursday. Jack had just emerged from the Interior Department building, and even as he held the door for Babyface Hansley, who came behind, his eyes searched for a taxicab. Hansley cleared the door and Jack advanced toward the curb waving for a cab.

The two men had just concluded a very successful meeting at Interior on the New Mexico Plan, and Jack was in the best of humor.

In the last several weeks, he had learned to appreciate Karl Hansley's political talents. Hansley was a Nixon protege and looked like a child, but Jack now admired him. In the jungles of bureaucracy, Babyface had turned out to have the ways of a tiger and a snake combined in perfect proportions. Today, more than ever, Jack was proud of Hansley.

A tremendous see-saw battle had developed over the New Mexico Plan of late, with several agencies tearing at the project like hyaenas on a carcass. ERDA, Interior, EPA, NRC, Commerce — not to mention lesser powers — had all latched on to the Plan, and it had looked as if Jack's cherished project would become the casualty of a jurisdictional war.

But Babyface had done some magic shuffling behind the scenes, and in a brilliant alliance with Interior, he had vanquished all the other contenders. A deal had been struck. Commerce would plan the site and control all press announcements until groundbreaking time. Interior would build and operate the site. In exchange for that, Interior had agreed to "sit on" the Bureau of Indian Affairs and to "neutralize" the other agencies. Jack had to hand it to Karl Hansley. Karl was a real smoothie!

A cab pulled up and picked up the passengers. As it surged forward, Jack turned to Hansley. "That was great, Chief. I never would've thought that you could pull it off."

Hansley smiled, his eyes closed. A sprinkling of light and shade passed over his childish face as the cab rolled toward the Commerce building.

It was a short ride and nothing was said. They had nearly arrived when Hansley opened his eyes and turned to Jack.

"Jack," he said, "remember that Future Now proposal we got a while back?"

"Oh, that." Jack felt a little chill in his guts.

"Aspic called me yesterday," Hansley said. "He says we've had the thing for over a month. He was wondering . . . I meant to call you about it, but it slipped my mind."

"I've read it," Jack said carefully. "To tell you the truth, it's a little on the sleazy side."

Hansley nodded. "I know. But go easy on the guy, will you? He's been pretty helpful to us on the Hill."

They rode in silence. Hansley's words echoed in Jack's mind. Teddy Aspic. Future Now. The thing had slipped his mind entirely, displaced by *real* concerns.

A dreadful thing, Jack now recalled. It was called "An Exploration of the Institutional Aspects of Long Term Intensive Care of Nuclear Waste Products," a deceptively innocent title. The rest of it was couched in similarly unreadable jargon. One had to know what Aspic meant before the word "priesthood" jumped at you. Aspic avoided talking of priesthoods. He spoke instead of "waste-dedicated cadres." The cover letter had been clearer. In it Aspic had dropped the names of powerful members of the California congressional delegation.

The cab arrived. "I'll take a look at it again," Jack said. He sounded unhappy. "Any particular time you want the evaluation?"

"Try to get it out before you take off," Hansley said. "I'd like to wrap this up — one way or the other."

They left the cab and Hansley paid the driver.

Jack reached his office in a despondent mood. Airline tickets clipped to a typed agenda waited in the center of his empty desk. His packed suitcase stood beneath the National Guard poster against the wall. His plane left at six-thirty tonight. He was headed for Kansas City for a week's vacation, a time he hoped to put to use wisely for once. He had to mend fences with Betty Ham, his fiancee. He had to get Evelyn out of his mind. Nothing had "happened" between Evelyn and Jack. Jack could still look Betty in the eye. But they had something going, he and Evelyn, and it wasn't love. Since that time when they had seen *Superstar* together, the sparks had flown. Jack hoped that his trip home would cure him of the dreadful infatuation he felt for Evelyn.

But given that he left tonight and given also that Hansley wanted the evaluation before Jack took off, the time to act on Aspic's devilish proposal was here . . . and now!

It was unnaturally quiet in the office. Jack's secretary, little Tania, celebrated a birthday in the conference room down the hall. The staff had left to taste the cake. Jack sat down heavily, extracted the proposal, and read it again.

Time had not improved it. Its phony sociology disguised a revolting idea. Aspic proposed manipulating people into a kind of compulsory atomic service. Jesus. The concept cried out for a paper shredder —

but shredders had lost popularity in Washington these days.

Man, Jack thought, *it's simple. This is just a piece of shit. I ought to say so and get it over with.*

He had the power to destroy this concept. It would be *his* decision and he knew it. If Jack said No, Babyface would have to back him. Karl Hansley couldn't risk a leak, not on a study like this. Jack had the power to make or break the project.

If he broke it, Hansley would be pissed — and the taxpayers would save a bundle . . .

But Hansley would be definitely pissed. And Hansley had backed the New Mexico Plan — all the way. He had stuck his neck out for Jack's project. Hansley had done his raunchy best to keep New Mexico alive. Jack had not complained — because the Plan was *real!* It would serve the people of this land. Could Jack be prissy about the Future Now proposal seeing how Hansley hadn't shied from kicking groin for New Mexico? It was a very shitty business . . .

Jack stood up. He walked back and forth in his office like a caged animal. He stopped before the New Mexico map at last. He wished he could be out there now, away from filthy politics. Get his hands dirty. Honest work. He walked to the door, opened it, and stepped out into the corridor. Down the hall voices sang Happy Birthday to Tania, Happy Birthday to You. Jack's mind was empty.

And then, suddenly, half angrily, he made his decision.

Oh, what the hell, he thought. *Why do I have such goddamned scruples. I might as well be reasonable, not a stickler. I've got bigger fish to fry. I can't screw up important things over some small detail.*

He sat down at his desk again and took a fresh pad from a drawer. He selected an exquisitely sharpened pencil from a cup and began to write.

"One of the most troublesome problems associated

with waste management," he wrote, "is the need for 'perpetual care,' i. e. the necessity for ensuring that the wastes are properly attended to throughout their period of slow decay.

"Most solutions to this problem proposed to OEA heretofore have been inadequate in that they have not attacked the key element of the problem, the institutional aspect.

"This proposal represents the first holistic approach to perpetual care we have ever seen . . . "

Jack felt a little sick when he finished an hour later, but a decision was a decision, by God. He took the sheets and went looking for Tania. He wanted to send the memo before the close of business.

7.
Regression At Carmel

The funding decision having thus been reached, Jack took an airplane to Kansas City and spent that evening with his aging mother. He rose early the following morning, dressed himself with more than normal care, and then he went to surprise Betty Ham. Betty worked the night shift at Menorah Hospital, and she didn't know that Jack was in Kansas City. Their meeting, as a consequence, was more animated than most.

As Jack and Betty embraced in Kansas City, Jack's memorandum arrived in Karl Hansley's office in Washington, D. C. It lay on Hansley's desk until late afternoon; Hansley had meetings on Capitol Hill. He came across the two-page item right around closing time and quickly scanned the pages. He then called out to Lulu and asked what time it was in California now. Hearing that it was just one p. m. out west, he placed a call to Future Now.

He couldn't have picked a worse — or better — time. Aspic sat in his office at that hour. The venetian blinds were tightly closed, the lights were off, and Aspic resembled a shadow seated before his desk, his elbows on the surface, his face cradled in his hands. He had spent the entire morning alone, secluded, rising sometimes to take a turn around his office, reclining at times in his high-backed chair, slunk forward at times as he was now. He tried in this manner to throw off the deep depression that the onset of his malaise had triggered three days ago, and while he made progress, the progress was slow.

Outside his office people spoke in whispers. Fritzie had been told to hold his calls. She had orders not to disturb him. Aspic was working on a big proposal and needed his privacy . . . but Fritzie knew better and so did the rest of the staff. Aspic's malaise was Future Now's most public secret.

When Hansley's call came in, Fritzie decided to honor Aspic's orders in the breach. Hansley was a client; he was also one of Aspic's more valuable contacts. Fritzie knew this because Hansley's name was on the "A" list for Christmas cards; he got one of those gold-engraved jobbies with a personal note. Fritzie knew that Hansley would be calling with good news — else he would have had someone else call — and good news was just what her boss needed. So reasoning, Fritzie buzzed Aspic while Hansley was on hold.

Aspic started. Several buttons blinked on his console. He punched the intercom.

"Mr. Hansley is on the phone," came Fritzie's voice. "I thought you'd want to know."

"Thanks," Aspic said. His voice was hollow. "I'll take the call."

"On twelve," she said.

Aspic pulled himself together and punched one of the flashing buttons. "Karl!" he cried, simulating a cheerful tone.

Hansley sounded very far away. They exchanged comments about the poor connection and each other's health. Then Hansley said:

"I've got some good news for you, Teddy. I thought I'd make your weekend. Your institutional study, you know the one I mean — it's been approved for funding."

"Say again," Aspic shouted. Hansley's words had faded behind a rush of static. "Did you say *approved*?"

"Yes. It's a go situation." Hansley sounded *very* far away. "You'll get the formal notice later, but I thought you might want to hear right away."

"Yes, indeed. Thanks. Karl . . . did Jack Clark recommend funding?"

"Yes. He thought it was a pretty nifty study. He called it a 'holistic approach.'"

"I'll be damned. You know, I didn't expect that."

"Didn't you? Clark's all right. He knows how to play the game."

They tried to continue the conversation, but the line was so poor that they broke off.

The call had a salutary effect on Aspic. He rose from his desk. He walked around the room and raised the venetian blinds one by one. For good measure he clicked on the light. Then he unlocked his door, stuck his head out, and asked Fritzie to get him a cup of coffee. "And rustle up a sandwich for me," he added. "Roast beef should do. And ask Mr. Templar to come and see me."

As a consequence of the interchange that took place between Aspic and Templar a few minutes later, Templar got up early the following morning. He packed himself an overnight bag. Then he caught a cab to Palo Alto. Having paid the driver, he turned toward Aspic's spacious mansion. Aspic gestured from behind the picture window's glass. The garage door rattled up in less than a minute. Aspic backed out a silvery Mercedes, and the two men were soon underway. They headed south to join the sparse traffic on scenic Highway 1.

It was a bright, glistening morning and cold enough so that Aspic turned on the heater. The air seemed unusually clear; the sky was bright; they drove amidst dark greens, bright sunlight, and pastel colors.

Templar wished that he could feel as cheerful as the day looked. Instead he trembled with his usual apprehensions. Aspic had announced to him the day before, out of the blue, that his, Templar's, advice had been accepted.

"What advice?" Templar had asked.

"Remember our conversation in The Whittler a while back? You told me then that the only way I could get to the bottom of this thing of mine was by regression. Well, I'm ready to risk it. I've made arrangements with a friend of mine. We have the use of his chalet down on the coast for the weekend. Helen has gone off to New York. I've finally found the courage to do it. So we're starting tomorrow morning."

"But . . . what has that got to do with me?"

"I can't do a thing like that alone. You'll have to help me. You know what it's all about. And you're qualified. Incidentally, Commerce just called. They've funded the priesthood study. Jack Clark approved it. What do you think of that?". . .

I don't have the courage of my convictions, Templar told himself. *I should have refused him. I should have told him no. Flatly. No.*

"Are you sure you want to go through with it?" he asked Aspic now.

Aspic glanced over at Templar. "Yes. Now that I've finally gotten up the courage, I'm going all the way. I don't plan to stop until I'm at the very bottom of this thing."

Templar said nothing. He sank back into the soft

grey seat of the Mercedes and recalled a biblical injunction. *"Resist not evil . . ."*

Aspic had been musing about Project Psychotron, and his thoughts returned to that subject now. As always after an attack of the malaise, he felt cheerful. And when in good spirits, he spent much time pondering that project. It was still only a vague idea, nothing definite. It dated back to his Eureka moment in The Whittler. By "psychotron" he meant some hypothetical technology designed to catch the human soul. Souls were "psychons" in his new jargon, and he had created the jargon in order to find study money in Washington. He could no more talk of "spirit" than of a "spirit catcher" to those folks. The key to funding lay in knowing what to call a thing.

Now Aspic reviewed his progress to date. Health, Education, and Welfare had said No. The National Science Foundation had called his idea "daring." Which also meant No. The Ford Foundation had referred him back to HEW. But his last call had yielded promising results. Just before his malaise had struck again, he had reached a man in the Defense Department's sprawling R&D empire. The man had listened quietly while Aspic talked about potential breakthroughs in the "occult nexus." Then Aspic mentioned "psychons" by the bye, expecting a rebuff. No rebuff came. "Drop by," the man said. "Try us. You might be surprised how up to speed we are." Which reminded Aspic. He turned to Templar.

"I'd like you to go to Washington with me next month."

"To Washington? To do what?"

"I think I've found a funding source for Project Psychotron."

"Your're not really serious about that, are you?"

"Dead serious," Aspic said.

Templar took off his glasses. He began to rub them

with the end of his tie. "I get a bad feeling about all this," he said.

"Sure you do. Change threatens you, Cam. You're the worst kind of conservative of all. An astrologer. That's the oldest profession save only one."

"My feelings never lie," Templar insisted. "When I feel trouble up ahead, it's bound to come."

Aspic just chuckled.

They arrived in Carmel by the Sea late that afternoon. High amidst mountain crags nearby, above the Pacific shore, a friend of Aspic's owned a small chalet. They reached it by a steep and winding road.

Aspic walked around the property, stretching in the sun. He had used this place before — though never for an LSD session. He had entertained a lady friend up here, and the place stirred memories of vigorous sex and languid contemplation. From the edge of a small, Japanese-style garden, he saw the Pacific. Crashing waves spread snowy foam over the deep-green ocean surface of a rocky inlet far below. Up here silence reigned. Only the wind moved among fragrant pines. Aspic sighed. Then he turned to help Templar unload.

Less than an hour later, Aspic swallowed LSD mixed with water. Accompanied by Templar, he left the kitchen and walked to the room they had chosen for the exercise. It was a small and nearly empty corner room. Aspic would lie on the couch, Templar would sit on the chair, and the tape recorder they had brought along already waited on the end table. A single window in the room opened on the view of an ancient Joshua tree.

Templar sat down while Aspic paced. They spoke about inconsequential matters. For some period of time Aspic felt nothing unusual. But then he noticed that the Joshua had come alive. It flickered, oozed, and seemed to want to speak. He watched it for a long time, entranced by the phenomenon. Then he turned to Templar.

"Everything is alive," he said. "It's simply amazing."

"Blake said it first," Templar answered. " 'When the doors of perception are cleansed, everything appears as it is — infinite.' But now you best lie down and try to concentrate."

Aspic didn't want to rest. His experience was not altogether new, and yet it seemed fresh. Freedom, wisdom, happiness — they bubbled up like a mountain spring inside him. He began to vocalize his feelings while Templar watched the tape recorder's bubble. Aspic's voice caused a succession of green tremors on its surface.

Aspic grew more and more animated as he talked, more and more dramatic. He saw the world of boxes bursting. The categories lay around his feet in "ruined smithereens." He said goodby to airplane trips, proposals, and the talk-talk-talk. Life was a single line of poetry, he said. This went on for a while.

Then Aspic saw that Blind Man Templar led him toward a very, very, very distant and curiously undulating couch. He looked down-down-down at tiny little pudgy Templar. Templar shimmered in a light mysterious.

"Your face is glowing," Aspic said, "but only on one side. I see a man behind you. He wears a pointed hat."

Templar pushed Aspic gently down on the sofa. "Lie down and close your eyes," he said. "Close your eyes."

Aspic didn't want to close his eyes. He wanted to talk, he wanted to see. He marvelled at the beauty of the wall, the rich gorge of the redwood panelling. He saw a tiny spider in the corner. "What a comic," he said, "what a consummate comic! No — a consummate *cosmic!*" The thought tickled him; he found it exquisitely true and funny; and he laughed until his eyes watered. Slowly the cosmic hilarity ebbed away. Aspic reclined and closed his eyes.

"Now you are going back," Templar said. "You are

calm, you are relaxed, your muscles are letting go, your thoughts are flowing freely. You are ready and you are receptive. You are waiting . . . waiting . . . patiently waiting . . . knowing that you can do it, knowing that all is well . . ."

Templar continued talking in his manner, soothingly, hypnotically. Aspic did as Templar told him. He relaxed and let go. Exquisite feelings surged through his body. He experienced his muscles. He circulated with his own blood. He watched his heart beat and heard its stupendous sound. Then suddenly he saw a vision. He went into it more or less willingly, a chaotic yet marvellous hurly-burly. Templar's voice, asking him what he saw, came from far away.

"I am in a kind of storm," Aspic said. "It's . . . it's like a bubble chamber. I see flashes and streaks of light."

"How did you get there?" Templar asked.

"I don't know. Tornadoes of force. Scary. If I hadn't been here before . . ."

"You're in the Bardo."

Aspic nodded. "A whorehouse full of energies. Tremendous. I'm flying."

"I said Bardo, not bordello."

"Bardo?"

"Your soul is disembodied. You're in the spirit realm. You're on the death plane."

"It's like a bubble chamber," Aspic said, and then he fell silent.

A huge inferno drew him — a blazing furnace of thermonuclear energies, perhaps a sun. A vast dish of tomato soup lay below, a steaming redness filled with coiling, living noodles. The inferno terrified him, the tomato soup disgusted him. And then he was inside his knee.

He *knew* that he was in the knee. The knee belonged to Dr. Mahler and Mahler was in Hermsberg, Germany. A blow had just shattered his kneecap.

"Oh, my God," he cried aloud. Far off Templar urged

him to describe exactly what he saw, but Aspic couldn't do it. Pain tore his nerves and exploded in his brain. He fell toward up-rushing ground. Naked hands went out and tore on frozen dirt. He lay face down on ice.

Then a brutal force cracked against his spine, its origin a boot tip. The heel blasted down into his kidney. Aspic no longer cared, but his stupid body tried to crawl away and hide — but where could he hide? He lay in the midst of a frozen snow-scape dotted with black stumps.

The boot then cracked against his skull and he disappeared in darkness only to return. He looked up and saw the sky. Massed clouds hurried across its reaches toward Russia. Then the shadow of the Beast advanced and loomed over him. Heavy boots, a mud-smeared coat...then he beheld the Beast's red face under the helmet. The Beast snarled with an open mouth, called him a lazy swine...told him to get up...but he couldn't rise with a shattered knee.

The Beast's red face now turned to purple, and he screamed in a shrill voice. The rifle butt rose up toward the clouds and came down again. Aspic had no breath left. He simply saw the rifle butt rise up, come down, rise up, come down. It rushed through the air with a loud roaring and landed with such force that the earth trembled and shook.

Then he no longer saw the rifle, only the Beast's blazing eyes, and the eyes burned like twin laser beams, with concentrated energy. Fire pierced Aspic, fire burned Aspic, and fire flung him free of that snow-covered scene.

He was back. The tape recorder hummed. Ice broke somewhere as a tray was cracked. Cubes clinked into a glass. Water rushed. Then Templar's steps approached.

Aspic drank the water greedily, aware now that he had asked for it. He merged with the ice crystals and felt their desperation as the room's heat advanced on the attack. To melt or not to melt — that is the question. He didn't want to melt. He longed for crystal structure; he feared that blazing flame.

Templar stood above him. "You must rest now," Templar said. "Then we must try again. You didn't go far enough back. You must try again, otherwise we've just been wasting time."

Aspic shook his head. He wanted nothing more to do with that awful past. But then as Templar began to murmur suggestions again, Aspic found himself once more sucked away into a vision. He flew again. Templar disappeared, the glass disappeared, and the tape recorder's hum faded into a melody.

Aspic tried to understand all this. He struggled as if with demons. He tried to stop the whirl, the flow, but couldn't. And then, with a muffled little scream — his body trembled on the couch — he plunged back down again. He was an excruciating pain inside his knee. He was Dr. Mahler again, the place was Hermsberg, Germany, and the Beast stood over him, intent on murder.

But this time the vision changed. The scene careened around and round. Aspic experienced a lifetime as in a flash. He remembered every scene as it swirled past him, but he didn't stop the crazy tumbling although he knew he could. He knew that he was seeking something, a particular event, an explanation. Dr. Mahler's early life — his studies, the move to Berlin, his marriage, the hospital, the practice, the marches, the Reichstag fire — none of these had anything to do with his malaise.

Then, abruptly — as when someone stops a runaway film and freezes a single frame on the screen — a certain vision crystallized. Aspic saw a frozen landscape. He had done it himself. He had found the spot along the coils where It began. He didn't know what "coils" he had in mind, nor what "It" really was.

The scene began to move, and he was an integral part of it.

He stood at a railroad siding. His arm lay protectively around his daughter's waist. Eva shivered, and he could feel her body trembling. Snow hid the earth as far as the eye could see. White plumes of vapor came from the mouths of shouting, helmeted Nazi guards. The prisoners lined up. Poor Eva stumbled; Aspic caught her. Beneath her coat she wore only the flimsiest of nightgowns; the Gestapo had come for them during the night.

They stumbled away, marching through the snow. Guards walked on either side. One of them — it was the Beast — oggled Eva lecherously. Then came barbed wire fence, miles and miles of fence. At last they were herded through a gate into the camp and then toward a giant concrete building. They mounted steps and entered a cavernous, echoing hall. Harsh voices shouted. Men to the left, women to the right. Against the walls. Off with coats and shoes. Aspic parted from his darling. The look in her dark eyes made him want to die.

A sergeant walked front and center. He had a long, droopy nose. He rubbed his nose with an extended index finger, moving his finger rapidly back and forth. He sniffed twice. Then he took folded papers from a case, unfolded them, and began to read.

Aaron Flink stood next to Aspic. Flink had haunted Aspic throughout the trip, feeding off the doctor's moral courage. Now, again, Aaron was near. His lips moved in silent, babbled prayer; his eyes were wide with terror. The sergeant said that all would go into the delousing chamber as their names were called. Flink babbled about poison gas. His whispers were hysterical.

Aspic would have welcomed death. He sought Eva's eyes across the room and saw her against the wall in her flimsy gown. Her eyes evaded his. She cringed away, out of sight, still shivering. She tried to hide behind the other women.

The sergeant called names. The names echoed, louder and louder. More and more people moved out — women to the right, men to the left. Aaron Flink's turn came. He walked out, wringing his hands. And then came that cursed commotion. Flink's voice screamed in agonized tones. Aspic heard it even before it sounded. The memory rushed ahead of its replay. The sergeant sniffed, folded his papers, and ran out of the room to see what the disturbance was all about. In disgust, already sure what he would see next, Aspic turned toward Eva.

The Beast. Yes, he was there. The vile memory was ready. No sooner was the sergeant gone than the Beast pounced. He stood near Eva, on the women's side. Now he turned toward her, grabbed her, and tried to force a kiss from her. She resisted, struggled, but the Beast was stronger. He pressed her rudely against the wall; his helmeted head moved as he tried to catch the poor girl's lips. And then he began to make ugly, obscene dog-like motions with his midriff. Faster and faster. The watching guards laughed.

Aspic felt consumed with searing passion. He rushed across the empty gap between the men and women. He grabbed the Beast by the collar and jerked him away from Eva with such force that the Beast's helmet came off, crashed to the concrete, and rolled away. Aspic held the Beast by the collar with his left. With his right he slapped the pig across the stupid peasant face — left, right, left, right, left, right, left. Then others grabbed him from behind and dragged him away . . .

Then Aspic toiled in ice and snow, scratching the frozen earth. The Beast marched in his direction. Jack-boots squeaked on snow. Lazy pig-dog, the Beast snarled at Aspic. Aspic fell down with a blow. Get up, pig-dog. All right, if you want to be like that! Crash came the rifle butt, and Aspic was once more inside his knee.

"Rest, now, Teddy. Just relax and rest," said Templar. "And then we'll have to try again."

Aspic sat up. "No need," he said; he felt calm and clear as glass. "No need," he repeated. "I understand it now."

When Aspic awoke the following morning, he heard a far off sizzling sound and smelled bacon. Bright light came into the bedroom. He put on the sunglasses Templar had thoughtfully left on the bedside stand. Then, slipping into a robe and tying the belt as he walked, he went out into the kitchen.

He didn't answer Templar's greeting. Templar stood before the stove, a spatula in hand.

"Did you notice an encyclopedia in the house?" Aspic asked.

"An encyclopedia? I don't know, I didn't look."

Aspic marched out again. Presently he returned, carrying a volume.

Templar watched him from the stove. Aspic was leafing through the book. He found his spot, stopped, and began to read. Suddenly he slapped the pages together.

"That's it," he cried triumphantly. He laid the book on the kitchen table. "There *is* a place called Hermsberg," he said. "And it used to be a concentration camp. And guess what, Cam. Today it's a uranium mine — in East Germany. I think we've got our man."

Templar asked Aspic to explain.

"Isn't it obvious," Aspic cried. "If I have lived before, and as a scientist of sorts, and if I'm drawn toward science in this life — why, then Jack Clark, if he has lived before, would be attracted to the atom. And there he is, the little son of a bitch, messing with nuclear wastes!"

8.
RICHARD'S ADVICE

That Sunday morning at eleven, sixty-seven hours had passed since Jack's departure from Washington, a time span that Evelyn had experienced as a liberation from a nightmare. Since the night of Jack's departure, she had entertained three lovers in succession. She had laid her problem before each man in turn and had solicited their advice. Why did she feel so oddly about Jack? And how could she break that weird relationship? None of her friends had been much help.

Now Evelyn sat on the crumpled covers of her bed, her back against the bed-board. A pink robe draped her naked body. A glass of orange juice tilted in her right hand. She gazed fixedly into the distance, calculating. Another hundred and sixty-some-odd hours of liberty still lay ahead. Then the telephone would ring, and there would be Jack again. Ludicrous that her mind was still on Jack . . . after such a weekend. An unfaithful wife spent less time thinking about her husband than she wasted on Jack — and they hadn't so much as kissed.

Richard lay next to Evelyn. Naked to the waist, the rest of him under the covers, he read the Sunday edition of the *Washington Post*. The morning, like the night before, had been amorous. Satisfied now, Richard paid her no attention, and Evelyn felt irked.

"Richard," she said. Richard continued to read. "Hey, you," she said, and she nudged Richard's shoulder with an elbow. Richard grunted and kept on reading. "Richard! I want to talk."

"What about?" he asked, still reading.

"About my problem."

Richard put the paper down. "Not *again*," he said. "I thought we were finished with that."

"You might be finished," Evelyn said, "but I still have my problem."

Richard tossed the paper on the floor, threw back the covers, and got out of bed. He stood for a moment in his shorts.

"Evelyn, you know you really do try a man's patience. Do you know what I mean? You call me up. You invite yourself out to dinner — and that after playing frigid for a month. You do the night cap bit, we do the Ooh-la-la . . . and then you keep me up half the night bending my ear about your kinky love affair with another man."

"Where are you going?"

"To the bathroom. If you don't mind."

Evelyn sipped her orange juice. Men were not the liberated swingers they pretended to be, she had discovered. Herbie had been furious with her; Sid had begun to sniff and yawn, sure signs of discomfort; and Richard, who was an industrial psychologist over at the Labor Department — and therefore the most likely of the three to help — refused to dialogue with her.

Presently Richard returned. He had fixed himself a Bloody Mary and smoked a cigarette. Not finding an ashtray, he left again and returned with one. Back on the bed again, he reached for the paper.

"Just tell me one thing," Evelyn said. She waited until she had his distrustful attention. "Is it possible to 'fall in hate'?"

"I really don't feel like psychoanalyzing some strange man and his feelings for you on a Sunday morning right after we've made love. See what I mean?"

"Be serious, Richard. I really want to know."

"There is no such thing as falling in hate," he said gruffly. "But there *is* such a thing as sex repression, and that's what you've been practicing. Who is this character? Some sort of defrocked priest?"

"I told you," she said. "It's nothing like that. The question never came up."

"Sex, you mean?"

"Yes. Sex."

"You've never invited him up? For one of your famous 'night caps'?"

"I'd die before I'd do that," she cried. "I *loathe* him."

Richard took several drags on his cigarette and then snuffed it out with vigorous motions. He shook his head.

"Evelyn, you're either not telling me something or something else is wrong. Let me get this straight. You loathe the man." Evelyn nodded. "And yet you go out with him?" Evelyn nodded. "Frequently." She nodded again. "All right," he said, "could you tell me, as simply as possible, *why* you go out with him?"

"I thought that you could tell *me*."

"How can I? Normal, sensible people don't consent to keeping company with people they *loathe*. That's an awfully strong word, you know." Richard's eyes grew wary. "He's not your boss, is he?"

Evelyn laughed. "No, no. Nothing like that."

"Then why?"

"I enjoy it, in a way. All we ever do is fight, but I

enjoy it. We're so different. He's a redneck, in a way. Very straight, very patriotic. We get into it. We tear at each other. The way it turns out, we never stop. We'll go out, and then, by the time he takes me home, the argument isn't finished yet —"

"And so you start again the next time," Richard said. "And I suppose that in between — between these cozy little get-togethers — you hone your weapons, you sharpen your blade, you make up devastating arguments . . . ?"

Evelyn nodded, smiling.

"When did all this start? *How* did all this start?"

Evelyn propped herself higher against the backboard of the bed. "He bugged me for a long time — to go out with him," she said. "Well, about a month ago I did. We went to see *Superstar*. It was playing over in Arlington." Evelyn adjusted her hair. "You know me," she said. "I'm not very religious. Nobody in my family is. Bible reading isn't exactly . . ." She gestured. "Anyway, I was kind of surprised by the play. It was so *real*, so *now*. You know? I don't cry very easily, but this time I did. And afterwards, out in the car, I felt so calm and mellow. I guess that's what they mean by catharsis. Anyway, we drove along — he was driving. Neither of us said anything, and I thought that he felt the same way I did. We were crossing Key Bridge. I still remember that. I remember looking at the moon in the water. So I said something like . . . 'What a great experience,' words to that effect."

"And he blew up."

"Yes. How did you know?"

Richard waved a hand. "Go on," he said.

"Just like you said. He blew up. He turned to me real sharply, and of course I looked at him. I noticed his hands. He was trying to strangle the steering wheel. His knuckles were turning white. And I thought, what the hell? And then he said that, as for him, he'd never seen a worse distortion of The Greatest Story Ever

Told . . . Had he known how they would cheapen the Gospel, he wouldn't have given those filthy hippies a nickel of his hard-earned money. Words to that effect."

"And then *you* blew up."

"I certainly did!" Her eyes flashed with recollection. "I let him have it. I tore him apart."

Richard smiled. "Classic," he said, bounding from the bed again.

"What do you mean, classic. — Where are you going now?"

"To get a cigarette. Be right back."

Evelyn waited impatiently. Telling the story brought back the emotions of that night. She experienced again that mixture of rage and exhilaration she always felt when battling with Jack. The feeling no longer pleased her. She didn't like the direction in which she moved with Jack.

Richard returned. He stopped in the door way. His left arm, laid across his chest, propped the elbow of his right. The cigarette smoked in his right hand. He leaned against the door post.

"Have you ever read a book called *Games People Play?*"

"Probably," Evelyn said.

"Probably not. Or else you've read it carelessly. Your thing with this man is a classic 'game,' right out of the book. It even has a name. It's called 'Got you, you son of a bitch.'"

Evelyn looked at Richard uncertainly.

"Very simple," he said, exhaling smoke. "Men and women associate with one another for a reason, and that reason should be no mystery to you. For some reason the two of you don't click on that level — you want to, but you don't. So instead you play a game. It's a kind of substitute for sex."

"I couldn't possibly have sex with him," she said. "He is too much of a boor. If it ever came to that, he'd try to lord it over me. You don't understand him. He'd think of me as his property after that."

"So why don't you just break it off?"

"I've tried to, but it just never seems to work out."

Richard thought about that. "He attracts you sexually," he said, "but you don't want to face up to that."

"That's not true."

"Then why have you been so . . . continent lately?"

Evelyn gestured; her gesture took in the crumpled bed and items of clothing tossed carelessly on the carpet.

"I haven't been exactly continent."

"True. But he is out of town, and you're just human too." Richard tapped his naked chest. He smiled without humor. "Erotic Services Incorporated. Just telephone, and we'll send out a man."

"That's unkind, Richard."

"Unkind, perhaps. But true. Take my advice, Evelyn. Hop in bed with your lover. That's what he *is*, you know. As for me, we have a pleasant arrangement, but it certainly doesn't go as *deeply* as your relationship with Mr. X."

Evelyn didn't hear Richard's sarcasm. "But if I do . . . What if he starts to get possessive? What if it gets even worse?"

Richard was sucking smoke. He exhaled a stream. "Tell him he is a lousy lover," he said, speaking to the ceiling. "Tell him about your other friends. Tell him about me. If he is the kind of man I think he is, he'll run so fast you'll never catch him again. And then you'll be *really* sorry, I would guess."

Again, Evelyn refused to hear the guarded injury in Richard's voice. She thought about the meaning of his words, her lips pursed, her eyes on the rumpled covers.

Silence. Then, carrying his cigarette so that the long ash wouldn't fall, Richard went to the ashtray on the bedside table.

"If you're satisfied with the consultation," he said, "I think I'll take a shower. Believe it or not, I have a tennis date with a certain Miss Z." He gave her a sideways glance. "We just love to slug it out over a net."

Richard waited for a reaction, but Evelyn was still absorbed in thought. He shrugged then and left the room. The sound of rushing water soon issued from the bathroom.

9.
The Intersection of Another Technology

Outside it was a cloudy, windy September day. Inside the small conference room too many bodies had heated the air and turned it smokey with tobacco. At the head of the table, Jack gathered his papers and rose.

"Well, gentlemen, I guess that's it — until the next time. Thanks for coming; and thank you for your contributions."

While everyone rose and a hubbub of talk began to fill the room, Jack put the papers in his briefcase and closed the case with a click. Then he waved to all and sundry and hurried from the room.

Another meeting of the Interagency Committee had passed uneventfully. The Commerce-Interior axis now held New Mexico in an unyielding grasp, and these meetings served one purpose only — to let the vanquished agencies save face. They were still "involved," could still make "inputs." But all that was sheer formality.

The meeting had been held across the river from Washington, in Crystal City, on neutral grounds, and Jack had trouble finding the elevator in the unfamiliar office building. He found it at last and punched the button to summon the car.

Today not even New Mexico could hold his interest. Other and more exciting prospects loomed ahead. He reviewed his day while waiting.

Aspic was due in thirty minutes — to present the first progress report on the priesthood study. A dreary prospect — and Jack resolved to keep *that* meeting short and sweet. Then would come lunch time, and time to get away to buy the wine. He didn't plan to do much work this afternoon. He smiled inwardly. *I'll be saving up my strength,* he thought. He would be saving up his strength because he planned to *score* tonight!

He was sure that he would score. Three days ago Evelyn had called. "Jack," she had said, "about Wednesday night . . . Listen, I got to thinking. Why don't we have dinner at my place. You bring the wine. Afterwards we'll just laze around and talk and such. And if it gets as hot and heavy as usual, we can sleep late on Thursday and to hell with Uncle Sam."

Since his return from Kansas City, Evelyn had acted oddly — and all of Jack's resolutions about breaking with "that Bantry bitch" had evaporated instantly. She had begun responding — to *him.* Hot dog!

The elevator came. Jack got on thinking that it was really a kind of basic thing. Face it. They had a real hot for each other. How else could he explain it — all those vicious fights . . . like cats on a roof. An animal thing. It happened to every man once in his life. After it had burned itself out, it would enrich his life with Betty . . .

He caught a cab in front of the Marriott and sank back into the seat, grateful to have escaped the chill. It was a very bitter, very windy, overcast day.

The cab had just turned out of Crystal City and was

moving along Highway 1 when Jack glimpsed Fred Jones standing by the roadside in a trench coat. One of his hands covered an ear. With the other he waved at every passing cab, but all the cabs were full. Jack told his driver to stop.

Jack had worked closely with two men in the Aerospace section before his transfrer to the OEA. Jones was one of the two, a giant, bearish man, a merry man with an infectious laugh and a booming voice.

Being as jolly as he was today, Jack greeted Jones with unusual bonhommie. He even slapped the giant on the knee, expecting a similarly merry response. But Jones, so full of good humor as a rule, did not respond as expected. He nodded to Jack, smiled thinly, and then began to blow into his gigantic fists to warm them, eyes on the back of the cab driver's head.

"What brings you to Crystal City?" Jack asked.

Jones glanced at him quickly, gave a single, soundless snort, then shook his head.

"What's up? Something is up. You're not yourself."

Jones gave Jack another look, hesitated, and then said: "I was over here interviewing for a job, as a matter of fact. With the environmental boys. Their Noise Program is over here. I'm getting out."

Jack looked surprised. "You," he cried, "leave Aerospace? Just now that they gave you a promotion? Why?"

"It's a long story."

"Well, tell it!"

"It's too weird, too hairy, too unbelievable," Jones said. His voice had a gravelly quality. "I don't really want to talk about it."

"Come on. We're supposed to be old buddies."

Jones stared ahead. "All right — but later." He made a gesture toward the driver.

The cab wound its way toward Fourteenth Street Bridge by a series of ramps. Interstate 95 was in the final stages of construction, and no one could make sense of the traffic pattern now. The sky was lead grey and it was cold enough to see the steam of exhaust pipes although it was already mid-morning.

They rode along in silence for a while. Then Jones turned.

"What about you? How are you taking it? Hansley is still in command, I hear, still boondoggling like crazy."

Jack chuckled.

"I hear," Jones continued, "that he foisted off a real lulu of a contract on you. Something about a plutonium priesthood? Sid always refers to you now as the 'plutonium priest.' Is it as bad as it sounds?"

"I don't know," Jack lied. "The proposal was far out, but I haven't seen any of the work yet. As a matter of fact, I've got the first progress report meeting this morning at eleven. The consultant is coming in. God knows what he'll have to say. I haven't tracked the contract too closely. It's Hansley's baby, so I just let it ride."

"You really surprised Sid."

"Surprised him? How?"

"Sid used to say that you and Hansley would butt heads one of these days. You're his hero — Sid's hero, I mean. No compromise, that sort of thing."

Jack squirmed. "You can't win them all," he said. "I've got much bigger programs to worry about than that one contract. I wasn't going to let everything go to hell just for one silly pet project Hansley was going to fund no matter what I did. It has nothing to do with heroism."

Jones raised a huge hand. "I'm not putting you down, Jack. It's just that Sid was surprised. He is up in arms now, even worse than I am. We're both involved in this thing."

"That thing? Jack asked, gesturing vaguely.

"Yeah," Jones said. "I'll tell you about it in a minute."

The cab stopped in front of the Commerce Department and the icy wind caught and almost turned the two men as it whistled down 14th Street. They struggled to the sidewalk, bending into it.

"You want to go someplace and have a cup of coffee?" Jack asked. He still had twenty minutes until his appointment with Aspic.

Jones shook his head. He guided Jack to a streetside tree whose trunk provided a minimum of shelter against the wind.

"I'd better tell you out here," Jones said. "It's probably best that way." He looked about furtively. His face expressed some kind of inner discomfort. "Jack — you're still in the National Guard, right? So you understand it when I say that this is hush-hush."

Jack wondered what might be hush-hush about the economic reporting and research functions of the Aerospace section. He nodded.

"You won't repeat this to anyone? For God's sake, don't. It could be my neck. Literally." Saying this, Jones touched his nostril and sniffed. The cold wind made his nose run.

"I've got an AEC clearance," Jack said. "Not that it matters. I won't breathe a word. What are you into?"

"It's a very long story," Jones said, speaking quickly now, "but in a nutshell, you know how the Department can call in all sorts of industry groups for consultation, all part of our mission, and how — "

"They can all collude, sort of, without fear of antitrust?"

"That's it. Well, a couple of months ago, three guys came in. They were in civilian clothes, but you could tell that they were military. They were with some obscure DOD research command, you know, with a name so long even the initials spell a word?"

"I'm with you."

"Well, in a nutshell, they wanted us to call a secret meeting of several small companies in the medical electronics field. No big deal. But they wanted us to get secrecy agreements from all the companies in advance of the meeting."

"Spooky," Jack said.

"That's what we said. I didn't commit us to a thing, just listened. Afterwards I checked with Charlie House — my boss. But he just winked and said, 'Do it.' He told me not to ask too many questions. The Secretary himself had cleared the project."

"So?"

"So we did it. It took three weeks to negotiate it all."

Jones stopped and waited until a bus that had pulled up nearby had disgorged some passengers and the people, leaning into the wind, holding down skirts and hats, had dispersed.

"You swear this won't go any farther?" Jack nodded. "You know the rules of the game. At a meeting like that, someone from the shop has to attend to make sure there is no collusion and such, and Sid went because he's a lawyer and still has a clearance from his time at Defense. Sid told me what went on in there. The DOD cats asked these people to form a joint venture for a very hush-hush but very profitable long-range research project. They want to experiment with brain transplants."

Jack waited. He thought that the punchline was yet to come. When Jones did not continue, he said, "Is that so bad? I thought that transplants were all the rage. Hearts, livers, eyes. Why not brains?"

"They want to transplant brains into machines, not people."

"Are you serious?"

"Dead serious. The rationale is that the Chinese are supposed to be doing it. Nobody seems able to get a computer small enough — mechanical computer, of course. So they want to try to use organic brains."

"Human brains?"

"Not at first. But that's the whole thrust of the project."

"Where would they get them from?"

Jones shook his head. "I don't know; but it scares me shitless. If they really want to use them — the brains, I mean — hell they can't use old people's. They're likely to be senile. So your guess is as good as mine."

"How did they react?"

"Who? The companies? You know that bunch. They drooled. Dollar signs in the eyes. The Aerospace business is way the hell down; and the medical electronics types have been starving worse than most. They went frantic looking for the dotted line."

"They never learn, do they?"

"No. And Watergate is hardly over. Sid and I went round and round, trying to figure out what to do. See, there's nothing *illegal* here. They were careful, the people from Defense. That's why they asked the Department to arrange the meeting. By the book. And rhesus monkeys don't have civil rights. If we blow the whistle, we just get clamped in the jug for violating security regs. But the implications . . . "

Jones rubbed his ears while Jack stared pensively. Everything was grey — buildings, street, the sky.

"So you're getting out?"

"Yeah. I want to be as far from this shit as I can get. And Sid too . . . Jack, not a word; don't even hint, please?"

"I won't say a thing."

"It's hell, keeping it inside," Jones said. "Sometimes I think I'm too sensitive for this work. Me. Sensitive. But when I think about it . . . "

His conversation with Fred Jones had tarnished Jack's excellent humor. He was reminded that Washington was a cesspool of corruption and that none could quite escape, not even men who made

integrity their guiding light. He was guilty too —
though only of wasting the taxpayers' money. He took
the elevator up, gloomy at the prospect of meeting
Aspic and determined to keep the meeting short.

10.
The Progress Report

Across the hall from Jack's office, in the room Tania shared with two other secretaries, Aspic already waited. He wore an elegant grey coat with a black fur collar. The room was hot, but inwardly Aspic felt a chill.

He had been in Washington since the day before. Templar and he had visited John Burdick at Defense — the same Burdick Aspic had found while beating the bushes for money to fund the psychotron. That part of the trip had been successful. Templar and Burdick — so unlike each other — had hit it off immediately and had talked for hours about psychic research and other odd phenomena. Aspic had left the Pentagon practically sure that DOD would fund a Phase I study of the psychotron. But the meeting that now lay ahead filled him with apprehension.

He felt obscurely that all his thoughts about the Beast, all his schemes of retribution, might be visible in his face. Jack Clark might guess it all; Clark might already know. The Nazi guard was very real to Aspic at the moment, and so was an echo of the fear of death.

When Tania's buzzer sounded, and Tania told someone that Mr. Aspic was here to see him, Aspic shuddered involuntarily. He wished he had insisted that Templar come along. He felt a need for allies. But Templar was back at the hotel. He had begged off saying, "I don't want to get into that karmic tangle, Teddy. I pray to God that I'm not part of it already."

Aspic picked up a mapcase full of charts and crossed the hall. Jack stood behind the desk, coat off, his moon-face stiff, his pig-eyes staring.

"Morning, morning," Jack said. They shook hands across the desk.

Aspic took off his coat. "Do you want me to close the door?"

"Naw," Jack said. "It's too late for that. Everybody seems to know about the study. I just found out that they call me 'plutonium priest' around here." Aspic detected no hint of humor. "Well, what have you got?"

Aspic had charts meant for an easel. He had expected to make a presentation to five or six people, but apparently there was to be no group. The study might be widely known, but Clark had no intention of spreading the news farther.

Aspic pulled out the charts.

"Oh. A presentation." Jack looked unhappy. "Well, never mind. I'll make some room here and you can lay those things on the desk. We're all out of easels at the moment."

Aspic arranged the charts on the desk, and after some preliminaries, he began his presentation. He explained the charts one after the other, bent over the desk, reading bulleted headlines upside down. At first he used his index finger as a pointer, but his hand trembled so much that he stopped.

The meeting was a mere formality called for by the

contract — and no occasion for nervous shakes. But the man across the desk had murdered Aspic long ago, and that awareness reverberated like a gong in Aspic's mind.

Moreover, he had a secret agenda. He meant to talk about — his Project Psychotron. If the Psychotron developed as Aspic hoped it would, it would be the central feature of any atomic priesthood. With a smidgin of good fortune, Clark wouldn't be in charge by then. But just in case he was, Aspic had to lay in some foundation . . .

He launched into this task as soon as he reached the chart showing project objectives. He emphasized one of these: TO IDENTIFY A FAIL-SAFE MECHANISM THAT WILL ENSURE INSTITUTIONAL CONTINUITY.

"In other words," Aspic said, "we've got to find some fool-proof way to bind the priesthood to the job. That's critical. There is no special magic in starting new institutions. That's done every day. But how can we be sure today that the institution we start now will last as long as the nuclear waste? Unless we can find some sort of fail-safe mechanism, this project will be nothing but an exercise. But such a mechanism may call for a new technological breakthrough, and that's the problem."

"What kind of breakthrough?"

"I'm thinking of some sort of behavioral technology."

"What? Some kind of compulsion?" Total rejection gleamed in Jack's eyes.

"I don't like that word — or the idea," Aspic said. "I was thinking of a system of incentives, built-in incentives."

"Built-in? Why not robots?" Jack smiled unpleasantly. "This whole project is a little bit like science fiction anyway. Why not go the whole hog?"

Aspic let that pass. "Robots are an option," he said.

"But I don't think that we could build robots today that'll be able to adapt themselves to circumstances as they might be centuries from now."

"Why not implant human brains?" Jack asked, smiling.

Aspic looked at Jack. The meeting was going splendidly considering that the pig-eyed man across the desk was a Nazi. But Aspic would not be baited, rattled, or "punished" by this character. He would damn well keep his cool and bide his time.

"That sounds gruesome," he said, "but you're making a point anyway. You're identifying a problem in this study. Just about anything we might come up with in the way of behavioral inducements is likely to violate civil rights."

"So what do you suggest? Contract cancellation? — Ted, could you just get on with it? I'm a little pressed for time."

Aspic continued. He felt nervous and on edge and realized that Jack meant to make him feel that way. Jack drummed his fingers on the desk. His eyes wandered. He nodded rapidly before Aspic had finished making his points. He waved his hands at charts and told Aspic to go on to the next one — he had gotten that one. From time to time he glanced at his watch, or at the wall, or at papers that had been shoved to the side to make room for charts. And thus twenty minutes passed.

Then came a sudden and unexpected interruption.

Aspic heard steps running down the hall. And in the next moment a young woman stood in the doorway, a touch breathless. Her auburn hair flowed freely; her unbound breasts heaved gently.

"Jack, about that wine I asked you to bri—"

Aspic broke into a smile of pleased surprise. "Evelyn," he cried. "Evelyn Bantry, for God's *sake!*"

"Teddy!" She was as pleased as he was.

They embraced affectionately.

"Harvard Square?" Aspic asked, holding her at arm's length. "Sixty-nine?"

"Has it been that long? — Teddy, what a pleasant surprise. Are you —" She glanced at Jack. "I mean — is this business?"

Aspic nodded. "But you — you wouldn't be working here, by any chance, would you?"

"Sure," she said. "This is my turf, Ted. And you? Are you on your own? Or are you still with — was it General Electric?"

"Free as a bird. I'm on my own. I've formed this small consulting group on the West Coast — but say, Evelyn. This is no place for reminiscing." He glanced at his watch. "What about lunch? Can you make it?"

"Why not?" she said. She glanced quickly at Jack. "Let's catch up on things on my time — rather than Uncle's." She turned. "Sorry to barge in on a meeting like this, Jack, but your door was open and so I . . ." Her eyes went back to Aspic. "Just pick me up when you're ready." She gave her room number and turned to Jack. "Jack, I'll give you a ring later." And then she was gone.

Aspic looked at Jack. "Well . . ." he said. "That was a pleasant interlude. Evelyn and I go way, way back. Are you two friends?"

"Colleagues," Jack said. His voice sounded hoarse.

Aspic continued his presentation. But now he felt a good deal less nervous than before. Evelyn's interruption had affected Jack. Something more than formalities between colleagues linked Evelyn and Jack . . . which was surprising, odd. She couldn't be his girlfriend, could she? How could she put up with *him!* Aspic meant to find out. His own relations with the girl had been brief but intimate — intimate enough so that he expected her to tell him all. Nothing unlocked the tongue so much as reminiscing about old loves over the third martini.

11.
The Murderer

Evelyn's sudden entrance had violently unsettled Jack's equilibrium. That casual embrace, the light tone of the conversation, Evelyn's agreement to have lunch — all this told Jack what he had always known: those two lived in another world. They put him down, they shut him out. He was a stranger in his own office. It had cost him weeks of effort to get a date with Evelyn. Aspic had succeeded in a minute. And the filthy bitch. Off she went with Aspic — hours before another date! She had rammed one into him!

Jack somehow kept his cool. But after Aspic left, he went into a small collapse. He didn't leave to buy the wine. He sat behind his desk and stared at the wall. His thoughts were racing.

He settled down after a while and convinced himself that it was nothing. They had known each other, those two. No big deal. It didn't change a thing. Evelyn had a hot for him and not for Aspic. Aspic was not desirable, not in that way. He was an ugly thing — made of wire and wadded paper, a guy with hormone problems. They would have lunch and that would be that, and it was ridiculous to worry.

He went out and grabbed a sandwich. Back in his office, he waited until one o'clock. Then he rang Evelyn's extension, but she wasn't there. He tried again at half past one; and then again at a quarter to two; and then again at two. After that he was too embarrassed to call her any more. Evelyn's secretary had become pointedly nasty. Instead Jack began calling her apartment. At first there was no answer. Then the phone turned busy. It stayed busy call after call after call. Three o'clock, three fifteen, three thirty.

Jack felt numb. His head hummed like a fluorescent lamp gone bad. His whole body was one heavy, dull excitement. He was separated from his thoughts. His mind conjured up ever more vile scenes of copulation. He could see them on the bed, doing it, doing it. The princess-style telephone hung by the cord down to the carpet and made cricket sounds.

At last he exploded into action. He couldn't take it any more.

Ten minutes later, he stumbled from a cab and ran into the ornate hall of an apartment house. He vaguely saw a man in a red uniform talking to a girl before a switchboard. Then he had reached an elevator. He jammed the button with such force that his finger ached.

He raged silently as the elevator rose. He rushed from the box before the doors had quite opened. He stopped before her door and rang the bell. He held his index finger on the button.

They were in there and he knew it. The hallway lay in deathly silence, a dim, carpeted length with doors. It smelled of dust. The walls had been well insulated. He couldn't hear the bell ring on the other side.

He pressed the button, let up, pressed. And again.

And again. Then he lost control. He hammered on the door. His fist grew numb. The heavy, solid wood absorbed his blows with a dull sound — like something very strong and very stupid. The door seemed alive and taunting. Jack began to kick it.

At last he heard a metallic noise on the other side followed by the turning of a lock. The door opened a crack, stretching a safety chain across the gap at the level of Jack's eyes. Evelyn's face peered out. Her eyes showed fear.

She held her body out of sight, but Jack saw enough nevertheless. Her face had a puffy, faded look; her chin and cheeks were red with whisker burns. Jack saw the flimsy fabric of a nightgown at her neck.

"Let me in," Jack demanded, his voice dark and guttural with passion. He grabbed the door and shook it so that the safety chain rattled angrily. "Open it up."

She tried to close the door from the other side, pressing herself against it. "Go away, Jack," she said, almost in a whisper. "You're out of your mind."

"You don't have to whisper," he shouted. He wedged his foot into the gap. "I know you're in there, you son of a bitch," he yelled at the top of his lungs, and he threw his shoulder against the door with such force that, on the other side, Evelyn staggered back from the impact. But the chain held.

"Goddammit, open up," Jack yelled into the dark gap, and he pounded the door again. Now that the door was partially open, the sound reverberated and echoed in the hall.

"You heard her, Jack. Go away. You're not wanted."

Aspic had appeared in the gap, naked to the waist. He was very thin. His ribs showed. He had a dark fuzz of black-grey hair across his chest and belly.

"You — cockroach! You filthy, dirty rat," Jack hissed. Completely beyond himself, he pulled back an arm and punched out toward Aspic with all his force, but the gap was too small and his aim uncertain. His knuckles caught the wood, and a jarring pain travelled back up his arm.

The pain merely heightened Jack's rage. He pulled back from the door in preparation for a full-force body lunge meant to tear the chain device from its hinges.

He would have leaped and crashed against the entry, but at that moment two things happened. Aspic quickly slammed the door and rammed the lock home. At the same time, Jack became aware of the fact that he was no longer alone in the hall. Faces stared at him from several open doors. A man in an overcoat came toward him warily. The man carried a briefcase in a peculiar way — as if he meant to use it as a weapon.

"You wait! You just wait," Jack yelled at the impassive solidity of Evelyn's door. Then he ran, away from the approaching man, toward the red glow of an Exit sign.

He ran down the stairs, through the lobby, out of the building, and down the street. Then he hailed a cab and went home to his place in Alexandria. His car was still at Commerce, but he didn't care. Upstairs at last, he found some Jim Beam bourbon and took a drink right from the bottle. It burned his throat and watered his eyes, and he had to spit into the sink. The warmth spread quickly. He drank again. This time it didn't hurt so much. In fact it felt damn good.

The bottle was a fifth, two thirds full. He had touched it last to mix Betty a drink more than a year ago when she had been in Washington to visit. The seven-up he had bought as mixer was still there too — four dusty bottles out of six. Jack was not a drinker, and the bourbon had a quick effect.

He experienced a mixture of feelings. He felt worthless and destroyed, angry and restless. The world belonged to other people, not Jack Clark. You worked, you slaved — no use. Work didn't count. Was he a physicist? No, sir. A garbage jockey. Nuclear garbage, to be sure, but what difference did that make? He didn't have the *class* to be a physicist. No Havahd, no MIT, no daddy with friends on the board of Morgan Guarantee Trust. Could he go out and rip off a hundred thousand bucks — legitimately, at that? No, sir. If he did it — into the slammer. And how come? Because he didn't travel in the right circles, that's how come. His picture on *Time's* cover? Never. Would *he* ever head up an office. No way. Babyface was twenty-seven. Babyface was one of the *real* people, not one of your "honest folk." Not his world. Made in the USA. But for other people.

Goddamned, he wouldn't take it, wouldn't take it lying down. He would do something — something drastic. No other way. Just a slave. A comfortable slave — but still a slave. He was in government, but he was governed by other men — men like Aspic.

And then, having thought the thought of drastic action, something floated into Jack's mind, something he had read or heard. Only a genuine *act* could redeem a man. A *genuine* act. All else was meaningless.

Jack didn't know where the notion had come from. Vaguely, in the back of his mind, he sensed echoes of his days at Kansas University, a philosophy course he had been made to take to enrich his engineering curriculum . . . existentialism . . .

Wherever it had come from, the phrase held a magic charm. A genuine act. It reconciled him to the world. He felt in charge again. He was not altogether impotent. He still had this freedom — he could act.

The yellow pages on his lap, he began calling hotels. Soon he found Aspic at the Hay-Adams and got Aspic's room number. Then he waited. He sucked bourbon, sprawled in a chair. Then he dialed the hotel again and asked for the reservations desk. A male voice came on the telephone, and Jack booked a room for himself under the name of Donald Hamelin. The last time he had stayed at the Hay-Adams, he said, he had been in

Room 311. He wondered . . . The clerk told him that there was no problem.

Jack found his suitcase and threw several sweaters and sweatshirts into it to give the case some weight and to cushion his bottle, which would go along. Then Jack found the service .45 he had been issued as a captain of the National Guard. He put the thing in with the sweaters and the sweatshirts. Then he was off.

Jack didn't think of killing Aspic as he was setting out. He took his .45 because he would be facing conflict. If he had anything in mind at all, it was beating Aspic to a pulp. The thought of murder came somewhat later. He turned murderous as a consequence of drinking and waiting.

He arrived at the Hay-Adams at around seven. He entered the room fifteen minutes later. He spent better than four hours in that room, brooding and waiting, and in that time he convinced himself that nothing short of wasting Aspic constituted a genuine act. By then he had reached and passed the peak of drunkenness and was sliding toward sobriety. Existence seemed a burden too heavy to carry, a worthless joke, and his rage at Aspic had turned icy.

Room 311 was not directly opposite Aspic's room as Jack had imagined it would be. With his own door slightly ajar, he could see part of Aspic's door. The rest of it was blocked by the corner of the corridor. The elevator was around that corner, and while Jack couldn't see it, he could hear a hiss-and-roll when its doors slid aside.

He spent much of that four-hour span peering from his darkened room into the corridor. Every time the elevator stopped, excitement gathered in his throat. The excitement abated when he heard voices or when steps moved off in another direction. Meanwhile he could hear the hotel around him — muffled sounds of television sets, voices, the ring of telephones. Time crept and tortured him.

His waiting had taken on an icy rhythm of its own when the time finally came. He had been aroused so often by the elevator that nothing stirred in him at its hiss-and-roll. But he was alert. He heard steps, and this time they came in his direction. But the approaching party didn't round the corner. Instead the pattern of light changed on the wall next to Aspic's door. Jack heard a key. Someone fumbled mightily to find the lock. Aspic was drunk! Jack waited until the key went in. Then he burst from his room and hurled himself forward with a force and momentum such as he hadn't displayed since his days as a fullback at Centralia High.

Seconds later he picked himself up from the floor. He was inside Aspic's room. He rose with a bound, quickly closed and locked the door, and turned on the light.

He started with surprise.

The man he had tackled and flung inside wasn't Teddy Aspic. He was a small, pudgy man, presently on the floor on hands and knees. Part of him was in a large sitting room, part of him in a narrow entry hall. The man swept the carpet with a hand looking for a pair of glasses dislodged from his face in the fall.

Jack began to back away, terrified by his mistake. Backing, he stuffed the .45 into his belt. His feet stumbled across the key the pudgy man had dropped.

"No, don't go!" cried the little man. He had found his glasses and blinked uncertainly in Jack's direction from a kneeling position. "Come back, man; maybe I can help you."

Contrary impulses paralyzed Jack momentarily. The encounter had jolted him back into a more ordinary state of consciousness, and now he felt a need to murmur some kind of explanation or apology before he disappeared. Good God! What was he doing here!

At the same time, Jack simply wanted to flee. But what if the pudgy man raised the alarm?

The pudgy man had risen, and now he advanced. His eyes looked strange through the thick lenses. His nostrils faced out, two black apertures.

"You're a troubled man, and I'm a healer," said the pudgy man. "Let me help you. I think I can help you. My name is Camilio Templar. What's yours?"

Templar —

Shock washed over Jack as he recognized the name. Templar was one of the consultants assigned to work on the priesthood study. Jack recognized the name because it was unusual. He realized that he was in a suite with more than one bedroom. The desk downstairs had not deceived him after all.

Jack mumbled out an explanation. He had wanted to play a practical joke on a friend, he said. So sorry for the stupid error. It was really inexcusable . . . Then Jack quickly left.

But Templar came behind.

"You're a troubled man. Please don't ignore me. I saw your gun. You need help, my friend, and I can help you. I have no motive but to help."

Templar took Jack by the arm and forced him to stop.

"I'm terribly sorry," Jack said, "but really, it was nothing — a practical joke. I'm fine."

Templar peered at him. "You're Jack Clark, aren't you?"

"Don Hamelin. Don Hamelin from Oklahoma City."

"You came to kill Teddy Aspic," Templar said. He moved his head slowly up and down in an affirmative gesture. "Chained by your karma, the two of you . . . What a deplorable situation. Mr. Clark, I won't take no for an answer. I must have a talk with you. That's a favor you must grant me. You nearly broke my spine back there."

After a moment of tense silence, Jack said, "Where do you want to talk?"

"Not here, of course. Let's go out and find some place where we can be undisturbed."

If anything the icy wind had grown colder and more intense since morning. At this late hour downtown Washington was usually the prowling world of hookers, pimps, bums, and police, but tonight the streets were empty, and the topless place where Jack and Templar soon settled was deserted. A girl took their order. Another one, glad to be doing something, uncoiled herself from the bar stool, stepped up on the platform, and soon was dancing slowly, bobbing her breasts and grinding her hips. Her face was a mask of boredom.

"You were going to throw your life away, back there," Templar began. He rubbed his glasses with a paper napkin. "Now I want you to give me your gun. Then I want to know the reason why."

The .45 pressed against Jack's hip. It felt immense and dangerous, but he couldn't give it up. He was sober now. He wouldn't harm a soul. The time span between Evelyn's appearance in his office and the sight of Templar on the floor seemed now like a mad, crazy, and unbelievable dream. And like a dream, it had left behind a bitter residue of feeling.

"I'm not about to harm a soul."

"You don't know that," Templar said gently. "A man in your situation is not accountable."

"What situation?"

"You're in a karmic bind. You soul is chained."

"I don't understand you." Jack said. Ordinarily he would have said a good deal more. "Karma" marked Templar as a kook, and Jack had no use for the greening of America. But he withheld this observation. He continued to be in a state of shock, and Templar exuded a kind of innocence that Jack could not attack.

Templar replaced his glasses. "No man who is responsible for his actions lurks around in hotel corridors waiting to kill someone. If it could happen to you once, it can happen again. It must have happened countless times before. Unless you stop it and get some help, it's bound to recur. Over and over again. Remember Hermsberg?"

"Remember what?"

"Hermsberg — now give me that gun."

Jack felt confusion, dizziness. He had never drunk a fifth of whiskey at a single sitting. The feeling came from the alcohol. He lowered his head and shook it rapidly, trying to clear the cobwebs.

"I'll have your gun," Templar said, "at least until I've gotten Teddy safely out of town. Do you know Dr. Mahler, incidentally? I would recommend him to you. Remember the name. Dr. Mahler. Now may I have it, please?"

Jack could not explain it. The dizziness returned. He felt nauseous. He would have to vomit in a second. He took the .45 out of his belt and laid it on the plastic seat of the bench they both occupied. He placed it on his left, away from Templar. He had the irrational conviction that Templar could make him give up the weapon.

"Let me see your hand," Templar said.

Still dazed and confused, Jack put his hand on the table. Templar took it, opened the palm, and leaned over the lines. His thick glasses almost touched Jack's skin.

The girl arrived with bourbon for Jack and orange juice for Templar. She thought that the men were holding hands and snickered as she left with her empty tray.

"Hmm," Templar said, peering. "I'm surprised. You're on your way out of the bind, Mr. Clark — unlike that friend of yours and mine, the Dr. Mahler I just mentioned." He released Jack's hand. "Your lines say that you've turned your psychic eyes away from evil and toward the good. Your lines speak of atonement. You're on your way out of the tangle. You've put Hermsberg behind you. You could escape, my friend. But I must have your gun."

Jack gulped his bourbon and Seven-up like a man dying of thirst. The glass crashed back on the table, two-thirds empty. The ice cubes jumped. The girl on the podium stopped momentarily to peer in their direction.

"Stop it, whatever you're doing to me," Jack said to Templar. His tone was pleading, his face white.

"You're fine. You're all right. Too much excitement, too much liquor. Just relax, Mr. Clark. I want to help you. Look at me."

Jack's eyes returned to Templar. A part of his mind noted that Templar was an ugly little creature — but kind.

"Listen," Templar said. "Do it. Get out of this city. You don't belong here. Get away from here. It's for your good, believe me. You're all right. It's obvious from your hand. Something happened to you, back in Hermsberg, something woke you up. You chose a good life for yourself this time around, a life of service and of love. You're not the Nazi killer any more, and Hermsberg is forgiven. But don't let it happen again, break the chain, burst out . . ."

Templar never finished. Moisture had collected rapidly in Jack's mouth. Nausea overwhelmed him. He ran for the men's room, burst in, and was sick over the bowl. His stomach emptied in several convulsions spaced apart in time. In between he staggered about — from a dirty sink to a waste can with a flapping door in its domed lid. His face had a blue coloration in the merciless neon that hung loosely from a frame over the dirty mirror. Sweat beaded Jack's solid face.

At last his sickness passed and he felt close to normal again. He washed his hands and face and went out. But Templar was gone.

PHASE II
Breakthrough in 1992

12.
The Dedication

That troubled September day in 1974 brought drastic changes in Jack's life. He resigned his job with the Commerce Department within days of his encounter with Templar. He packed his few belongings in his car, and he left Washington — forever, as he saw it. He married Betty within months of his arrival in Kansas City and went to work for a small strip mining company with land holdings in Kansas and Kentucky. Four quiet years passed. Two boys were born. Jack's modest income, combined with Betty's earnings as a nurse, secured a decent enough life for them, but Jack was not too happy. He felt restless in the profit-making sector. He had always yearned to be in public service — and in atomics. But he had left that life behind, and he kept his sorrows to himself.

But while Jack lost touch with his previous occupation, the governmental mills continued grinding very slowly. The New Mexico Plan turned into the New

Mexico Project. Engineering studies, design work, environmental assessments, and budget battles succeeded one another year after year. Then, early in 1978, Commerce handed the project over to the Department of Energy for construction, and the search for an initial facility cadre began.

The New Mexico site was in the middle of nowhere, equidistant from Phoenix and Amarillo and south of Albuquerque. The new town to be established — to be called Perpetual, N. M. — lacked everything at that time. Everyone would live in trailers. There were no sewers, much less schools; no electric power, much less movie theaters — and DOE had a hellish time attracting qualified people. The Department turned to the Civil Service Commission. Computer searches were run. And in due time, like a bolt out of the blue, Jack received an offer letter from the government.

He accepted by telegram on the same day. He moved his family to New Mexico a month later. And he was still there fourteen years later, in the Spring of 1992, on the day when the recently completed articaverns were to be dedicated and Jack was about to be rewarded for his long and loyal service at the New Mexico Nuclear Waste Processing and Ultimate Disposal Complex. He was then forty-eight years of age.

That morning, around ten o'clock, he entered Articavern Alpha and mounted steps to a brightly decorated podium. The years had added weight to his stocky figure. His face was red; his cheeks had developed saggy jowls; his heavy beer gut overhung his belt; and he walked with a slight waddle.

He stopped at the lectern, and while pretending to be checking the loudspeaker system, he quickly surveyed the waiting guests. He looked for Betty's familiar, rectangular face.

The cavern lay bathed in mellow light. A red silk ribbon divided the space into unequal halves. On

Jack's side of the underground enclosure, Perpetual's prominent citizens settled into rows of folding chairs. The men wore suits, the women formal dresses. Both sexes wore white hard hats bearing the emblem of the Department of Energy. Jack didn't see Betty anywhere.

He fussed with the microphone a little longer, still hoping to glimpse her. One of the media teams chose that moment to test its lights, and Jack was momentarily blinded; but then the lights faded away slowly. He gave up his search for Betty from that raised perspective and walked to the chair he was to occupy during the ceremony. He carried an oblong case; he placed it on the chair. Inside the case reposed a pair of golden scissors. Jack would hand the scissors to Stanley Morgan later — after the speeches were done. Morgan would cut the ribbon, thus opening this latest addition to the Complex.

Jack left the podium. He headed for the elevators but then he changed his mind. Instead he turned toward a freshly painted yellow front-end loader. It stood near the ribbon, under Fredrickson's loving care. A 200-liter barrel painted shiny black rested on its fork lift. The barrel held cemented nuclear waste.

"Everything ready?" Jack asked.

Fredrickson wore a pair of brand new overalls and had scrubbed himself lobster pink for the occasion. He told Jack that everything was set to go.

Jack lingered, still searching the crowd. He turned to leave at last, but people had noticed him, and three couples converged on him. They insisted on shaking his hand.

"I'm not general manager *yet,*" Jack protested, blushing, but he smiled with pleasure at all the attention.

"Not yet," said Charlie O'Brian, Perpetual's chief of police. He was a tall man with a balding crown, a droopy nose, and merry eyes. He poked Jack's sizeable beer gut with an index finger. "Not yet, old boy," he said. "But rumor has it that the Big Man will announce the good news during the luncheon."

"We can't keep any secrets around here," Jack said with mock regret. Then he looked about again with a nervous, distracted expression. "I appreciate the good words, and all," he said, "but I've got to run. Did any of you see Betty?"

No one had seen Betty, and Jack went on.

The arti-caverns lay deep underground, smooth-walled hemispherical caves carved from bedrock by plasma technology. Vertical shafts linked the caves with the surface, and Jack made for one of these. An elevator took him to ground level and then eight stories up. He hurried back to the conference room where Throckmorton was still briefing Stanley Morgan.

Jack slipped into the darkened room and took his seat again. Throckmorton lectured, a pointer in his hand. He was boring Morgan. Morgan hadn't come here to learn that the bedrock had left the caves as ionized gas . . . Morgan fingered a stack of index cards. He peered at his watch — pointedly, Jack thought.

Matter of fact, Jack thought, why *had* Stanley Morgan come? A new technology had been used to carve the arti-caverns from the bedrock, but the Secretary of Energy didn't fly two thousand miles to a miserable little place with ten thousand people, in New Mexico, at that, which had no electoral votes worth mentioning — just to bless some arti-caverns.

Jack's thoughts wandered back to a discussion held the night before at Puccini's bar. Ray Pisciotta of the *Gazette* had said that Morgan was coming to make a major policy speech. "Either that," Ray had said, "or Morgan has picked Perpetual to break with the Administration on foreign policy. That's certainly in the cards."

"Come on, " O'Brian had cried. "In Perpetual?"

"Sure. There is a tradition about so-called major policy speeches. Remember Churchill? He gave the Iron Curtain speech in some godforsaken little hole in Missouri. So Morgan picks Perpetual, which isn't such a bad idea. There is lots of symbolism in that name. And we're a nuclear facility, meaning power, energy. My bet is that Morgan wants to send a little message to our yellow brothers in Mao-Mao Land."

"He can't do that," Jack had said. "The policy is non-intervention."

"Sure it is. But who says that Morgan wants to toe the line. '96 is just four short years away, and you've heard all those speculations about third parties."

A major policy speech, Jack thought, eyes on Stanley Morgan. *Maybe.* Morgan sat curled forward, like a spring, and looked the way the papers described him — slim, dark, and intense. New York State had not produced a top-ranked politician in nearly two decades. Now that such a man had finally emerged from that bankrupt region, he turned out to be the most exciting political property around. Both parties curried his favor, but he steered carefully between them. *He might be president one of these days*, Jack thought — but he wished that Throcky would get on with it. If Betty didn't show . . .

Throckmorton's droning finally ended. Morgan, uncoiling, instantly rose. Jack moved forward to get Morgan's attention. "Mr. Secretary." Sharp, cool eyes caught his. "This way, Mr. Secretary." Then Jack led the way out of the conference room.

A glass-covered corridor ringed the top floor of the Administrative Tower. It gave a good view of the Complex. Morgan had passed that way on his arrival, but a dust storm had obscured the view. Now the Complex lay below, fully revealed. Morgan glanced out and saw the vista; he hesitated, looked at his watch, turned, and gestured.

"So that's it," he said. "Quite an operation for such small quantities of waste."

Jack turned a little red. Morgan echoed a carping theme the nation's media never tired of playing. They called the Complex a white elephant and worse. The outside world had no real understanding of the issues.

Although he disagreed, Jack said, "Yes, sir. Most of this was built in the late 1970's. Back then we expected quite a flood of nuclear waste."

"But the industry never took off," Morgan said, nodding. "Well, that flood will start soon." He seemed to become aware of Jack just then, glanced at him, and said, "How long have you been out here?"

"Since 1978, Mr. Secretary."

"You like it out here?"

"Yes sir. It's the kind of work I like — and remote locations go with the job."

Morgan considered that, nodded. "I guess that's right. What are those things, over on the left?"

Morgan pointed to a cluster of buildings partially hidden from view by one of the many dome-like rises that dotted the landscape.

"That's hydrafracture unit three," Jack said. "It's the one we use routinely."

"And all those ponds?"

"They're evaporation and cooling lagoons, Mr. Secretary. We hold low-rad waste in some of them — wastes we generate in the detoxification plant." Jack pointed. "Over there. But most of these are cooling ponds."

"Not for fishing," Morgan said. And he gave a quick, bright, flashy, theatrical smile.

"No sir."

Morgan glanced at his watch and nodded. "Very nice," he said, dismissing the scene.

"This way, sir," Jack said. He led the way. Morgan, his entourage, and the Complex's staff members followed him to the elevator.

The crowd stirred and then subsided when Morgan

entered Arti-cavern Alpha and, led by Jack, mounted the platform. He sat down on the chair Jack designated and shook hands with the governor who was already there. Then the other dignitaries settled down as well. Finally Van Thie Tran, public affairs director for the DOE, approached the speaker's lectern to make the introductions and to kick off the ceremonies.

Jack saw Betty finally and experienced relief. The old girl had come. They had quarrelled that morning over Jack's suit. He had refused to wear the new pinstriped job she had bought in Albuquerque just for this occasion, preferring the old reliable blue suit he now had on. She had said that he looked ridiculous, had outgrown his old suit, had turned "grossly fat." Then, in a sudden fury, he had flung the hair brush against the mirror, and while the mirror had survived the blow, some of Betty's glass animals on the dresser had not.

She still refused to look at him, but at least she had come, which meant that she would get over it. She wouldn't give him the silent treatment as she had, for fifteen days — yes, fifteen days — back when he had quit his job in Kansas City and had dragged her and the children west.

Donald Duncan rose now to applause; he was the governor of New Mexico. The governor was proud, he said, to be a part of this dedication. The great state of New Mexico was proud to contribute to the solution of the Nation's ever-mounting energy problems by hosting the New Mexico Nuclear Waste Processing and Ultimate Disposal Complex — this proud aggregation of the most modern technology and dedicated people . . .

Blah, blah, blah, blah, Jack thought. *Get on with it, will you; move it.* Jack wanted to hear Stanley Morgan who, at that moment, sat leaning forward, his eyes on index cards.

Jack looked in Betty's direction again, and this time

she looked him in the eyes. Her rectangular face, framed by black hair, still had a forbidding expression, but then her features softened, and she winked at him. Jack winked back. Then he took a deep breath and expelled it slowly. All was right in his world.

The governor wound up at last, saying how proud he was. And now it was his pleasure to introduce an illustrious colleague and an ex-governor of the great, proud state of New York, a man who needed no introduction, his very good friend — blah, blah, blah. And Morgan rose, holding index cards, as applause echoed in Arti-cavern Alpha. Jack settled back to listen, filled with curiosity.

Morgan began with congratulations, little bows to right and left. He mentioned names, Jack's among them; he noted the occasion; he commented on the facilities... Then, pausing, Morgan began again. He asked his audience to contemplate the wider meaning of this day. He asked them to recall to mind the reasons why they were all here. The media turned on their lights and started taping.

Jack listened to the historical sketch that followed wondering where Morgan would end up. Morgan retraced the energy crisis from its beginnings in the 1970's. He started mildly, but his tone grew increasingly more harsh. He listed policies one after the other. After each one he asked and answered a question. "Did that policy put gas in our tanks? No, my friends, it did not."

Then came another pause. It seemed like a pregnant pause. Morgan appeared to be hesitating. He moved his cards. He took a deep breath. He coiled the spring of his tense body. Then, exhaling, he continued.

He wondered whether, against that background, the current Administration policy — a policy unchanged in nearly a quarter of a century, the Kissinger tradition, the strategy of negotiation, the policy of "Mister

Nice Guy" (if he was permitted to label it thus) — whether that policy was still viable vis-a-vis the Arab-Peking axis. He didn't think so. *(Hear, hear!)* And in its place he proposed to put another policy — proposed to throw it open for public discussion. What was that policy? It was the policy of "No More Mister Nice Guy."

In the pause that Morgan now made to let his words sink in, Jack tried to find Ray Pisciotta in the crowd. The editor had been right. Morgan was breaking with the Administration's stand. This would create an uproar in the nation! Jack couldn't find Pisciotta, and Morgan resumed.

Force, he said, had been despised too long — far too long — by both of the major national parties. US military might had increased in the last decades. We had weapons systems now, thanks to the power of research and native ingenuity, such as the world had never seen before. Morgan couldn't talk about them, but he knew what lay in our arsenal. And knowing what he did, and seeing the world beyond our shores mounting an ever more successful economic war against our shores, he couldn't understand, he found it incomprehensible, why one administration after the other embraced the policy of Walter Mitty rather than the policies of John Wayne!

Then, pausing again, Morgan laid his index cards aside. He drew himself up and his eyes swept imperiously over the audience.

"America is tired," he cried. "America has had enough. Americans want leadership. Americans demand that we strike back at our enemies — yes, ladies and gentlemen, our *enemies*. Let's call a spade a spade, for once. When foreigners step on our necks, let's yell, let's scream, let's fight back, for once. When the people who eat our grain, and drive our cars, and fly our planes — when the folks who lobby in our congress for more aid — when the people who accept our medical and social help—when those same people cut our pipelines and send our tankers back to us empty—then, my friends, it's time to *act*! To act instead of negotiating. To act in place of apologies. And I'm ready to act, I am resolved to act. At this very hour, my resignation is being handed to the President. Yes, my friends, I am leaving the cabinet, I am leaving this administration. And I shall lead a national crusade to regain the honor we have lost over the decades!"

Jack sat, stunned. One thought kept repeating in his mind. *This'll put Perpetual on the map. This'll put us on the map.* He wondered how the people would react, what the networks would report, what statement the White House would issue. Here he was, about to hand the golden scissors to a man at what might well be the start of a new era. "No More Mister Nice Guy." The phrase would echo for years to come—especially if Stanley Morgan was elected president.

Morgan had picked up his cards again. He read the concluding paragraphs now. He rattled them off. Pisciotta had been right. Morgan had spoken for the cameras, to the nation, not the assembly of smartly dressed Perpetual VIP's. The media wouldn't carry the final remarks. Then Morgan was finished. He stepped back amidst applause.

Jack waited until the applause died down. Then he touched Morgan's elbow. "This way, sir."

He led Morgan off the podium and then down the aisle between the folding chairs toward the shiny front-end loader. The guests had risen and resumed applauding.

Embarrassed and foolishly grinning, Fredrickson showed Morgan how to operate the fork lift. Then, while Fredrickson withdrew, Jack and Morgan positioned themselves before the red ribbon. Cameras flashed. The TV crews taped. Jack opened the case and held it out to Morgan. Morgan took the scissors. He cut the ribbon. The people clapped. Jack took the scissors and replaced them in the case while Morgan mounted the front-end loader and, amidst yet more applause, drove it across the invisible line where seconds ago the red ribbon had hung.

13.
The Prophecy

Secretary Morgan's eight-passenger jet zoomed down the runway and rose swiftly, steeply, into the sky. It was now three in the afternoon. A few strangers still lingered in Perpetual, but on the whole things were back to normal again — with one difference. Jack was now formally General Manager of the Complex. He drove Betty home from the airport basking in the glory of it all.

"I think I'll change," he said, guiding the station wagon down the empty road. "Then I'll just go out to the Complex and look around a little." His kingdom. He wanted to inspect it through general manager eyes.

Betty looked benevolent. The morning's fracas was forgotten. "You do that," she said.

He put on a comfortable khaki outfit after they got home. Early that morning, while Betty had been in the shower, he had filled a picnic cooler with cans of beer on ice. He put the cooler in the dusty jeep he used for his official rounds. Betty didn't see him do it, which was just as well. He went back in the house and gave her a kiss. Then he drove off.

The Complex occupied nearly six hundred acres of what had been — and legally still was — Shashtuk Indian reservation. A double chainlink fence went all around the Complex. Rough tracks on either side of it were suitable for vehicular traffic, and Jack decided to drive around the outside first. He set a leisurely pace, rolling up and down little hills, the Complex to his right.

The country had a greenish-yellow tinge around here and, like much of this desert region, it was empty and silent. Small bushes and tall cacti sat amidst sand and scrub, waiting, waiting — Jack couldn't guess for what. Rain, maybe. But there wouldn't be any rain until the fall. The land was dry, bone dry, and the slightest wind could raise huge carpets of dust that coiled away into the unforgiving blue of the sky.

Jack liked it out here. He didn't miss the cities, he didn't miss the hustle and the bustle and the grind — least of all these days. Inflation being what it was, and with the chronic energy shortage, who could afford to buy a house any more. People flocked back to the inner cities. They lived like sardines, packed in thick. Even on his salary he couldn't live in the suburbs of Kansas City any more — not to mention Washington. He was glad that he had escaped all that. *And*, he thought, *if Stanley Morgan should succeed, and we adopt an aggressive foreign policy, we'll have to tighten our belts still more. And then those of us out in the sticks will be much better off. Let 'em call us hicks as much as they like. We'll still have our houses and yards — even if nothing much grows out here in the desert.*

He stopped the jeep, opened the ice box, and took out a cool one. He was about to open the can when he saw a dust cloud in the distance. He put the can back, guessing that he saw a security patrol — and it wouldn't do to drink in front of Indians.

Jack had guessed correctly. His own jeep's dusty trail had attracted one of the patrols. The vehicle arrived, stopped and two men got out.

Security guards serving the Complex came from the Shashtuk tribe. Jack knew the boys who now approached him. Joe and John Bull were brothers. They looked remarkably alike. Both had big round faces and long, glistening, blue-black hair. But Joe was ambitious and rowdy, John reticent and shy.

"Hey, Mr. Clark," Joe cried. "I thought it was you. It's so dry we saw your dust from way back — from Purple Sage lagoon." Joe held out a hand. "Congratulations, boss. I didn't have a chance earlier. The place was crawling with VIP's."

"Thanks," Jack said.

John Bull came up. "Me too," he said. "Best of luck, Mr. Clark."

They stood about and discussed recent events. The media people had left a deep impression on the security men. They told stories about the pushy ways of the network crews. It appeared that a team from CBS had gone down to the Shashtuk village to get background stories. The old folk, Joe Bull said, had refused to be filmed, and there had been hassles. Another team had been caught filming the facility from Custer's Rim, and when Fred Cactus tried to take away the film clip, one of the men had pulled a gun. Jack couldn't believe that story, quite, but he let it pass.

The men were about to break up when John Bull said: "You know, Mr. Clark, we knew you'd be the one."

"Yeah," Joe chimed in. "It didn't come as no surprise for us."

"Well," Jack said, "I'm glad to see you had such confidence in me."

"That's not it," Joe said. Then he nudged his brother with an elbow. "Go on, Horse, you tell him."

John Bull, however, had suddenly turned shy. He looked down at the dusty tips of his scuffed cowboy boots.

"All right," Joe said. "Horse don't want to tell you, but it's no big deal. It ain't no secret. You've heard about Chief Walk-on-air, haven't you, boss?"

Jack narrowed his eyes and looked up at the sky. He had a vague recollection of some ancient Indian witchdoctor whose roundhouse had had to be moved somewhere to the east of what was now the airport — but that had been ten years ago. It surprised him that the old man was still alive.

"The medicine man? Is he still around?"

"Chief Walk-on-air will never die," Joe said with a twinkle in his eye. "Or so they all say. Me, I don't know. I think the old man is a little off his rocker, but he's a damn good fortune teller — no denying that."

Among the security guards, Joe Bull was by far the most Americanized. He did his best to put a distance between tribal ways and his own behavior, but obviously he didn't always succeed. His voice betrayed respect for the medicine man.

"What did he do?" Jack asked. "Did he predict that I'd be the next general manager?"

"Not exactly," Joe said. He looked at his brother again. "Horse heard him tell it, Horse ought to tell you. Go on, Horse, tell the boss." But when John Bull continued to stare fixedly at the ground, Joe shrugged. "Horse ran around with Chief Walk-on-air a few years back. The Chief was teaching Horse all about sorcery. Chief Air told John that you'd be general manager around here some day. You and some guys were running a survey back around Devil's Point. Horse and the old man were out collecting herbs not far from there. Suddenly old Walk-on-air points to you and says that you'll be the last general manager of the Complex."

"The *last* general manager?"

"That's what he said. I don't know how he figured that, but that's what he said."

Joe gestured toward the visible portion of the Complex as he spoke by way of saying — How can all this continue to exist without a general manager?

Jack understood the gesture and had to agree. He saw Hydrafracture Unit Two, parts of Liquid Processing Gamma, and between them the bright mirror-surface of Charlie Horse lagoon. Domed hills hid the rest of the Complex.

Just the part Jack saw was huge — a clustering of giant concrete bunkers, silvery storage tanks on stilts, graceful towers linked by pipeways. The Complex would last forever — much longer than Jack Clark.

"Well, I don't know," Jack said. "Chief Walk-on-air might be a pretty good guesser, but as for 'last,' I don't know about that. That sounds a little crazy."

Jack's statement aroused John Bull at last. The young man looked up. His eyes were bright. "Chief Walk-on-air is never wrong. I know it. He knows things."

Jack had learned not to argue with fanatics, and this boy seemed taken with his sorcerer. "Well, maybe," Jack said, evading a confrontation.

"Tell him about the other thing," Joe said. "Tell him what the Chief said about the Dying."

Jack looked at John, then back at Joe. "What Dying?" A tinge of irritation had entered his voice, and he wondered fleetingly what he was doing here, on his day of triumph, talking to a couple of superstitious Indians. This was no time to talk about "dying."

"I'm not much for this sorcery stuff," Joe said, once more distancing himself from tribal ways, "but I've got to go along with Horse on this. Chief Walk-on-air really does know things about the future. That's why I wanted Horse to tell you about the Dying. The Chief said one time that someday all of this will be gone."

Joe gestured in a circle, his Stetson in his hand, encompassing desert and Complex. "And when that day comes, he said, it'll be dangerous to die around here."

Jack made a face by way of reaction. "Dangerous to *die* here? I'd say that any place is dangerous to 'die' in, if you ask me." He scratched behind his ear. "It sounds all mixed up. He probably said that it'll be dangerous to *live* around here."

John Bull once more roused himself. "Chief Walk-on-air says what he means. We don't understand it either, but that's what he said."

"Well," Jack said edgily, "you heard him, I didn't. Where does he live nowadays? Still out beyond the airport? I might just go out there and ask him myself."

After the Bull brothers had driven off, Jack opened his can of beer. He drank most of it down. He felt thirsty and irritable. He didn't like the conversation he had just concluded with the Indians. It didn't fit his conception of his first hours as general manager. Besides, he had a very low opinion of prophecy and such. Betty was keen on astrology. She was forever trying to read his horoscope to Jack, but Jack refused to hear it. He didn't want to be influenced by what it said in the paper — and no matter how convinced he was that astrology was a crock of shit, it *did* influence him if he knew about it.

He finished the can and opened a second one. The dust cloud raised by the security jeep was settling down over the rolling, rippled ground immediately adjacent to the fence. It was hot out in the desert.

He drank about a third of the beer — enough so that it wouldn't spill. Then he heaved himself back into the jeep, groaning a little — he really was a little heavy, though "grossly fat" was an exaggeration — started the engine, and continued the tour.

No matter where you went or what you did, Jack thought, you couldn't quite escape them. He meant the "crazies" — people who speculated about things you couldn't know about. He had had it with the future years ago, in Washington. All he wanted was to live his life, to live along, quietly, minding his own business, serving the little people of the world. But the crazies were never very far away.

After a while the empty stillness of the landscape — which seemed unaffected by the roaring of Jack's jeep — the rhythmic-random bouncing of the vehicle, and the soothing effect of alcohol combined to erase his temporary irritation. He stopped from time to time and meditated on the Complex from various perspectives — the place he had conceived in his mind as a bureaucrat in Washington, the place he had helped to build in various capacities, rising slowly through the ranks. The place, above all, whose manager he had at last become.

The work seemed good to him. The future held no drama — just quiet efficient work. Chief Walk-on-air was just a crazy injun. The Complex — all that metal, all that concrete, all those shimmering lagoons, the slender administration needle far away, up on the hill, now catching the afternoon sun — this was reality.

Jack's cooler was empty by the time, having completed his circuit, he entered the Complex by the front gate. He waved to the security guards full of good humor and generosity. He drove up the hill and parked the jeep in the slot marked General Manager.

He got out. Then, yielding to an impulse, he wrote WASH ME into the thick dust layer on the hood of his jeep.

14.
Batch 381 (Mice)

Theodore Aspic sat in an armchair in a dark, windowless room. The room formed part of an apartment, and the apartment part of Future Now's Mountainview Experimental Research Station. The Station resembled a large private residence from the outside — the house, perhaps, of an eccentric, reclusive, and hypochondriac bachelor. It had a tall bamboo fence on three sides, and it was immediately next door to Santa Lucia General Hospital. It bore no corporate sign on the entrance. It had its own power supplies deep underground. Neither state nor county had approved the construction plans, thanks to discrete federal intervention. And the mailman had learned long ago that no one ever wrote to 6238 La Hacienda Drive.

Aspic sat with his head tilted back. Beads of sweat had formed on his forehead. It was morning. He had spent the night in Mountainview. He had risen less than thirty minutes earlier, had put on the bathrobe he still wore, and then he had picked up the special mail a messenger had brought out from the city early in the morning.

A part of that mail — a large yellow envelope, several typed pages, and six large photographs — rested on Aspic's lap. He had been reading the report and looking at the pictures when It had begun again.

Sweating, eyes out of focus, Aspic tried to find the inner resources he needed to rise from the chair, to walk to the bathroom cabinet, and to give himself the injection. It took a long time to muster so much force, to concentrate his will to that extent. But he succeeded finally. He rose. He laid aside the package he held on his lap. Slowly he walked to the bathroom.

Moments later, with trembling fingers, he sucked drug into the hypodermic from a small flask. He held the needle into the light and squirted a hair-thin stream into the air. He swabbed his arm with an alcohol-impregnated ball of cotton, clumsily — he still held the hypodermic. Then, with gritted teeth, he injected the drug into his arm.

The drug was a proprietary formulation known as Philotran. It was a palliative for schizophrenia. It had been on the market for six months. Dr. Bermogen, Aspic's personal physician, had urged Aspic to use the drug. "Philotran has its dangers, Teddy," Bermogen had said. "I have in mind the manic episodes that sometimes follow its use. Nevertheless, with a case like yours, we have to take a few chances." Aspic had resisted using the drug. This was only the third time in as many months. Using the drug implied at least that he was mad — and he knew that he wasn't. But his malaise had worn him out. Even the implication of madness no longer bothered him, and as for manic episodes, they didn't frighten Aspic nearly as much as these crippling depressions.

On schizophrenics Philotran worked like a flash. But Aspic suffered from karmic memories. The drug was not specifically indicated for such an ailment. Such an ailment was not officially recognized in any lexicon of psychic illness, and Aspic had no intention of submitting himself to analysis more rigorous than that provided by Dr. Bermogen — who worked for Future Now. Karmic malaise — Aspic's Syndrome — would never be described.

Back in his armchair, half seated and half reclining, Aspic waited a long time for Philotran to work. Relief came very gradually. Bermogen said that adrenalin was one of the components — or one of the components stimulated adrenalin flow. But the chemical system had other effects as well. Aspic experienced a fading of his malaise. It disappeared behind a curtain of numbness. At the same time Aspic's mind grew sharp and piercing. He felt keenly alert — and inclined to listen for a sound that could not be heard.

He opened his eyes at last, sat straight up in his chair, and once more picked up the package he had been studying.

The package was a report, including several color photographs taken through a telephoto lens. At roughly annual intervals, Aspic commissioned a detective agency to give him an update on the appearance, doings, and general status of Jack Clark. This report had been ordered more than a month before, days after Aspic had seen a photograph of Clark in the *San Francisco Chronicle.* Clark had been shown handing a pair of scissors to Stanley Morgan on the occasion of Morgan's outrageous No More Mister Nice Guy speech. With some alarm, Aspic had noted that Clark was getting unusually fat.

Now the report was in. Aspic had his own pictures. Though they had been taken from a distance, optics and photography had so improved during the last decade that Aspic might have been looking at close-ups done in a studio. Even without the fine detail, he could have seen the signs he was looking for — the thick, red, swollen neck; the bluish, saggy cheeks; the nose heavily colored by tiny, bluish veins.

Aspic shuffled through the photos, studying each one in turn through the pleasant numbness of Philotran. A heavy, gross, fat man — the Beast grown middle-aged.

Next he took up the written report and found that it confirmed what Aspic could see for himself. Jack's physical condition was deteriorating. The man ate too much of the wrong types of food; he drank a great deal; he didn't exercise. And now, it seemed, he was on drugs as well.

Aspic reread the pertinent paragraph.

"In checking on a rumor that has begun to circulate around Perpetual recently," he read, "subject was observed entering the dwelling of a Shashtuk Indian medicine man where, according to reliable local sources, drugs (predominantly peyote but possibly others) are dispensed to the medicine man's 'disciples.' It was not possible to ascertain whether or not subject is a 'disciple,' but gossip here claims that subject 'has gone native.'"

Aspic laid the package aside. He stared into the room's darkness for a while. The only light came from a lamp on the table where Clark's pictures now lay. Aspic didn't like the agency's report at all. Despite Philotran's numbing effect, he experienced a twinge of anxiety, a touch of that rage engendered by helplessness.

Presently Aspic rose to shower and to shave. Shaving, he commented unfavorably on the face that looked back from the mirror. The years had been unkind to him — a haggard man who had a tortured look. The whites of his moist eyes were shot through with red. His hair had turned completely white.

Success, he thought, feeling bitter. In Wall Street circles he was thought very successful because Future

Now had joined the ranks of the New Technology Conglomerates and NTC's were all the rage these days. But neither Future Now's success, nor Aspic's personal accumulations of wealth, nor yet his success thus far with the psychotron — which was enough for two, three Nobel prizes if he cared to publish, which he did not — could change the fact that thus far he had really failed in the experiments that meant the most to him. Nor could "success" cure his malaise. He was in a race against mortality, and just now it looked as if he would lose that race. Clark looked like a candidate for a coronary. *And those goddamned mice,* he thought, splashing water on his face, *are not producing, not producing . . .*

Wearing a fresh lab coat, he entered the super-secure office he maintained adjacent to the apartment. The small room — all the rooms were relatively small owing the expense of psychon shielding — had a safe-type lock. Aspic sat down behind the desk and turned on the recording device. His secretary's voice came over the speaker.

"Good morning, Mr. Aspic. This will remind you of the Executive Committee meeting at 1:30. A call came in last night from Miss Evelyn's lawyers. They want to talk about the alimony escalation clause. Mr. Horowitz said that you would understand. And then there is a telex from Japan. I'm afraid it's bad news. They say that test series 204 has come out negative. The explanation is unstable polymer chains. I'd like to know if it's all right if I take off early Friday afternoon. My mother is coming to San Francisco. Have a nice day, Mr. Aspic."

Aspic had a momentary sensation of guilt. He should do the right thing today — go downtown and take charge of his life rather than hiding here in Mountainview chasing illusions. He had become reclusive, almost people-shy. And this place was driving him nuts.

But Aspic's guilt died away. He picked up the telephone, punched a series of numbers, and spoke into the activated dictaphone.

"Patti, tell Mr. McKee to take the Executive Committee meeting for me. I won't be able to get away from Mountainview. Call Mason at the law firm and tell *him* to deal with Miss Evelyn's lawyers — and tell them I don't care where Mason is, I want them to handle it. Have them put another lawyer on the case if Mason is in Europe again, but tell them that I don't want to be bothered. Please send me a copy of the Japanese telex on the telecopier. And have a good time on Friday afternoon."

Aspic then rose and crossed over to the wall opposite his desk. The pictures of thirty-some women hung there in identical frames. Several were turned around so that only the cardboard backing, secured by staples, could be seen. Aspic reached for one of these and turned it. For a moment he stared at a photograph of Evelyn, thinking uncomplimentary thoughts. Then he replaced the picture, the face once more against the wall.

He left the room thinking that everything connected with Jack Clark had caused him either pain or loss of money, Evelyn along with everything else. Their marriage had lasted less than a year. She had claimed that he was impotent, and he had charged her with adultery. But she had won against him in the courts, and since then she had sucked resources out of Aspic at an increasing rate to support her wilting playgirl career in Washington, D.C.

It was after that divorce — to show himself that she had been wrong about him — that Aspic had begun to photograph and mount on his wall pictures of women he had satisfied. Indeed. He had been impotent with Evelyn, although not immediately, only toward the end. While his divorce from Helen was in the works, he and Evelyn had lived like wild lovers. But then . . .

Without success, he tried to wipe away the memory of his first and last sexual failure with Evelyn. Soon after their marriage. They had visited friends that evening, had just gotten home. She sat on a round stool at the kitchen counter sipping coffee, . . . *no,* Aspic commanded himself. That damnable scene. Turning toward him, lips parted, ready to be led upstairs, she had suddenly brought to his mind that frightful nexus of memories of Germany, and he had realized with a rush of panic that she might have been his daughter once and that he might be skirting on the edge of some kind of weirdly incestuous act. The thought was ridiculous, the notion truly bizarre, but that momentary wonder — and the feeling that another person shone or radiated from behind Evelyn's down-lidded, lip-parted, pleasure-seeking face — sufficed to freeze his passion. He had feigned the sudden, debilitating onset of a crippling headache. He never touched her again.

Aspic took a deep breath. Why did he have to relive that experience over and over again? He forced himself to concentrate on the present.

This'll be some day, he thought. *Jack Clark looks like he won't make it through the summer. I have the malaise again. Evelyn is suing again for more alimony yet. And the Japanese have failed on yet another formulation of that damn memory enzyme . . .*

Aspic had no appetite for work today. He steered away from the animal labs and entered a laboratory to his left instead. The room housed the central psycho-magnet and the psychon storage tanks.

Much of the room, the portion to Aspic's left, was dominated by a gigantic cube of glass. It might have been an enourmous ice cube, but on closer examination it revealed itself as a structure made of small hexagonal glass cubicles piled one on top of the other in tier after tier. Small instruments extended from each of these glass aquaria, and tiny luminosities glowed inside a few of them.

A middle-aged woman on crutches stood before the beehive of glass and recorded instrument readings on a clipboard. Like all the help in the Mountainview facility, Mrs. Gerber was handicapped in body as in mind. She believed, they all believed, that the flickering, blueish lights behind glass were cosmic rays that Aspic captured on behalf of the Weather Bureau. Instead they were psychons, caught as they escaped from the adjacent hospital.

"How many did we catch last night?" Aspic asked. He spoke loudly. Mrs. Gerber was hard of hearing.

She held up a hand, fingers apart.

"Five?"

She smiled angelically, nodded, and went back to her work.

It had been a slow night. They had seen a richer harvest when Santa Lucia's nurses had been on strike a month ago. Or could the magnet be decaying? This model was virtually indestructible. The Japanese had succeeded in this case. He approached the magnet to check its instruments.

The magnet itself was an artificial ovum, slimy in appearance, and the size of a grapefruit. It floated in a hazy, golden liquid, in a rectangular tank. Arranged on the four corners of the tank were devices that resembled, and had been modelled on, electron beam guns. A constant but invisible bombardment reached the ovum from the guns. A funnel-like construct suspended from the ceiling drew the ovum's excitations upward and channelled them to "broadcast" baskets mounted inconspicuously on the facility's roof. Psychons "heard" the excitation, entered the facility, and were diverted and caught in the glass beehive whose innards were cooled to cryogenic temperatures by liquid nitrogen.

Aspic checked several instruments arranged on a

separate but nearby console. A plaque on the console said: "Dedicated to the Scientists of Tibet."

Aspic had mounted the plaque in 1985, a month after the first psychon had been frozen in a layer of gas — a triumphant time. He owned his triumph to Tibet — therefore the plaque. He had solved the riddle after years of failure while reading *The Tibetan Book of the Dead.* He had tried every type of electromagnetic radiation by then. Then, reading the ancient text one night, he had learned that he must use sex. Sex drew souls to be reborn. They heard or felt people copulating — it was there in black and white. Souls perceived the ecstatic "cries" of an ovum about to be penetrated by a wiggling sperm. The idea was Aspic's, its execution Japanese. Osaka dominated genetic engineering in the world these days. Osaka had created the first artificial ovum for Aspic — and also the pseudo-semen with which he bombarded his eggs.

The ovum was in tip-top shape. Still, Aspic lingered a little. The drug had toned down and flattened his emotions — but not enough to kill the pain — and Aspic felt nothing but pain these days when working with the mice.

He moved at last into an adjoining room, still procrastinating. He went to inspect the conditioning drums. "Doc" Sturm greeted him loudly from behind a work bench to the left of the door. Doc worked from his wheelchair. He assembled one of the newer versions of the drum. He had an insufferably loud voice and crude manners, but his hands were deft.

"How are you coming?"

"Not coming at all," Doc bellowed, winking. He had just delivered one of his standard lines. "Too damned old to come," he shouted. But he held up half of a drum for Aspic to see.

The drums were shaped like cornucopia, wide-mouthed at one end, tapered at the other. Doc fitted tiny flakes of plastic to the inside of the drum in an intricate pattern. Each flake contained a minute particle of ovum inoculated with a conditioning agent.

Aspic praised the work, but he was gloomy. He had achieved great things thus far — but catching souls seemed routine. They did it at the rate of at least five souls a night. Quite something else to condition the little buggers. Six years. And as yet they still hadn't taught a single psychon one last blessed goddamned thing!

To Aspic's right stood eight turning cornucopia, their wide mouths facing out. *Like a line-up of agencies*, he thought. Defense sponsored the first two on the right; next came Interior's machine, then Labor's; Health, Education, and Welfare had its own project; the Treasury. The last drum, heavily shielded on all sides, belonged to Commerce. It was the continuation of a project begun a long time ago — the priesthood proposition. Psychons in that drum were getting healthy doses of ionizing radiation.

They all want to condition souls, every last one of them . . .

Aspic watched madly twirling balls of light inside the drums, coils of psychons turning round and round. They strove to reach the magnets embedded in the drum walls, but they couldn't do it. Each agency had its pet conditioning agent and its ultra-secret research budget to support this work. The rich profits allowed Aspic to pursue his own research. *His* objective was immortality. But the Japanese kept failing on that project. They kept finding analogues to the right memory enzymes — but they couldn't stabilize them. Reborn mice just wouldn't remember skills that Aspic taught their predecessors.

"See you," he said to "Doc" Sturm.

"Don't lay anything I wouldn't lay!" Doc shouted.

Aspic now entered a very large room. He had spent far too much time in this hall-like expanse of late — trying to *force* the experiments to succeed, convinced that he was racing death, Jack Clark's or his own. Despite the Philotran, he felt disgust.

Three long tables to his right held intricate mazes, wheels, towers, and cages. The mice learned unusual skills in those devices. A heavy, padded door in the right corner led to a miniature gas chamber where trained mice expired in cyanide fumes; their psychons were captured and conditioned in drum after drum with agent after agent. They were "decanted" into "mouse conceptions" inside a complex of wire cages to Aspic's left. Tier upon tier of mice, one pair to a cage, charged up with hormone shots, copulated inside those cages at decantation time. The newborn mice went back to the mazes, wheels, and towers to show whether they remembered anything.

Aspic walked between the training tables on his right and the feeding tables on his left toward a huge display panel mounted over computer consoles opposite the door where he had entered. He heard the metallic banging of pans and the lilting but monotonous singing of Karesh Gapurti, the animal tender. Gapurti worked in an adjoining kitchen. Soon it would be feeding time for Batch 381 (Mice).

Aspic punched buttons and reviewed the data on the latest batch as words, tabulations, and graphs appeared on the huge screen.

Why did he even bother with this batch? The mice were hopelessly incompetent. They had failed every test — not once but often. They were reaching sexual maturity now; and based on the results of nine of the most recent batches, even those tantalizingly vague hints of conditioning disappeared after the mice were fully grown.

I'll go to the office and tend to the business, Aspic thought. *God knows, I should.*

But he modified this decision, thinking that he would stay to watch the feeding.

Karesh Gapurti entered now, still lilting. He wheeled

before him the first glass container filled with mice. Gapurti was an exceedingly shy young man, happiest when alone with mice. Seeing Aspic, he looked away, stopped singing, and his dark cheek began to twitch.

Aspic knew better than to address Gapurti. He waited until the man had rushed out again, then he went to the glass cage and looked down at the hungry mice. The small furry creatures already crowded that side of the cage which faced the feeding table. They pushed, shoved, and crawled over each other. They did not behave like proper mice — and they were mice only in body.

Aspic looked at the tiny eyes and once again wondered what these pseudo-rodents were thinking. No doubt about it — they were thinking, and not the thoughts of mice. Cam Templar's horrified outcry echoed again in Aspic's mind: "To do *that* to Christian souls!" Ah, yes. How moldable, manipulable, and malleable was man — if he couldn't have a human body (and he couldn't in this shielded building) then he chose any available creature for his incarnation, even mice.

Gapurti pushed in and positioned at the ends of the feeding tables eight more glass containers on wheeled stands. Aspic watched. Then Gapurti disappeared again, and when he returned he wore a face mask, gloves, and a protective gown. He carried two feeding trays; they were open at one end and came equipped with little ramps to allow the mice to reach the grain. One of the trays held irradiated barley meal.

Gapurti went back and forth until each table had its set of trays. Aspic watched. The mice squealed excitedly.

The cages were made of perforated glass so that the mice could be observed and filmed. Gapurti adjusted a wall-mounted camera. He turned it so that it faced Table No. 1. Bright lights flooded the table, and the mice squealed louder than ever.

Gapurti walked to the first cage and reached for the sliding glass door of the cubicle. With a tortured expression on his shy face, he looked up at Aspic.

Aspic nodded. Despite the Philotran, he felt a faint clutch of excitement. He told himself bitterly that hope never died, did it? Batch 381 had failed this, the simplest of all tests, so often that hope was purely wishful thinking — and that Aspic stood here now, expectantly, was just a measure of his desperation. He had to get away from here and think about the basic theory again rather than digging a dry hole deeper.

Gapurti lifted the glass, and with a dry rustle of tiny feet on the plastic surface of the table, the mice rushed forward.

Aspic was so accustomed to failure by now that he didn't even notice at first that the mice, having sniffed the ordinary barley, had turned in a body toward the irradiated tray. Only Gapurti's agitation woke him up.

"What?" he cried. Beneath the heavy blanketing of Philotran, emotions stirred. "Are they really — get a Geiger counter, quickly. I bet you made a mistake."

Blushing and blanching in quick succession, Gapurti rushed from the room. Aspic took the device when Gapurti returned and personally made the measurements. He couldn't understand it. The mice were devouring irradiated grain. But why now and not before? What had happened? Aspic repeated the measurements again and again. Through his confusion and the Philotran rose a dulled feeling of elation.

"Don't move anything; don't touch anything," he ordered. Then he went to a telephone and dialed a number. So great was his excitement that he misdialed three times.

15.
Prosthetics for Peace

Cam Templar left his apartment very early that morning. Ordinarily he didn't reach his office much before eleven. He had no reason to be an early bird. He had no real work to do most days. For the last three years or so Aspic had turned into a veritable Howard Hughes who lived secluded at Mountainview. Templar had been spared the terrors of "consulting" with Teddy about the mice — a consultation which always ended with Templar on his knees begging, *imploring* Teddy to put a stop to his blasphemous experiments. So Templar had no reason to go to work at 9 a.m. sharp. But he went in anyway, if a little later. He had to do something to earn his handsome salary, and he could usefully fill the time by corresponding with the many occult associations to which he belonged.

This morning, however, Templar had another and more personal mission than serving Future Now. He was about to carry out a plan that he had secretly nurtured for the last four years, the time during which he had been completely blind.

Ronald Kubrick led him out of the apartment and into the elevator. They went down and then out into the garage. Templar noted that Kubrick had changed the brand of his after-shaving lotion; and Kubrick was cross about the early start.

Templar sank into the back seat of the company sedan while Kubrick's steps shuffled on concrete as he went around to get behind the wheel. Templar sighed. Great corporate surpluses made all this possible — Templar, Kubrick, and the sedan. All three were useless. Templar did not work; Kubrick's only work was taking care of Templar; and Future Now leased the sedan only to cart Templar around — or Kubrick's girl friends when Kubrick was off duty. Traces of their odors sometimes greeted Templar in the morning.

The engine started and the car lurched forward violently. Kubrick signalled his irritation.

Templar sighed again. He was a kept man, Aspic's indulgence, Aspic's court jester, Aspic's toy. Why had he stuck it out at Aspic's side? Because he was a coward, an abject, despicable coward. After years of living plushly on Future Now's profits, he could no longer face the world, no matter how vile Aspic's experiments were becoming.

With a scream of tires the car raced up the ramps of the garage and, having arrived at the street outside, it stopped so suddenly that Templar was nearly thrown out of his seat. Then the car surged forward like a rocket, and Templar was pressed back into the cushions.

Amidst his sinecures and luxuries, Templar endured small tyrannies. Kubrick had no fear of Templar because Templar never complained. He viewed Kubrick, sedan, and generous salary as undeserved gifts one didn't criticize. But this morning, mindful of what lay ahead, Templar gave vent to a much repressed side of his personality.

"Kubrick?"

"Yeah," Kubrick said. Insolently.

"How much do we pay you?"

"Not nearly enough," Kubrick said.

"If you keep this up," Templar said, and his voice broke with unaccustomed aggression, "you'll join the ranks of the unemployed in a hurry."

"Keep what up, Mr. Templar?" Kubrick asked. Deferentially.

"You know exactly what," Templar said.

The car wound its way through downtown San Francisco. Kubrick had abruptly changed his driving style. Stops were smooth, accelerations imperceptible. The man's auric state, wisps of which reached Templar in the back seat, contained traces of apprehension. Then they reached the freeway system, and Templar rode in the midst of a great rush of air and tires, out to the Peninsula.

He rode toward a Defense Department "institute" not far from the San Francisco airport. He had a nine o'clock appointment with Major Robert Simon, to be followed by a physical. Templar was fifty-eight years old in 1992, yet he was about to join the Army — if all went well with the physical. He had pondered this step for years; he had dreaded this step; he had had the worst of premonitions about it. But in the end he had decided to take the plunge. He so wanted to break away from Aspic's influence.

The Prosthetics for Peace program was twelve years old, but Templar had become aware of it only after his eyesight had completely failed four years ago. He had changed his life-style then — acquired a pair of parrakeets, had his first chauffeur-companion, and became an avid radio buff. One morning over breakfast, listening to a nonstop talk show, he heard an ad for PFP. New space and military technologies had been perfected, said the ad, capable of restoring virtually any human organ. The procedures were still very expensive, but the Department of Defense stood ready to bear the costs of prosthetic operations provided that the volunteer agreed to serve in the military at "remote tracking locations," for a minimum of ten years. Age and physical condition were no deterrent. DOD was an equal opportunity employer . . . sex, race, national origin . . .

Templar called the number that same day and spoke to Robert Simon, then still a captain. "What about blindness," he asked Simon. "No problem," Simon said. "Eyes we can give you." "What kind of eyes — will I have to wear some sort of heavy pack on my back?" "Not at all. The system is completely integrated." "What do I have to do?" "Fill out an application and obtain some other documentation for us. We will evaluate all that. If you qualify based on those data, a physical is the next step. Are you aware of our requirements for ten years of active duty?" "Yes, yes. That doesn't bother me." "Well, then, let me shoot you some forms."

Throughout that exchange, Templar had felt nothing unusual — no warnings, no alarms, no premonitions. Simon sounded cheerful and competent. But when a set of forms arrived a week or so later, and Templar settled down to fill them out, assisted by his secretary, Caroline, a dull unease took possession of his mood. The application forms gave him no trouble. But the liability disclaimers Templar was asked to obtain and submit frightened him. All his relatives had to sign forms releasing DOD and holding it harmless against any and all claims, of whatever nature and kind, arising from the prosthetic operation, it being explicitly understood and acknowledged that the volunteer's action in submitting to the operation was a free act, completely uncoerced, etc., etc.

Templar had two living relatives — a cousin and a

sister. They signed the forms without comment. Templar wasn't close to them. His was not a family in any real sense of the word, more the echo of a family in the process of dying out — two bachelors and an epileptic spinster . . .

Despite his dull misgivings, Templar sent the documents to Simon. Two months passed without reaction. Then Simon called at last — and he had called or written to Templar at intervals ever since, urging him to go through with it, to report for his physical, to claim his prosthetic eyes.

Riding now toward the "institute," ready to do what Simon had urged him to do for years, Templar wondered again why Simon was so insistent. Why so eager to help an old man? Surely DOD could find more vigorous individuals for its various "remote tracking locations" . . .

They had almost reached the airport when Templar felt the first of those unpleasant flashes in the region of his solar plexus. He had expected something of the sort that morning, but he had awakened without a single prophetic premonition. At the time he had been glad and had thought that he might be doing the right thing after all. Now he was not so sure.

Kubrick eased the sedan off the freeway. The car swung in a lengthy loop. A jet was taking off. Its roar submerged all other sounds. The sedan stopped after a while — at the gate presumably. Kubrick exchanged words with the guard. Then they drove on.

Simon had told Templar that an audio signal issuing from tiny microphones embedded in the walks of the institute would guide Templar unaided to the doors. "We deal with many blind people," Simon had said.

"Wait for me here," Templar told Kubrick. Then he got out of the sedan, picked up the signal, and began to walk.

The air was thick with jet fuel smells. Templar felt the heat of the sun on his skin. He noted that he had started sweating. And those electric flashes in his belly had intensified to such an extent that a terror possessed him and slowed his forward motion to a crawl.

Di-ing-dong; di-ing-dong, went the signal.

The operation will kill me, Templar thought. *That's what all this means. It's going to kill me, and my body knows that in advance.*

Nevertheless, he went on. Whether he lived or whether he died, going on was the right thing to do. Every step carried him toward his future and away from Aspic's.

But then he heard his name called from a distance and recognized Kubrick's voice. He heard as well Kubrick running toward him. The steps came, air rushed, and Kubrick had caught up.

"Mr. Templar."

"What is it?" Templar could almost taste Kubrick's excitement and anxiety.

"Mr. Aspic just called on the telephone. He wants you to come to Mountainview. Right now."

"Did you tell him that I have an appointment?"

"I sure did, Mr. Templar, but Mr. Aspic told me to get you out. He has to see you *right away.*"

With a sinking sensation, Templar slowly turned. He thought he understood now why his solar plexus had begun to flash just now. Aspic must have succeeded in his conditioning experiments. Teddy had to share his triumph, and Templar was the only man with whom he could really share it.

I'm not meant to escape my fate, Templar thought, back in the car. *I should have left him years ago — back when he still played with magnets, before he caught his first soul.*

Desolate now — cringing at the prospect of seeing Aspic in the flush of victory — Templar felt a touch relieved at the same time. His premonitions of disaster had no connection with Prosthetics for Peace, it seemed. He was not yet on the brink of death.

16.
The Fire in the Aura

With Kubrick's hand at his elbow, Templar approached the Mountainview facility. The flashing pains in his solar plexus had subsided somewhat, replaced by a dull sensation of despair. As so often since, greedily, he had left his humble teller's job to join Future Now as a "consultant," he deeply regretted having cast his lot with Aspic's; occasions such as the one that loomed ahead were the price he had to pay.

A door opened up ahead.

"There you are, Cam. Finally." The voice was Aspic's. "I'll take it from here, Ron," Aspic told Kubrick. "Why don't you take the rest of the day off."

"No, Teddy, I — "

But Aspic cut short Templar's protest. "Go on," he told Kubrick. Then, addressing Templar: "I'll get you wherever you want to go, Cam. But now I want you to be my witness."

Templar felt a hand at his elbow. He stepped up and passed inside.

They paused before an inner door. Aspic punched numbers on a dial-face, and a faint electric hum signalled that the door was open. Templar walked past Aspic, well inside Aspic's aura, and noted that Aspic was riding high. An alien something interfered with Aspic's auric emanations, possibly a drug; but underneath that Templar sensed elation.

"So you've succeeded after all," he told Aspic as they walked down a corridor toward — Templar assumed — the training and feeding room. It had been years since Templar had actually seen this place, but the layout hadn't changed. "I don't see how," he went on. "Didn't you tell me just last week that Batch 381 had failed? And 382 isn't due yet. Not for another month. What happened?"

"It's Batch 381, all right," Aspic said; Templar heard the smile. "The same one; the one that failed."

"And now they've passed the test?"

"You'll see. You'll see."

"Which test? Alpha or Beta?"

"Alpha — but it's still conditioning."

"But not immortality."

Aspic laughed. "You absolutely *insist* on seeing everything from the dark side. We've got conditioning. It took six years. Immortality is next. Like the popular saying has it, 'The difficult we do right now; the impossible will take a little longer.'"

They had stopped. A door opened, and Templar felt a nudge.

"I still don't understand how it could be," Templar said. "How can they pass the test today — if they failed it weeks ago?"

"I don't know. I'm puzzled too. But it's something I'll figure out in due time. Carefully now. There are some cables on the floor. There. Now this way, Cam."

Templar knew himself inside the feeding room. Faintly he heard the squeak of mice.

"You stand here," Aspic said, positioning Templar. "Give me your hand. No. The left one. Now touch this."

Templar touched something cold and metallic.

"This tray holds the irradiated grain," Aspic explained. "Now your right hand. All right. This tray has the regular grain."

"Do we really have to through with all this? I believe you, Teddy — even without a demonstration."

But Aspic said nothing. Templar heard him move. A click sounded, and Templar felt the heat of lamps. The demonstration would be recorded on tape — but even without tapes of any kind, Templar knew, these dreadful events would be etched indelibly into the very substance of the world; they would be written into karmic history.

No matter what I do, Templar thought, *I'm already caught.* He contemplated with a feeling of dread the kind of karmic retribution he had already merited as a result of his participation in Aspic's experiments — however reluctant he had been. But then he remembered what he had nearly done today. He had come within a centimeter of escaping — and he could still do so, *would* do so! Even late was better than not at all.

"Now," Aspic called. "Are you ready? Remember what I told you. The left hand is the irradiated stuff. Now just wait and tell me what is happening."

A glass panel scraped. Templar couldn't see, of course, but he heard and imagined mice stampeding from the perforated glass containers — thirty or forty snow-white furry creatures with fine reddish feet and bright black eyes. They came. They scratched their way across the table. And then Templar felt unmistakeable vibrations in the left-hand pan.

A momentary silence — only the feeding of the mice could be heard.

"Well," Aspic asked, "Tell me what is happening."

Templar sighed. "They're eating from the left-hand tray, just like you said they would."

"So they are," Aspic said. His voice carried a curious undertone. "So they are. But go ahead, Cam. Make sure. Reach out and touch them."

A shiver passed over Templar, a feeling of utter revulsion. He released the pan and stepped back. He understood abruptly why Aspic had wanted him to come. Aspic wished to humiliate him. Templar had opposed these obscene and blasphemous experiments with all the power of his not too vigorous nature for years. And now that Aspic had at last reached the nadir — now that he could control as well as simply capture souls — he wanted to flaunt the power of science over the realm of religion of which Templar, willy-nilly, was the representative.

"All right, Teddy," Templar said. "You've made your point. Now please call me a cab. I want to get back to the city."

"Wait," Aspic cried. "Not so fast, Cam. This calls for a celebration. And I know just the place, too. Let's go to that little joint on El Camino where it all started. Remember?"

Templar said nothing. But he knew that his humiliation for the day was not yet done.

In the course of nearly two decades, The Whittler had undergone modifications. It was now a bustling but also a much more swanky place — or so Templar judged based on Aspic's conversation with a man, no doubt the maitre; on the general timbre of the sounds; on the feel of the tablecloth; and on the weight of the silver.

Aspic ordered champagne. Then, while it came, he launched into a speculation. Why had Batch 381 first failed and finally passed the conditioning test? Not the mice had been conditioned, he argued, but the souls incarnated in the rodent bodies. The *souls* loved radioactive stuff, not the mice. The souls had been *in* the mice from the very outset, even before the mice had been born. So why the change in behavior at this late date? What was the linkage between body and soul. Had those souls been *asleep*? What had awakened them?

Without thinking, quite impulsively — it was just a hunch — Templar said: "Sex?" He mentioned sex because his own puberty had been so painful, because he had been a cheerful, happy, and outgoing little lad until his own sexuality had come like a heavy, menacing pressure and had turned him shy and sensitive.

Across the table Aspic was silent for a moment.

"You know," he said at last, "you've probably hit it. I have to bow to you, Cam. You're sometimes extraordinarily perceptive."

There came another silence, and with the silence a change in Aspic's mood, a darkening. If Aspic's aura had been a bright fog until that moment, suffused with sparkles of excitement, now a black smoke seemed to spread through it.

"Damn," Aspic said. "I do believe you're right. The whole conditioning apparatus is built around sexual attraction. The last batch of synthetic enzyme I used finally worked — but not until the mice reached puberty. Damn. Do you know what that really means?"

Templar shook his head. He didn't care. He felt sickly once again. He was always doing this — triggering insights in Aspic. He *had* to get away before Aspic went on to even more unthinkable abominations.

"Well, I'll tell you," Aspic said. His voice dropped to a whisper. "Even if I could start on human experiments tomorrow, the soonest I could really be sure is by 2007 — fifteen years from now. By then I'll be sixty-three. Sixty-three. God. What a battle this has been, what a battle . . . And the memory enzyme isn't even synthesized yet."

Templar said nothing. He hoped — and God forgive his hope — that Osaka would be turned to rubble in an earthquake before the Japanese synthesized the substance Aspic sought. Templar had but a vague idea of the biochemistry Aspic used in his experiments, but Aspic's objective had been clear enough since 1985. He hoped to condition souls to remember their past lives upon rebirth in new bodies — and thus immortality would be achieved. A dreadful perspective. One life was burdensome enough, and the more memories he had, the more Templar groaned under their weight.

"What will you do? Wait for the enzyme or go ahead?"

Aspic laughed dryly. His aura darkened even more. Red flashes, as it were, zig-zagged within the smoke.

"I can't afford to wait. I guess I'll leave my ivory tower, put on my selling hat again . . . I have to package a full-scale experiment with human subjects, and that'll take some very fancy dancing."

"What will you try — the priesthood thing?"

Another laugh. Then the air moved as Aspic gestured. "The priesthood thing doesn't interest me any more, but it still tickles the fancy of some people high up in Commerce. I will accommodate those folks, if they'll let me — but only for one reason: I want Jack Clark."

"Are you saying that just to make me feel bad? If so, don't waste your energies. I can't believe that you could possibly still hold a grudge against a man who has never done you any harm in this life. Teddy, why do you get such a kick out of torturing me?"

But the real question, Templar knew, was why he allowed himself to be tortured. He had no answer — unless he, like Clark, had harmed Aspic along the way . . . Redemption. Templar might be paying karmic debts.

Across the table Aspic seemed to have withdrawn into a shell of silence. Then Templar heard the waiter. The champagne had arrived, and the ceremony of uncorking took its course. The cork popped; the liquid ran into glasses. But Templar didn't reach for his.

Then Aspic leaned forward and his mood enveloped Templar.

"To answer your question — I guess I'm just perverse. Somewhere deep down I'm a hunter. I'm like those Nazi hunters of the fifties and the sixties. Or maybe I have an exaggerated sense of justice — take your pick. I see Jack Clark getting away with it. He is a big chief now — a big fish in a little pond. He has made it in this life, you see, and I have not."

Could Aspic really mean that? Templar wondered. Aspic? His far-flung interests, his several mansions, his yacht, his unprecedented discoveries? Aspic? Comparing himself with a middling bureaucrat?

But Aspic went on. "Jack Clark has made steady progress for a man of his endowments," he said. "He is married — the lady is no beauty, but at least she's loyal to him. They have two sons. I have no offspring. My only legacy is a tribe of mice. I have my curse, my malaise — and a few drugs that keep it in control; very poorly at that. I have my work — but I never would have made these discoveries without Jack Clark. He led me in this direction. I even owe him my success in science."

Templar heard Aspic drink greedily. Wine splashed as he filled up again, drank again. Something was breaking inside Aspic. A barrier fell. Out of the smokey aura of the man flames burst forth and licked the psychic ether, reaching toward Templar.

"He has managed to destroy me," Aspic said. "Without even trying. I fell into Jack Clark's trap. You know me as a cynical sort, Cam. I've always had a flippant strain, I admit it. But you know what? You know why I started Future Now? To be independent? — not at all! To make lots of money? — not at all. Deep down I always felt that I could do great things for mankind, that I could improve the human lot by having my eyes open to the future. But Clark derailed me. The son of a bitch led me astray. One thing after the other. That damned malaise — it's on me now, didn't you notice? But modern science, bless its soul, has given me sweet Philotran to mask the pain."

He drank again.

"Then Evelyn. He thrust her on me. Not literally, of course. He didn't want to do it. In fact he didn't want anything to do with me. But everything he did just dug a deeper hole for me. Do you understand? I had no use for Evelyn, but Clark had driven her into a corner, and so she threw herself at me, and God knows why, but I married her, and that too turned into a curse. And that's not all. The very thing I've spent my life on, the psychotron — it's really a death trip." Aspic laughed. "That's right, a death trip. It's a great scientific breakthrough, all right, but it won't lead anywhere. And do you know why? Because it's wrong in its conception — I conceived it, all along, as a way to get back at Clark. And now that I've finally got the means to do it, it seems so foolish and so meaningless."

"But, Teddy!" Templar was greatly agitated by Aspic's sudden and unprecedented revelations. Aspic was clearly not himself, and Templar saw a chance such as he had never had before. "Teddy, for the sake of God! Do you hear what you are saying? If that's the way you really feel, for heaven's sake, man, why do you go on? Give it up. Take a sledgehammer and destroy the thing. Forget it, turn to something else — but don't go after Jack Clark now. Don't you see what that'll do to you? It'll tie you even closer to the man. And you could stop this sad charade right now, today!"

"Too late for that."

"Too late? Teddy, it's never too late to start again."

His own words startled Templar — they were as true for him as they were for Aspic. He waited for Aspic's response, but Aspic had fallen silent. His aura had changed. Smoke and flames had yielded to a turbulent, blazing fire.

"Listen to me," Aspic said. "Just listen to me talk. I sound — I certainly don't sound like a man who has just made a major breakthrough. It must be the drug I took this morning. Forget what I just said. It's not me talking so much as my malaise."

"What you said is *true*! Don't turn your back on your true self. Do it, Teddy! Destroy the psychotron. Start all over again. I'm sure that even your malaise will disappear. Please."

Aspic chuckled. "All right, Cam. I'll think about it. I'll certainly think about it. But now, drink up. We're here to celebrate and not to wallow in depressing contemplations of the past."

Templar reached out and found the slender stem of his champagne glass. He sipped a little of the wine although he never drank; now he wanted to seem obliging. He had reached his own decision. No matter what Aspic did or didn't do, Templar would act. It was never too late to start again.

"A toast," Aspic said. "Let's drink to science and the human mind — that penetrating power and its conquest of the universe."

"I too offer a toast," Templar said with sudden courage. His hand trembled as he lifted his glass. "To the indomitable spirit — that spark of God in man which, however much it may be tortured and dragged in the mire, shall triumph in the end."

Aspic laughed with abandon. Obviously his mood had suddenly shifted.

"You drink to yours," he cried, "and I'll drink to mine."

Aspic gulped champagne; Templar sipped. Then Aspic started talking, excitedly and furiously, though in a low voice. He spoke about "Psychotron Alpha" and the many intricate maneuvers he planned to use to bring it into existence. Templar listened, biding his time.

At last the maitre d' arrived to take their order. Templar dissembled. He questioned the maitre. He lingered over this and that selection on the menu and strongly signalled the obvious intention of having a complete meal. But when the ordering was done, he requested a favor of the maitre. Could someone lead him to the men's room? One of the lesser waiters was assigned this chore, and Templar left the table without so much as a word to Aspic.

On the way, Templar stopped. He had a billfold with compartments. He took a twenty-dollar bill from the appropriate slit and handed it to the waiter.

"On second thought," he told the man, "why don't you take me out front and catch me a taxi."

PHASE III
The Spirit Capture

17.
Chief Walk-on-air's Farewell

The sky was brilliantly blue, the land lay green. From time to time a fickle wind picked up the dust of distant country roads and flung it skyward. The year was 2004, the place Perpetual, New Mexico, and on this late August day a funeral was in progress.

A shiny black hearse led the way, moving very slowly. Strung out behind it like a kite's tail walked the people of Perpetual, those directly behind the hearse in silence and with a stately tread, those at the back hurrying and talking in low tones.

The road went up steeply at this point making for the crest of a hill. The new hospital crowned the rise up ahead, to the left; facing it on the right, circled by barbed-wire fence and partially hidden from view by imported shrubbery, stood a hexagonal building the people of Perpetual called "the Factory." Beyond these buildings and down the other side of the hill lay Perpetual's cemetery, the objective of this procession.

Uniformed policemen pushed their bicycles immediately behind the hearse. They had this honorable spot because the man inside the coffin was Charlie O'Brian, lately Perpetual's chief of police. But the chief mourner on this day was Charlie's oldest friend, Jack Clark. Jack walked behind the troopers, all alone. He wore a faded blue suit. He huffed as he walked, carrying his now very heavy frame. His face was fiery red. And from time to time he wiped his forehead, cheeks, and neck with a large white handkerchief. Other notables of Perpetual walked a step or two behind him.

Much too nice a day, Jack was thinking. *Much too nice for a funeral at least. Too pretty a day by far. Or else the Lord above rejoices to see Charlie up there in that great police station in the sky. Old Charlie has done it*, Jack thought. *He sure has packed it in.*

His sadness over Charlie's passing and the pain of climbing this steep hill combined in Jack into the same feeling of trauma. He had attended quite a few funerals over the years — but lately they were getting to be a chore. Gas rationing had come some years ago, but DOE had really cracked down hard six months ago when China had crossed the Yalu River and the Russians had stopped exporting fuel to have enough for war ... Jack could still get gasoline without a card, but he couldn't ride in this procession while others had to walk. Only Charlie rode, but Charlie had stopped caring ...

Jack fished out his handkerchief again and wiped himself as he wobbled along. The Factory approached slowly to his right, and he eyed it suspiciously. In an odd way he feared this mysterious facility.

The Factory had been completed about a year ago. And it had gone up behind a shroud of such uncompromising secrecy that it simply had to be one of Stanley Morgan's little tricks. Morgan was a consistent bastard — not a nice guy, far from it ... In disagreement with virtually everyone in Perpetual, Jack believed that the Factory was part of Morgan's rearmament scheme. And if Morgan did in the future what he had done in the recent past, the Factory would be the target of enemy attack — and then who would mind the perpetual care of wastes? Besides, Jack had sons to think about. And he didn't like it one tiny bit that Morgan had managed to postpone the national elections under the guise of "crisis." What was the U.S. of A. coming to? Where was the world going? Down the tubes, down the goddamned tubes . . .

Through a line of tall bushes planted just inside the forbidding barbed wire fence, Jack now glimpsed the two-story hexagonal building. An armed guard circled the place. On top of the building odd-looking wire baskets shaped like trumpets turned on a tall pole. They might have been some kind of new-fangled radar.

The official name of the place was "Experimental Weather Station, Region VIII," but no one believed the words. Soon after the facility had been completed, young men and women had arrived by chartered planes. Buses had whisked them to the facility, and they were seen no more. A month later these people left, and a new batch came to take their place, and so it had gone ever since.

Word seeped out — no one knew how — that this was not a weather station. A new kind of electronic birth control system was being tested here, part of a super-secret scheme to keep South America's birth rate down. Soon a beam would issue from those turning baskets and stop Latinos from having babies. The people named the facility "Stanley Morgan's Pill Factory" and later simply the Factory. They laughed about it. The machines inside the plant were just like everything else these days — they didn't work. All the girls were said to be pregnant when they left Perpetual — another of those federal boondoggles. But Jack had another idea.

The hearse topped the hill at last and the driver, who had done this thing before, stopped the car to let the people catch up and catch their breath. Jack stopped gratefully and began to wipe himself again. Fred McMurty then advanced. Fred was Perpetual's mayor and also an old friend. He stood next to Jack, took off his Stetson, and began to fan his face.

"You still don't trust it, do you?" he asked Jack, his head inclined toward the Factory.

Jack was breathing heavily and had to gasp a little before he could respond. "Sure don't," he said.

"But you won't say what you think it is."

Jack shook his head. "I can't. Not that I really know, Fred, but I *think* I know. You remember how much concrete they put into that thing? And how deep the hole was underneath? That thing was built to last forever, and if I'm not mistaken it has a couple of small breeder reactors down below. I think I know what it is, but if it's what I think it is, then I'm not free to say."

"I'll take your word for it," McMurty said. They had had the same exchange before.

The hearse started up again, and Jack set himself in motion down the hill. The Factory was an anti-psycho station so far as he was concerned. Everybody whispered about psycho — a weapons system with computers so unbelievably smart that the missiles in which they were installed could practically think like people. The Chinese had such weapons too. And the Factory, Jack was certain, was a defensive installation against Chink attack. Pulses of madness came from those turning trumpets. The madness rose into the sky and set up a shield or barrier up there. The Chinese missiles would be disoriented and would drop harmlessly in the desert.

Jack could have said this much to Fred McMurty without violating confidences. Everybody repeated rumors about psycho. But Jack had inside information he had sworn never to reveal. He recalled a windy day in Washington, the day Fred Jones had told him about brain transplantations, and Jack was sure that psycho had to do with that. And if it was really so . . . he didn't want to talk about psycho, not for a minute. If *that* ever got out . . .

Jack could see the cemetery now — a small, ugly compound surrounded by a wire fence to keep out the coyotes. What a sad resting place for good old Charlie!

Sure enough, I'm going next, Jack thought. He shuddered. His own funeral would be identical — with one difference. He would be in the shiny hearse rather than old Charlie . . .

Death made him think of other mysteries — half revealed and half obscured by Chief Walk-on-air. The Chief had never talked about the final destination of the soul. The Chief had talked darkly about Jack, of course. Jack would be "all right," he'd said; Jack's spirit would "soar very high." But he had never said what all those phrases really meant. Where was Charlie now? Was there a heaven, was there a hell?

The funeral wound its way down the hill and stopped at last outside the fenced compound. Charlie's troopers opened the gate. Then they extracted the long black coffin with gilded decorations on its top and, three men on either side, their round hats off and over the heart, they carried Charlie in toward a mound of yellow dirt.

The people filed in and took up positions. They made deferential room for Jack at the grave's end, directly facing the Reverend Hajt Groend on the other end. Then the brief ceremony began.

Hajt Groend, whose ethnic origins were not too clear to anyone around here, had come to Perpetual to escape what he called "dat oh-shawn ov bornogravy" by which he meant all other areas of the United States. He was an angular, blond man of few words.

"Here lies Thy servant," he said, his accent heavy.

"Charles Kefin O'Brian. That served thee well, Oh Lord. That gave this small community the law and order. We know him well. We won't forget him. We beseech Thee, Lord of Hosts. To receive Thy servant into Thy everlasting Love and Mercy. Now and Forever. Amen."

Someone nudged Jack. He took a clod of earth and threw it down on Charlie's coffin.

Jack escaped the wake after an hour. Betty was ailing . . . People shook his hand and accepted his excuse — but their eyes knew what Jack also knew. Betty's ailments were of the mind; she would not recover soon, and his presence at home didn't matter one way or the other. He drove home thinking about Chief Walk-on-air. Tonight was his night to visit the old man again.

Betty sat in the kitchen, before the portable TV. She wore an old robe. Her hair was up in curlers — it was always up in curlers; curling her hair was the only activity Betty seemed able to pursue.

"Could you feed the cats?" she asked when Jack walked in.

He nodded, took the catfood box, and rattled it one or two times. A pair of cats came streaking in, side by side, with identical motions. They stopped silently and waited with noses pressed against the screen door leading to a backyard patio.

Betty hadn't moved from her television perch since morning — or if she had moved, she gave no sign of it. Once Jack had thought of mental illness as a form of raving and ranting, but he knew better now. Betty *looked* sane, but she was not. He poured catfood into a dirty plate while the cats hovered expectantly. He straightened with a little groan and then stood there, eyes absently on the feeding cats.

Life . . . Sand between fingers. Betty deteriorated and Charlie was gone. Budgets were shrinking year by year. He had come to loathe the atomic business and this dirty little backwater of a burg. He had lived once in high style, in Washington, and there had been a woman once the likes of whom his Betty never could be . . . Yes. And high ambitions to be an atomic engineer. He had come close to his ambition — *but, hell, face it, buddy,* he now thought, *you blew your life, pretty much, and there isn't much more left of it, either, Charlie popping off like that!*

He went inside and busied himself at the sink.

"You don't have to do that," Betty said, but it was a mild protest and not repeated.

Jack did the breakfast dishes, put them away. Then he looked into the refrigerator, but the jars and cups and foil-wrapped little packages did nothing for his appetite. If anything he felt a kind of weight on his stomach.

He closed the refrigerator and went to change his clothes thinking — *Stupid of me. Wash the dishes in my Sunday best* . . . And this reminded him of a Sunday supplement article where it told how many umpteen thousand braincells you lost each year — or maybe millions? — and how he wasn't getting any younger.

He put on his trusty khakis — nice and loose — and felt better right away. The pressure in his stomach eased. Tonight he would experience peace, and he told himself that there was still that in his life — that strange peace and quiet he always felt when he was around the Indian. *And that, my friend, is a consolation,* he muttered under his breath. *It's a consolation.* He didn't know precisely what he meant.

He puttered about until the sun was nearly down. Then he climbed into his jeep and drove off in an easterly direction, toward the airport.

Jack had made this trip with great regularity for at least eight years — ever since he had become Chief Walk-on-air's disciple in earnest. He had become the Chief's disciple because his life had come unravelled in those days. His youngest son, John Kevin, had been caught with drugs. Charlie had arrested John and had released him into Jack's parental custody — but Jack had been unable to hold the boy, who had run away from home. Then Betty had her nervous breakdown. And less than a week after that, consoling himself at Puccini's with a cool one, eyes out on the street, Jack had seen Teddy Aspic riding in the back of a car — or could've sworn he had seen Aspic. He thought that he was going batty, had failed as a father, as a husband. And so he went out to see Chief Walk-on-air, in earnest this time and not just as a paying customer. He went to learn something, to let the Chief help him somehow — Hajt Groend sure couldn't help him; Hajt Groend could barely speak American. And since then he had been driving out, like this, year after year.

The desert was alive with blooming vegetation out this way. It had rained recently although it was not the season yet. Seed upon seed lying in dormant wait for just such an event had sprouted with that total abandon desert life displays — the boundless urge to have its hour in the sun.

In a moment of rare loquaciousness two months ago, Chief Walk-on-air had predicted that the rains would come. He had also said that Arti-cavern Lambda would be flooded. And it had been flooded. The Indian knew the future, no doubt about it. Did he know when Jack would die? Probably. But it wouldn't do to press him to say so. The Chief talked when it pleased him and not otherwise.

Some miles beyond the airport, Jack turned off the highway. The wheels spun in sand and raised a trail of dust. The sun had completely set when the roundhouse appeared up ahead in the bobbing beam of headlights. Smoke curled from its center. Dogs yelped and then, recognizing Jack's familiar scent, they turned to tail-wobbling welcome.

Jack alighted with a groan, heaving his big gut. He

had been athletic once. He had to diet. But it seemed a little late for self-improvement. He went into the hut, bending to clear the low door. Dung smoke and Shashtuk odors mingled in his nostrils. An ancient crone squatted by the fire with a pan. A young boy sat on a cot.

"Hi there, boss."

Jack nodded to the boy. "Where's the Chief?"

The boy gestured into the darkness outside.

"Up on the rise?"

The boy nodded.

Jack went out again and trekked slowly up a slight elevation marked by two large cacti resembling hands stretched to the sky. The dogs followed him for a while and then dropped back.

He found Chief Walk-on-air seated between the giant plants, hands on his knees, his face turned west where, on the horizon, a faint line of crimson still separated darkness from darkness. The old man had a wrinkled Indian face and jet-black hair bound into a braid in the back. His eyes were closed.

Jack caught his breath a bit and then sat down on the bare ground. He noticed a bundle next to the old chief. Had Walk-on-air been out collecting peyote? Or was he bound outward now? In the darkness Jack couldn't see whether the bag was full or not. It was just a spot of darkness on the ground.

Jack waited. The old man would speak when it pleased him.

Slowly he fell into a peaceful reverie — as always in the old Indian's presence. His mind lingered on the few, rare times when they had had a conversation — like the time when Walk-on-air had said that he had "hunted" Jack's spirit and had found it good. Or the time when he had introduced Jack to the Holy Mushroom. And how then he had had visions such as he had never forgotten. His fortune had never been told, not in so many words. Instead the Chief had given him another thing — a kind of peace. The peace didn't last for long, but at least he felt it when he was here.

A long time passed. Then, across the bit of rock-strewn dirt, Chief Walk-on-air opened his eyes.

"Good-bye, old friend," he rumbled in a guttural, hard tone.

Good-bye? Jack sat still and didn't answer. He would let the Chief say what he had to say. Questions only dammed up the thin trickle of communications that came from the ancient.

"The Big Sky will come now and fetch Walk-on-air."

Silence. The crimson line on the horizon had disappeared. Now the cacti were like shadows. The first stars had stirred out of darkness and blinked in rising heat.

"This is a bad place for dying. Walk-on-air is going south. Far away."

Why? Why is this a bad place for dying?

They sat in silence again for a long, long time. Then the Chief stirred again.

"White man has spirit-catcher. Very evil machine. Walk-on-air go south, die, come back to Shashtuk land."

"What do you mean — spirit-catcher?" Jack blurted out. He slapped his hand to his mouth, but it was too late. He had disrupted the flow.

For a long, long time Jack waited, but nothing more would come from the Indian. The sky slowly thickened with stars; the Milky Way dusted across his vision when he lifted his head. At last he rose.

"See you, old chief," he said. Then he went back to his jeep.

On the way home he had a bad moment. Suddenly he felt in the pit of his stomach a kind of burning pressure he hadn't felt in years. Could Walk-on-air actually leave? No! He would be off peyote hunting deep in Mexico. He did that every year. His bag had looked very flat on the ground, come to think of it. He would be back in a couple of weeks, and Jack would see him again on Wednesday nights as usual. That talk of dying and of spirit-catchers had to be a bunch of nonsense. Chief Walk-on-air liked to kid sometimes. Jack felt a little better.

As he passed the airport, he noticed that a sleek, white business jet had landed during his communing with the Chief. He had been so absorbed in his experience that he hadn't even heard the plane approach.

Whoever had landed was someone very big, very important. Lesser figures couldn't jet about in small planes like this one — not nowadays, fuel being what it was. Jack guessed it was a Pentagon big-wig come to visit the Factory.

He was still thinking about the private jet when he heard the high speed whine of tires to his rear. A big sedan zoomed by him, rocking the jeep a little as it cleaved the air. Jack recognized the Pill Factory sedan.

He had driven several hundred yards before it hit him. He thought that he had glimpsed a face — that face: unmistakable, memorable, shocking. It had flashed by too quickly for certainty, just like that other time, glimpsed out of Puccini's window. Nevertheless he was sure that he had seen Teddy Aspic — or someone very like him, very like him.

Emotions gripped Jack, and he pulled the jeep to the side of the road. He heaved his beer gut out of the vehicle and stood for a moment, breathing hard. He felt sick. The pain in his stomach had returned.

A vast array of speculations gathered at the back of his mind, but Jack refused to let the speculations surface.

I've got to get away from here, he thought, over and over again.

Slowly he calmed down a little and decided not to be too hasty. He would wait for one final session with Chief Walk-on-air. He would ask the Chief what he should do. He would ask him whether or not the flitting shape he had just seen was Aspic. And if yes, why he was here. He would make the old man talk somehow . . .

Something moved out in the desert, stirring dry brush. Jack shivered. Then, in a hurry, he got into his jeep again and drove away.

18.
Revenger's Arrival

The beautiful, sleek jet touched down, steadied, and taxied to a stop, and for the second time in four weeks, Teddy Aspic had arrived in Perpetual, New Mexico.

He had come the last time on a routine inspection and as part of his contractual obligation with the Department of Energy. Future Now operated Psychotron Alpha on behalf of the DOE. He came this time on his own volition, as a private citizen, and he was bent on a very private mission. He came in answer to a summons Dr. Goldblatt had sent out. And he came to fulfill a promise he had made himself many long years ago.

The plane that had brought him had come illegally. Aspic had simply commandeered it, using the reflected power his association with the Southern Political Coordinating Organ gave him. SPCO was one of Stanley Morgan's more recent administrative creations, and Aspic was a SPCO consultant these days. He supervised a crash program to build four psychotrons in as many southern states. The memory enzyme still eluded his grasp, but his powerful supporters had asked him to start building anyway. If the enzyme was ever synthesized, they wanted to be ready to use the technology. The jet belonged to them. And Aspic's time also belonged to them at present. Aspic should have been in Atlanta, working, rather than here.

But he was here now and sat alone in the twelve-passenger cabin. Several drawings and the contents of a good-sized file lay spread out over several seats around him. He had been studying the file, prepared years ago and labelled, only half in jest, "Project Karmic Comeuppance." Now he gathered the sheets and placed them in an attaché case. Then he rolled up the drawings. They showed the construction details of Psychotron Alpha.

Indeed, he thought, his mind on SPCO, if those gentlemen knew how he planned to spend the next few days of his precious time—they would have a collective hemorrhage. World conditions being what they were, SPCO's "immortals" were pulling out all the stops. They blithely risked political and legal necks; they were going for broke. They wanted all those psychotrons in operation before Stanley Morgan pulled the plug on dear old USA. Well might they worry, Aspic thought, even the younger ones: Morgan steered the ship of state toward a sure collision with the Chinese axis. War would touch the USA in a very physical sense this time. Aspic knew it, SPCO knew it, even Stanley Morgan knew it—had to know it. But when they had elected Stanley Morgan to a second term, the people had still not known how madly Morgan believed in his own policy of aggression.

One way or the other, something would soon give. SPCO had diverted massive quantities of manpower, material, and energy from Morgan's "Mission Readiness" to support the psychotron projects. If war didn't break out soon, a scandal would certainly erupt. Stanley Morgan wouldn't be a nice guy about it, and some people would be tried for treason, would hang by the neck until dead . . .

Aspic peered forward. A single cloud hung in the distance, positioned between the pilots' heads. The cloud moved out of sight as the jet turned off the central runway.

Aspic was still lost in thought. *I am a madman*, he decided.

He was mad to turn aside from his tasks in Atlanta in favor of a thing like Project Karmic Comeuppance. Mad but thoroughly consistent. He was the victim of his own plans. He had invested so much energy into Perpetual's psychotron (not to mention Future Now's money) and had thought about Jack's capture and "recycling" for so long that abandonment of the plan was simply unthinkable.

The squat, grey airport building now swung into view. For a moment Aspic saw a man in yellow overalls guiding the plane. Behind the man he glimpsed Sid Goldblatt's portly, balding, waiting figure. Then the plane swung again, erasing this scene.

The jet stopped at last, the engines died, and the copilot, removing his headgear, entered the cabin to unlatch the door. Aspic put the drawings under his arm, picked up his suitcase and briefcase, called thanks to the pilots, alighted, and hurried toward Goldblatt.

Goldblatt was bald on top but wore a thick, black walrus mustache by way of compensation. The mustache gave him a sad expression, but he was not a sad sort of man. Young and competent described him better, loyal and competent. He had the technical gifts Aspic sought in his closer subordinates and had a trait Aspic especially valued: Goldblatt asked very few questions. That's why he managed Psychotron Alpha and was in charge of tracking Jack Clark.

"How is he?" Aspic called before he even reached Goldblatt.

Goldblatt made a circle with his thumb and index finger and nodded reassuringly. "Can I take that?" he asked, trying to take Aspic's suitcase. But Aspic shook his head. "Maybe these drawings?" Aspic let him have the roll of drawings. Then the men walked toward Alpha's waiting sedan whose rear wheels and open trunk were visible around one end of the building.

"Well, Sid," Aspic said as they took off with Goldblatt at the wheel, "tell me all the nitty-gritty details. I gather that Clark is hospitalized, in poor condition, and that it's stomach cancer. Beyond that I know nothing. Fill me in."

"I didn't want to put too much on the air," Goldblatt said. "You've always stressed how sensitive . . ."

"Right. Very sensitive," Aspic said quickly. "Stomach cancer surprises me, you know. I always expected a coronary. Years ago, already. But he has proved unusually durable. How did it happen?"

"It's quite a story," Goldblatt said. "Something of a disquieting story." He glanced furtively at Aspic. "But I'd better start at the beginning."

Aspic nodded, eyes on the black-topped road. Greenish-yellow desert flanked the highway; the sky was dark with clouds.

"You know about Chief Walk-on-air, of course . . . Well, it seems that the old man decided that his time had come. The chief was quite a figure around here. No end of weird stories about him, all of them highly improbable to say the least, and one of these was that he had lived for two hundred-some-odd years, so it was high time for him to go. But to make a long story short, he just disappeared the other day. The old Shashtuks do that. They're like wild animals when it comes to dying. Chief Walk-on-air wandered off into the desert. He had told several people that he'd be going, and Clark seems to have been one of these.

"Well, Clark took it very poorly. He was a kind of part time disciple of the chief's and very attached to him. Then, of course, another old friend of his had died, about four weeks ago. I think you had just arrived on one of your visits on the day of the funeral, and I showed you O'Brian's psychon in the tank."

"The police chief."

"Yeah. The police chief. Anyway, Clark and O'Brian had been drinking buddies. And Clark and the old Indian were soul-mates or what have you. In any event, Clark's friends were dead. So then, after that, Clark began complaining about stomach pains, and then he started acting strangely."

"Doing what?"

"Well, for starters, he couldn't believe that Chief Walk-on-air was really dead. He organized a search party. The party combed the desert for several days, but of course, the old man couldn't be found. And no wonder. It doesn't look like it — " Goldblatt gestured at the landscape. " — but the desert is filled with all kinds of caves and burrows. Then, of course, Clark used his own security guard. They're Indians for the most part, and they didn't really search. They're very shy about death, and Chief Walk-on-air scares them shitless, if you'll pardon the expression — especially Chief Walk-on-air's *ghost*! Clark had fits. He ranted and raved. He threatened to fire people, and things like that. Finally he called off the search, but he continued on his own."

Aspic shook his head slowly.

"He drove about," Goldblatt said. "He spent days driving across the desert in various patterns. It was the talk of the town. You could see Clark's dust clouds all over the map.

"Well, of course, the people were starting to get uneasy. The general manager of the Complex is a big man around here, and Clark seemed to have lost his mind. Every time he came into town, he looked a little worse. He had stopped shaving. He looked wan, awful. He lost a lot of weight. And he walked about with a stoop, especially toward the end. He was forever touching his belly, testing it, probing it.

"People tried to help him, of course, but he refused. His wife had been mentally ill for years, so she wasn't much help. Finally someone wired Clark's oldest son, Gerald, in the Army. But before the son arrived, Clark took off."

"Took off?" Aspic asked.

Goldblatt nodded. "He was trying to get away from something. In the last days he had grown quite wild. He went around town telling people to leave the city. He said that something dreadful was happening in the 'factory,' and that the chief had told him so, and more intriguing nonsense like that. That's when they wired his son."

"Odd," Aspic said, feeling troubled. But at the moment he did not pursue his thoughts. He wanted to hear the rest. "So what happened?"

"Like I said, he took off. It happened on Monday. He went right after the banks opened. He took a thousand dollars from his savings. The money was still on him when they found him — plus a suitcase and a shotgun. His jeep had run off the road on the way to Albuquerque. He was unconscious and doubled over with pain."

"That was yesterday?"

"No. The day before yesterday. We didn't get the word until yesterday morning, and then it took some time to confirm it, to code the message, and all the rest."

"How far did he get? From here."

"Thirty miles, roughly."

"Not very far."

"No. Lucky for him, they found him right away. He was nearly dead when he arrived here. They had to operate right away. They took out two thirds of his stomach."

"I thought you said he was all right!" Aspic said, surprised a little and recalling Goldblatt's Okay signal at the airport. "He sounds in poor shape to me."

"He's alive," Goldblatt said. "And much better than yesterday."

"But what's the prognosis."

"Fair to low," Goldblatt said. "Clark isn't helping, the doctors say, and nature alone won't do the trick. Clark doesn't seem to want to live."

The car topped a rise and Perpetual now came into view — a flat, drab line of billboards, signs, and buildings on either side of the highway. Psychotron Alpha, the hospital, and the municipal building were still hidden behind a line of sickly trees. Goldblatt eased off on the gas.

Anxiety flickered somewhere in Aspic's guts— contrary impulses. Goldblatt's story of Jack Clark going mad had had a numbing effect. Clark had known something. Something had warned him that a race was in progress, a race that Aspic might still lose. Others knew also. That old Indian, alive or dead, seemed ominous just now to Aspic — more than just a simple peyote picker and brewer of herb tinctures. And Aspic didn't like the desert nor this dismal one-street town. He had the urge to get the hell away, back to lush Atlanta and Project Immortality. And leave well enough alone!

But he didn't act on the impulse. Inertia and the sedan carried him forward. They turned to the right and began to climb a steep hill. The psychotron was on the right. On the left stood a two story hospital. It was, despite its modest dimensions, too big for a population like Perpetual's. But it had been built a year before Psychotron Alpha thanks to a very large contribution from an anonymous "friend."

19.
The Spirit Trap

Wearing a one-piece work suit, his tall, thin frame bent over a desk in the central control room of Psychotron Alpha, Aspic surveyed the work to be done. An hour had passed since his arrival; he had eaten and changed; and he felt a little better now. A technical challenge lay ahead, and Alpha's humming and vibration shut out the world of Indians and deserts he had just crossed. In a way he was home again.

He stood in the heart of the facility, a circular room. A thick column in the center of the room supported the ceiling and also served as a conduit for psychons attracted by the broadcast baskets on the outside. Psychons moved down through the column and then by way of so-called psychoskids under the tiled floor of the control room. They reappeared as flickering entities in the nitrogen tankage that covered two thirds of the control room's walls — a giant, curving beehive of glass on either side of the entrance. The souls were eventually released from the nitrogen and conveyed to conditioning drums that turned deep underground in a chamber next door to the magnets.

Opposite the entrance, fifteen control consoles filled out the remaining space. Aspic stood at one of these, studying construction plans. Each console had its own closed-circuit television screen. Through these could be observed activity in the "guest rooms" where the experimental subjects lived. Drum devices in each console, each equipped with a paper sleeve, recorded telemetered data on each couple. Pressure sensitive devices installed in the experimental beds could feed a constant, realtime reading on the couples' more intensive activities. Mini-computers in each console were programmed to assimilate, integrate, analyze, and synthesize all input data — and to record on finely callibrated chronomats the exact moment when impregnations had most likely taken place. These data, in correlation with information about captured souls, could be used to determine with precision exactly which psychon, having received which type of conditioning, incarnated in which woman.

Alpha was a far cry from the crude methods Aspic had used in Mountainview back in the beginning. The system was very precise, very well engineered, and fail-safe. But it left too much to chance, still too much, and Aspic had no intention of leaving anything to chance — not where Jack Clark was concerned.

He pulled up a chair, sat down, and swivelled around toward the central column, arms raised, hands folded over the nape of his neck. He stared at the column and saw a caricature of himself in its stainless steel surface. *The disappearing man*, he thought. In the distorted reflection he appeared even thinner than he was — a slender thread of a man with white hair and spidery joints. He was an old man — too old for such a caper as he had in mind . . .

He didn't like the column, and not because it reflected his own figure.

For best results he had to tear into its stainless skin, open the insulated ducting, and fit an identity screen over the sex-selector assembly. Aspic had developed a workable ID screen some years ago, but Alpha lacked this refinement. The assembly in the column was discriminating enough. It screened for psychons with male tendencies while it routed female souls to accelerator guns mounted in the eaves; these latter were shot out into space, well beyond Alpha's range. But the assembly couldn't tell one male psychon from another.

Yet Aspic's plan of "recycling" called for such discrimination. He planned to capture Jack Clark's soul and then to hold it in suspension for ... for as long as the psychotron would last. Templar had once described that realm between death and rebirth as the world of purgatory, a time as well as space of testing, a region of desire and of the gnashing of teeth. Clark would reside in that world for as long as it pleased Aspic to hold him there.

The question now, however, was strictly technical — how to get the job done. If he cut into the column, the magnet had to be shut down. But Jack might pick that very time for dying, and Aspic couldn't risk that. And if he left the magnet on and Jack's death coincided with that of other people in the region, Aspic would be unable to tell Jack's soul from that of the others. He had to find a neat way out of the dilemma.

He swivelled back to the console's desk, scratched behind his ear, and pondered the matter for some time. Then he had found the solution. It was neat and simple, although it had a certain cost. He would capture Clark alone and no other soul. He would put Jack Clark on ice. And then he would fit the ID screen at leisure and route it to a special circuit designed expressly for his friend. Then, on all successive rounds of Clark's eternal recirculation, the screen would guide the Beast into a special tank, into a special drum...

Aspic picked up a telephone and dialed Goldblatt's extension.

"Sid? I want you to release all the psychons. Route them to the accellerators and shoot them out of our attraction zone."

Goldblatt was silent on the other end. Thunderstruck, Aspic supposed.

"I mean it," Aspic said. "The system must be completely purged — and kept purged. Sorry about your schedule, Sid, but my protocol must have priority. Can you do it?"

". . . Sure," Goldblatt said. "But what about new captures? You can't keep the system purged, not for very long."

"Right," Aspic said. "Here is what you do. Turn the magnet to minimum broadcast. All I need is a hundred meters. Just the hospital, nothing more."

"Just the hospital," Goldblatt repeated. "Clark must be something very special. Teddy — this will set our program back *six months!*"

"Clark *is* special," Aspic said. "And one of these days I'll tell you why."

Then Aspic went to work. The tools and special instruments had already been assembled and lay in tidy piles and packets in the center of the control room — lengths of conduit, sensors, several small conditioning drums, circuitry, laser welders, wiring, diamond drills, and much else besides. Armed with a selection of tools and supplies, wearing a plexiglass helmet, Aspic approached a wall panel separating the nitrogen tankage from the consoles. The panel yielded to pressure and slid aside, revealing a narrow opening. Aspic slipped in and worked his way behind the tankage. Soon he was rearranging plasticcladded conduits that rose, like a wall of pipe, out of the floor.

Soon Aspic fell into a rhythm of work. Minutes became an hour, several hours. It had been many years now since he had worked like this, using his hands—not since the Mountainview days. He didn't have the energy he had had back then, but now a long-dormant purpose impelled him forward. Alpha hummed all around him. Cryogenic nitrogen rushed through capillary pipes to cubicles of glass as he adjusted pressures, as he bled tanks, temporarily covering surrounding surfaces with artificial rime. He welded wiring from time to time filling the dark space in which he crouched with sharp, clear sparks. He stripped cladding from conduits and psychoskids and replaced the cladding with foam that rushed dryly from tubular containers to solidify instantly, thus sealing its own bubbly pores. He drilled into cubicles, slowly and carefully, and filled the holes with stems of delicate sensors around which he packed expanding elastomers using syringe-like applicators. When he crawled out again toward early morning, one area of the beehive had been isolated from the rest. Six hexagons of glass, dark and empty, surrounded a seventh hexagon, brilliantly lit and filled with gas. Jack Clark's home had been prepared.

Aspic rang for coffee. He wasn't tired. Far from it. Rather he felt an exhilaration — and the urge to carry on. So much work still remained. Goldblatt was still asleep. Aspic had no news of Clark's condition. Clark might come at any time, and Aspic wanted to be ready. By the time a woman from the cafeteria downstairs arrived with coffee and some rolls, Aspic had torn up a portion of the flooring, had exposed a line of flat psychoskids, and was engaged in testing them with an instrument.

"Just put it down somewhere," he told the woman, gesturing toward a console.

She placed her tray and left, and Aspic kept working. He forgot all about the coffee. It steamed for a while and then grew cold.

The work entranced and hypnotized Aspic. His thoughts ran idly over this and that — the looming war, the past, Mountainview, Templar's strange disappearance, and how it all began and how now brown cow it was ending here in this brilliant room in the middle of a desert where next door a big fat Nazi who had gone native lay in a coma, waiting one presumed, to give up the ghost. Where exactly did these skids fork? Here? Or there? Test it to be sure. Seven point nine. Six point oh. Make that six point one. There. All right. Put in the bridge now, nice and eeeasy does it. Right on, partner.

Goldblatt came around nine, and Aspic took a break. He wolfed down the rolls but didn't touch the tepid coffee. Goldblatt had no word yet about Clark. Alpha had one of the nurses on its payroll, but she didn't go to work until noon. Well, noon was soon, Aspic said, grinning. He was a little punchy now — but full of good humor. He told Goldblatt to wire San Francisco. He wanted an ID screen — specified the model — and asked that it be hand-delivered as soon as possible. And Goldblatt departed again.

Fatigue caught up with Aspic around midday. He had finished with the psychoskids. The loosened tiles had been placed back into position — so and so, not very tidily. Next came the conditioning drums. They had to be assembled, wired, linked in, tested, and armed. Hours of work — but Aspic had no reserves left.

He went to the bathroom and splashed water on his face. Grey stubble covered his emaciated face. Grey, grey, grey. His skin was grey, his hair was grey. He felt grey. His tongue — he stuck it out — also grey. The old grey mare, she ain't what she used to be.

He tried to smile, but suddenly it all seemed dreadfully tedious, all this. Ridiculous. Not to say ludicrous. He was an old man, playing games. What the hell for? It didn't matter. Even immortality seemed . . . ludicrous! Why carry all these grey old thoughts over into a fresh, new body? What benefit was that? So that at age fifteen, sixteen (whenever puberty came, like a crash) suddenly he would remember — this? An old man playing Nazi hunter? Memories were just a curse, an utter curse. *Or am I just calling the grapes sour?* he wondered. Immortality was, after all, still just a dream.

Aspic left the bathroom. The elevator opened just as he reached it, and Goldblatt came toward him.

"We've got a report," Goldblatt said, stopping.

"And?"

"They've just put him on the critical list. The nurse said it was just a matter of hours now. That's her opinion, mind you; but she's experienced."

Aspic closed his eyes tightly, opened them wide, screwed them up again, opened them wide. The word echoed about. Hours.

"All right," he said. "Thanks. Let me know if there is any change." Then he went back to tackle the conditioning drums.

He worked feverishly now, a man possessed. Echoes of his malaise trembled on the edge of his awareness. Bits of hallucination garbled his thoughts and mixed up his hands. Malaise. It had died away slowly years ago. Even his malaise had grown old and weary, but memories of it were present like this squirming salamander — *wire, wire* — that he had to wiggle through that dilatory opening.

From time to time an icy clarity settled over him. He saw as through a crystal, sharply. He made a deal with himself each time, one part agreeing with an other. This act, this concluding act, would be his last deed on the psychotron. He would leave here and go home to San Francisco. No more mad science after this. He promised it to Templar, seeing very clearly now, almost seeing Templar, over there, on his knees, pleading . . .

All this while Aspic worked, competently enough. He placed the drums into the narrow area behind the tankage. He led power to them, checked the motors, the rotation, and the bio-magnetism inside them. Two of the drums gave faulty readings. He adjusted, whirled, adjusted, whirled. Once more hours passed. His stomach made angry, prolonged, gurgly noises. His back and neck ached. Figures danced in the murk. Small cuts on his hand smarted. But he kept on.

At six o'clock he rose at last, finished finally. But as he looked over his handiwork, he noted that he had wired the drums to the wrong psychoskids. He was too far gone now to record any emotion. He went down again and did it over. Then he looked again — eight o'clock. Everything checked. But to be on the safest safety side, he stumbled from the recess, shuffled through his case until he found the checklist, the pencil, and then, keeping himself under very tight control, he went over it again one . . . step . . . at . . . a . . . time. And then again.

At Aspic's request a comfortable armchair was brought up from the downstairs lounge, and Alpha's resident doctor, upon some coaxing, gave him stimulants. Then, seated before the cubicle where Jack Clark would soon show, if all was rightly wired, taped, linked, latched, and plugged, Aspic sank down for his final vigil.

He waited for hours, half dozing, half awake. Things happened around him, but he was not fully aware of his surroundings. Goldblatt brought a telex at one point, a telex from SPCO. It was around ten at night. The telex had just been received and decoded in the cipher room downstairs. For reasons Aspic couldn't fathom and didn't care to worry about just now, Goldblatt was in a great state of excitation. He urged

Aspic to read the message and said wild things about the Chinese, Stanley Morgan, and mobility. Mobility? Aspic mused about the word "mobility." The rest of the message did not register on his tired and now mildly drugged brain. He dropped the cable to the floor. When he next became aware of the control room, Goldblatt had disappeared.

Then, very much later, Aspic started up.

He had been arguing very lucidly and elegantly with someone in a dream. With himself . . . ? The subject had been Immortality. There had also been something about the mobilization of psychons.

But Aspic now heard a low *beep, beep* and forgot all about his dream. The sound came from an instrument he had installed himself — it seemed like all that was last year sometime. *So* . . . he thought. *So you are here at last. Well, hello!*

He rose slowly and walked toward the beehive, toward that single, isolated cubicle in which a psychon rested now, held immobile by the cryogenic temperature within. Aspic watched it for a while. Then he leaned closer. His eyes virtually touched the glass. Jack's psychon looked like any other — a tiny fish made of some kind of fire, a bluish firefly.

20.
Kidnapped

Jack's moment of death came as an experience of levitation. One moment he was inside the body, aware of it as a vague pressure. Then he was up above and looked down on the body of an older man. The eyes stared without focus. The mouth hung open, the chin sagged. Rubber tubing still linked an arm to a bottle filled with sugar solution; the bottle hung from a silver bar. Jack saw the scene clearly, although not with his old eyes. A night-light glowed. Somewhere a compressor hummed. Nothing had changed except the focal point of his observation.

The experience lasted only briefly. Then Jack realized that the corpse below was his. That pasty, obscene, naked face was his face, the heavy gut his gut. But who was he? How could he be there, watching from above?

Something in him panicked. The sensation was not a sensation, the emotion unlike an emotion but analogous to it. Desire or fear, whatever it was, caused him to move with incredible swiftness. One second he hovered above his own mortal remains. The next he was suspended in the sky. He had no memory of passage or of the lapse of time.

At first he did not recognize the scene below. It had been many years since he had toured Perpetual in a helicopter — back when fuel had been plentiful. Even then he had only done so by day. Now it was night, and he was higher up than ever before. Perpetual, when he recognized it, was a smear of darkness in a faintly yellow expanse. The sky above was filled with familiar constellations.

Jack had no need to "look up" to see the sky, nor to "look down" to see Perpetual. Various viewpoints came into being as he shifted his attention. Thus when he thought about the Complex, he saw it down below without "turning around."

While looking at one of the evaporation ponds, he became aware of a new phenomenon. Faintly at first, then more and more clearly, he perceived "lines." The pond, from this height, had appeared to him initially like a large, dark surface. But now he saw that from it emanated or into it fell "lines" of light differently constituted than the "lines" which rose from or fell into other parts of the landscape.

The lines multiplied around him the more he looked for them. They went in every imaginable direction. They filled up all space. They disappeared into the heights and into the depths. They glowed, had directional motion, and soon obliterated everything else.

Jack found himself travelling along one of these lines, slowly at first and then with increasing speed. He rose higher and higher, as on a rail. He accepted this as a natural thing. The "coils" began to loosen from around his center. They trailed behind him like multi-colored ribbons in the wind.

A shock of recognition interrupted Jack's passive motion. He suddenly understood why this "trip" did not surprise him. He had been through all this before. And he knew that in a moment now he would be vaulted, flung —

Yes. He was vaulted and flung into space. The line of light he had been riding abruptly disappeared. Some kind of momentum carried him beyond the world of lines and into a free-floating void. He fell or tumbled without a sensation of falling or tumbling. He knew of his own motions because the "coils" trailed now in this direction and now that. They seemed to have weight and to be subject to gravity. They had no "substance" in the ordinary sense. They were "attached" to his center and threw of a multichromatic light. They were tightly packed images filled with a radiance, an energy.

Out of a new awareness which had come to him mysteriously, Jack knew that he must examine the coils now. Important consequences would flow from that act. It appeared to him that a "pattern" would emerge from the examination of his past lives and that he had to catch the pattern before it was "decision time." He understood — was it a memory? was it an intuition? — that he had very little time in which to act. He concentrated on the nearest coil and immediately found himself displaced in space and time.

The room refused to come into focus at first. He saw a bed, but it was not a proper bed so much as a table of sorts. A woman lay on the table, legs spread wide apart. She was naked below the waist but clothed in white garments above it. Figures, also in white, stood about her, wearing masks. Excruciating pain distorted the woman's features to such an extent that Jack failed at first to recognize his mother. Then, suddenly, he was in the picture. His mother's pain became his own. He felt on the edge of suffocation. He struggled to be free of her body, in a panic. He was as eager for this awful thing to end as she was. Her outcry of anguish was his anguish. Then he was born. The world hung upside down. Something stung his rear, and he let out a yell.

More rapidly than in any movie, yet with a great deal more clarity and excruciating "inwardness," Jack then experienced his entire life, all over again, in strict chronological order. The emotional toning of this experience made him smile, frown, cringe, strut—until he realized that he mustn't. He must observe dispassionately. He must resist the magnetic attraction of mere mortality. He must seek a *pattern*.

The coil at last ran out. The bitter taste of Jack's last days remained and lingered — the irrational conviction that some evil something hovered over Perpetual, a something he must escape. His new awareness told him not to fret about the past; it urged him to articulate the pattern.

Jack tried. At last he thought he saw it. Service was his pattern, public service. He had wanted all his life to help humanity.

But why, something asked.

Why? Why not? Wasn't it the natural thing to do?
There is another reason. Look at the next coil.

Jack still floated in the void, but now his apparent motion had stopped. Coils floated around him, partially revealed, irridescent strands of recorded experience, the experience of seemingly countless lives. One of the coils seemed closer to his center of awareness than the others. It glowed with a brighter inner fire. It was his Schweinhirt existence, he well knew, and now he had to look at it quickly before it all began.

Before *what* all began?
Don't hesitate, act!

But Jack hesitated. He had no detailed recollection of his Schweinhirt life, but he knew that it was a cloud of darkness. He anticipated pain and humiliation from that coil. He had looked at it before — one life ago. He didn't want to look at it again.

In midst of his hesitations, he became aware of a light in the void, a vortex of luminosity. Tiny at first, it grew and grew and came toward him with inexpressible speed. Jack was frightened at first. Then he recognized Chief Walk-on-air with an inward jump of joy. He didn't see the Chief in any conventional sense. He simply knew that the Chief was present inside the blinding light.

Below (in a manner of speaking), underneath the light, a carmine red ocean had formed simultaneously. It was repulsive, viscous, and covered by pink froth from many rushing waves. He didn't like the ocean and turned instead toward the vortex of light.

But then, as he approached the vortex, it began to blaze with terrifying force. It was a single eye, Chief Walk-on-air's left eye, a diamond, a pure, white, hard, blinding emanation. The force appeared to pierce through Jack. Its power shattered him into a thousand pieces. The pieces appeared to scatter in ten thousand directions.

Go! something urged. *Complete it!*

But Jack could not comply. He experienced the analogue of a shudder and fell back. He "turned" away. He fell toward the ocean of blood.

Almost instantly he felt an almost unspeakable surge of desire. He felt breathless, jolted, and stupefied with longing. He had been light, totally weightless, but now desire made him heavy, groggy, and gorged with want. He fell toward the red like a stone.

The ocean disappeared as if it had been a mirage. Instead he found himself inside the maze of lines again. Some of the lines were red. They curved toward him like the stems of flowers; they seemed to beckon. When he concentrated on their tips, the tips enlarged; they became the size of television screens, and in those screens Jack saw couples making love. The numbing desire he felt came from those couples. He couldn't tear his "eyes" away from these scenes of sexual activity. As he concentrated on now this and now that "screen," the screens turned into doors, the lines became wide channels, and powerful lusts impelled Jack to enter.

A faded, weakened residue of his earlier awareness urged him in a whisper to choose carefully, to incarnate with care. He realized that he could go wherever he pleased and choose exactly the pair he needed to complete his "pattern." He sensed mysteriously where the couples presently lay — and he noted that they resided all over the world, represented all the races, all the combinations of all the races, all the social classes, and all degrees of quality from gross unconsciousness all the way to the highest refinement. He tried to make a selection, but a frenzy of desire appeared to spread a layering of blood before the pair of eyes he no longer had. He decided on an impulse and hurled himself through one of the doors making toward a couple of generally solid merit. Little sounds of joy escaped him involuntarily, and he hastened, he rushed, through a cloud of humid fume, toward his own conception.

Jack had barely begun this trip when something harsh and gross, a terrifying vacuum, a rude stormlike pressure tore a hole into the channel he was striving down. He was sucked out and away from his chosen trajectory. He fought with all his might against this intruding power, knowing that something had gone terribly wrong. But whatever had him wouldn't let him go.

Just before an unbelievable cold embraced and crystallized his awareness, he saw rushing toward him the randomly glowing wire cups that turned on the pole atop the Pill Factory's roof. *Spirit catcher*, he thought. Then he was inside.

21.
The Spirouettes

The cubicle was filled with some kind of gas, and the gas had been deprived of energy to such an extent that its molecules were virtually immobile. A long time passed before Jack realized that he was held in a cryogenic prison bounded by a specially formulated silicate-based barrier. Light entered through the barrier.

Jack strained his "senses" and gradually he became aware of all manner of phenomena. Faint electrical twitterings sounded nearby. Gasses scraped against piping. Dull throbbings, very far away, hinted at powerful machinery. Light "sang." This play of sound was interrupted and overwhelmed suddenly by the onset of a very loud, rhythmic, insistent *beep, beep, beep* that sounded for all the world like a telephone's busy signal. The sound went on and on. Then the light entering his prison began to change, to fill with motion. A play of light and shadow replaced the earlier diffusion.

Jack "stared" at the new pattern that had formed against the side of his "room," and he thought he saw the outline of a gigantic face, much like Chief Walk-on-air's face beheld inside the vortex — but this face lacked all inner fire. It was, instead, a field of deep opacity, a dark composite of continent-sized masses of flesh and enormous craters or caves which, after some puzzlement, Jack recognized as pores. Over the continents floated two immense, glistening domes of moisture.

Jack had never seen a face in such a way before, and it took him a while, especially in that almost fiery cold — which slowed down the usually instantaneous manifestations of his thoughts — to reorganize the light impressions into a more conventional array. When he had done it, he saw a man he knew.

The effect on Jack of seeing Aspic was cataclysmic. He made a supreme effort to get away and expended immense stores of "energy." Instantly more gas poured into his prison to compensate for his effort. He sagged back into a kind of exhaustion. But inwardly — if one could speak of an inwardness in his case — he was consumed by an unspeakable rage and fear combined. He grasped — not with total clarity but with sufficient clarity to experience unspeakable anguish — what his condition signified. Moments earlier, up there in Paradise, he had relived that time in Washington when Teddy Aspic, his moist eyes staring much as they now stared, had spoken of "behavioral compulsions" by which he hoped to fetter men to the service of atomic wastes. Moments before he had heard Joe Bull expound on the dangers of dying in Perpetual. And he had heard Chief Walk-on-air warn against a "spirit catcher." In an instant Jack saw the potential of all these events, saw the turning baskets on the factory's roof, and felt again the impossibility of escape. Then the face receded, and a still diffusion of light took its place.

Time passed, time rolled. Using changes in sound and light, Jack tried to keep track of its passage. By day the sounds intensified, by night they faded. Some kind of commotion filled spaces near his prison by day. Oddly patterned echoes resolved into voices he couldn't understand. Sharp reverberations meant the clang of metal. The rushing sound, as of an ocean, could have been acetelyne torches. Faces came — Aspic's and others' — and looked at him from time to time. Then it all grew still again. Instruments twittered. Dull throbbing grew more audible. The light was still.

This cycle repeated at least five times. By night Jack gathered his energies. Once a day he squandered them completely in hopeless tries to "will" his way out of the prison. But ever and again the seering cold drained away what little power he could muster.

On the evening of the sixth day — if it was evening, if it was the sixth day — Jack fell into an uncontrollable excitement. The clanging and the banging had stopped around midday. The instruments had warbled oddly ever since. He had heard unusual machinery murmurs — not unlike the purr of cats. And now Aspic's face was back. It lingered and lingered.

Jack tried to control his "feelings." But yet — how could he put down the only hope that he could have? He hoped for change, any change at all. He feared above all having to continue in his present, unchanging, unmodulated state. He could do nothing. His prison had no handle. He couldn't move, he couldn't even "kill" himself. He had no future, and his coils, invisible in this environment, couldn't console him with his past. Would a change come? Would something happen?

Something happened. The change came abruptly, without warning. Jack "sat" in his prison one moment. Aspic's face hung before him like a continent. The next moment he was torn from his cryogenic chamber and felt himself hurled through a flat, narrow channel at such a speed that the coils around his center flared out behind him like a comet's tail. Then he was plunged into a total darkness.

Or not quite total. He had a sensation of rotation. He turned in the midst of a darkness, but here and there he saw clusters of ... spirouettes? Jack didn't know what they were. He called them spirouettes. They were shaped like corkscrews — white, tiny, and fibrous — as if made from tightly twisted, bleached flax. The spirouettes danced in the darkness. They were in motion, as was Jack.

Jack turned for what seemed an endless time. He "thawed out" slowly, losing his stiff rigidity. He regained his suppleness, picked up the rotational energies of the thing that held him now — and then it came, something he had forgotten all about in prison: he felt the blinding shock of sexual desire.

Jack crashed against the invisible, moving barrier in his eagerness to escape. He bounded back and forth. At one point in his frenzied motion — which he recognized for the compulsive madness that it was, a moth's blind rush against a pane of glass — he skirted the edge of a clump of spirouettes. One of them turned. It might have been a predatory fish sensing prey. With a spiralling motion, picking up speed, it came at Jack, touched, held, and began to burrow in. Jack fought to rid himself of the spirouette, but he had no adequate means of defense. He lacked arms; he had no hands. The spirouette sat tightly, like a leech. Jack "felt" nothing as a consequence of its adhesion, but he knew that this collision boded ill. His motion attracted another spirouette. It also came toward him. But before it had a chance to burrow in, Jack was sucked out of the darkness and ejected into freedom.

In a way it was just like having died again, but this time Jack hovered over a patch of ground next to a brick wall. A sickly dandelion plant lay dusty against the sand. Then came the slow crunch of a pair of boots. A uniformed guard moved into view. A weapon hung from his shoulder. He walked past.

Jack felt a joyous sense of relief. Free again. The sexual compulsion had vanished. It occurred to him that he could move about now, if he wished, keeping close to the ground, looking at this and that forever. He also knew that that would be an error and useless waste of time. Instantly he moved himself to heaven and waited for the lines to form. He rode one of the lines up, into infinity, and rocketed out into the Void.

He was determined to do things right, this time. Whatever suggestions reached him from the deeper wisdom that seemed to blossom in the Void — he meant to follow it to the letter. The awareness came. It urged him to examine his coils. Jack did as he was told. Once more he was born and lived his life. But this time he was in slightly better control, and when the time came he did not shy from looking at his Schweinhirt experience.

More of the pattern opened up. Jack understood a little more. He had decided on a life of service to erase Schweinhirt's brutalities. The Schweinhirt life lay before him even before he had lived through it a second time. He wished to turn his eyes away, but his awareness urged him on. He had to find the "moment" when, as Schweinhirt, he had turned aside from the "true path." He didn't know that moment, therefore he had to suffer the review.

Reluctantly, Jack entered the Schweinhirt coil.

An odd body with a different feel . . . Schweinhirt's had a coarser make-up than the body Jack had more recently owned. A simpler and more elemental man — a kindly peasant boy, so innocent, naive, so readily led. He hated the simple village where he lived, dreaming of escaping into the glittering town. His father was a grim, humorless man who demanded too much work. The war came with its bands, recruiting posters, and exhortations on the the radio. He joined the army. (But that was not yet the wrong decision; he had to look further.) He trained. He marched through soggy, snowy forests. He pushed a vehicle stuck in mud. The men grumbled about army life. It wasn't the adventure of the posters. Rumors floated about the SS. The SS wanted volunteers. Storm troopers had more prestige, and better pay, and better food. Girls never refused their smart advances. He listened to these rumors with a kind of longing — but knew deep down they weren't true. Why then did he want to go? Why did he wish to volunteer? Why *did* he volunteer?

Jack had found the "moment." The rest unravelled like a knitted glove. Deep down inside those Schweinhirt guts something had known that Teddy Aspic waited somewhere on the end of an SS career. And wherever Aspic was, there also would be Evelyn. And Schweinhirt had been unable to resist that tug, that pull. He wanted to find Aspic-Mahler, he wanted to hurt Eva-Evelyn.

I should've bolted at the prospect, Jack thought. *But no. I went. I wanted to meet them again although I didn't know a thing about them — Schweinhirt didn't. I wanted to pay them back for the time before . . .*

Hey! Wait a minute. *What* time before?

Wait. You'll see that too. That was your Balog life.

His Balog life. It had a darker cloud around it than even his Schweinhirt life. Jack couldn't face the prospect of opening that coil. When Schweinhirt died at Stalingrad and the coil, a short one, finally ran out, Jack hesitated. He couldn't get himself to look at Balog, sensing yet other crimes. And beyond them, other crimes yet? Life after life? A churn of crimes, a flood of hatreds?

The vortex formed above him, the ocean of carnality below.

Jack knew that he was lost again. He couldn't face

the fire that bore Chief Walk-on-air's features. He had to fall into the soup below. But he could still choose, couldn't he? He would go to China; he would pick a door to India, to Russia, to anywhere but here.

He fell; he fell into desire. He chose a door — a Japanese couple somewhere in Kobe, far away from the factory. He entered the door, sure of his escape. But the rude force came and sucked him out. Once more — the cubicle.

22.
Caught in Time's Amber

The stages of Jack's sojourn in Paradise divide into four periods. He had no adequate measure of time. He measured it by the number of cycles he underwent, but eventually he lost count, or no longer cared to count, or despaired of counting. But the urge to relate his existence to some objective absolute was overwhelming, and so he divided his "enduration," as he called it, into periods, into cycles of cycles.

The earliest time he called The Struggle. During that age he learned and relearned that he was hopelessly captured. He couldn't be reborn again — Aspic's devilish machine prevented that with unfailing efficiency. Neither could he give himself up to union with the Fire Vortex, his only other alternative. So he cycled endlessly — from cubicle to spirouettes to Paradise and back again — collecting spirouettes until his soul acquired a groggy, soggy weight and the analogue of physical pain appeared from the spirouettes' apparent "bite."

Next came a brief period, a kind of intermission, a kind of pause. Jack experienced this time as positive not because the compulsions of his captivity diminished but because the world changed — and for a while at least he found distractions. He called this time The Change.

He noticed The Change in that brief interval between release from the Rotation where spirouettes attacked him and his compulsive flight into the Void. Then, very briefly, he was free and could observe — much as on his first release he had observed a dandelion and the uniformed guard.

The Change puzzled Jack for many, many cycles. It came rather swiftly, or so at least it seemed. But the world's transformation was so radical, he couldn't believe his "senses" and had to conclude that geological times had passed even while he subjectively experienced the period as no more than a score of years.

Next came a time he called The Desperation, a long stretch of utter horror. Nothing changed. Nothing gave relief. Spirouettes multiplied; the icy cold stung; the Vortex terrified; the vile ocean of carnality tortured him with longing.

He had experienced all of his past lives by then — many times over. Clark, Schweinhirt, Balog, Manousse, Pappalos, Burke, Heinrich, Heikkonant, Martial, von Eisenstiel, Lummus, Habib, and on and on. He had learned the "pattern" a long, long time ago. He knew that his current suffering in this artificial hell was the direct result of crimes committed in the dawn of civilization, beginning with a petty thing, a ludicrously petty thing that had repeated thereafter in one form or another in every life. It was always the same shoddy conflict over a woman — she being Evelyn by many names but always the same basic identity. The antagonist was always Aspic, whatever he was called.

This sorry drama had its bit players as well. Templar had been the original go-between, intriguer, pimp — catalyzing violent events. Charlie O'Brian, bless his soul, had also played a role at times. Betty, dear Betty, was the one he always betrayed, the woman he loved. And God had watched the drama from the side, most recently as Chief Walk-on-air.

Jack knew all this when he entered The Desperation. Every detail of all his lives lived in vivid color in his awareness now. No mysteries remained to be uncovered. The environment around him no longer changed. Therefore he fell into desperation and remained there for ... decades? They seemed like eons.

Finally came the period in which Jack now found himself. Originally he had called it Death, but lately he had begun to will that Death might turn into Escape!

Outwardly the world was still the same as it had been during The Desperation. The factory still lay deep inside some kind of hole. Dirty, freakish, degenerate creatures worked in the pit. They scraped dust, soot, and dirt from the side of the building, loaded it in buckets, then hoisted the buckets out of the pit by ropes. The land around Perpetual was still a lake of fire and smoke. Volcanoes had formed and spewed dust and lava. The great cluster of egg-shaped buildings still stood where once the Complex had been, surrounded by a moat. The sky was still a sewer of flying debris and drifting dirt. There was no change in the physical world, but a monumental change had taken place in Jack's own psychic sphere.

The period that Jack called Death had come as a decision. There had come a point when something had snapped. Jack had simply given up. He gave up all thought, feeling, and striving at one point. He no longer struggled or resisted. He simply let it be. He cycled and cycled, withholding any "comment" or participation. He expected nothing, wished for nothing, and for a long time, indeed, nothing happened.

But then, so gradually that he didn't become aware of it until the process had run its course, he found himself surrounded by a bubble.

He had cycled inside that bubble now several thousand times. The surprise and suspicion the bubble had aroused at first had faded into watchful expectation. Jack's ego, scourged and perhaps hardened during The Desperation, was now awakening again. A grim watchfulness characterized Jack best. All softer emotions and states of mind had been ground away a long time ago. Grim. Determined. Even his hope of escape had about it a fierce willfulness. It was less a hope than a demand. Whatever crimes he had committed during his many sorry rounds on earth had been atoned. His punishment had far exceeded his crime. If anything he had a bank account, a goodly reserve, a credit of atonement. If only he could get away from here, he could — and by the gods he *would* — spend some of that accumulation.

His ego grew stronger and more self-assured because Jack suspected that the bubble was his own creation. He had somehow made it by his decision to "die" and to be done with it. Energies uselessly squandered until that time in fruitless resistance had gone to work for him. They had formed the bubble out of floating psychic detritus. The bubble in turn protected him: the cryogenic cubicle no longer froze him; the carnal ocean no longer stirred his lust; even the spirouettes bounced off the bubble; their sharp tips could find no purchase. Only the Vortex still frightened Jack — and he waited for strength. The Vortex, he knew, was his only chance of salvation.

Then the time came. It was the start of yet another cycle — tens of thousands, hundreds of thousands, perhaps millions of cycles now lay behind him, but this time, he knew, the last one had been endured. Jack felt that his strength was at the full. Never in any of his lives, nor ever in the Afterworld, had he felt quite like this — reckless with abandon. At that moment he travelled up a line of light toward the Void again, and he already knew what he would do. Without hesitation, without a thought, he would plunge into the Fire Vortex. He hoped only that his bubble would hold up and would protect him.

He sailed into the Void, "looked" up, and saw the Fire. He willed himself into its midst, and instantly he "flew" into the center of that seeming face.

The Vortex caught him like a storm — yet unlike any storm he had ever experienced in scores of lives. Incredible forces flung and tore him. His hope of a moment ago appeared for what it was, a wishful thought. The bubble reached incandescence, cracked, flaked, and was torn away. Naked now, Jack burst into flame and screamed unheard in the tumult. The test was too great. He couldn't meet it. He was still too heavy, still too gross, still too much dross, too little metal. If he had experienced psychic pain during his cycling, it appeared now like an itch compared with the relentless torment of this purifying, transcendental fire storm. It burned away whatever Jack had been and was — coils, ego, spirouettes. It began to consume Jack at his center — and in that moment Jack cried out and begged, begged in total desperation, to be released once more. *Let me try again, please, let me try again*, he cried, unheard, it seemed. But no. It happened. He was alone. The storm had disappeared abruptly. The ocean frothed below, red, steaming, pink. The constellations glimmered overhead.

In his many cyclings, Jack had learned to know his corner of the Afterworld. Free of the Vortex, he saw that he was in another portion of the world. *Look at the lines* ... The lines had changed. He also saw what he hadn't seen around Perpetual — crowds of disembodied spirits. They jostled and fought desperately to gain access to active lines, those glowing red.

Too many spirits, not enough bodies. Some great dying had taken place during that century or centuries he had spent cycling back and forth in Paradise. *Look at them competing!* The spirits fought for the privilege of being born again, a mad flash and spark of energies.

Jack gathered up his powers. The dread that he had just experienced inside that fiery tornado had already begun to fade, replaced by the dawn of lust and the awakening of all manner of desires.

Free again. Free to be embodied. Free to hunt that devil, Aspic. Free to pay the bastard back with interest for all those centuries of torture. *Here I come, Aspic, you son of a bitch. Ready or not* . . .

Maddened by desire and light without his spirouettes, he scanned the active lines, seeking a compatible couple. Oh, God, how they screwed down below. Pumping, clawing, groaning. Squishing and slapping and grinding and beating on those hot, those moist, those palpitating anvils of real flesh!

He glimpsed through the window of a red hot line a couple rising up toward orgasm in the dark cubicle of some underground city. The violent fury of this pair drew him, compelled him. He bit her shoulder. She gouged holes into his buttocks with her fingers to force him deeper into her pulsating cave. The ricketty cot on which they labored rocked flimsily beneath their violently thrusting bodies.

A hundred or more souls obscured the apperture, each bent on incarnation. Jack dove down into their midst, filled with the energy of hundreds of years of deprivation. He scattered them apart. He plunged into the window and down that snaking corridor to become an impregnation. He didn't feel the rude suck of Aspic's devilish machine this time, and in a moment, sighing with infinite relief, he dissolved into a quaking, palpitating, biological bliss.

PHASE IV
The Magic Show

23.
Two Caravans in Cactus

The town of Cactus lay at the termination of the Lower Caravan Route. Not far to the west of it began the California desert, and to the south extended the badlands known as The Shashtuk. At one time in its history, Cactus had been a busy waystation on the caravan route, the route continuing on into California proper across the desert, but twenty years before this date the western lands had separated from the mainland and had moved far out to sea. California had turned into an island, the trade had disappeared, and Cactus had remained behind, a shrunken residue of its past.

Now the thirty or so rude huts that formed a circle around the Sweeper's Haven housed scores of mutant hunters who plied their trade in The Shashtuk. Cactus people hunted antler-beef as well, tanned leather, and brewed a liquor known simply as "cactus." In support of their liquor trade, the Cactus people bought Golden

Age bottles of all sizes and shapes — such was the extent of the local economy.

This clustering of squalid, dome-shaped huts lay like an aging pile of manure left by some giant horse in the midst of an almost limitless ocean of swaying, silvery mutagrass. Smoke rose thickly from the village into a sky perpetually dark with volcanic dust and other planetary detritus. The Holocaustic War dated back some hundred and fifty years — it was now 2159 by the better calendars — but the Age of Dust showed no sign of abating, and Cactus rarely saw the sun except as a sickly, moving lamp above the murk.

Very few caravans ever came to Cactus. The people herded their mutants or hauled their liquor, dried beef, and hides to the Phoenix markets. Very rarely did a glass merchant come with rattling wagons to sell his load for Henriettas or some bales of leather. Otherwise Cactus was left alone. The arrival of a caravan, consequently, signalled a general holiday, and today was one of those days.

Children had sighted the caravan in the morning. It came from the east, a small but respectable train. It followed a faded line across the prairie, its vehicles swaying on the rough terrain. Mutagrass had taken over the caravan route; only traces of its well-trampled and wheel-gouged surface still remained.

By mid-afternoon the caravan was close and most of Cactus had marched out to greet it — and the townfolk led the caravan back now, considerably excited and intrigued. The caravan contained a Show-Biz, and not just any Show-Biz. For a period of months now stories of this magic show had circulated on the Route. The show belonged to Magic Jack, a strange and shadowy figure from the east. His entertainment was said to be the most unusual and exciting ever to hit the routes, upper or lower.

Why had this famous magic show come all the way to Cactus? Few shows ever even came to Phoenix. But to Cactus? It was too good to be believed, and the people speculated all the way back about the reason.

They had another reason for puzzlement. When they had marched out to greet the caravan, the Show-Biz crewmen had ridden forward and formed a line to block the people's path. A huge balding man with a thick, red beard had told them in a gravelly voice to stay away. Magic Jack didn't like people crowding his fancy vehicles, so everyone should keep his distance lest Magic Jack order the train to turn around. Of Magic Jack himself there was no sign.

Like every other settlement with a smidgen of pride, Cactus had a caravan terrain, a wide, muddy expanse surrounded (like the town itself) by a water ditch. Mutagrass blanketed the world these days — a tough, long-stemmed silvery growth, the source of most food, fodder, fuel, and fiber. Mutagrass thrived despite diminished solar radiation, but it was a relentless conqueror and only water could keep it at bay. Mutagrass was water-shy.

The train moved across a hang-bridge onto this terrain — two colorful vans, three smaller wagons, twenty horses, and eight men. The vans rode on genuine Golden Age wheels. Vivid pictures painted on their sides aroused most of the curiosity. The crewmen opened one of the wagons and placed a portable fence around a sizeable space. Then they began to raise a canvas tent of generous proportions. They refused all help.

The people gathered on the far side of the fence and talked excitedly about the pictures painted on the walls of the vans. Those who knew the most gave explanations.

A giant, milk-white rabbit — as big or bigger than a man — took up a portion of one of the pictures. Rays of light came from the rabbit's eyes and fell on an audience shown seated inside the same tent that the crewmen were raising now. Bubbles rose from the heads of the audience, and inside the bubbles were shown all manner of scenes from the Golden Age.

The rabbit's name was Evelyn — maintained those in the know. She was a giant mutant from the east and had an art called Hip No Tism. She could crawl into your mind; and once she was inside, she could make you see the Golden Age as if you had actually lived in that blessed time.

The people held look-out for the rabbit's owner, but they still saw no sign of Magic Jack. They had to content themselves with the magician's picture. He was also shown on one of the panels of one of the vans. He stood with a short-handled whip in hand — a powerful man in a one-piece woven suit, a round black hat on his head. He had a scowling look on his face and eyes almost as brilliantly shiny as the rabbit's.

The people concluded that Magic Jack had to be inside one of those colorful vans — and Evelyn in the other.

In this judgement the people were correct. Magic Jack stood inside his van, the one nearest to the crowd. He stood in darkness — if not in total darkness. Scores of tiny peepholes riddled the walls of the van, too small to see from the outside — but sufficiently large to see the world if you stood inside and were peering out. Magic Jack was busy doing exactly that. He spied. Thirty or so people crowded the fence — Cactus loomed behind them, dirty, domed, and smoking — and Magic Jack looked in turn at every face. He examined the people slowly, thoughtfully, methodically — but he didn't see the one he was seeking.

He was a man of thirty-two, a sturdy, powerfully built, middlesized figure. In many ways he resembled the man he had once been, his namesake, Jack. But the current Jack had a somewhat thinner, leaner face and look, and his nose was slightly twisted, having been broken several times.

He had been born in a community called Atlantis far to the east of Cactus. He had come to life unknowing, ignorant, and normal in most ways. His parents had named him Buddy Brandon, an old-fashioned, Old Order Name — common in Atlantis, which had strong links to the Golden Age. Thirty years had passed before he had awakened to his true identity on an island in the Mississippi. Since then he had journeyed west, ever west, using his current name. Cactus, for him, was the end of the line.

Standing in the darkness, spying, secluded from the world — such an activity suited Jack well. Whether now or earlier as Brandon, he had never been a cheerful or gregarious sort. His awakening had turned him into an even more menacingly dark and harsh man than he had been. He seldom left his van. Big, bearish, bearded Tovarish ran the crews. Jack came from his hiding place only when he had to do the magic show or, rarely, to deal with dangers along the caravan route.

He stood, slightly bent, and peered at faces. He had looked at a thousand faces in the same way since his awakening. He had seen better towns than Cactus and greater crowds — but nowhere yet had he seen a face or figure suggesting his enemy and prey — the man who had once been Teddy Aspic. He still didn't — even though he had arrived at the end of the line.

From Cactus he planned on heading south, into The Shashtuk. He meant to find the place he had known as Perpetual, the place people called Plutonium now. He had hoped that he would meet Aspic here in Cactus if not before. He figured that Chief Walk-on-air owed him that favor. But it seemed that it wasn't in the cards. No one out there mattered. He saw only common faces — no one outstanding or even halfway memorable. Aspic — he knew this in his bones — would stand out in some way; he would reveal himself.

Jack was still spying a little later — he moved from one peephole to the other to get different angles on the crowd — when some event, disturbance, or happening stirred the people. They turned from the Show-Biz van and faced toward the north. They were looking at something. Then Jack heard a sound very characteristic of this age — the distant scream of greaseless axles turning.

He put a bench into position and clambered up to get a better look. He could see above the crowd through peepholes placed just beneath the roof. From that perspective he now spied a caravan approaching. The ground rose slightly to the north. The caravan had just become visible as it reached the top of the rise. The train was still a goodly distance from Cactus, but Jack saw several small wagons, numerous horsemen wading through waist-high mutagrass, and . . . it was something, presumably an object. It had a silvery glint. A swarm of little figures carried it; the figures would be mutants.

Jack had learned a good deal about the Lower Caravan Route and the settlements along its continent-spanning reach. He knew that Cactus was a dump, an isolated, wretched place too poor even to need a city wall. He knew that caravans seldom came here, least of all a big one such as the one that now approached. That a caravan approached, the second one this day, had to be a sign, an omen, and Jack couldn't help but feel excitement. Maybe the Chief had acted after all — and why not? If karmic chains had pulled Jack to Evelyn, why wouldn't the same chains pull Aspic toward the scenes of his old crimes?

Jack began to sweat. Sweat ran down into his eyes, and he had to wipe his itching eyeballs from time to time. Meanwhile he strained to see, but the distance was still too great. He decided on an impulse to leave his van for once; he had to see this caravan from closer up.

His van had two doors, one in the side, the other at the end. His dark hat pulled over his brow, dust goggles over his eyes, he left the vehicle by the end door, the one farthest from the crowd. The creak of his door alerted Evelyn; her colorful abode stood end to end with Jack's. She emoted instantly, and Jack felt enveloped by her cloying emanation. Sexual tingles passed over his body and visions rolled across his eyelids. He felt transported in time for a moment. He was in the Golden Age, in Washington, D. C. He sat across a table from Evelyn, and they snarled at each other over Bloody Marys.

But Evelyn's telepathics no longer touched Jack as they had in those early days, two years ago. He shook off the feelings she aroused and moved out of the reach of her emanations. A residue of her emotions lingered temporarily and then faded — her sexuality, her sadness, and her dark wish to die. It occurred to Jack that six days had passed since he had whipped her, and she was growing desperate again. *Well,* he thought, *both of us will get a little satisfaction before the night is out* . . .

He passed the tent on his way. Hammering sounds came from within. Tovarish and the crewmen were assembling the stage. Jack heard his foreman's gravelly voice giving some direction.

The crowd had moved to face the approaching caravan, and Jack joined the people at the rear, disregarding their curious looks; he scowled and made a forbidding face, and no one ventured to address him. But despite his stern exterior, Jack was aroused. The approaching caravan was a sweeper's train. He saw that already — light wagons designed for very rough travel across the uncharted reaches of the mutagrass ocean. But if this was a sweeper's train . . .

Since his awakening, Jack had often wondered what kind of man Aspic might turn out to be — and had as often concluded that Aspic would turn out to be a sweeper. No career resembled science quite as much as sweeping did these days. The vast structure of objects and constructs that had been the Golden Age lay buried now beneath the ice cap or under mutagrass prairie. Sweepers were the pioneers and discoverers of the Age of Dust. They dug up metal, plastics, artifacts, and "gaso-lean." They were tinkerers, traders, and "restorationists." Aspic could well be one of these.

Then the caravan came close enough to be observed, and Jack's excitement grew. These people carried unusual bounty, very odd bounty. The object Jack had glimpsed earlier, that silvery thing — it was a missile, by God, a bomb, a warhead, and unexploded dud. *Son of a bitch*, Jack thought. He had never seen anything like this, not in the Age of Dust. The object was a long, silvery cylinder, perhaps eight feet long and sharply pointed at one end. It rested on a crude framework made of roughly hewn logs. Twelve or more mutants carried the thing — they staggered under its weight. They led the way; the small wagons came behind them in a curved line.

The people of Cactus had recognized the caravan now and spoke about it excitedly. Jack gathered that the train belonged to a sweeper by the name of Golden Arm and that Golden Arm had "returned." It seemed that he had not been expected to return. The people spoke as well about a thing called "Godbod." Jack didn't understand the term, but he gathered that Golden Arm had "left" claiming that he could find "Godbod"; that Cactus had not believed that he could do it; that now that Golden Arm had "returned," it meant that he had found his "Godbod" after all. And if it was so, Golden Arm would sure be filthy rich one of these days because "they" liked nothing better than "its ineffable perfume."

All of this was a bit mysterious and confusing, but Jack meant to get to the bottom of it. He singled out the man who seemed to know the most about this

Golden Arm — a fellow with freckles and a prominent Adam's apple. Later he would question the man, but for the moment he turned his attention to the caravan.

He saw now that behind the missile on its wooden cradle walked another group of mutants. Behind them rode eight or nine men on horseback. Yet other men guided the wagons, flailing with their whips. Presently the mutants stopped and lowered the shiny bomb to the ground. Other mutants advanced and picked up the load. Thus the caravan advanced.

"Sweepers," said a gravelly voice.

Tovarish and the crewmen had left their work to join the crowd. Tovarish towered over Jack, a giant of a man and in some ways a mysterious figure. Jack guessed that some karmic debt bound Tovarish to his service. The man was loyal to a fault. They had met somewhere before, in some other life, but Jack couldn't place the man.

"Nice chunk of metal." Tovarish pointed at the bomb with a bushy chin. "Too damn big to melt, though."

Jack gave no response, and Tovarish fell silent. "All right, men," he said after a while. "Back to work. There isn't anything to see." He led the crewmen back toward the tent.

Soon the caravan reached the terrain. The mutants crossed the water ditch struggling to hold the missile and its frame above the water even as they sank chest deep into the muddy muck. They clambered up again, pulled the framework up over the bank, then sank exhausted to the ground. The village dogs instantly formed a madly barking half-circle around them. The rest of the sweeping train, meanwhile, had turned and approached one of the raised bridges some distance to Jack's left. Villagers ran toward the bridge to lower it over the channel.

Jack looked at the mutants one by one — more from habit than anything else. He didn't think that Aspic would turn out to be a mutant. Most of these creatures were colorfrees, a few were beemen. Colorfrees had bright red skins and snow-white hair; hairy holes served as their noses; missing or badly-wired nervous systems made them into jerky, twitchy creatures whose faces changed color rapidly with every movement of thought — from deadly pale to purple. The beemen had multi-faceted eyes. None looked even remotely like Aspic.

He turned his attention to the sweepers themselves. Most of the men had stayed behind to supervise the crossing of the wagons, but three men approached riding abreast. The sun had begun to set. The east was already black, but the western sky resembled a vast coagulation of blood. The light came from behind the sweepers and their faces lay in shadow. Nonetheless Jack focused instantly on one of the men — and so intently that for a moment he forgot to breathe.

The man rode in the center — an inordinately tall, thin creature. He was seated on a midsized pony, and his legs dangled just above the mud. The people knew him; they addressed him with cheery calls. He waved to them, he grinned at them, his white teeth flashed.

Jack controlled himself. Encounters not unlike this one had disappointed him before. Appearances . . . One had to have more than appearances; one had to have a sign. But dammit all — the man looked like Aspic, leastways from a distance: tall, thin, and a little stooped. He was Golden Arm, the leader of this train, and Jack now knew why the sweeper had that name. Arm wore a leather jacket of the Hell's Angels type — black leather (or it might have been plastic, for that matter) studded with bright silver stars. The jacket was too small for him but also, paradoxically, too loose. When the sweeper waved his arm, his sleeve dropped back. A dozen golden watches circled his arm — and Jack would have bet that every watch on the sweeper's arm was a "working mystery."

The man was evidently popular. He dismounted near the framework with the bomb. In effect he stepped off his pony; his legs were so long. The crowd immediately made a circle around him and bombarded him with questions. Where had he been? What was that thing? How had he found it? Did it work? Golden Arm grinned, flashing his teeth; he waved, flashing his arm; he told the crowd that they would hear all about it in good time, in the Sweeper's Haven, over a glass of cactus. Then his eyes caught the colorful vans. "Hey," he cried, "What might that be? Travelling Henriettas? That's what this boy needs just now — red hot Henriettas." The crowd laughed. Then they told Arm about the magic show.

Jack moved a little so that he could observe the sweeper without being observed in turn. He saw a long face — thin, dark, lined, and burned by wind. It was a northerner's face; a man who had spent many years up on the Ice, tunnelling and seeking buried cities. The face combined hard features and a general tone of merriment. And it had about it a puzzling something Jack could not quite place. Then, abruptly, he understood the source of his unease. Golden Arm was squinting. He had squinted all along. He looked out at the world through narrow slits, as from behind fortifications. He squinted perpetually, it seemed — even when he laughed, and that last habit gave the sweeper a peculiarly wolfish look.

Jack observed a little longer, careful not to come directly into the sweeper's view. He listened to the banter, analyzing the sound of Arm's voice. Arm spoke with a clear, sharp, leader's voice — and with a northern twang. What was he doing this far south? What did he seek in Cactus? What was meant by "Godbod"? Jack meant to get answers to those questions before the night's magic show began.

He moved deeper into the crowd, reached out, and tapped the shoulder of the man he had singled out earlier—the freckled fellow with the Adam's apple.

"Would you mind?" Jack asked, "I'd like to talk to you. Could you come along?"

The man had been listening to a spirited exchange between Golden Arm and several thin but animated village women. Amusement still molded the Freckled Man's features even as his eyes questioned Jack. Then he evidently judged Jack to be a less amusing fellow than this Golden Arm. "Just a minute," he said and turned front again.

Jack calmly pushed his goggles to his forehead. His eyes had a peculiar power, and he knew how to use their hypnotic depth when it suited his purposes. He tapped the man's shoulder for the second time. The Freckled Man turned with an expression of irritation, but his face sobered instantly when he saw Jack's staring eyes.

"Now?" Jack asked.

"All right," the man cried. "All right, I'm coming. Don't get excited." And Jack led him off toward the magic caravan as if he were a lamb.

24.
JoAnn the Ursula

The Freckled Man followed Jack not because he wanted to but because Jack's eyes had a commanding and peculiarly menacing depth. But Jack's effect on people came only partially from his memories of many lives. He was also an Atlantean, and in this Age of Dust, Atlanteans were a breed unto themselves. They remembered more of history, they had a closer contact with the Golden Age, and they had something resembling a culture while the balance of the population still struggled with survival and had regressed to a primitive state. Atlanteans resembled the Mennonites of the Golden Age with this difference: they were technologically more advanced than the people who lived around them. They were reclusive not in order to shield the purity of a religious faith but to protect themselves from "barbarian" attack.

Atlantis lay in the east, a large community for this day and age. But little of Atlantis was visible above ground. Atlanteans lived in an extensive system of caves deep underground. The caves had been burned from bedrock in the Golden Age — using the same technology that Jack had used to make the articaverns in Perpetual, New Mexico. The cave system had been an air raid shelter, one of the underground command posts of the Strategic Air Command. It had survived the Holocaustic War more or less intact. Portions of the old technology still worked — geothermal steam drove the generators; telephone communications linked the various caves; an ingenious waste disposal system recovered sewage and fed nutrients to hydroponic algal tanks; and Atlantis could still use a variety of mining machines that had been stored deep in the shelter to permit its inhabitants to dig out again if they were ever buried by a direct atomic hit.

In Jack's day Atlantis had had sixty thousand people. The community had grown sharply in the last few decades — so much so that a portion of the people now lived above the ground. Despite these numbers, Atlantis was too small to sustain the know-how it had inherited. Atlantis lived in the Age of Dust like every other community. Sheer survival drained off most of her energy and talent. When bulbs burned out, candles replaced them; when machines malfunctioned, they could no longer be repaired. The know-how was decaying rapidly. There was no time for sustained education. Atlantis had to sweep for metal and high energy fuels like all the rest of the world. Atlanteans collected mutagrain, hunted antlered-cattle, and grew vegetables. They wove fibers of high quality, made candles, forged iron, and traded carefully with the "barbarians" through numerous agents. And they defended vigorously a territory far greater in extent than the immediate environs of Atlantis.

Jack returned to earthly life in the midst of this community. He was not remarkable in any way as a child — perhaps quieter than most. In his early teens, however, he came into conflict with Atlantis. He failed to "blossom," as Atlantis put it. He refused to "open." No amount of counselling worked in his case. He turned surly and withdrawn and, when pressed, he tended to be violent. He seemed encased in a thick block of stone, and when it came to "sharing," he flatly refused.

Jack himself had no idea why he felt like a stranger among his own, but he knew what he liked and hated, and he disliked Atlantis intensely. He dreamed of the world "outside," of "hinterland," as it was called. Stories of barbarians and the adventurous life of the caravan routes consumed his interest, while the persistent call to join in the "communion" filled him with disgust.

Atlantis combined the strains of two contrasting cultures — a spartan military ethic which had evolved early in the community's history and a strong utopean tendency in social relations, a reaction to the now dimly remembered horror of the Holocaustic War. Hence also the community's name. Jack chafed under the discipline and cringed back from the constant "giving" that utopia demanded. He had come back to earth in order to wreak vengeance on an enemy. He didn't know that at the time, not consciously. He was antisocial because he rejected social betterment. He had opted instead for retribution, the cruel law of eye for eye.

Early on, Atlantis marked Jack for an "outside" career. His graceless nature and violent tendencies might best be used in armed conflict and the arduous labor of sweeping. He was "sent up" at age fifteen and joined a sweeping train.

Not long after that, Jack became well known. It seemed that he had "the talent." The talent was a gift for finding buried Golden Age facilities in the midst of that vast ocean of mutagrass. Jack had "nose," he had "the touch." He could sense the presence of antiquities by odd and random clues — a wobble in the ground, the placement of clumps of woods or rock outcroppings in the mutagrass, or the course and shape of dark-green waterways that cut across the silver prairie. He could not explain his talent either to himself or others.

Other people with "the talent" would have risen rapidly in the Atlantean sweeping service. Not so Jack. He also had a talent for making enemies of all who favored and furthered him. His temper and insubordination became as famous as his finds. And by the time he reached age thirty, shortly before his awakening, he was still only a "scout," a respected position in sweeping circles but one devoid of all authority. Train commanders wanted Jack because he could find "the goods." But their eagerness to "shaft" rich digs was tempered by the price they had to pay — Jack's violent tantrums and inexplicable moods. The price grew too steep, eventually, and Jack's periods of "rest and recuperation" grew longer than those of work.

One day, while once again between assignments, Jack was summoned to the Coordination Cave by telephone. In those days people called him Brandon — never Buddy.

"Brandon," said his segment leader, "something has come up. We're about to send a train into the Quadrant Lake region. The train is ready to march, but two of their scouts have taken ill. We need an experienced hand, especially in that area. You are the man. Report to Captain the Ursula at the head of Tunnel Nine. Can you get ready right away?"

Jack nodded. He had spent six weeks back home, which was exactly six weeks too many. He went back to his quarters, gathered his roll and pack, and took off for Tunnel Number Nine, one of the few with a working elevator.

Captain the Ursula, he mused on the way. *Captain*

the Ursula ... He knew a Captain the Bakey and a Captain the Fore, not a Captain the Ursula. *Must be a new one,* he thought, *or from one of the other segments* ...

He emerged from the dark, dripping tunnel after a short walk and saw the train nearby, a string of light wagons and several clusters of lounging sweepers. He made for a small bunch seeing Lieutenant Paddy Horse, a huge, redfaced, beefy man.

My luck, he thought. *That son of a bitch Paddy* ... He had swept with Paddy Horse before and, like most others with whom he had worked, Paddy had earned Jack's contempt.

Lieutenant Paddy Horse stood with several others. All listened to someone Jack couldn't see. But as Jack's approach was noticed, the people turned to look at him, and as they did so Jack saw a woman.

She stood there, slender and young. Dark hair framed a pretty, slightly rectangular face. Rich embroideries, no doubt of her own design and execution, covered her one-piece uniform. On her red beret gleamed a single silver star — the captain's mark. So this was Captain the Ursula, a woman and still young — she couldn't have been over twenty-five or six — and they sent *her* to the Quadrant Lakes?

Heaven help us, Jack thought, approaching. *A woman and so young. And pretty.*

Her femininity startled and confused him. He wanted to be angry with the leadership — he was usually angry when he heard about the promotion of people younger than he was — but this captain, even from a distance, had a strange effect on Jack. He suppressed his usual carping internal mutters.

As he approached she looked at him squarely, fully — in the best Atlantean tradition. But as he stopped before her and dropped his heavy pack into the dust, her eyes gleamed up momentarily, as if in recognition.

"Jack . . . ?" she asked, a little tentatively.

"Brandon," Jack said. "Buddy Brandon. Are you Captain the Ursula?" She inclined her head. "Why did you call me Jack?"

"I am not sure." She continued looking at him as if she were searching for some clue. "You look like someone . . . " She shook her head decisively. "I guess not. You reminded me of someone, but now I'm not sure who."

"Well," Jack said, "Atlantis is a big place." He was a little cross with her. Buddy Brandon's name was well known in Atlantis, but she had not reacted in the slightest. "I'm to be your scout," he said.

"Is someone else coming?" She seemed to be looking over Jack's shoulder. "We asked for two replacements."

"Lady," Jack said, staring at her, "I'm Brandon When I'm along, you don't need any other scout."

Lieutenant Paddy Horse now intruded into the conversation. "If they sent Brandon, they won't send anybody else — and not because Brandon is so great, JoAnn. Brandon can't stand competition."

"Stay out of this, Horse's Ass."

"You better watch your tongue . . . scout."

"I'm not yet under your command, " Jack said, "so don't give me any orders until we hit the grass."

"Gentlemen," the youthful captain said. "If you two have personal hangouts with each other, don't work them out under my command." She turned to Jack. "You were sent alone?"

"That's right."

"In that case . . . Paddy, a good horse for our scout. Welcome, Brandon. Let's go out there and have a good sweep. And you two — stay in communion. For the duration."

The sweeping train left Atlantis and took a southerly course. Their orders were to follow the Mississippi river to the Quadrant Lakes Region, a badlands infested with radiation. The Quadrant Lakes had once been Memphis, but that city had turned into a giant series of craters during the Holocaustic War. Badlands made good sweeping. Barbarians avoided such areas; they hadn't been swept clean. Only mutant hunters and their swarms of dogs plied their trade in such reaches, and they were no competition for an organized train.

Jack had made many, many sweeps — but none ever like this one, under a woman's command. And what a woman she turned out to be! Jack couldn't understand her, and during those first weeks of dusty marching, he spent much of his horseback musing-time thinking about JoAnn the Ursula.

She was a good commander — simple, direct, decisive, and fair. Atlantis had many women like her, but they tended to take "inside" jobs. All women served on sweep rotations — this train had six or seven — but the grime, the dust, the incessant wind, the filth, and the monotony, above all the monotony, discouraged a continuing career . . . unless, like Jack, you liked it out here with the dusty antlered herds, coyotes, and ever-circling carry crows.

But while JoAnn was a sharp commander, she also had another side, and Jack's puzzlement arose because he saw that side of her as well, by nights, around the fire. She could sing, dance, embroider, tell stories — and she had a clear, sweet, silvery laugh. Her laughter struck Jack the first night out and echoed in his mind throughout the following day. After that he waited for the nights to hear the ringing of that bell. He behaved like a model sweeper in her honor and stayed clear of Paddy Horse — even though the lieutenant had picked a half-lame pony for Jack, half-lame and blind in one eye.

They had been underway for three weeks or so when it began to dawn on Jack that the captain might be sweet on him. On many a night he caught her looking at him across the fire with an expression such that . . . no! He couldn't quite credit what he saw, but repetition of such momentary eye collisions ultimately forced a conclusion — and then a soul-shaking excitement.

Jack watched her now through eyes cloudy with unbelievable hopes, and it seemed to him that she sang for him; that she told her jokes and stories for his ears; that her laugh tinkled for one man alone. In the day time, when she turned crisp and cool again, it seemed to Jack that her orders to the scout had a special softness absent from her voice with others.

All this had about it something of the fairy tale, too good to be believed. Jack had had a miserable time with women — especially Atlanteans. Atlantis believed in open mating. Men approached women, or the other way around, and asked for sex in the "open mode"; sex could be shared without sanctions and often blossomed into love. No woman had ever asked Jack to share sex; very few had ever said yes to his advances. His few experiences of real pleasure had come far from Atlantis with barbarian women or, more frequently, in mutant kennels on red-hot Henriettas. Atlantis forbade such couplings — they produced colorfrees, the mutant world's most abject slaves. But when you had no other choice . . . That a woman of the Ursula's beauty and character should show an interest in Jack — it took him by surprise, it tore him in two.

Toward the end of their fifth week of travel, Jack spied some odd lumps in the ground not far from the muddy river that flowed to their right. They were still some distance from the Quadrant Lakes, but Jack asked for a shaft. The shaft hit an ancient bridge abutment, encouragement enough to stop, to set up a permanent camp, and to sweep the area in earnest.

Three days later a shaft found rich treasure, a seeming complex of buried structures. Nearly a ton of metal, some plastic, and several small motors came up that day, and Jack was in his glory. There might be gaso-lean down there, and ato-*mo*-biles even, and clothing, oil, and glass. Jack's talent hadn't failed him.

That night JoAnn's eyes glowed warmer than ever across the crackling flames, and Jack decided that he would have to chance it. Field discipline prevented JoAnn from making an approach. Jack was her subordinate. But he could go to her even if she couldn't go to him. At the first suitable opportunity; at the first suitable opportunity . . .

He approached her two days later in the evening. There had been an awesome hurricane that morning. The dust had dropped out of the sky. The day had been a "blue," the sun brilliant and unobscured, and it had been hot, sweaty, and muddy in the shafts. JoAnn knelt by a small, clear stream and washed after the day's work. She was naked to the waist. She had soaped her face, neck, torso, and breasts and now splashed herself, leaning forward.

Jack squatted down next to her. He felt very shy and ill at ease, and to compensate for these feelings, he had assumed an easy-going, cocky air.

"Hi there," he said.

She looked up, face red and wet. He looked at her nipples in such a way that she would know exactly what he meant, so . . . with eyebrows a little raised and his mouth a little puckered. She continued washing. Then she dried herself while he watched and slipped into the upper portion of her one-piece embroidered suit; it had hung down about her waist.

"What about it, JoAnn?"

Her eyes were dark and cautious. "What about what?"

"What about you and me slipping off somewhere for some serious copulation?"

She shook her head. She didn't look at him. Her chin was bent. She looked at the buttons she was fastening.

"Why not?"

"Just no. I don't feel like it."

"Now — or ever?"

"Let's just say now — for now." Then she shot him a look that any man, dense or bright, had to interpret as a promise.

Two days later Jack renewed his request. A coolness had come between them in the intervening time. She had avoided his eyes. She had been subdued around the fire by night, and her laughter had had a forced and tinny sound. Once more she said No, and when he insisted on an explanation, she gave him the formula response: "Free to ask, free to shake." — meaning that traditionally the shake of the head was enough to end the conversation.

Days then passed — days of dark brooding for Jack. He recalled every slight he had ever experienced and he computed in his memory all the metal, plastic, mysteries, wire, glass, food, liquor, books, and gasolean Atlantis had obtained as a consequence of his talent. It seemed to him now that Captain the Ursula had merely teased him along. The promise of her favors had kept him docile and obedient — despite Paddy's constant rain of snide remarks. Now that Jack had found the treasure, she became like all the rest. "Free to ask, free to shake." How often he had heard those words. They echoed in his mind now much like her laughter had tinkled weeks ago.

He came to a resolution at last. He would ask her one more time — a final time. If she said No, he would leave, depart, disappear. Why serve Atlantis like a mutant when his talent could make him rich and powerful? He could start a sweeping train himself, he could found a presidency, create his own Henrietta stables, live like a lord, in charge, not merely a scout for others, handing promotions to people ten years younger.

During the digging of the last few days, an aluminum boat had been found, well preserved and serviceable. It had been used for fishing the day it had come from the shaft and lay on the flat muddy Mississippi shore. On the evening of his decision, after dark, Jack took his pack and sleeping roll and laid them in the boat. He didn't want to build up hopes he didn't feel, and if JoAnn consented to a sharing of the bodies, he could always fetch his things again before the dawn. This done, he went back to the fire.

That morning a small instrument had surfaced from the latest shaft, a silvery object whose letters spelled "Harmonica." It made sweet music even if the man who'd found it and now played it was the Horse's Ass. Paddy clowned around the fire, the instrument against his mouth. He jumped about in rhythm with the music while everyone else clapped.

JoAnn was there with all the rest, smiling and clapping, and when her eyes crossed and met Jack's, he saw the promise once again. A tightness formed in his throat.

The merriment lasted later than usual — or maybe it just seemed like that to Jack. He cringed every time a sweeper threw more mutaroot upon the fire and the resins in the darkish fuel began to crackle. He wanted people off to the tents, off to bed.

The fire burned out at last and ash was heaped on the embers so that they might survive the night. The men went left, the women to the right, and JoAnn, shielding a burning twig against the breeze, went to her wagon.

She slept by herself in the center of the camp in a small vehicle where records and the most valuable objects were kept — the batteries, bulbs, false teeth, Golden Age matches, Golden Age soap, and books.

Jack followed the Ursula when no one was about. Bits of light came from the wagon — she had lit a candle from her twig. She moved about inside. He heard boards creaking and saw the flitting of shadows.

Don't expect a thing. They've always treated you like dirt; why should they change now?

But he *did* expect success. He couldn't help himself. His heart had moved into his throat. He swallowed hard and stepped up to the wagon.

A single movement pulled aside the leather flap at the vehicle's end, and Jack looked in.

"JoAnn — "

There was a sudden violent scramble inside. JoAnn was naked as on the day of her birth. A bowl of water stood on the floor, next to it a towel and a piece of soap. JoAnn had jerked up from a squatting position...

She stood now toward the back of the small vehicle, where her simple cot extended across the width of the space. She had grabbed her embroidered suit and held it across her body.

"JoAnn, I — "

"Get out," she cried. Then again, angrily, stamping a naked foot: "Get out, get out, get out!"

Jack had to say it. He had to let her know that he had not intended either to frighten her or to observe her at intimate toiletries. Dammit all!

"JoAnn, please listen — "

But JoAnn the Ursula, driven to extremity by embarrassment and Jack's stubborn insistence, flew into a rage.

"Paddy!" she shouted. "Hilton, Jackson!" Her raised voice carried far. She called her lieutenants.

Furious in turn, livid, exploding, Jack slapped the cover shut. Steaming, he headed away into the night. Steps came running in his direction. The beam of a precious flashlight zigzagged through the darkness, crossed Jack, then came back and rested on his face.

"You!" The voice was Paddy's. He blocked Jack's advance.

"Get — out — of — my — way!" Jack had found an object for his rage. He didn't wait to see whether or not Paddy Horse meant to comply with the order. He lunged forward and hit out with all his pent-up fury.

He was striking at Atlantis and his past. The jar of his fist as it drove into Horse's face gave him a joy he hadn't felt in months. People tried to grab him from behind. He kicked, elbowed, and swung. Gasps told him that he was succeeding. The darkness was total. The flashlight had gone out.

Free of his attackers, Jack ran. He knew where the river was. He just followed the grade down. Moments later he waded knee-deep in water and mud, pushing the boat. He jumped into it when it had cleared the bank, and the current slowly took him away.

25.
The Island of Awakening

He drifted all through the night and most of the following day, and throughout this time he shifted in mood from anger to despair and back. At times he told himself that he had acted stupidly and hastily; at times he congratulated himself on his courageous break with Atlantis; at times he almost sobbed, remembering the Ursula, sure once more that she had loved him and that he had fumbled his chances like an idiot. Twice during the day he changed his mind, but by then he was too far committed to be able to return. The river resisted even though Jack was willing.

The river ran high and fast. The hurricane of a week ago had swelled its waters, and once out in the central current, he couldn't go upstream again. Masses of debris obstructed his movements — tree trunks, dead animals, and submerged plugs of dead mutagrass. His paddling succeeded only in stopping the boat's downward rush, and the current was so strong, he couldn't make the eastern shore.

Gradually he resigned himself to his chosen path. JoAnn had teased him merely. He recalled how she had yelled for Paddy Horse — for Paddy Horse! He put the tinkle of her laughter out of his mind and recalled instead how she had tossed her head when saying — "Free to ask, free to shake."

Later yet he fell into reveries of the future. He recalled the fluting of the Henriettas he had mounted and the thrill of the odor of their invisibly squirted, acrid effluvium. He imagined himself at the end of his adventures as the master of a score of caravans. He turned practical matters in his mind — how he could convert this boat into metal and buy horses, and tools, and hire a few hands . . . his talent would surely do the rest.

Thus the day passed.

Late in the afternoon, the wind rose. Dust flew so thickly that Jack put on goggles. The muddy Mississippi ran with froth. A storm might be brewing, darkness would come soon. The long ride in the cramped boat had stiffened his limbs. He didn't want to spend another night out on the water. Thus thinking, he roused himself from daydreams and took a paddle. Several islands loomed ahead, heavily wooded islands. He might make it to one of those even if he couldn't reach the shore.

The current helped him this time. A little paddling, a little luck, and he was moving swiftly past the eroded bank of one of the islands. He reached out, grabbed an exposed root, and brought his boat to a stop. Muddy water towered up as the boat strained against the current, but Jack succeeded in tying the boat; he threw his gear up, and then he scrambled ashore.

The wind died soon thereafter, suddenly, abruptly — not unusual in this day. The western sky turned almost clear. The sinking sun was unobstructed, bright. Minute bits of silicate glimmered in the air as they slowly settled out.

Jack considered going on, but on reflection he decided to stay. The densely forested island promised shelter, and it was too late to start again. He had been chilled by the wind, and though the sun was bright, its rays were weak. A nice warm fire, a little dried meat toasted on a stick... He hauled some of his property up and then crashed into the underbrush to find himself some kindling and fuel.

Moments later he distinctly felt or heard a warning. Something or someone told him to go back. It was not a voice so much as a feeling in his chest and groin.

The feeling shocked, puzzled, and intrigued him all in one, and he thought at once of Old Order machines. He had never experienced anything remotely like this, and he had learned to associate the Golden Age with all things strange and unusual. Whatever it was he felt, it had to come from the past. Where was he now? How far from the Quadrant Lakes? He couldn't guess.

He stood unmoving, careful not to make a noise. He had visions of a great discovery, something no sweeper had ever found... A little apprehensive, yet also resolved to grasp his chance, he moved deeper into the island. Maybe it was meant to be, he thought, meaning his break with Atlantis.

The peculiar feeling intensified and grew as he progressed. Heavy undergrowth blocked his path. He moved into darkness trampling amidst many types of ferns with delicately serrated leaves. Animals scurried on either side. Birds flapped invisibly in the crowns of the trees. With every step he grew hotter. With every step the voices in his head grew more insistent and multiplied in number.

Jack felt fear but overcame it. He was certain that a treasure of great value lay on this island and that the voices in his head were guardians meant to scare him off. A sweeper who trembled never found a treasure — much less still-working machinery. He could not afford to fear a thing — not when his talent called.

The island was not large. He had observed it from the water. Ordinarily he should have been able to cross it in ten minutes or so. But he made very slow progress and soon realized why. His body resisted. His lungs worked to suffocation. His legs had the weight of stones. He walked slower and slower. And the heat intensified.

Then came a point when he couldn't move any more. Voices seemed to scream inside his head. His view was unobstructed and nothing prevented the next step, but he was up against an invisible skin or membrane. If only he could break through that ... if he could do that, he was sure that he would win.

Jack stood and strained against the barrier. Earlier he had been chilled. Now he sweated. Sweat drenched his chest and sides. Beads ran down his face and under his collar. He tried to lift his legs, his arms, but he couldn't do it.

I've got to move, he thought. *This is ridiculous.* By sheer luck, by chance, he had come upon something. He could just hear what they would say about him in the caves after he reported this. But somehow he had to go on.

At last he thought of a stratagem. He would let himself fall forward. He wouldn't try to walk. He would just fall. He carried out this intention immediately. He let his body fall without resistance. It worked smoothly. In an effort to prevent the fall and to restore his equilibrium, his legs followed along. He had broken through the barrier.

Almost at once he felt a change. The voices had retreated. He still heard them, dull and faint. They still urged him to turn back. But now he felt an overwhelming sensation of love and affection. It dominated his awareness and caused twinges of sexual excitement. Curious. Really odd.

He moved on. The land rose up ahead, and as he approached the slope, he noted that the trees were thinning out. The setting sun burnished their tips. Eagerly, now, he ran the rest of the way and stopped at the crown of the hill. A clearing lay beneath him.

At first he saw nothing unusual. It was just a clearing surrounded on all sides by trees. A little fog lay in the bottom. An outcropping of white rocks, boulders, lay in gathering shadow. Then he saw a movement, and he realized that he had deceived himself. The huge white objects he had taken for boulders were living shapes. *Mutants. Mutants . . . ? Telepathic mutants!*

Until that moment the word "telepathy" meant nothing to Jack, and yet he understood the word now. He understood as well that the strange beasts below had been "broadcasting" the feelings he had experienced. The word "broadcast" caused a tumble of visions in his head. He saw "apartment houses" with "TV antennae" on the roofs. He heard a "crooner" singing a "hit." He understood as well what the mutant broadcast meant. It was a "survival adaptation." The beasts sent out telepathic messages to protect themselves from his approach. But now that he had penetrated their protective zone, they tried to make him love them!

He started down the hill. Involuntary sobs began to rise out of his throat, and visions began to tumble through his mind. Memories rose in mad profusion. They would have been incomprehensible had Jack been an ordinary man, but he had seen all this before, countless times, in Paradise.

At last he had approached the shapes closely enough to see them. He stared with some amazement at giant rabbits. The beasts were as tall as he was and considerably heavier. Their fur was milky white yet phosphorescent at the tips; each beast stood in an odd nimbus of radiance. Some had been grazing while others had been sitting alertly on their haunches, ears raised. Now all were sitting up. They beamed a cloying telepathic pulse toward Jack. It was so powerful in its effect that tears of love flowed down his face.

Nevertheless, he kept on going. Involuntary affection for these strange and isolated mutants made him lift his arms — as if in anticipation of an embrace. But he walked slowly, like a soldier behind a coffin. Meanwhile images raced through his brain.

With a portion of his fractured awareness, Jack saw that the rabbits were in a state of fright and tension. They trembled on the edge of action. Suddenly all but one of them darted off in all directions with a speed and agility he would not have thought possible. They disappeared into the woods ahead.

Why had that one rabbit stayed behind? Jack had no idea — nor time or leisure to reflect. Momentous changes tore his brain. Information flooded him and emotions bombarded his chest. Yet he walked on relentlessly until he stood two or three feet in front of the animal.

The beast trembled visibly. Its fur stood on end, the phosphorescent tips at maximum extension. Jack thought of ghosts.

Then his eyes locked with the rabbit's eyes, and he felt as if sucked into a trance, a waking sleep. The rabbit's thoughts probed and touched his own. Then, without warning, the sad world of the animal, visible in its reddish-greenish eyes, appeared to open like a flower in Jack's mind. Within that flower was another. It shot up and opened in its turn. Then another. And yet another. At last, with an inward gasp, Jack recognized the rabbit. Suddenly he knew the being hidden beneath that fur, those trembling whiskers, and those long, tufted ears. The recognition coincided with changes in his own awareness. The storm of images he had experienced was sorting into patterns. He was awakening.

"Evelyn," he cried. "Evelyn Bantry!"

The rabbit didn't answer, and Jack knew at once that it couldn't; it couldn't speak. But the rabbit eyes attempted to communicate, and telepathic pulses conveyed to Jack a mass of emotion in which horror, desire, and despair were mingled in like proportions. Then, abruptly, Evelyn Bantry, or that which she had become, bolted in her turn.

Jack stood for a moment. He experienced vertigo. His legs seemed to fill with lead. He sank to the ground, fighting the swoon that held him. He didn't want to go to sleep now. He needed time to think. But his body sagged. He lay down, feeling drained. And he closed his eyes . . .

26.
The Bunny

Jack woke with the morning's light and found himself lying on marshy ground. His body shivered. He trembled with the cold. His flesh was icy and his clothing clammy. Fog lay in patches in the clearing. It boiled out of the surrounding forest like porridge from a forgotten pot. The sky above had dusted over once again, and the light was faint.

At first he took this for a dream. Only slowly did his memories sort out, but when they did he felt profound surprise and shock. He remembered everything now. He recalled his immediate past as Buddy Brandon, his time in the Afterworld, his pathetic Jack Clark existence, his time as Helmut Schweinhirt, and many other entities stretching back through the reach of time like a dark gallery of his discarded masks. He remembered, above all, the reason why he had returned to this desolate and ruined world.

He sat up and took stock of that world now, seeing it

through Jack Clark's eyes. An ice cap covered one half of America. Volcanic eruptions all over the world had obscured the sun with dust. The population had shrunk so much that — no wonder souls were forced to incarnate inside weird creatures, like Evelyn inside that, that Harvey hare. Education, knowledge, science, culture — the whole colorful, vibrant, throbbing world had turned into the dark and devastated scene Buddy Brandon found so normal and Clark so unbelievable. Mutagrass, savage traders, endless caravan routes, mutants and mutant hunters, Henrietta brothels, packs of wild dogs, antlered cattle, awful hurricanes, and a sun barely strong enough to illuminate a portion of the sky. Men lived in a twilight of the gods, and if mutagrass had not adapted to this godawful environment, even fewer could survive. He had come back to this?

Yes. He had come back to this. He understood now why he had been surly, moody, and rebellious; why he had not fit in back home in Atlantis; why he had been restless and unhappy. He had returned because he had a mission, but he hadn't known that until now.

Shivers passed over him, and he rose. He rubbed himself to move his blood through arms and legs. He jumped up and down where he stood. Then he turned away from the faint light in the east and toward the darkness in the west.

Across the clearing, inside a patch of fog, his motion was now answered by another. He felt it. He didn't see it. A pulse of involuntary affection touched him — lightly. He understood. *One* Harvey hare, and only one, lurked in the fog.

"Go away," he shouted. His voice echoed through the surrounding woods.

The answer was a cloying telepathic pulse, and momentarily Jack felt the hatred he had always felt for Evelyn, a hatred mixed with lust. Something warned him, but he put aside the warning. *Yeah, yeah,* he thought. *I know all about that. But I've got a bank account.* Evelyn and Aspic marked the road he must avoid, but he had no wish to give up his plans of vengeance. Why else had he come back? Why else had he accummulated all that credit in the Afterworld? This time it would be different. But, indeed — he had no business with Evelyn. He was after Aspic.

"Go away," he shouted again, addressing the patch of fog where Evelyn seemed to be lurking. Then he set out for the island's western shore, glad to be rid of the freakish creature.

He discovered after a while that he hadn't shaken Evelyn. He had walked some distance through the heavy underbrush surrounded by the noise of his own passage as by a bubble of sound when a mosquito chanced to bite him. He cursed and slapped his cheek, pausing for a moment, and as he paused, he heard the loud rustle of leaves and the crackling of dry brush behind him. He turned and saw her — a huge, white, hulking shape. She was poised for another hop. Her paws were lifted and hung down like those of a begging dog. Her ears also nodded forward. She was a pitiable vision.

Jack felt angry. She aroused him against his will. A peculiar excitement played over him at the sight of her, only partially sexual. A new reality superimposed itself on the murky forest, dead trees, moss, and bright green ferns he saw: the vision of a concentration camp filled with huge white rabbits. He sat in the driver's seat of a giant machine with spiked, metal wheels. He drove the machine over the rabbits, grinding and killing them. Blood and fur caked the wheels.

Jack shook his head to banish the vision. Excitement warmed his loins. *She wants to die! She doesn't want to be a "bunny" any more.* It was confusing and frightening. Without consciously intending it, Jack broke into a run. He crashed and stumbled from the spot through the thick undergrowth.

Out of breath, heaving, he stopped at last and looked back. Evelyn was gone. He continued with a feeling of relief.

He came upon his things up on the shore at last, but when he looked for his boat, he found that it had been ripped away during the night. A floating tree-trunk must have hit it. The weak Old Order rope by which he had secured it was torn and hung slack from a root.

Jack cursed. The river was wider than he remembered it and, at this early hour, it presented a confusing vista of water and mist. The swollen red mass of the rushing water did not look inviting in the least.

He still stood there hesitating, trying to discover what to do, when he heard the distant crash of branches behind him. She was still coming! Jack dropped his pack and began to undress.

Moments later, shivering, he lowered himself into the water. His roll — which held his clothing now and which he had secured using his belt — floated behind him as he swam out into the mist.

Soon the chilly water began to feel almost warm. Jack grew accustomed to its metallic taste. He made good progress against the current. Nonetheless, he swam for a long time before, at last, he glimpsed the opposing shore through a break in the mist. Relieved now — he had wondered where all this might end — he made greater efforts to put the river behind him and to reach firm land.

As he labored in this manner, he heard what sounded like a grunt behind him. With a rush of irrational fright, he twisted his neck to look back. God *damn!* There she was. Fur plastered close to her rabbit skull and reddish from the Mississippi mud, her eyes wide open with animal terror — there came Evelyn! She came, gasping with the exertions of her swim, rapidly, trying to catch Jack. Then her telepathic emanations touched him again — a frenzied love-lust and a suicidal wish.

Jack could do nothing about it — nor about his own reactions. Entirely against his will, he experienced sexual arousal in the most literal form. He gagged with disgust at himself and the ludicrousness of the situation. Reflected against his twentieth century memories, all this seemed insane, a nightmare. Would the damn rabbit follow him on, would she *hound* him like a fury?

He made it to the shore as fast as he could, crawled on all fours over a shallow shore, then out on the muddy bank.

His last exertions had calmed him somewhat. Grimly, he took the belt from his soggy, muddy pack; its buckle dangled in the mud. Thus he waited for Evelyn to come on shore.

She came, head plowing through the water, ears back — like some giant rodent, some monstrous, long-eared rat. Any moment now Jack expected her telepathic pulse to hit him. He braced for the shock and — yes, no denying it, he looked forward to it!

Ridiculous!

There he stood, stark naked like some savage, waiting for a woman in a rabbit's body. The hare sent out emotions urging him to kill her — because she longed to be reborn a person rather than a bunny. And she was someone he had known and had shared Bloody Maries with in Washington, D. C.

"Get back," he shouted at her. "Get the hell away from here!" And he made a little run toward her with a threatening demeanor. But she kept swimming.

He knew that in some way he couldn't understand, she sensed his thoughts. She answered them with wordless emotions of her own. Her enamations embraced him. He experienced again a tumbling of visions — his lives flashed up, all mixed and jumbled. Sexual passion gripped him as if he were a soul falling toward that red ocean of carnality.

Evelyn clambered ashore dripping. She shook herself. Ten thousand tiny droplets flew in all directions. Then she came hopping toward him, a little tentatively. Jack barely saw her. His head sang with rage and passion.

He screamed at her. The belt flew through the air. The buckle tore into Evelyn's side. Instantly Jack experienced the feedback from that blow — Evelyn's emotion of pained pleasure. It urged Jack to do more, more, more of the same.

Jack lost his bearings. The rabbit held him in her spell and for a brief time forced him to do her bidding. Jack beat her furiously. The heavy buckle tore and gashed her fur, then cut her flesh. Jack's kicks sent her reeling. She bled and gasped. And still she urged him on with visions and with murky, wordless, telepathic orders.

Jack was beside himself. The pleasure she took in her approaching death enhanced his own blind excitement. She caused him to see her as Evelyn Bantry, naked and spread-eagled on an enormous bed, chained to its four posts by her wrists and ankles. She induced a vision in his mind wherein he knelt between her outspread legs thrusting with all his power at her madly bucking, blood-red orchid of a hair-ringed cunt. Each blow of the belt buckle that he landed on the rabbit was a thrust into her illusory vagina. The two scenes overlaid each other: furry rabbit, violently flailing, naked man; naked woman in shackles crazed by passion, kneeling man. Incoherent sounds gurgled from Jack's throat. Kill, kill, kill. He beat her with all of his power.

Suddenly he shuddered. It was over. His loins jerked with one, two, three pulses of relief. What Evelyn had denied him in the twentieth century, a hare with Evelyn's soul inside it had granted Jack. In a manner of speaking, he had scored at last.

She lay, a tortured, bloodstained heap of fur. She still emoted. Her eyes stared at Jack imploringly. Jack sensed her emotions — she still wished to die. But now her pulses had no effect on him. Jack understood the nature of her telepathics: they worked on hormonal centers in the receptor body. His glands had been driven to peak production. They had done their work, and it was over.

Once more Jack shuddered, releasing pent-up tensions. *Life is incredible*, he thought, meaning his own experiences as a man through many lives and many crimes. Here was another one to add to that long list — a river and a muddy bank and an act of sadism on a goddamned rabbit woman!

Profoundly disgusted with himself, he walked to the water and washed himself as carefully as the muddy water allowed. Shivers continued to pass over his skin; goosebumps came and went. Up above carry crows had gathered, smelling Evelyn's blood.

Then Jack dressed and tidied up his roll. He glanced at Evelyn as he worked and saw her lie in an unnatural, contorted position. Her head was hidden by her heaving belly. Her telepathics were weakening. Soon the crows would swoop and make a circle about her. By night she'd be a skeleton . . .

"Good-bye, Evelyn," he said, ready to go. Then he left as quickly as possible, never expecting to see her again.

27.
Talisman's Fenwick

But, of course, he did see her again — or else the Show-Biz, parked now outside of Cactus, would not have come into existence. Jack had left Atlantis meaning to become an independent sweeper, not a freak-show impresario, but the decision had been forced on him by Evelyn's relentless pursuit and his own inability to kill her. So he had made the best of his lot and carried Evelyn inside that colorful van. She earned his living and gave him unholy pleasures, a devilish marriage, a heavy drain on his karmic credit balance up there in the Afterworld.

Leading the Freckled Man toward the Show-Biz tent, Jack made sure that they stayed out of the range of Evelyn's "ambient" emanations. She emoted mildly at all times, especially when she sensed the proximity of crowds and the impending moment of another magic show — each show being yet another chance for her, another chance to die, another chance to goad

Jack to excesses of punishment so that she could depart her bunny body for the skies . . .

Jack entered the magic tent, the Freckled Man at his heel. He nodded to Tovarish, and the foreman understood the gesture. He gathered the crewmen and left the tent to Jack and his guest.

It was an empty tent and gave little for the eye to hang on — a crude stage at one end, a dirty curtain at its back. From the stage portruded a heavy iron ring — like some mechanical mushroom. Near it lay Jack's short-handled whip, its long leather lash laid in coils. There was no sign of magic anywhere, and the Freckled Man was evidently disappointed.

He was a long, lanky fellow of light complexion, sparse reddish hair, a chinless face, and busy little eyes. He seemed to be a talker and a gossipper, lacking toughness and character — the very reasons why Jack saw him as a good informant.

Jack turned to the man, introduced himself, and learned that the Freckled Man was Baldwin's Carpet. A leather tanner by trade. Which explained the slightly pissy smell Carpet gave off.

"Let me tell you why I wanted to talk to you," Jack said. "The man who just arrived, the sweeper, the one you all call Golden Arm — he looks very familiar, like someone I've met before, but I can't quite place him. Where does he come from?"

Baldwin's Carpet had overcome the intimidation Jack's eyes had occasioned moments ago. He had obviously understood the possibilities of gossip early acquaintance with Magic Jack offered to him later in the Sweeper's Haven, and thus he displayed an eager attitude now. He leaned back against the stage.

"Fenwick, you mean? His real name is Fenwick. Talisman's Fenwick. You ever hear about Talisman's Motel?"

Jack shook his head.

"I guess you haven't travelled the Upper Route.

Talisman's Motel is up on the Colorado Ice Edge, a pretty famous place. Fenwick is Talisman's oldest — an icepeditioneer."

"An ice hound. What's he doing this far south?"

"That's a long story," Carpet said, and in preparation for telling his story, he pulled himself up and sat on the stage. Jack faced him, arms folded across the chest.

"Do you know something about The Shashtuk?"

"Nothing worth mentioning," Jack said. "This is my first time west."

"Have you heard about Plutonium?"

"Only the name."

"Well, sir," Carpet said, evidently pleased to have found someone as ignorant as Jack, "Plutonium is quite a place — though I wouldn't advise you to visit. It's a place — and it's a brotherhood of mutants, but not the kind you hunt, leastways I wouldn't advise it. There are three or four hundred of them, and they live inside the Volcano Ring — you ever hear about that?"

"It's a ring of volcanoes; that's all I know."

"That's exactly what it is — a line of mean spouters. A half of a ring, actually, facing east. The valley behind — that's where the plutojacks live."

"Plutojacks?"

"That's what they call themselves."

"You said that they were mutants . . . ?"

"They are, sort of, but not the ordinary kind. Some say that plutojacks have a disease, others say it's a madness. Fact is, people *turn* into plutojacks — not all, but some. It happens when they're still young. Suddenly they'll start to bark — I mean, really, like a coyote — and then they just kind of double up, and then they run off into The Shashtuk to find Plutonium. People around here — you know, them with sons who've gone off and turned plutojack — you better not tell *them* that plutojacks are mutants; them's fighting words for some. But now my family — we've never had a barker; it happens mostly with hunters who spend time inside The Shashtuk. We, meaning my family, we kind of *lean* to thinking that plutojacks are mutants. See what I mean?"

Jack nodded. "What do they do in there?"

"Do? Nothing mostly. A plutojack has one thing on his mind — and only one. That's Godbod. Some of them even forget to eat — they don't *need* to eat; they just worship all the time sniffing that ineffable perfume."

"Godbod? What on earth is that?"

"That's just it. Nobody really knows. It's stuff. Anything. Dirt, rocks, rags anything. Only a plutojack can tell you. It has ineffable perfume, something you smell, but not with the nose so much as down here." Grinning, Carpet touched his crotch.

"Down . . . there?"

"It's true," Carpet said. "They call it gutsniffing, but it's really down there that they feel it. For plutojacks, Godbod is like a woman. Hard to believe, but it's the truth."

"Strange people," Jack said. "But you were telling me about Fenwick. What has he got to do with all this?"

"It's a long story, didn't I tell you? Fenwick is a sweeper, and you know what sweepers are like. They're not happy just to be finding things. They want mysteries — working mysteries. Or they want to make dead things move. Fenwick is worse than most when it comes to mysteries. Do you know why? It's because he grew up in Talisman's Motel; and that place is a nest of restoration. Old Talisman feeds ten or twenty readers, and all they ever do up there is read and talk. Fenwick has his head full of the Lore. He has a dream . . . Fenwick dreams big."

Carpet extended his arms in both directions to indicate the size of Fenwick's dream.

"What is his dream?"

Carpet chuckled. He rolled his eyes up toward the roof of the tent to show how crazy Fenwick's dream really was. Then he said:

"Fenwick wants to find and dig up Old New York."

"That's some dream," Jack said. "But Old New York is to the east and under the ice someplace — or so I've been told. Fenwick came the wrong way if he came south."

"That's right. But Fenwick didn't come down here to find New York. He came to see the psychotron."

"The — *psychotron?* Did you say — *psychotron?*"

Carpet nodded. He was enjoying this. "Psychotron," he said. "That's right. You want to hear about that?"

Jack indicated that he did.

"One day, about two years ago," Carpet said, launching off, "Fenwick is home at Talisman's Motel. He has just come back from an icepedition, and winter is about to set in. They're sitting around talking, Fenwick and a bunch of other sweepers, and sweepers being sweepers, they're telling each other lies about the mysteries they've seen, each guy trying to outdo the next. And Fenwick is louder than the rest. He has quite a reputation as an ice hound, and it seems like he deserves it.

"Well, as they're swapping stories, suddenly this southern guy, a trader, he pipes up and says, 'You folks can talk all you like about the Ice, but when it comes to working mysteries,' he says, 'we've got one in The Shashtuk down south that beats all your mysteries to hell,' he says, 'and it's not some little piece of clicking junk but a whole building full of mysteries.'"

"The psychotron?"

Carpet nodded eagerly. "So Fenwick looks at the trader and says, 'What kind of building?' And our man says, 'It's called a psychotron.' 'A *what?*' goes Fenwick, and right off he calls over to one of the readers, and the man comes over, carrying a bucket of beer — they know how to drink, those readers. Fenwick says, 'You ever hear about a psychotron?' And the reader shakes his head and says he hasn't, but he'll look it up in one of those books they've got mountains of at Talisman's Motel."

Carpet moved adjusting his rear on the hard planks of the stage.

"While the reader is off to sniff around in his books, Fenwick turns to our man and wants to know all about the psychotron — what it looks like, what it does, things like that; and when the trader tells him, he makes a face and won't believe a word of it. Then the reader comes back, still toting his bucket, and he doesn't even stop at the table. He just shakes his head as he's passing by. Then Fenwick turns to the trader and says, 'I'll make you a little bet, my friend. If you can show me that psychotron of yours, and if it really works,' he says, 'I'll give you the ten kegs of gaso-lean I just come back with; but if you can't, you'll let me have those five red hot Henriettas of yours that nobody wants to buy because you want an eye and a tooth for each.'

" 'Its a long trip,' says our friend.

" 'Tell you what,' Fenwick says. 'I'll provide the horses and the keep, and we'll start tomorrow morning at first light.' "

"Who was that trader," Jack asked. "Was it you?"

"No," Carpet said. "My brother-in-law. He's still using some of the gaso-lean he won off of that bet."

"And . . . the psychotron? I suppose it's something down in Plutonium? A big building with a pole on top and baskets turning on the top of the pole?"

Carpet glanced at Jack sharply. His eyes expressed surprise and disappointment. "You know about it!"

"I had heard something about a working mystery down in these parts. I didn't know what it was called."

"That's it," Carpet said, for once frugal with words. Jack had spoiled his fun; he suspected that Jack knew more than he was letting on he knew.

"But after Fenwick saw the psychotron . . ." Jack pursued, "what happened then? It looks like he stayed down here, or he came back, or something."

Carpet stirred back to life a little. "Well, you see," he said, "that gets us back to Fenwick's dream. Fenwick went down there and stayed with the brotherhood a while, and as you may already know — " here came a suspicious glance " — the plutojacks have a lot of metal down there, in their caverns, and all around the place. So Fenwick figured that he could get that metal. It takes a hell of a big train to dig up Old New York — supposing you can even find the place."

"How did he figure he could get the metal? By stealing it?"

"From the plutojacks? I wouldn't advise it. No. Fenwick figured that he could trade for it. The way he put it to my brother-in-law was like this: 'I'm a sweeper,' he said, 'the best damn icepeditioneer this side of the Coloradoes. You tell me what you want, and I can find it for you.'"

"Godbod?" Jack asked.

Carpet nodded. "That's it."

"But how can Fenwick find Godbod? He is not a plutojack!"

"Now there you've got me," Carpet said. "I don't know how he did it, but he did it. He went out that winter, two years ago, and by spring he was back. He had a bunch of old metal drums chock full of — nothing; just old cement. He claims he found them in the California desert."

"But then he left."

"Well, yes. He did. He found the Godbod but it wasn't much. And then, talking with old Hamster's Shoe, he figured out why."

"Who is Hamster's Shoe."

"Oh. That's right. You wouldn't know him. He is the head plutojack. He calls himself general manager. It's some name out of the Golden Age."

"General manager."

"Some sort of title," Carpet said.

"All right," Jack said. "You were saying that Fenwick found out — what?"

"He found out why he couldn't find much Godbod in these parts."

"Why couldn't he?"

"Well, in the old days, when the caravans still ran through Cactus, the plutojacks used to sweep around here every year in Spring. The area has been swept clean. The plutojacks got everything many years ago. So Fenwick went up north. He wanted to find a place where there are no plutojacks — and never have been any."

"And now he's back. That big piece of metal he brought back. Do you think it's Godbod?"

"Sure," Carpet said. "Otherwise Fenwick wouldn't have come. He might have lost that bet with my brother-in-law, but he is smart. He'll get rich off of the plutojacks one of these days. And no man before him ever did. I wouldn't be surprised if he finds Old New York some day. But I wouldn't bet on it."

Jack shook hands with Baldwin's Carpet a little later. Carpet would see the show for free tonight, Jack promised, seeing how Carpet had helped him out — even though this Fenwick didn't seem to be anyone Jack had known. Then Carpet left and Jack entered his van. He spent a precious Golden Age match to light candles on either side of a huge, cracked mirror mounted over a Golden Age desk at one end of the vehicle. He sat down before the mirror and communed for some time silently with the only friends who had a chance to understand his immortal mind — Me, Myself, and I. But he couldn't stand to sit for long. Agitation made him rise, and soon he paced the length of his van, walking back and forth, back and forth. He was still walking two hours later when a fist drummed on his door. He opened the door and took in a bucket of steaming water. Then he took off his clothes and began the ritual washing he never neglected before a magic show.

28.
The Magic Show

Talisman's Fenwick went into Cactus as the light was fading. He meant to drink a little cactus and a lot of beer, and once he had slaked the thirst of weeks, he planned to satisfy his other needs in the company of red hot Henriettas. The last thing on his mind that evening was to attend the magic show, and later, in the Sweeper's Haven, he gave a low opinion of it. He spoke to Cactus people and those of his sweepers who had followed him into town.

"I've been around this dusty world for forty-some-odd years," he said, gesturing with a half-filled mug. "I've been east and I've been west, on the Ice and off. And I grew up in Talisman's Motel, where people know the Lore. Let me tell you. In all my years I've never heard about a giant rabbit. Now as for Hip No Tism, that's an art, all right. But Hip No Tism comes from the magician. The right magician can make you see a giant rabbit even if there isn't one. Jack might be doing Hip No Tism and then again he might not. A big man dressed in ice-bear fur can look like a man-sized rabbit in the dark. I don't deny that that is entertainment, but entertainment isn't worth five measures of copper. Magic Jack sounds like a conman — a clever conman and all that, but that's not worth a lot of metal."

Fenwick was popular and especially admired now that he had returned. Nonetheless, the people listened with skeptical expressions. They had heard only good things about this Show-Biz. Con or not, they said, the show had come to Cactus. Five measures seemed like a lot of copper, but not for a high class show.

Fenwick shrugged. His mind was on Henriettas.

After dark, just as the mood was getting good and rowdy, the rattle of a heavy drum came drifting into the Haven. The show was starting. The people drank up and hurried off to see that imaginary rabbit. As gullible as all the rest — they were good boys but not very smart — Fenwick's people went right along.

Fenwick didn't mind. He ambled over to the bar and asked the shrimpy, balding Haven's master where he might find some Henriettas. Cactus had no parlor; the town was much too small for that. But scores of mutant hunters lived in Cactus, and you could almost always find a hot one stashed away in the back of a stable waiting for the Phoenix auctions. To hear the fluters flute — now *that* was entertainment.

The Haven's master stared up at the cobwebs, pursed his lips, then shook his head.

"You're out of luck," he said. "I don't think we've got a single Henrietta in Cactus now. But wait a couple of days. Ticky's Toe is due back soon; he'll be sure to have some."

"Damn!" Fenwick cried. And he ordered a glass of cactus.

He sipped the liquor in disgust. *Wretched little*

place. He finished his beer, tossed down his cactus, took his hat, and left the Haven. If he couldn't get a Henrietta, a woman would have to do. He didn't like the scrawny, bony Cactus ladies, but they were easy-going. Their men were always gone, and you could get a humping by just winking your eye and tilting your head.

But once he was outside and looked around, he saw no light in any of the huts. Even the dogs had left. Every soul in Cactus had run off to see the magic show — all except the Haven's master. The master was a miserable miser and scared to leave his property unguarded.

Oh, what the hell, Fenwick thought. *I guess I might as well.*

He checked his sack to see if he had enough metal left. Yep. He had enough. Then he untied his pony — it hung its head all alone in the faint orange light that issued from the Haven through stretched sheets of cattle-bladder. Then, long after all the others had left, Fenwick also headed for the caravan terrain to see the show.

The tent was tightly packed. People sat on the ground, shoulder to shoulder and stared expectantly toward an empty stage. Candles burned around the periphery of that raised platform. Tiny mirrors propped behind them at an angle reflected light against the sloping roof. A black curtain hung behind the stage, and from time to time it seemed to move.

Evelyn hid behind the curtain. She could sense the presence of the crowd, and the nearness of so many people aroused her anxieties to the extent that she emoted lightly. Her telepathic emanations passed over the crowd in waves, inducing a mild sense of affection mingled with a tingling of sexual arousal.

Fenwick sensed that subtle something the moment he entered, and he was immediately on his guard. He had never experienced Hip No Tism himself, but he had heard enough about it to know this wasn't it. For one thing, he saw no magician; the stage was empty. Villagers sat on the ground, their backs to him. They were unnaturally still. He thought he might be smelling something, and he sucked air through his nostrils; but it was something other than a smell. Damned if he didn't feel a — a something in his head, just like the people said he would.

Fenwick had no love for situations he couldn't oversee or grasp, and consequently he stayed well back, near the spot where he had entered. And he kept his back against the canvas.

Then time passed. Jack was still in his van at this time, concluding his preparations. Evelyn emoted behind the curtain. The people floated on the lukewarm waves of her emotions. The candles flickered at the foot of the stage. And shadows danced against the tent roof.

Fenwick relaxed little by little. The pleasurable sensations Evelyn induced in everyone began to take effect on him as well. Sexual fantasies bubbled up inside him. He remembered — fleetingly and then more vividly — love feasts he had enjoyed in the past, and he began to feel a warm affection for everyone inside the tent.

Suddenly, jarring and startling everyone — like a knife slicing the air — came a sharp, shrieking note of music from some instrument. Jack had entered the tent. Blowing with puffed cheeks on a set of bagpipes, he passed quickly through the crowd, toward the stage.

Fenwick was badly rattled. At the sound of the bagpipes, Evelyn emoted in a spurt, and the people felt a temporary rush of visions — confusing, jumbled, odd. Fenwick recovered quickly, but by that time the magician had already passed him. He saw Jack mounting the stage — a short figure in a silvery suit carrying an odd instrument.

Fenwick felt more uneasy than ever, but now his curiosity was roused. He guessed he had been hasty in the Sweeper's Haven. Something odd was happening, something really odd . . .

Jack laid down his instrument; it sagged down with a sigh — like a dying beast. Fenwick had never seen bagpipes before. He squinted at these "udders" curiously. Then Jack stepped forward, arms folded across his chest, and for a long, suspenseful moment, he stared out over the crowd, eyes moving, probing, seeking.

"WELCOME, WELCOME, WELCOME," he suddenly shouted. People laughed, releasing tension. "Welcome," Jack resumed. "Welcome to the Show-Biz of your servant, Magic Jack — and a lucky bunch you are, yes, sir. Ladies and gentlemen, you may have cried a little, parting with your copper, but you won't be sorry that you did — no, sir. 'Cause there ain't no Show-Biz quite like this one; nor will you meet a stranger man than me, yes, sir, yours ever truly, Magic Jack. Nor has there ever been, nor shall there ever be, not in ten thousand years to come, a Harvey hare like Evelyn. She's hiding behind that curtain right this minute, folks, waiting to come out. And when she does — look out! You'll start seeing pictures in your head, all about the Golden Age — and I don't lie, no, sir. Evelyn and me, we go a long ways back — we've been pals for hundreds of years. That's right, you heard me — hundreds of years. You believe that, sir? How about you, sir? You're smiling, sir. You don't believe me. I don't blame you, sir. Didn't believe it myself. Step closer, sir. Why so shy? Let me come down and say hello. Put it there, sir. Mine is Magic Jack. What's yours?"

Jack had jumped off the stage and now pumped the hand of one of the villagers. The man turned his head in every possible direction, a sheepish grin on his face. Then, bantering and chattering, Jack continued moving through the crowd.

Instinct told Fenwick that some hidden purpose impelled Jack to mingle with the crowd. Then he got the notion that Jack moved in his direction — and he felt a mild alarm. Why? Had someone told the magic man that a well-known icepeditioneer stood in the audience?

Puzzled and a little irritated, Fenwick moved slowly along the back of the tent in such a manner as to remove himself from the magician's apparent path. But Jack also changed direction.

During all this, Evelyn's emotions had grown perceptively stronger. Fenwick experienced confusion. It seemed that pictures flashed across his eyelids but at a speed too fast for him to glimpse them. He felt a touch of fear; he felt the urge to flee. Obedient to that urge, he began to slide along the canvas toward the exit. But he didn't get very far. Jack stopped him with a call.

"You, sir," Jack cried. "Yes, you, sir. The tall gentleman in the back, the gentleman in the straw hat."

Fenwick turned involuntarily. The magician made toward him waving a hand, crying: "You, my dear sir — just a moment. Let me introduce myself. You must have an opinion on the subject I was just discussing with that gentleman back there. Are there ice dragons in your opinion? Or are they just a fairy tale? Ah, here we are, sir. I am Magic Jack. Your servant."

Fenwick squinted at the grey face before him. The lights were behind Jack, and shadows hid his features. Nevertheless, Fenwick saw Jack's left eye staring. It stared with penetration. It had a menacing expression — as cold, hard, and devoid of human warmth as that of a bird of prey. Jack's hand extended toward Fenwick in proferred greeting.

"Your name, sir."

Fenwick perceived the words as a command. Despite his strong reluctance to enter into any kind of contact with this man, he gave his name and shook Jack's hand.

"Fenwick, eh? You must be the famous sweeper the people here call Golden Arm. The pleasure is all mine, sir. Entirely mine. A deep gratification; a humble, burning joy; a glorious honor; an overwhelming bounty."

Jack bowed in the grand manner, one leg forward, one pulled back. He swept the floor with a flourish of his hat. His words and gestures communicated a comic intent, and the audience laughed.

They laughed at Fenwick's expense, and Fenwick was not pleased. Nonetheless, he smiled. He framed a suitable reply, but he didn't get a chance to give it. Not pursuing his question about the legendary ice dragons any further, Jack abruptly turned. He walked back to the stage, clambered up, and began to blow out the candles.

As the candles went out one by one, the silence in the tent deepened more and more. Evelyn's emanations grew in intensity, and all those in the tent felt the heat Jack had experienced on the Mississippi island.

At last came total darkness. The audience stirred and then grew still again. Then, in a shrieking, wailing voice that sent shocks through the people, Jack yelled, E-E-E-E-V-E-LYN-N-N!" Immediately the curtain rustled. The sound of a chain could be heard as it was dragged across the boards. Evelyn hopped out on the stage — a giant beast. Her fur stood on end and spread a greenish, phosphorescent light. In that light Fenwick saw Jack on the stage. Jack held a short-handled whip, its lash trailing on the floor. Another man was bending down. He attached the end of the long chain to a hook. The chain terminated in an iron collar around Evelyn's neck. The man then left the stage.

For a moment longer, Jack appeared to wait. He lifted his whip at last. Then, in a slow, measured, but imperceptively accelerating rhythm, he began to whip Evelyn. The rabbit hopped in huge, wild, frantic motions about the stage. The chain brought her up short again and again. Her collar choked her. She made strange noises. And her telepathic emanations grew with every lash of Jack's whip.

Fenwick experienced flashes of intense white light. Sweat drenched his skin. Panic and curiosity held him in a kind of paralysis. But the physical discomfort that he felt soon fled. He found himself caught up in visions, carried into realms at once familiar and strange.

Since he had died in the Golden Age, Fenwick had lived five other lives — each one short, painful, and brutal. Twice he had starved to death as a child in what was then a terrible time of chaos and transition. Two of his subsequent existences had been as mutants; he had been hunted, enslaved, and cruelly used each time. During his last life but one, preceding his birth as Fenwick in Talisman's Motel, the laws of karma had relented just a little. He had lived longer and in relative peace as a fiber weaver in Atlantis — the reason why Jack's vengeful spirit had been drawn there years ago. By then Fenwick was an old man living a humble life of service, preparing himself, as it were, to resume his cosmic career as an inventor and discoverer.

Each of these lives now opened up before Fenwick's eyes — each life a pack of cards flung into the sky by a tornado, and Fenwick a disembodied eye among the cards. When that eye beheld a card, a scene from the life that he was viewing unfolded in his consciousness at an incredible speed.

Pack after pack opened and flew up. Fenwick saw events in random order. Even if he had had time to think about all this, he would have been confused. But everything rushed by him much too quickly, and his body was wrenched and convulsed by monumental emotions — caused by the visions — which succeeded one another at a breakneck pace.

In time the scenes changed. Fenwick found himself back in the Golden Age. He saw it all in vivid colors. A part of him marvelled at all this. That legendary world had the same heavy feel as the current day — despite its mad plethora of "working mysteries." He travelled in flying ships. He spoke to others through a wire. Needles squirted liquids into his arm. Mice ran about in boxes made of glass . . . and then his life was over, and he went yet another step farther back.

It happened now that as Fenwick experienced his Mahler life in random snatches, his disembodied, swirling eye chanced to see a snowy scene. It looked to him like an icepedition camp. Thousands of starving mutants were penned up in that place, and he was one of those mutants. He worked with a pick-axe in a frozen field. Then came the Beast wearing a pot on his head . . .

Of all the scenes of his past lives, Fenwick knew this one. Something in him recognized the experience, and instantly he felt a brutal shock of illness, of malaise. The emotion was so strong that he dropped out of his peculiar, telepathic trance.

There came a brief moment of total confusion. Fenwick's heart beat furiously. He gasped in giant gulps as if he had just run up a steep mountainside. Not one part of his body was dry. His skin shivered under a layer of evaporating sweat.

Then the place, time, and occasion of his experience clicked back in place. He stood in a dark tent amidst moaning, groaning, swaying shapes. Sharp came the crack of a flailing whip. A chain rattled angrily, again and again. A giant rabbit hopped. Deep obscene groans of pleasure — uttered with abandoned shamelessness — came in Fenwick's direction from a half-crouching Jack.

Fenwick understood vaguely what was happening on the stage, and it caused him outrage, fury. *That lovable, sweet rabbit. That dirty son of a bitch!*

Before he fully grasped what he was doing, he had made a lurching movement forward.

"Stop it," he yelled. "Stop it, damn you, stop it!"

Jack immediately stopped, and Evelyn collapsed on the boards. She transmitted an emotion of excruciating sadness and disappointment to the audience. Many people began to sob — sad along with Evelyn that the death she sought had once again escaped her.

Jack stood for a moment on the stage. He gasped; he stared. Fenwick had interrupted the magic act at its very height, just before it was to end in a explosion of pleasure. Jack lurched forward. Bent down somewhat, he peered out at the audience.

"That's you, isn't it?" he called. "That's you, Fenwick, isn't it? I knew it, buddy. I just knew it."

Fenwick didn't answer. He turned and bolted from the tent. All around him the people of Cactus stirred uneasily in a dazed awakening.

29.
Another Proposition

Jack paced from one end of the van to the other. The magic show had ended without satisfaction. Sweat drenched his body, his blood ran rancid with roused lust, his mind steamed with schemes. Fenwick was Aspic — and vengeance would be his. Fate pointed to Plutonium. In the shadow of that cursed "psychotron," in the shadow of those turning baskets, Fenwick would be handed over to his fate. It was to be, it had to be. Jack had known it all along, and now he felt supported in his quest for vengeance by Heaven itself. Chief Walk-on-air, after all, had made all the arrangements...

He paced and plotted, feverish with plans.

Outside his van the fires of two camps were dying; men and mutants settled down to sleep. From Cactus came the faint noise of carousing in the Haven, but even that tumult died down in time. The Haven's guests left or retired, Fenwick among them. He staggered after the Haven's master. The master lighted Fenwick's way up a set of rotting stairs with an upheld candle.

In the darkness of a room where he had slept before, Fenwick dropped heavily down on a cot. He felt dizzy. The room began to turn in circles when he closed his eyes. Ordinarily he would have dropped into deep sleep in moments, but tonight he couldn't do it. His mind, like Jack's was feverish. But while Jack pondered Fenwick's fate, Fenwick thought about the rabbit. He couldn't get her out of his mind. Her image had fused mysteriously with that of every woman and fluter he had ever touched. Shaken by the Hip No Tism, he tossed and turned on the narrow cot. He felt desire. And he was angry and afraid — emotions he seldom felt. Boldness, good humor, and a sharp intelligence were his predominant traits. Boldness had made him a successful sweeper, good humor a leader of men, and his intelligence had made him secure. But his time in the magic tent had shaken his security — which angered him. And Jack frightened him.

He found himself between the ocean and the bear — as they said up on the Ice. He had to have that rabbit. He had a dream — the dream of finding Old New York. But now that dream seemed lifeless in comparison with her! He would gladly buy the rabbit. He would take her if he had to! She held mysteries more potent than that buried city; she was more woman than any Henrietta he had ever had. To want a mutant animal was madness, and he knew it, and he didn't really care.

But how could he get her? Magic Jack stood in his way — a strange, dark, menacing figure. And it angered Fenwick that he should be afraid. It made no sense at all. The bold icepeditioneer — fearful of a Show-Biz man? But yes, he was. And he would have to overcome that fear before the rabbit could be his.

He tossed and turned. The straw beneath him rustled. He heard the scurry of rats' feet inside the hollow walls of mud and thatch. Distantly coyotes howled. Sometimes he closed his eyes; then the room whirled. He opened his eyes, squinting even in the darkness. With open eyes the whirling stopped but sleep receded; and without sleep his thoughts went on and on.

Morning came at last. The sky was dark but the wind was down. Dust rained gently on the land. Out on the caravan terrain, men and mutants stirred. Fires came alive in Fenwick's camp — a big one for the mutants, a small one for the men.

Tovarish awoke late. He borrowed fire from Fenwick's mutants and soon stood over a flame-licked pot. He sliced winter onion into bubbling grass-seed meal; his eyes watered as he did so. From time to time he glanced toward Jack's van. His master still paced in there, back and forth, back and forth.

When the light had risen sufficiently so that Jack could see it through his peepholes, he snuffed out his candles and left the van. Tovarish and the other crewmen sat around the fire. They waited for the meal to cook. Jack passed them without greeting and made for a small wagon next to the tent.

The wagon held a good many things — metal, cans of precious gaso-lean, furs, and bits and pieces of machinery. Jack came for none of these. He opened a large wooden crate. Inside it lay two submachine guns carefully wrapped in separate layers of leather, cloth, and Old Order plastic sheathing. He took out one of the guns, unwrapped it, and began to disassemble it.

He worked methodically — dusting, wiping, oiling. The weapon was filthy. The Age of Dust covered all things with grit and grime, even objects carefully wrapped. Jack reamed the bore. He inspected its helically grooved interior against the brightening eastern sky. He assembled the weapon, clicked a long, curving clip into the aperture, and slid a bullet into the chamber. Then he went to work on the second gun.

He was still engaged in this task when he saw Fenwick approach. Fenwick rode a pony. He had just emerged from among the steaming pods of Cactus. He had spent the night at the Sweeper's Haven, Jack observed. Jack felt blood pound in his throat. Soon, he thought, would come the confrontation.

Jack expected Fenwick to return to his own caravan. Instead he rode past the silvery missile on its wooden frame. Using a gap in the portable fence around the Show-Biz caravan, he came in, dismounted, and addressed some question to Tovarish by the fire.

Jack wiped his hand on a rag. With a glance at the sky where now, as every morning, carry crow flocks flew in black squadrons, rising, dropping, he came to meet his visitor. Fenwick saw him and advanced; Fenwick's eyes were hidden behind the slits of his squint. "Morning," he said to Jack.

Jack stopped and nodded back. "To what do I owe the honor? Are you paying me a neighborly visit — or can I be of service?"

"I came to talk business," Fenwick said, and he sounded on edge and guarded. "I want to make you a proposition."

A proposition? The word raised echoes of the past.

"A proposition?" Jack pointed to the magic tent. One of its sides had been rolled up. "Let's talk in there," he said, and he led the way.

Fenwick followed; and although the meeting had taken place at his initiative, he walked uncertainly. He had hesitated until the last moment before approaching Jack. He still hesitated, still not sure that he should do this thing, still wondering whether to change his mind. Magic Jack looked as menacing to him in light as he had looked in darkness; he still frightened Fenwick with those eyes. Fenwick felt a shiver at the other man's mere presence. He wanted to back out of this... but there was that rabbit...

They arrived inside, and Jack invited Fenwick to sit. Both men settled on the edge of the stage, half facing one another.

"So you have a proposition to make?"

Fenwick nodded, eyes on the dirt. He nodded again, still gathering his thoughts, still unsure. Then he plunged ahead.

"I am a sweeper in these parts," he said. "Mostly I deal with Plutonium. Have you ever heard of that place?" He darted a quick glance at Jack.

Excitement throttled Jack's throat. Fate itself seemed intent on delivering Fenwick. "That's the mutant colony south of here," he said. His voice trembled slightly with emotion. "They worship some kind of stuff."

"Godbod." Fenwick nodded. "Godbod. But I wouldn't call them mutants. They're people just like you and me. Peculiar people, but they're not mutants." He waited for a reaction, but when none came, he went on. "Anyway, I trade with them — not many people do. They are hard people — tough to deal with until you get the hang of it; but once you do, it's worth it. The plutojacks are rich. I've never seen a richer town or presidency. They have caverns underneath the pods they live in — filled with metal. And there is metal all over their valley too, in other places. If you know how to deal with them, it's worth the long trip and the bother."

Fenwick wouldn't look at Jack, and Jack felt irritated. Aspic sat before him, yet the man was absent — absent because a man lived in his eyes. And Fenwick's eyes were hidden — dark slits in that long, thin face, dark slits with a gleam of light inside them. Jack wished to see the soul behind the body with the loudly ticking golden arm.

"Are they the people with the mystery?" he asked. "The thing they call the 'psychotron'?"

Fenwick hazarded a glance in Jack's direction, nodded. "It's something to see. And it's more than just a mystery. It's a building from the Golden Age with a mystery up on its roof—"

"Turning, turning, turning? Like baskets?"

Fenwick looked at Jack and met the full chill of hard yet cloudy eyes. For a moment he thought that Jack might be a plutojack himself.

"You've been there."

"Not me," Jack said. And suddenly he grinned, without humor, like a snake might. "Not in this body, anyway." He grinned some more and slapped himself on the thigh. "But I've heard about it. I've heard about the psychotron. But you were saying—a proposition."

Fenwick nodded, ill at ease. A grinning Jack was worse than a staring Jack.

"It came to me last night," he said. "You've got quite a show here, Jack. The plutojacks would like it. They'd pay you quite a bit to see it, more than a place like Cactus. So I got to thinking. Why don't you go down there?"

"And you would provide the introduction?"

"That's what I thought."

Jack pretended to think about it. He had spent the whole night plotting how he might take Fenwick captive. His own caravan was puny compared with Fenwick's train; his own crewmen no doubt less eager for battle than Fenwick's sweepers. Reluctantly, he had decided to make a display of his armaments if need be—his submachine guns and his hand grenades. But none of that would be necessary now, least of all in front of many witnesses. He might not have to risk an all-out battle, not in Cactus, anyway. Fenwick offered to deliver himself to Jack of his own accord; the lamb came to its own slaughter.

"Well..." Jack said at last. "What sort of fee have you got in mind?"

"A tenth."

"A tenth of . . . how much, roughly"

"I would guess that you could take in half a ton of copper," Fenwick said.

"Hmm. A half a ton?"

"That's my guess," Fenwick said.

Jack still pretended to be hesitating. Then he stood up. "That's your caravan next door, isn't it? I'll tell you what. I'll think about it. I'll come over and tell you what I'll do before the day is out."

Fenwick also rose. "Fair enough," he said.

Then he followed Jack out of the tent debating with himself. Should he go ahead and ask? It might tip his hand — but then again the thought of Evelyn burned in his brain like a fire.

"I wonder if you could do me a favor?"

"What favor is that?"

Fenwick gestured toward the vans. "Could you show me that rabbit of yours? I would sure like to see her in daylight."

"You don't believe that Evelyn is real, do you?"

Jack grinned again; he grinned like a coyote.

"I believe she is real, all right," Fenwick said with conviction. "I would just like to look at her in the daylight."

"Sorry," Jack said, but his grin was not a grin of sorrow."I can't show her to you. Evelyn's asleep and I can't disturb her now. The magic show is hard on her. But maybe later. Or you could come and see the show again tonight."

Fenwick had no wish to experience all that again. "Not likely," he said; "not at your prices."

"What happened last night?" Jack asked. "Weren't you the one who stopped the show? 'Stop it,' you yelled. Did something bother you? A terrible vision?"

"I don't remember," Fenwick said lamely. He spoke to the ground and still avoided Jack's penetrating gaze. Then he gestured by way of changing the subject. "You have quite a show here, Jack. What happens? How do you do it?"

"Trade secret," Jack said.

Fenwick tried to look at Jack but didn't quite succeed. "You can't show her to me now?"

"Not now. But maybe later."

Fenwick shrugged. "Well, then, I guess I'll be on my way. You'll let me know today?"

Jack nodded, and Fenwick left.

Gazing after Fenwick, Jack thought, *Evelyn has captured him; I didn't have to do a thing. This has happened before in lives past. She never fails to snag the one or the other of us, and usually both* . . . Then Jack went to fetch his submachine guns and a sack filled with hand grenades. He carried these items to his van and stashed them carefully under his bed.

PHASE 5
Plutonium

30.
In The Shashtuk

The two caravans were joined — joined end to end, not mingled — and then Jack and Fenwick entered The Shashtuk, bound for Plutonium.

Jack's train took the lead for the simple reason that his heavy, painted vans moved slowest of all; they set the pace. In the center came the missile carried by two groups of mutants who relieved each other from time to time. Then came the long string of Fenwick's light prairie wagons, sometimes straight and sometimes curving stiffly like a reptilian tail.

The Shashtuk looked no different from many other parts of the world these days — outwardly — yet it was clearly a badlands by the feel of it. The mutagrass ocean extended into the distance, rolling, swaying. Here and there, resembling giant ships, black dense forests floated on the silver of the grass. Here and there mountain peaks — rough ragged rock bright with smears of a mutated yellow lichen — stood forth from the prairie resembling islands. Tan clouds of dust marked the whereabouts of giant herds of antlered cattle breeding here with minimum molestation from man — like once the extinct buffalo. Sometimes the wind brought the stench of mutant nests hidden in the vastness. Carry crows in black squadrons provided air-cover to the caravans and fought in noisy, glistening masses over the sparse leavings of the column after every stop.

The mutagrass reached higher here than elsewhere. The antler-beef was more abundant. The coyotes howled louder and displayed more daring by night than in more populated regions. But these outward signs did not account for everything. Jack felt a silence in The Shashtuk — a silence undisturbed in any way by the din of cricks, the sharp "kee-haw, kee-haw" of crows, the coyote laughter, or even the incessant, maddening scream of ungreased axles.

Jack felt in The Shashtuk what he had often felt in the New Mexico desert long ago — a listening presence. This land no longer looked like desert, but Chief Walk-on-air was still around. He seemed to lurk somewhere above the layerings of dust; or else he brooded over the horizon; or he came mingled with the breeze as an odor of distant mutant nests; those smells evoked sharp memories of an Indian roundhouse. At times Jack shivered in that noisy silence; he didn't like the feeling of being watched. Why now and never before? Did Chief Walk-on-air want to make sure that Jack carried out his mission, his mission of karmic retribution? The Shashtuk was eerie. No wonder people avoided it.

Since leaving Cactus, Jack rode a horse — the better to observe. All day long he circled the column; he watched and spied like a predator. He wanted to understand Fenwick, Fenwick's ways, and the nature of his people. Inevitably his and Fenwick's forces would have to clash, and Jack was looking for a suitable strategy.

At first he disliked what he saw. Fenwick was an able leader — echoes of the Ursula. He moved about a good deal too, but unlike Jack he was forever chatting, joking, and horsing with his men. Whenever some trouble struck — Fenwick was instantly on hand. When antler-beef was sighted he led the hunting charge, screaming like an eagle and brandishing the long stiff lance called "steak harpoon" in these parts. He was entertaining around the fire.

And his people obviously liked him — liked him as a man. Jack felt twinges of resentment and jealousy not in any way connected with the soul of Aspic in the thin and bony Fenwick body. Fenwick brought to mind again Jack's Buddy Brandon days. Fenwick would have been a captain, Jack still only a scout. Jack's crewmen didn't like him. They served because he paid them well — and because Tovarish had a fist the size and hardness of a boulder.

The confrontation will be bloody, Jack told himself during those early days. He didn't like that prospect. He had credits up above, but his balance was declining. He didn't want to have the blood of innocents on his hands. If it had to be, it had to be, alas; and it looked like it would have to be. Fenwick would not just hand himself over. And so long as he commanded his people's loyalty — and even his mutants liked him! — they would make trouble when Jack made his move.

But some time after Jack made these observations, Fenwick's behavior changed. When it became apparent that Fenwick had been struck down, as by a curse, the mood around the caravan began to darken. By contrast, Jack turned cheery.

It happened after an axle broke on Evelyn's van. True to form, Fenwick arrived on the scene and took charge of the situation. Jack stood by, arms folded across his chest, and didn't interfere — although Tovarish clearly didn't like this abdication of authority. Fenwick enjoyed these crises of equipment. He yelled orders; he sent people running. They came with tools, metal, and several long wooden shafts. Then Fenwick set to work, evidently stimulated by the task ahead.

During this time Evelyn stood in the grass some distance from the van. Jack didn't like to see people within her telepathic range. Only the half-wit he employed as the teamster of Evelyn's van could endure her constant emotings without turning ill. The half-wit now held Evelyn's chain. After the van was fixed, Jack and the half-wit nudged and prodded the rabbit back into its fetid darkness. Evelyn resisted. She always resisted. Jack locked her door using an Old Order lock. Then the caravan started again.

Fenwick stayed by the wagon. He rode beside it squinting at the right front wheel. He wanted to make sure, it seemed, that the axle he had fitted to the vehicle would carry the heavy load. Jack watched Fenwick, riding behind him.

They had stopped on the top of a rise and now they headed down again. Some time back a heavy rainfall had cut channels into the side of the hill they were descending; mutagrass had covered these depressions since then and hid them from view. But as the van reached the ruts, it began to wobble dangerously back and forth. Evelyn was thrown about; she emoted strongly in her panic.

Visions passed over Jack's eyelids and the usual emotions washed over his body — glands released hormones, the heart rate jumped, blood pounded momentarily. Jack was used to this. The feeling passed. He thought nothing more about it. Evelyn disliked the road. Any little bounce or sway, even a gust of wind, sufficed to make her send her telepathics — and Jack expected that. He rode along a little longer; then he turned his pony to ride back along the column. He wanted to sniff the last wagon of Fenwick's train again, a mysterious little wagon, and now seemed to be a good time to do it. Fenwick was still preoccupied with that axle.

Three hours later Jack had made a complete circuit of the column. Today he hadn't smelled the vile odor that usually emanated from the small vehicle invariably placed at the tail-end of Fenwick's train like some caboose; Jack still wondered why. Had its teamster, the repulsive mutant called Co-Cheese, washed the wagon down? Possibly. The caravan had camped last night next to a running stream at the foot of one of those mountain islands in the muta-seas.

At the column's head again, Jack was surprised to see that Fenwick still rode next to Evelyn's van. Still? By now the axle had clearly proved itself. Then he noticed Fenwick's posture. The sweeper rode slouched; his head hung down; his arms were slack; his pony's reins hung loosely in hands laid across the saddle. Fenwick seemed asleep, but Jack knew that he was not.

A thrill rose up in Jack, the consequence of sudden insight. He had nearly forgotten his early days with Evelyn, far to the east, when she had chased and then simply accompanied him. He too had felt what Fenwick would be feeling now. Evelyn could have an ennervating influence — the very reason why Jack kept people clear of her van.

He recalled the early days of their "unholy union." Within the pale of Evelyn's emanations the psychic ether throbbed with dreams, with stimulation. She exuded sexuality and whisps of karmic recall. When she emoted mildly, as she did now, a man could lose himself. The Age of Dust could disappear for hours at a time.

Nice at first. Very nice. And then very ennervating.

Later yet would come disgust and pain and the

angry wish to hurt her—a wish Jack had ritualized into the magic show. The anger came because she would not deliver what her telepathics promised. No, sir. Evelyn wouldn't mate, not even when she was in heat—because she wanted to be a person, not a bunny.

For the rest of that day's march, Jack stayed near the van and watched. He stayed out of Evelyn's range. He had come to loathe her telepathics. He wondered all the while. Would this last? Would Fenwick too become addicted as Jack had been addicted once? If yes, Jack's work might turn out to be fairly easy—later.

He was pleased to find the following day, and in the days that followed, that Fenwick had indeed become addicted. The sweeper spent his days hewing close to Evelyn's van. Later yet he began to sleep near the vehicle. Jact took the rabbit from the van each evening and led her on a walk; or else he asked the half-wit to exercise the hare; Fenwick was always near at these occasions. Once he asked whether he might take Evelyn's chain. Jack readily agreed to this, and after that Fenwick assumed this chore. But Jack always watched closely. He didn't want the sweeper to take pleasure in the rabbit in any active way. A plan began to dawn in Jack's mind; tied to the plan was a—well, yes: a wicked hope. Jack hoped that Fenwick might be "awakened" too. In due time. In time for his execution. Jack wanted to rouse Aspic out of Fenwick's ignorance. He hoped to raise Aspic's ghost.

Fenwick's infatuation with the rabbit soon began to have its effect. A vacuum of leadership developed. Jack encouraged Tovarish to assume command, and Tovarish did so readily enough. His gravelly voice began to shout the orders to crewmen and sweepers alike. The sweepers didn't like this, but when on one occasion one of them appealed to Fenwick, Fenwick responded in a manner so lackadaisical and so obviously distracted that Tovarish won the point.

Fenwick's sweepers had none among them with obvious leadership talent, but they smarted under this unofficial change in management and they sought out a most unlikely figure as their spokesman and representative — the mutant Co-Cheese.

Co-Cheese was a colorfree, an older man, an ugly, wrinkled, shrewish creature. He drove the mysterious, smelly wagon, but beyond that he hadn't seemed important to Jack. Now Jack learned that Co-Cheese had a modicum of power over Fenwick's men, a most unusual situation in the Age of Dust. They sought him out. It turned out that Co-Cheese hailed from the north. He had served at Talisman's Motel and had raised Fenwick from a boy.

Co-Cheese then shouldered the burden of Fenwick's leadership — but only to this extent: whenever the column stopped, he sought out the sweeper and argued with him in hoarse whispers. Jack watched the process day after day. Co-Cheese would stand or squat near Fenwick, fiercely arguing. His face turned a hundred shades of red, pink, purple, pale, and white. His body jerked uncontrollably. His arms flew into the air as if he were a puppet handled by a hapless puppeteer. Fenwick listened without expression; sometimes he nodded or shrugged. But the sessions always ended with some rough gesture from Fenwick, a harsh word of dismissal. Then Co-Cheese turned chalky white, then fiery red. And stalked off with a twitchy, sometimes buckling gait.

Jack tried to cultivate the mutant, but Co-Cheese would not respond. Like all mutants he had learned the habits of a slave. He gave no cause for outrage. He answered all questions courteously but with minimum information. He stepped from his mutant role only on one occasion, and that had to do with his wagon.

Jack approached that wagon one evening after weeks of travel. As always it stood a little apart and — Co-Cheese had an instinct for these things — down-wind from the camp. Jack felt secure in probing. Fenwick wandered through the grass leading Evelyn by her chain. He wouldn't interfere.

"Co-Cheese," Jack said, "I meant to ask you this. That wagon of yours stinks to high heaven. It's down-wind of us, but sometimes the wind turns. What have you got in there?"

Colors passed swiftly over the mutant's features. Fine hairs draped across his nose-less nostrils trembled.

"Coyote cubs."

"Coyote cubs? Why do you carry coyote cubs inside a wagon?"

"Because my master wants me to."

"And why does your master want you to?"

"I didn't ask him, Master Jack."

"But you must know."

"I know only what my master tells me. He didn't tell my why."

"They're very funny coyote cubs," Jack said. "I've never heard them bark; I've never even heard them *whine*. Let's just take a look inside there."

Jack moved swiftly toward the wagon, but Co-Cheese moved even faster. He leaped between the wagon and Jack in a single bound; yet he managed to snatch a root-cutting machette off the ground as he did so. The machette jerked in the mutant's lifted arms. He held it with both hands. The blade reflected the camp fire's flames.

"Fenwick told me not to let anyone inside there — and I do as I'm told."

"*You* — are threatening *me?*"

"I do as I am told."

"Step aside."

"I'll cut you, Master Jack. I'm not kidding." Then Co-Cheese yelled piercingly. He called for Fenwick.

"Shut up, damn you," Jack hissed, suddenly afraid. "I was only kidding." Then he quickly stalked away. From a new vantage point he saw that Fenwick had heard the summons. Waist-high in mutagrass — Evelyn phosphoresced near him, the light was rapidly fading — Fenwick stood, head raised, alert, listening. But when the cry was not repeated, he turned back toward Evelyn again.

Jack relaxed. He wasn't ready for a confrontation. Not quite yet. He liked to choose his own time of battle. He didn't want that goddamned mutant rat to wrest the initiative out of his hand. A few more days of march remained before they were to sight the Volcano Ring. Then and not before . . .

Damn that mutant. Damn that little rat. One of these days, Co-Cheese, I'll get into that wagon of yours and see about those coyote cubs . . .

That evening passed routinely. But Jack's exchange with Co-Cheese had an adverse consequence the following day. During the noon-time stop, Co-Cheese penetrated Fenwick's lethargy. After that, with evident pain, Fenwick stayed away from Evelyn. He shadowed Jack instead; his squinting eyes peered suspiciously, but he didn't say a thing. Fenwick's people grinned a lot that afternoon and yet more the following day. Fenwick had changed. He was not his busy, cheerful self. But at least he had come back to them again.

31.
The Storm

Fenwick gave up Evelyn. He gave up that mixture of bliss, excitement, danger, and the promise of lust satisfied in which the rabbit had bathed him for a span of nearly three weeks.

Not until he gave her up did he realize the power of her Hip No Tism. It was as if the world had suddenly collapsed and darkened. He had floated in an ocean of feelings and visions, a sunny world of visions, a tingling, exciting universe of feelings.

Suddenly he was plunged back into the Age of Dust, a shadowy realm. The Shashtuk, which had always seemed beautiful to Fenwick in the past, looked now flat, drab, and devoid of charm. And the outward pall was matched by an inner depression. Life had lost all meaning. He wanted to do nothing but sleep. His thoughts turned to death — its total oblivion had a kind of attraction.

Two factors kept him going. First of all, he hadn't

given up the rabbit forever, only for a time, and he could look forward to a future when she would be entirely his. Second, he now sensed that he might be in danger.

He watched Jack and wondered about the Show-Biz man; was Jack after the secret of Fenwick's Godbod trade? Likely, likely. Why else did Jack pry and prod around Cappy Bonehill's wagon all the time? Could he be a plutojack? He had eyes a little like the brothers — but without that Godbod hunger in their depth. If he spied for Plutonium, the more reason to be on guard. The monks would tear Fenwick limb from limb if they knew how he found his Godbod. In any case, Fenwick had to plan. They couldn't go on like this forever. Jack had to be overcome. He wouldn't yield that rabbit — not for metal, not for anything.

So Fenwick stayed from Evelyn's side, but it was painful . . . this deprivation. Pain within — a dull, flat, colorless, dark world without.

The caravan moved south for three days. Then the lush mutagrass began to thin out. Here and there patches of a dark-green scrub replaced it — the first sign that Plutonium was near. Little by little after that, the scrub grass took over entirely. Then the signs of volcanic activity appeared. Thin fissures could be seen from time to time. Steam curtains rose from these rocky cracks. Later yet they reached the region of geysers and marched for a day amidst intermittently spouting columns of mingled water, steam, and brine. That evening the dust was heavy and hid the volcanoes of the Ring, but their glow could be seen faintly on the horizon after dark.

Fenwick retired that night in a state of sadness and yearning more acute than ever. He had caught a touch of Evelyn's Hip No Tism as they were setting up camp, and the power of her pulsings had nearly overcome his determination. He retired with a firm decision that he would act in the morning. He couldn't wait another day. Tovarish would be teased away at the beginning on some ruse and overcome by three strong men. Then Jack. The rest would yield without a fight. Tomorrow night he would spend with Evelyn . . .

Fenwick had lately slept in a small wagon where his personal belongings were kept. He lay down on a pile of skins in the light of a candle he had lit from a flaming brand of mutaroot. He took a slender booklet from beneath the skins. Filled with radiant Golden Age pictures, entitled *A Walk Through Old New York*, the booklet had once served to ignite Fenwick's dream.

He gazed at the pictures one by one and tried to recapture his dream again. But tonight they lacked all power. He no longer cared for Old New York. All he could think about was her . . .

He fell asleep after a while. The booklet sank down to his chest. His candle burned down until it became a tiny bit of blackened wick in a shrinking and hardening pool of wax. Then it died entirely.

Toward morning the wind rose and blew with such strength that wagons rocked and creaked and the dust sizzled against leather and prickled against the wood. Fenwick slept through it all. Lately he slept regardless of disturbances. He clung to oblivion. Then the wind died suddenly.

Somewhat later Fenwick started up, and as he swung off his bed of hides, the booklet fell to the wagon's floor. The end-flap of his wagon had been pulled aside, and in the light of a burning bunch of mutaroot he saw Co-Cheese. It took a moment before he understood what Co-Cheese was saying.

"He is at it again," Co-Cheese repeated. "He is sniffing about again, prying and poking."

Several seconds passed. Then Fenwick understood. "Cappy's wagon?"

Co-Cheese nodded his head rapidly several times.

Fenwick groped about, still a little hapless, still a

little groggy; but his anger was rising. In a moment he found his hat. Then he poked about until a grass machete came into his hand.

He clambered from the vehicle. "Let's go," he said; and he strode off toward a dimly visible small wagon some distance from the circle of wagons that formed the camp.

It was still early in the morning and quite dark — unusually dark. But Fenwick was so angry and so intent on action that he did not notice the portent of the sky. He marched toward Cappy's wagon; Co-Cheese jerk-walked in his wake. Fenwick strode so furiously that he almost bumped into Jack. The latter was headed back toward the camp.

"What in the hell are you doing out here?"

Jack recoiled a step from Fenwick's fury. He wore goggles, and now he pushed them up over his forehead — but Fenwick had already dealt with Magic Jack in his mind; the ice-hard, hateful eyes failed to intimidate.

"I was taking a crap," Jack said. "Not that it's any of your business."

"My property *is* my business," Fenwick said. "You were poking around my wagon."

Jack raised his eyebrows. "What would I want with your wagon? Especially that one. I have no use for 'coyote cubs' myself. And as for property, Fenwick, I would suggest that you secure that precious wagon of yours before the storm hits and blows it apart. Your precious 'coyote cubs' might just escape."

Saying this, Jack pointed with his chin toward the sky behind Fenwick. Fenwick turned, saw the sky, and reacted immediately.

"Cheese," he said sharply. "Get some mutants and . . . " He gestured toward Cappy's wagon. Then he strode off hurriedly without another word to Jack. Wagons had to be reoriented, animals caught and tied securely, the Godbod placed down on the ground.

The sky had frightened Fenwick. A hurricane threatened from the west; it looked like a real killer storm.

He reached the camp and saw to his relief that work was already under way to batten down. The magic vans were being moved so that they formed an arrow-head facing the storm. Fenwick's mutants wrestled with the Godbod needle, lifting it off its framework. Crewmen and sweepers were pushing wagons.

Fenwick joined the work with gusto. He ran wherever a hand was needed, shouted orders — the fire; somebody douse that; the horses, somebody quickly catch them; move men, move. We haven't got much time.

Not a breath of air stirred now, but the sky seemed to be in motion. One part of it was rusty red, another black. The black mass advanced, jostling and moving. It crowded the red portion. It ate up, gobbled, and swallowed the dim morning light. Thunder growled.

Then the storm began. First came a wind so strong that men stumbled along under its blows like puppets. The silt it carried cut the skin. People stopped what they were doing and crawled, staggered, crept for shelter. The thunder roared. And then came the first masses of water; all light disappeared save for distant but rapidly advancing curtains of lightning. The sound of the torrent and the furious lash and whistling of the wind obliterated the cries and calls of men and mutants. Yet all this was just a prelude to the storm's main thrust.

Fenwick found shelter under Cappy Bonehill's wagon. It had been pushed into camp by mutants under Co-Cheese's supervision and now formed one piece of an arrow-shaped configuration of vehicles.

Fenwick felt great — as if he had just been awakened from a nasty dream. The very fury of the storm, the driving, slapping sheets of water that drenched him effortlessly despite his shelter; and the quick, intense work in which he had participated — all this aroused his old, cheerful, and good-humored self. He laughed at the storm, although his laughter was inaudible in that elemental roar. He wondered fleetingly how he could have been so sad these last few days. Life was good again.

Then everything changed — outside as well as inside Fenwick.

The central mass of the storm reached the camp. Lightning literally rained down. Thunderclaps rent the air with sounds as if the earth were being cracked apart. The wind tore and chewed the vehicles. Animals screamed in terror — and one animal in particular.

Evelyn was in a towering panic. She was confined, of course, and couldn't see a thing. She sensed the fear of men, of mutants, and of animals. She was certain that the end had come. A part of her exulted. Another part of her raged in a state of terror greater then any she had ever experienced. And everything that she now felt spread from her outward in slowly moving concentric waves of telepathic emanation that no amount of wind could touch, speed up, or deflect.

Fenwick nearly fainted when the first of those waves hit him. He had sensitized himself during the last three weeks. His brain exploded into visions, his body burst into a passion. The passion was so compelling that he began to crawl forward like a madman. He tore and clawed in the darkness. He tumbled over people. He slipped, slid, and came up hard against wheels and other obstructions. Yet ever and again he continued forward, possessed by a mindless lust.

During all this, obligingly, his brain rationalized his actions. What better time to take possession of that furry, maddening rabbit of a Henrietta than now, in the midst of this total confusion?

His forward motion carried him beyond Evelyn's van. Suddenly he saw empty landscape in a triple flash of lightning. He rose. Instantly the wind swept him off his feet. He reached out madly as he tumbled past the rabbit's van and arrested himself on the handle of her door.

But the door was locked. It was fastened shut by a Golden Age padlock whose key, Fenwick knew, never left Jack's person. Fenwick had forgotten the lock in all his frenzied crawling. He had felt that lock before, by night, in the weeks past, when he had tried to enter here.

He rattled the lock furiously, feeling impotent rage. He cut his hands in the effort. He tried to *will* the lock off the door.

Then, in the light of another series of lightning strokes, he saw movement over his right shoulder. The door of Jack's van opened — very slowly; the wind pressed against it. Jack squeezed out. He tumbled down, then forward. Fenwick saw him brandishing ... the key!

Fenwick was past all caring or reflection. He didn't wonder why Jack bothered bringing him the key. He didn't notice the crazy leer on Jack's features — visible in the jerky lightning's light. He grabbed the key roughly. He jammed it into the lock the way he had seen Jack do it. And in a moment he clambered inside the dark yet phosphorously illuminated, dry, acridly reeking rabbit hutch.

The wind shut the door behind him. In the supernatural din, Fenwick didn't hear the faint clicking of the lock as it closed again under the pressure of Jack's fingers.

32.
The Ghost in the Machine

In brilliant, unusual sunlight, masses of carry crows, their black feathers shiny like slivers of jade, feasted on a dead pony just outside the storm-devastated camp. The conical mountains of the Ring were visible sharply on the horizon in the now clear and cloudless air. Water lay everywhere in pools and puddles, and the scrub-grass was soaked with moisture. Steam poured copiously from crevices and spouted from geysers. The camp looked like an abandoned coyote kill; most of the wagons had lost their coverings; their exposed superstructures suggested ribcages stripped of flesh. All sorts of gear spilled helter-skelter from up-turned vehicles looked like the ripped-out inner organs of a score of victims.

On the edge of camp stood Jack. Two submachine guns hung from his shoulders. Hand grenades beaded his belt. His black hat pulled low to shade his face, he watched Fenwick's sweepers load a wagon. He resembled the Nazi guard he once had been; they behaved like sullen, frightened prisoners.

They transferred keg upon keg filled with reddish, glistening copper from one of Jack's wagons to one of their own. They peered at Jack frequently. They looked especially at his guns and at his hand grenades.

Earlier that morning they had seen one of those eggs explode and tear into a pony. The beast had staggered, buckled, and begun to scream. Then like sharp thunderclaps, quick and terrible, the stubby mystery Jack carried had spat a string of bolts over the ground, moving in an arc, until the bolts had pierced the horse's skull and it had sagged abruptly into death, its agonizing screams cut off as if with a knife.

The pony's fate would be their fate, Jack had told them after that. The copper they were loading now would belong to them if they did as they were told — if they went quietly back to Cactus . . . or wherever. Else they could share the pony's lot . . .

They loaded the copper — amazed at the mass of it, not sure at all why Jack would be so generous. He had the power to kill them, after all. Why part with gifts? Some of them expected to be killed as soon as the loading had been done; they tried to stay far away from Jack and his terrifying Golden Age weapons. All of them pretended not to hear Fenwick's voice as it called dully for help throught the walls of Evelyn's van.

They will kill each other in their quarrels when the time comes to divide this loot, Jack thought. *The stick first, then a carrot.*

His take-over had gone without a hitch. He had killed — but he had only killed a horse. The Age of Dust was ignorant of firearms, as yet, and the sweepers had been properly amazed.

"Hurry it up," Jack called. "I haven't got all day." And just to show that he still meant business, he fired another burst of bullets into the air.

The sweepers left at mid-day. They whipped the ponies hitched to their copper wagon and ran like hell beside the vehicle until they were a good distance from the camp. Even then they hurried on, disbelieving their own luck. They had gotten away! And they had struck it rich!

Jack watched them for a long time. Only when the wagon and the walking men beside it had coalesced into a single black dot in the distance did he turn toward the camp.

His own crewmen and all of Fenwick's mutants were hard at work repairing the storm's damage. A huge fire blazed in the center of the camp. Tovarish fed its flames with bundled mutaroot. Piles of provisions, kegs of metal, heaps of skins, barrels of beer, cakes of salt, leather gear of all sorts, jumbles of tools and weapons, and much else besides had been stacked around the fire to dry out.

On the way back, Jack stopped next to the Golden Age bomb, the Godbod. It was his property now, and he guessed that it would come in handy when he approached the brotherhood, ready to negotiate.

The bomb had been lifted from the soggy ground and rested in the saw-horse of its wooden frame once more. Sunshine burned its silvery surface, but the metal felt oddly cool under Jack's stroking touch.

They were two strangers who went a long ways back. They didn't fit this scene. Jack gazed at that scene, hands on the hull: a primitive camp, freaky mutants, smoking volcanoes in the distance, a steamy landscape. Then he moved on.

"Tovarish," he said, reaching the fire, "let's go and open up that 'coyote wagon.'" He grinned. "I want to *see* those little coyotes."

To see — because he already thought he *knew*. Fenwick's precious Geiger counter lay inside that vehicle, but Jack still had to see it. He had never seen a plutojack before.

The wagon had done well in the storm. Better secured than all the others, it still had its covers, tightly strapped. Rain had washed and drenched it; nevertheless it stank of urine and of faeces.

"Open her up," Jack told Tovarish as they arrived. "No. Don't bother untying. Cut the straps."

The wide blade of Tovarish's knife flashed. The end flaps soon hung loose. Tovarish draped them up over the roof.

Jack advanced through a cloud of pungent odor and peered into the dark interior. In a moment he saw a slender paleness deep within. The figure didn't move. "The other side, Tovarish. Open up the other side."

When light entered from the other side, Jack saw motion. A half-starved, naked boy — at most sixteen years of age — crawled rapidly on hands and knees toward the center of the wagon, equidistant from either opening. A tortured, long, and narrow face. Huge eyes glowed, peering at Jack. Long, filthy, matted hair hung down to the boy's bony shoulders. Gigantic, oozing sores — pestilential islands on sickly white skin — covered the boy's chest, stomach, and thighs. The boy's movement sent an odor of decay and putrefaction in Jack's direction. Jack had to gag. The boy pressed some kind of object against his genitals. In a second he had begun to rock rhythmically back and forth.

Jack stared speechlessly. He drew back with a shake of his head.

"Get some mutants," he told Tovarish. "Get that son of a bitch Co-Cheese. Clothes. Water. Buckets full of water. Hurry up."

Fury gripped Jack. *That son of a bitch Aspic. His goddamned creation. Institutional continuity —future generations . . . I might have turned out just like that. God damn! You son of a bitch Walk-on-air! Some fucking God you are, letting this happen. That wretched little kid . . .*

When Co-Cheese arrived, leading others, Jack let his fury burst over the mutant.

"Coyote cubs, eh? Coyote cubs!" He kicked Co-Cheese so violently that the mutant's spindly legs buckled and he splashed headlong into a puddle. "Coyote cubs! I'll give you coyote cubs!" And Jack sent Co-Cheese sprawling with additional, furious kicks.

"Get up you pitiful . . . Get up before I spill your brains . . . *Get* in there. Get that kid out of there!"

Moments later men and mutants had gathered to watch. Rude and simple creatures all, they guffawed loudly at the boy until Jack told them sharply to shut up. Then at Jack's direction, Tovarish tossed bucket after bucket of water at the mutely struggling boy. Co-Cheese held the youthful plutojack.

The boy struggled so furiously that Co-Cheese had difficulty subduing the youngster. At one point he lost his twitchy hold on the boy, the boy gave Cheese a powerful shove, and before the mutant could recapture him, the youngster bounded away. He burst through the circle of surprised watchers and ran toward the missile. He clambered up on the wooden frame and flung himself lengthwise on the bomb. His buttocks began to move at once in a copulatory motion.

The people laughed.

"Shut UP!" Jack shouted, beside himself. "Get away from here, you scum. Get the hell back to work. Tovarish, Goddammit!"

Tovarish had already moved. He grabbed Co-Cheese by the neck of his tunic and dragged the mutant to his feet. They hurried toward the silver needle and tried to pry the youngster from the missile. Meanwhile the others had scattered and pretended to work.

The boy resisted, struggled, bounced his buttocks. Tovarish lost his patience. His rocky fist moved swiftly and caught the boy's chin. The youngster slumped. Tovarish lifted him clear of the bomb.

The oldest behavioral compulsion of them all, Jack thought; he meant sexuality, not the force of Tovarish's arm.

"Put some clothes on him. And tie him up," Jack said, approaching.

"Hold him. *Hold* him," Tovarish growled, talking to Co-Cheese. "Don't let him go, this time." Tovarish waited until Co-Cheese had the boy in his grip, then he left to fetch the clothes.

Jack stepped up to the plutojack. The boy seemed dazed. The mutant's skinny arm encircled his neck and choked him.

"Hey, boy," Jack said. "What's your name, boy?" The boy did not respond.

"His name is Cappy Bonehill."

"I didn't ask you. I want *him* to talk."

"But he can't talk, Master Jack."

"Why not?"

"He hasn't got a tongue."

"He what — ?"

"He hasn't got a tongue." Co-Cheese was changing colors rapidly.

"He — " Then Jack understood. "You cut his tongue out?"

Co-Cheese turned grey. "*I* didn't, Master Jack. *I* didn't do a thing. Fenwick and the others — "

"You're an innocent. You're as guiltless as the driven snow. I've got a good mind to . . . " But just then Tovarish returned. "Open his mouth," Jack said.

Tovarish dropped the pants and leather poncho he carried. He grabbed Cappy by the forehead and the chin. The boy's eyes rolled in terror and he made a dreadful gurgling noise in his throat.

Jack stared into a black, toothless cavity and saw the cauterized stump of a tongue.

He drew back. "Dress him, tie him up. Get him away from here." He gestured toward the missile. It exerted an almost magnetic influence on the boy.

The wretched, miserable creature! They had used a flaming torch to cauterize the wound. Cappy's oral cavity had still not healed. Blisters still marked it. Why had the boy not starved? He couldn't have eaten in weeks, in months! Did the little bottle of Godbod he still clutched against his genitals suffice to sustain him? Vile technology! Foul invention.

Jack turned to one of the crewmen nearby. "Set fire to that goddamned wagon."

"Yes, sir," the crewman said, and he went off to carry out the order.

Jack watched as Tovarish dressed Cappy Bonehill while Co-Cheese continued to choke the boy. Using straps of leather, Tovarish bound the plutojack's ankles. Then he lifted the slender figure as if he had been a sack and carried him away toward the center of the camp. Co-Cheese jerk-walked stiffly after them, more to escape Jack's wrath than to be helpful.

Crewmen had moved the stinking wagon away from the other vehicles by now, and they held burning strands of mutaroot to its four corners. Jack waited until the fire had caught on. Then he went off toward his van. After this, he needed solitude.

The voice came as he walked — a loud man's baritone with a slightly mechanical inflection, speaking twentieth century American English.

"Chief of this camp, listen to me. Listen to me, heap big chief."

Jack heard the words. He was surprised, but he could barely respond with his emotions. The day had already drained him. He turned and looked at the shiny missile. *So. So it's a talking bomb. Wonders will never cease.* He sighed. He understood immediately what kind of bomb the wretched boy had found. Jack had been in on the beginnings, after all. A memory flashed: a windy, cold September day in Washington, D. C. Big, bearlike Fred Jones talked in whispers about the transplantation of brains into machines. And suddenly Jack understood who Tovarish was.

"Chief, leader, master — king of this camp. I'm calling you. Come and talk to me."

Jack began to walk toward the missile. Men and mutants stood in frozen postures all around the camp. All eyes stared at the silver needle. Only the campfire's flames licked, danced, and crackled as if nothing had happened at all. Bits of fluffy ash rose with the heat, wobbling like miniature kites. The last of the carry crows spread its wings and rose from the skeletal remains of what had been a pony.

It's more than just a talking missile, Jack told himself, advancing. His feet made sucking noises in the rain-soaked ground. *Nothing is just what it seems. Shit, man. You're living in a goddamned myth. You're a puppet on a string — and he up there the puppeteer . . . Fenwick found him. So who is he? I bet he has some bloody role to play.*

"Is that you, big chief? Are you coming, chief? Come close and touch me."

He can hear but he can't see.

The missile on its wooden saw-horse reminded Jack of the tale of Oz. *The tin woodman of my myth,* he thought and almost laughed. The mutants might be munchkins, Fenwick the scarecrow, Evelyn the . . . Then he had reached the missile and laid a hand on the cool hull. *Cool* hull — the thing gulped solar energy, had been energized during the morning's "blue."

"Hello," cried the voice. "So you have come at last. Can you understand me, chief? Say something, chief. Let me hear your voice."

Jack understood the missile — but only because he remembered all about the Golden Age. The language had changed sharply in a century or more. The missile would be anxious about that. Should Jack answer in the language of today? In the language of the past? He chose to play the primitive, at least for now.

"Who are you?" he asked.
The missile lay on its framework, silvery, inert. Dirty smears of water glistened on its surface — residues of Cappy Bonehill's presence. The bomb seemed to be working on Jack's question, translating the sounds.
"Who am I?" the voice then said. "Who am I, indeed. Moloch, to you. Moloch is my name. I am a big chief too. I am a Sky Chief. My makers called me Moloch. Do you understand that? I can do mighty wonders. Mighty wonders; do you understand? But tell me your name. I only speak to chiefs."
Jack didn't answer that. "Where do you come from?" he asked instead.
Pause. "From the sky. I come from the gods, big chief. Do you understand? The *gods*. They sent me down here so that I can do my wonders . . . for the sons of man. Did you get that? Wonders and miracles. I can even grant your wishes."
"What kind of wishes?"
Silence. "What *kind* of wishes? Any kind of wishes, chief. I am magic; I have heap great power. You name it, chief, and I can give it to you. Horses, women, weapons, herds . . . Moloch can grant your wishes. But, chief . . . ?"
"Yes," Jack said.
"There is something you must do first."
"What's that?"
. . . "I am captured, I am imprisoned, I am held inside that thing you're touching. I am inside this . . . bottle, chief. You must break that bottle. You must let me out of here."
"How can I do that? This thing is made of heavy metal."
A longer pause. "Metal. Ah, very good. Big chief, I see that you're an intelligent man. Now listen to me closely. Listen very, very closely. Do you understand — mountain?"
"Mountain," Jack said.

"That's right. Heap big mountain. You take Moloch up to a mountain. Take me to a cliff. A very high cliff. Have you got such mountains here?"

"Oh, yes," Jack said. Then he smiled to himself. "We have heap big mountain. Very high up. Tip of mountain touchee clouds."

Silence. "You've got it, you've got it, you've got it," cried Moloch. His intonation hadn't changed, but the repetition of the phrase meant to convey enthusiasm. "Now listen, chief. You take Moloch up on a mountain. Then you must take some rope, lots of rope, you understand. And then you must hang me down nose first. Do you understand that, chief? Nose first?"

"Nose first," Jack said. He tapped the hull. "I've got it."

"Good, good, good. You're bright, big chief. Brilliant, intelligent. Your wishes shall be granted. But you must do as I tell you. Big mountain, nose first. And once you've got me hanging like that, you must drop me from the mountain, straight down into a valley, from a steep cliff, nose first."

"Straight down," Jack said.

"Right, right, right. Right you are. Very bright. Then the bottle will break apart and Moloch will come out. Then Moloch will grant your wishes."

Men and mutants still stood in rigid attitudes and watched. From the direction of Evelyn's van came the sound of Fenwick's muffled moans. Heavy thumpings and bangings rocked the van erratically as Fenwick chased the giant rabbit in the dark, narrow confinement. *Lust-crazed*, Jack thought. But at the moment Fenwick's status didn't interest him. He turned to the missile again.

"I will take you up to a very high mountain," he said. He spoke very slowly now. He wanted Moloch to understand this. "Once we're up there, I take some rope. I hang you down over a cliff. Nose down. Then I let you drop down from the mountain. Nose first. Nose always first. The silver bottle will break apart, and Moloch will spring up from the ground . . ."

"Right, right, right!"

". . . like mushroom cloud," Jack finished.

Silence. A long, persistent silence. Then Moloch spoke again.

"What did you say?"

"I said — like a mushroom cloud. Now listen to me. Who *are* you? Who are you really? And don't give me any crap. I'm not some simple savage you can con with promises. Your name is no more Moloch than mine is St. Patrick. I want to know who you are, *what* you are, and how come you are here."

Jack said this in twentieth century English. His words silenced the missile. The silence lasted for such a long time that Jack grew impatient. He knocked on the hull. "Answer me!"

The missile made a hissing sound. It might have been a sigh. "Leave me be," the voice intoned; its volume had diminished. "Away, hallucination. I don't believe you. Go away. Go away. Go away." The voice died in a whisper.

Hallucination? Then Jack understood. The brain within that shiny hull had lain somewhere for more than a century. Madness must have touched it often in that time — madness and despair. *Like me*, Jack thought, remembering his time in Paradise. *Only worse, much worse . . .*

He tapped the hull again. "You're not hallucinating. I am a real man and you're some kind of bomb. You want to trick me into killing you — and thus into killing myself. You owe me an explanation."

The sigh sounded again, an eerie, mechanical hiss. "Why should I believe you? All I've ever heard is savage grunts. You're speaking English. And you sound like a memory of mine. Get thee behind me, Satan. Go away. Go away . . ."

"What happened to your visual sensors? You can't see, can you?"

The missile laughed — or meant to laugh. It repeated, "Ha, ha, ha." Then it went on in a low, hasty, urgent manner. The words hissed forth now, resembling whispers, and despite their mechanical quality, they suggested hysteria.

"Tempter, torturer, evil one! See? See! Of course I can't see. And you know I can't, you fiend. You led me on. You teased me with your promises. You whispered. You fed my sinful greed. You told me that you'd give me eyes again, but God would not be mocked. Blind, blind, blind. I had eyes again — they burned out on my virgin flight. You hear that, Lucifer? On my virgin flight. Ha. Ha."

"You are a brain," Jack said. "You're a brain inside a servo-mechanism. They killed you and they put you in. Or did you donate your brain?"

"Donate . . . Ha, Ha, Ha. I signed a contract, Mr. Devil. I signed right on the dotted line. But can a blind man read the fine print? Tell me that?"

"Then what happened?"

"Simple. I had a physical. Cardiograph. Encephalograph. They stamped me fit for my prosthetic operation. See Moloch in the dressing room. See Moloch naked. On the operating table. See Moloch swooning, swooning, swooning — away into Never-Never Land with a needle in his arm. See Moloch waking up. Moloch has his eyes again. Moloch can see as good as new. Moloch looks out over the Pacific Ocean from his missile silo. See the waves crashing against the sand? See the Russian trawlers trawling? See the fine probes in the brain. Feel the wonderful sex, sex, sex? That's what happened. Missile silo, Pacific Ocean, and sex, sex, sex inside the brain. If you were a good boy."

"Go on."

The missile sighed. "I shunned sex all my life, you know. I was a spiritual man. Sex? — I sublimated sex into awareness. Ha. Ha. But there I was, the virgin Moloch, with probes inside my brain. I caught up on all the sex I'd missed. Pacific Ocean, Russian trawlers, flight training, and sex, sex, sex."

"Are you still armed? Are you still lethal?"

The missile did not respond. It lay inertly, reflecting sun. Had its stores of energy run out again? Or had it lost itself in memories of the "golden" age? Jack rapped the hull.

"Please answer me," he said. "Are you a brain? Are you still alive?" Jack knew what he meant and hoped that the missile understood him. He knew about two kinds of life; he meant the ordinary kind.

Moloch hissed sadly. "Is a dead fly in a cobweb still alive? After the spider has sucked out its juices? I am caught inside a cage of artificial neurons. Brain . . . It turned to mush, and then to dust, a long, long time ago. I am just a sliver now, the merest ghost, my friend. And if you are really real out there and not just an illusion, for the love of God, release me, let me *die!*"

Movement caught Jack's attention, and he turned. Drawn by something — by his karma? — Tovarish had advanced. A forlorn, puzzled, frightened look disfigured his ordinarily stony face. A spot of sunlight burnished his balding skull. His bushy beard flamed in the light. His fate to behold his handiwork in this Age of Dust. He hadn't blown the whistle in the Golden Age and hence the missile talked. *And I approved that devilish contract and thus created Cappy Bonehill . . .*

"It's all right, Tovarish," he called. "It's talking mystery. The sun has made it talk." Then Jack turned to the missile again, suddenly eager to learn who lurked inside it.

"I will free you," he told the bomb. "So help me God. But you must tell me who you are." *You must tell me because we're all connected, and you too must be weighed down by guilt.* But Jack left that unsaid.

"My name?" the missile whispered. "My name? I

hardly remember it . . . My name, if it please you, was Camilio Ezra Templar."

Jack nodded to himself. He had guessed as much. Templar had been the only person missing from the party.

33.
The Brotherhood

Under a sky reddened by active volcanoes, the caravan struggled up the final hill. Men cursed; animals labored; vans and wagons swayed; mutants groaned under Templar's weight; Tovarish shouted orders; and Evelyn emoted faintly.

Jack rode beside the caravan, tracking its progress up the grade. When the caravan approached the top of the hill, he rode ahead. He wanted to be first to see the valley. He topped the rise, drew up his mount, and gazed down into a veritable hell's kitchen below. The valley gave off a random, peculiar glow. Volcanic forces appeared to be at work beneath the surface of the land. Huge patches of soil seemed to be lit from below. Strange lights played on thousands of plumes of rising steam. The sky itself reflected the volcanic irridescence of the valley floor and the ooze of cooling lava streams snaking in rivulets down the side of one of the cones. The valley teemed with writhing ghosts and stank of sulfur.

Jack stared at the fiery vista. The valley of the shadow of . . . Fenwick's death? Or was it the land of Oz they were about to enter?

Then the caravan caught up with Jack and they all descended into the valley together.

He was weary and yet tense, awed and yet determined, sure and yet also filled with fears. He came into the valley with a plan, carrying the man who had created the still distant and invisible monstrosity called psychotron. He had found an able ally in Templar — who, like Jack, blamed himself in part for the existence of the evil in this valley. They were as brothers now, bent on Chief Walk-on-air's mission. But Jack knew nothing about the brotherhood, and his clever plan might turn to dust. Hence his anxiety . . .

More than an hour's march through the sepulchral valley lay behind them when people heard the sound. Jack rode in the lead just then, guiding the caravan along tongues of firm land between fire lakes, and he was so intent on his pathfinding chores he didn't notice the faint and distant wailing. Tovarish rode up, took Jack's elbow, and told him to listen. Jack stopped. Then he heard it too — an unearthly barking, still some distance away. It issued from the glowing mass of steam ahead.

"Stop the column," Jack told Tovarish, and he found that he had whispered. "Tell everyone to stand by and wait."

Jack remained, listening.

The plutojacks were coming. Their voices resembled the wail of coyotes. Jack shivered and checked his weapons. He carried his submachine guns slung over his shoulders. Grenades hung on his Atlantean uniform like bulbs on a Christmas tree.

How could they have detected us? You can't see a goddamned thing out here, not in this steamy mess. Could they have smelled Templar's atomics? My God —what sensitive organs they must have...

The brothers came very slowly. Jack gauged the speed of their advance; then he rode back along the caravan. "Keep calm," he called, keeping his voice low. "Don't lose heart; don't do anything rash. I have a plan and you will all be safe."

He had a plan. He had meant to arrive under the cover of darkness — but somehow night had not prevented his detection. But even so, he had a plan.

He stopped by Templar. "Get away from here," he told the mutants lounging about the wooden frame. "Get back among the wagons." The mutants complied. Only Cappy Bonehill stayed with the missile. He had marched directly under Templar, his arms encircling the hull, his face pressed against the metal; he remained now in the same posture, apparently overcome by some kind of mysterious bliss.

"Are you ready?" Jack asked Templar, tapping the missile's hull.

"Ready," Templar whispered. "But you had better hurry. My power cells are leaking. I won't last very long."

Templar meant his voice. "How much longer?" Jack asked.

"Three or four hours. Unless the sun comes out in the morning."

"No chance of that," Jack said. "But there will be plenty of time. Stand by for my signal."

"Right," Templar whispered.

Then Jack returned to the head of the column and resumed his wait.

At last, heralded by a disturbance of many steam plumes along a narrow front, the monks appeared — thin, almost skeletal figures, bald, oddly dressed. They ran forward in short burst. They stopped abruptly, threw back their heads like epileptics, and emitted short, gurgling and then shrieking barks. Then they ran again.

A gust of arbitrary wind from the direction of this irregularly running mob brought the nauseating stench of decay. Then the monks glimpsed the caravan. Their barking took on a new urgency, and they hurled themselves toward the column.

Jack's pony paced, trying to back. Jack readied his weapons. Sweat glistened on his face.

Then the first of the monks had come abreast. He came at a run, stopped abruptly, barked, and ran on. Skinny, wasted, dreadful figures followed him. Even in the uncertain light, Jack saw the sores, blisters, and lesions... Weird eyes stared with fixed expressions — but they stared at Templar, not at Jack.

Masses of men enveloped him and passed him by. A cacaphony of shrill or gurgling barking — death rattles, crazy laughter — filled the air. The brothers' stench was suffocating. They crowded around the missile. They clambered on the framework in large numbers until the wood collapsed with a splintering noise and Templar crashed down to the ground. Yet still more brothers tried to reach and touch the hull.

For a moment the area resembled that of a kill. Predators mauled, growled, and tore at the victim. Then, as if a signal had gone out, a sudden hush fell on the brothers. The barking stopped. The figures withdrew from the missile. They milled about and then they settled. Templar's silvery skin, now tinted reddish in the light, became visible again.

With some amazement, Jack watched what happened next. The monks sat down; they formed tight circles. They stirred a little. One or two barked. Then came a silence, a profound silence, a stillness of such quality that its effect spread outward. Even Evelyn's frantic emanations ebbed away.

Jack had never seen such devoted worship. The

monks sat like statues. Steam hissed somewhere, water gurgled, horses stamped occasionally. But all the little noises of the night came from sources other than the plutojacks.

The echo of another time arose in Jack. Aspic sat across a desk, his big moist eyes full of persuasion. "We've got to find some fool-proof way to bind the priesthood to the job," he said. "That's critical..."

Should I act? Jack wondered. He decided against it. Daybreak would come soon. He wanted to see the monks before he faced them. He moved back along the column. "Settle down," he told his people. "Settle down and try to rest."

He followed his own advice. He dismounted, tied his horse, and sat down on the lukewarm ground. His back rested against a wagon wheel.

He didn't mean to fall asleep. He fought the urge for a long time. But the silence and the peace were such that he succumbed, little by little. At first he just closed his eyes. Then he dozed off, awakening with frightened starts. In the end a deep sleep caught him up, and he began to snore.

He still slept when morning came — brilliant on the horizon, a symphony of colors, as always in this age. A trillion bits of dust refracted the sun's rising rays. The light stretched up the sky-vault but could not quite reach its zenith. Darkness hung overhead, but the horizon shone.

Light slowly extinguished the glow of volcanic patches in the valley. They turned to islands of ashes. Steam plumes lost their reddish coloration. Tongues of frozen lava reaching down from the volcanoes reflected light in bronze shades. In the far distance stood Plutonium atop a hill, partially obscured by haze — five egg-shaped, silvery structures. Morning brought no stir. The plutojacks still worshipped.

Then, later, a faint breeze rose up. It carried the

odors of the caravan over the mountains and communicated the presence of dying bodies to carry crows over the prairie. Soon birds circled overhead, cawing. Jack jerked awake.

He shivered and stood up, his weapons clanging. He took in the scene — half remembering. He had seen all this through spirit eyes — silvery domes, ash, lava. He looked around and saw his people resting in tight clumps. Plutojacks sat rigidly. They didn't even seem to breathe. Templar still lay in the wreckage of his framework.

For a moment Jack collected his wits. He checked his weapons. Should he wait? The horizon was a mass of color, but the column still lay in shadow. He decided to go ahead. The brothers were quiescent, and the initiative would be altogether his. He took some sheets of dirty paper from his pocket — long lists of names he had prepared during the last few days. Then he moved forward.

He passed between the tightly bunched monks and gained the center of the circle. The litter of Templar's frame cluttered the ground. Jack cleared a space for himself. Then he looked out at the monks.

Even in the darkness of the night before, he had seen correctly. Dreadful creatures sat before him. They seemed like figures from a concentration camp. Bone, sinew, and desiccated flesh. Wide-open, glazed, vacant eyes stared ahead — too big in skull-like heads. Mouths hung open; bodies twitched. Most were hairless or carried only tufts of hair like mangy dogs. Like Cappy Bonehill, they had pestilential sores dreadful enough to kill all normal men.

And they wore suits. The vision of these creatures in Old Order suits, shirts, ties — it shocked Jack with incongruity. Most of the men were barefoot, but they wore ties! The ties were greasy, shapeless tubes; the shirts black with age and caked with pus and blood; the suits torn, ripped, or frazzled like sheeps' coats.

Nonetheless — the costumes pointed to some pathetic tradition.

Jack's eyes found the leader — a tall, gaunt, older man, completely hairless. He alone seemed awake and looked at Jack with an expression of total deference. It was a surprisingly shy and submissive look. Why? What did it mean? When Jack looked at him, the old man bowed. Jack bowed back. Then he waited for the monk to speak, but the hairless ancient now avoided Jack's eyes.

"Men of Plutonium," Jack called.

No response. The eyes stayed glazed. But then the leader gave forth a little bark, and instantly eyes began to focus all over the crowd. Like their abbot, they looked on Jack as if he were the object of worship rather than the atomic stuff under Templar's hull. Jack didn't mind. He relaxed. The plutojacks were not belligerent, thank God.

"Men of Plutonium," he called, "I come to you bearing a gift. I come to you with Godbod from the ancient past. I come to you out of your past. You don't know who I am, yet I remember all of you. My name is Magic Jack. I too know the worship that you practice — even if I do not wear your dress. I too have known the psychotron."

At the mention of the psychotron, the monks moaned. One or two wrung their hands. Jack had no leisure to assess that reaction. He had done well enough so far. He meant to carry out his plan. He glanced down at the sheets he held.

"I knew you once by other names," he said. "I knew Frank Capiello, Johnny Richards, Teddy Ardrey, Jim Sonow, Paul Taylor, Fred Zito, Billy Smith, Roger Underhill . . ."

He went on reading names, elated by the results.

The third name had evoked a groan somewhere in the audience. A plutojack had suddenly moved, as if stung. After that each name had evoked a similar response.

The plan was working. All these souls, sensitized in Aspic's devilish machine, responded to the stirring of their karmic coils; their reactions proved Jack's magic power — and at the end, Templar would do the rest.

Jack read faster and faster now, face flushed in triumph. His voice seemed like a wind among reeds. Plutojacks wobbled back and forth, swaying, moaning, barking. Their eyes rolled. Their arms flew up into the air. Jack was a ranting, raving preacher hitting them with rock-hard gospel. They were the congregation, reeling under the lash of the Word.

Tovarish, the crewmen, and the mutants stood by the wagons and observed this curious proceeding with puzzled yet pleased incomprehension. They knew that their master was in command of the frightening coyote-men.

Jack stared at the leader as he preached. The old man avoided Jack's gaze. He resisted Jack's odd railing. His name had not been found. Who was he? The figure looked unfamiliar, all these skeletons were strange, yet the leader's eyes had peered at Jack suggesting some old linkage.

Jack reached the end of his list. Only the names of notables remained now, names Jack hadn't written down. He called for Fred McMurty, Perpetual's onetime mayor. Someone answered with a cry, a flail of arms.

"I knew you too, Ray Pisciotta," Jack cried. Someone groaned. "And my friend, John Henderson." A series of muffled barks. "And my drinking buddy and old friend, Charlie O'Brian — "

The leader doubled over. He gasped. He held his stomach. His voice rumbled, as if in pain. Then he began to sway and moan like all the rest.

Jack stopped. He had worked himself into a sweat. His breath came hot and strong. His heart beat furiously. He had stirred himself as much as he had stirred the monks.

His own excitement subsided slowly, the plutojacks also settled. Their moaning and barking subsided; their sway and rock came to a stop. They looked at Jack, awe in their eyes, awe mixed with a touch of dread.

Jack looked at them. "Now," he said, "the prophet will speak." He leaned down and tapped Templar's hull with the barrel of a submachine gun.

Silence. Then came Templar's voice, delighting Jack. *Right on the button; right on the button!*

Templar's voice was weak; his energies were obviously low. But he spoke obediently, in accordance with their agreement. He began to say what Jack had taught him; he spoke slowly; he worked hard to bring forth the grunty twangs of this Age of Dust.

"Plutojacks and friends. I am Godbod's prophet and a portion of Its substance — sent to bring you more of Its ineffable perfume. That you may feel Its bliss more abundantly. Hear me, and obey my emmissary, the man who stands before you, Magic..."

The voice died. The voice died prematurely. *Damn!* Jack looked around with a rush of anxiety. And then he saw that he had already succeeded. Astonishment marked the hollow faces. Then the leader rose. He bowed to Jack.

"Welcome," he said; he bowed again. "Welcome, Magic Jack. We have been expecting you."

34.
Plutonium

Plutonium consisted of five structures, arranged like the eyes on a die, with a circular moat around the whole. Drawbridges crossed the water aimed at oval openings in the egg-shaped buildings. These gigantic pods were made of mud strengthened by thick strands of mutagrass. They resembled siloes from the Golden Age and not purely by chance. They had been built in imitation of constructs Jack had once seen daily from the top of this same hill. On the podroofs stood imitation antennae fashioned of wood. Above the oval entrances Jack saw crude inscriptions — Distillation Zone, said one; Hydrafracture Unit II, another.

Jack had just dismounted. He stood among the "managers" — as the brothers called the leaders. Charlie O'Brian, whose name was Hamster's Shoe these days, had led Jack up the hill, shy, silent. Now he pointed to a drawbridge and asked Jack to follow him.

"Just a moment," Jack said. "First I want to see my caravan settled — and the prophet bedded down."

He turned from the buildings and faced down the hill. Plutojacks marched up the steep incline in a dense bunch. Templar floated above them, held aloft by scores of hands. The brothers barked loudly; their eyes rolled madly. They trampled one another in their eagerness to touch the missile. Some distance behind them wobbled Jack's colorful vans, and behind the vans came other carts and wagons. The volcanoes now lay in the distance, the valley with its army of steam ghosts lay below. It seemed as if Plutonium itself stood just beyond the volcanic zone.

Jack looked at the entire panorama now. He saw dark woods to the west interrupted by tongues of mutagrass that looked like molten silver. Low but jagged ridges rose to the north like dragon's jaws — they were also new, like the volcanoes.

He turned to Hamster's Shoe. "The psychotron is over there, isn't it?" He pointed in a north-westerly direction.

The abbot nodded. Then his eyes rolled oddly and he wrung his hands. Mention of the psychotron appeared to cause him pain, but Jack felt it wise not to ask why. Not yet. Thus far everything had clicked. The first task, as he saw it, was to discover why or how he had been "expected."

The plutojacks then reached the hill top, and Hamster's Shoe turned to Jack. He made a little bow.

"Where do you want to place the prophet?"

"Over there." Jack pointed to a flat area next to the moat.

Shoe nodded to one of his "managers," and the monk went forth to supervise the prophet's placement. Once more Jack saw mad scrambling. Then a sharp call caused the brothers to settle in tight circles around Templar, and in a moment the only noise came from the approaching caravan — the wail of greaseless axles, the crack of whips, and Tovarish's voice urging the mutants to push.

Jack walked forward, whistled sharply, and waved an arm. Tovarish saw the movement, spurred his horse, and came riding up the hill. Jack stopped the horse by grabbing its bridle.

"They want to show me around the place," Jack said. He spoke in a low voice. "You'll have to manage by yourself. Set up over there, but don't raise the tent. I expect to move again tomorrow. Send your men into those woods — see them? All right. I want them to start felling trees. And another thing. Get some poles. Put the mutants on either side of Evelyn's van. Have them rock the van. Rock it hard. Don't stop. I want it rocked until I get back. And keep your eyes open. If something happens, yell."

Tovarish nodded. Then he turned his horse and rode back down the hill.

"I am ready," Jack said, rejoining the managers. "Could someone take care of my horse . . . ?"

Hamster's Shoe gave an order. Then he held out an inviting hand and led the way toward Plutonium.

They drummed across a rotting drawbridge and ducked through the oval opening into a large, dark hall whose only illumination came from huge smears of some phosphorescent paint on walls and ceilings. Shoe waited until all the managers had entered. Then he made another curious bow.

"Welcome again, Magic Jack," he said, bowed again. Jack returned the bow. "We thank you for coming. We have awaited your coming for five years." Bow. "We need your help." Bow. "You have arrived in the nick of time." Now came a final bow. Then Hamster's Shoe turned and led the way out of the reception hall.

Jack followed. He wondered where they had picked up this bowing habit — so reminiscent of the Japanese in the Golden Age.

Through yet another oval opening, Jack ducked into

a very low passage smeared with more phosphorescent paint. The corridor was circular. It suggested the inside of a giant snake. Fetid odors of decay, disease, and mold seemed to stream toward him, and he thought he heard low moans.

"*We thank you for coming,*" he thought, reflecting back on Shoe's ceremonious welcome. *How could they know about me? Why have I come to them "in the nick of time"?* . . . More reasons yet to be on his guard . . .

After a while the corridor widened and Jack straightened gratefully. Two submachineguns and a dozen hand grenades hindered his movements in this narrow place. The air grew hotter as they penetrated deeper into the pod — and the odors weren't getting any sweeter. Then he saw doors to left and right and glimpsed terrifying mockeries of human bodies inside dank dormitories bathed in greenish light. They resembled living skeletons — worse by far than the managers who surrounded him. They lay on the ground; they knelt on the floor embracing drums filled with atomic wastes encased in cement; they moved weakly along the walls clinging to the sides of bunks. Some of these miserables moaned. Some were obviously on the point of death.

Jack still labored to bring his own horror under control when Hamster's Shoe turned briefly. Gesturing toward the dreadful charnel rooms, he said: "The fortunates. They don't have long to wait."

The fortunates . . .

Soon they reached a pitch-dark shaft in whose center a circular stairway spiralled up and down, its boundaries marked only by luminous paint smeared on the railings. An updraft brought welcome relief.

They moved up the stairs in single file, presumably toward the managers' floor. Jack had seen a row of windows high up in each pod, small openings, oblong portholes . . .

His guess turned out to be correct. They left the

darkness and entered a circular room illuminated by dull, pale daylight. A moment passed before the furnishings came into focus. Then Jack saw desks. They stood in rows, as in a classroom, Golden Age objects, remarkably preserved. Each desk, astonishingly, had its own telephone. Piles of books and documents adorned each desk. Some desks had baskets. Some baskets still carried barely legible IN and OUT signs.

Jack felt Shoe's eyes and looked at the abbot. He saw an expectant, half anxious expression. He weighed the right reaction rapidly before he spoke.

"Magnificent," he said, embracing everything in a single gesture. "Truly magnificent. A proper office — the fitting office for Plutonium."

Evidently it had been the thing to say. Hamster's Shoe smiled. His eyes began to roll.

"May I look around?"

"Please, please," said Shoe, and once again he bowed.

Between the tiny, oblong windows hung pictures in frames. Jack approached these and saw very faded photographs of the ancient Complex at various stages of its development. They evoked an odd emotion — familiarity and strangeness all in one. Some of these might have hung in his old office long ago; some had served as models for the building of Plutonium.

As he slowly circled the room, he chanced to look out the window and thus saw the western side of Plutonium. Between two pods, beyond the moat, he glimpsed a miniature airport or something very much like it. Part of a runway with whitewashed markings on the dirt, a control tower made of mud and thatch, and a pole with an authentic windsock aswivel at its top . . . all this had to be the imitation airport of some cargo cult. Jack began to understand.

He walked all around the room now, impelled by curiosity, but he saw nothing else unusual. On the eastern side Tovarish directed his people as they set up camp. Toward the north, where the psychotron still had to be, Jack saw nothing but clouds of dust moved by an arbitrary wind.

"Magnificent," he said again, sticking to a sure thing. On his way back to the center of the room, he stopped at a desk and picked up a well-preserved manual in the blue plastic folder of the Department of Energy. The paper inside was leaf-brown, the type illegible.

Meanwhile a bottle had appeared from one of the desks or file cabinets arranged on one side of the room. Hamster's Shoe held it, and Jack saw that the liquor, like much else in this curious room, came from the Golden Age. Bowing again, Shoe handed this treasure to Jack — a virginal, unopened fifth of "Old Granddad" bourbon.

"Welcome yet again, Magic Jack."

Jack took the bottle. Gladly. He needed a stiff drink just now. A single twist removed the cap. He tilted the bottle and took a healthy swig. The liquor burned, evoking memories. He passed the bottle on.

As each plutojack sampled the whiskey, Jack pondered his next move. He felt uneasy despite his weapons. As Godbod's special emissary, he had to know his mission, after all, but all he wanted was control, unquestioning obedience. In all his planning up to now he had assumed nothing like this . . . this sham culture, these courtesies, this hierarchy. He had assumed that all the plutojacks would be like Cappy. Soon these men — they *looked* like Cappy but seemed a lot more sophisticated — would ask him to explain his embassy. Then what . . . ? He decided to wait. He would let old Charlie take the lead.

The bottle made three rounds before it emptied. A warm glow spread over Jack's chest. He leaned against the circular railing in the center of the room and watched the silent drinking.

The monks peered at him shyly from time to time. They were evidently still under the sway of Jack's odd sermon. What did they see in Jack? The fulfillment of some prophesy? What prophesy? Did they believe like certain of the restorationists that a few men of the Golden Age had escaped the Holocaustic War in airships and still lived on the moon? A safe hypothesis . . .

When the bottle was done, the managers scattered around the room. Each sat down. Each placed his feet up on the right corner of his desk — a ritual posture, obviously, no doubt copied from a photograph.

Shoe also went behind a desk, but he remained on his feet. "Magic Jack," he said and bowed, "I will tell you now why we have called you, but before I do, we have a question, asked in all respect." He bowed. "The question is this: Why did we have to wait so long?"

Jack saw Shoe's glance toward the telephone. *Their hot-line to Heaven,* it came to him, *their version of the prayer wheel!* He bowed toward Hamster's Shoe.

"You must know, Hamster's Shoe, that the dust interferes with communications. We heard you less than a year ago, and then only very faintly. It's a very long trip."

Shoe bowed in acknowledgement. "A second question, sir. We built appropriate . . . " Shoe seemed to be searching for a word. " . . . facilities for you. Yet you came by caravan . . . "

Facilities . . . The word had come with difficulty and had been mispronounced.

"My ship couldn't land here," Jack said. "You will recall a hurricane of several days ago . . . "

"Ah," Shoe said. "The hurricane." And he bowed again. "A final question, Magic Jack. This morning, before the prophet spoke, you . . . sir, you caused great confusion and pain to us. No disrespect, Magic Jack, but . . . "

"But why did I do it?"

Hamster's Shoe bowed.

"There are great mysteries that you have forgotten,"

Jack said. "You have forgotten all about your past, but I remember each of you. From the Golden Age."

Several of the managers barked. Shoe looked frightened.

"You have served Godbod since the Golden Age," Jack said. "You have passed from body to body through the psychotron, and I — "

Jack didn't finish. Loud barking drowned out his voice. The brothers' heads flew back in epileptic jerks. They wrung their hands compulsively — left hand attacked the right; right tore and gouged the left. The maniacal behaviour continued in diminishing pulses until the assembly settled again.

Trembling oddly, Shoe (inevitably) bowed again. "You speak of awful things, Magic Jack. We have sinned, but our sins are in the past. We are obedient and vigilant again. We have been punished enough."

Sinned? — How? Punished? — How? Jack decided not to ask. Godbod religion had mysteries he had yet to uncover.

"Tell me why you called for help," he said.

Shoe bowed several times.

"Magic Jack," he said, "when Canoe's Dugout merged with Godbod in perpetual union, and we placed his bones into the caverns, Plutonium had wandered far from the manuals. The employees dressed like ordinary people. The caverns were open day and night. Most managers couldn't even read the holy word — and the ineffable perfume was powerful and sweet."

Barks resounded as if to say "Hear! Hear!"

Shoe went on. "I followed Dugout into this desk. I was as blind as all the rest. I didn't see that we were sinning. Like all the rest, I chased after bliss and had no other thought. It had been like that more or less ever since I came here as an employee."

A scatter of barks.

"Two years passed before it happened. Then one

day, five years ago, fire came into the caverns. It ate right through the walls. Smoke and water rose up and filled the pods. Many brothers joined with Godbod that day, and the volcano claimed two caverns."

"Under us?" Jack asked.

"Under us. Magic Jack, the times then turned against us. The fire has been rising ever since; every year it swallows more of our Godbod. Only two caverns are still left. Most of our Godbod's gone. We've moved what we could, but the sweetest stuff we cannot budge, and it's so hot down there that we can't worship any more. Union escapes us. Most of us are growing old. The perfume is fading fast. Another year and we won't have any left — all swallowed by the fire."

The brothers, like a chorus, reacted to this dirge with barks of woe.

"We have worked hard to bring back the old piety," Hamster's Shoe continued, "and I think that we have paid for the carelessness of our past. Yet the fire rises. We don't know what to do. That's why we called and called and called. For three years now we have been calling, Magic Jack, without an answer. We had almost lost all hope. And then, last night, we felt Its sweetness wafting on the air."

Tumultuous barking.

Hamster's Shoe, evidently finished, sat down behind his desk. Unlike the others he kept his feet on the floor.

Jack stirred and stood up straight. The liquor was getting to him, or else this screwball scene. Odd feelings choked him up. He inhabited a dream — desks, papers, telephones . . . skeletal emaciated wretches scabbed over with awful sores . . . what diabolical compulsions imprisoned souls in such unlikely vessels . . . how could these men still be alive . . . how could they survive . . . did they have mutated bodies . . . the very scene mocked sanity . . . men calling Heaven through disconnected telephones . . . yet, mysteriously, God had heard them, had sent them a deliverer who would end their miseries.

"Brothers," Jack said, "fellow plutojacks, your troubled times are over. I have many remedies, and the prophet has such power that it will replace all the Godbod that you've lost. We shall begin the work at once. Today you must show me everything. Tomorrow we will start on the holy work. In due time I shall give you a perfume such as you've never smelled before. Take me first to the caverns."

He meant to add, "and then to the psychotron," but he thought it best to broach that subject privately with Hamster's Shoe. He did not want to make the monks sway, bark, and wring their hands again by mentioning Aspic's devilish machine. Indeed — these men had been punished enough for whatever sins they had committed in the present and in many pasts . . .

35.
The Factory

While Jack descended to the bowels of Plutonium, Tovarish endeavored to carry out the orders he had received. Members of his crew, equipped with saws and axes, had departed some time ago bound for the distant forest Jack had pointed out. The camp had been arranged suitably, with vehicles placed in two lines parallel to the moat. A fire had been lit. And the mutants were engaged in rocking Evelyn's van.

Jack's order that the van be rocked made little sense to Tovarish — but he didn't question his master's orders, sure in his mind that Magic Jack had a good enough reason. If Jack wanted the van rocked, it would rock.

Tovarish had placed six mutants on either side of the colorful vehicle. Each mutant held one of the poles which were ordinarily used to support the Show-Biz tent. Using these poles as levers, now one side of the van and now the other was tilted up. Tovarish gave rhythm to this work by booming shouts.

Tovarish stood a goodly distance from the van; all the rest of Fenwick's mutants stood behind him. The rocking motion of the vehicle caused Evelyn to bounce about inside; she produced telepathic emanations nearly as strong as during a magic show. Tovarish had no love for Hip No Tism, and the mutants were even more affected by it than ordinary humans. Those mutants immediately next to the van could carry out the rocking work for a short time only; soon they sank to their knees, the poles drooping in their hands; then Tovarish gave an order, and Co-Cheese, aided by another mutant, ran forward to drag the collapsed rocker back. Another mutant would take his place. Tovarish had to cuff and kick the creatures to make them move forward.

This went on for nearly two sweaty hours before Jack ducked out of the oval opening through which he had disappeared some time ago. He crossed the drawbridge, gestured toward Hamster's Shoe and another monk who came behind him; then he went off toward his caravan.

Jack walked to the end of his camp, toward the sound of Tovarish's shouting. He stopped beside Tovarish and watched the operation for a moment. Tovarish saw him and stopped his calls.

"All right," Jack said. "Let them rest a little."

Tovarish yelled appropriate orders, and the mutants scrambled away from the van with evident relief. As they retreated, Jack advanced. He entered the zone of Evelyn's telepathics. He tried to sense Evelyn's state of mind and to deduce Fenwick's from the former. Before he even reached the van, Jack knew that Fenwick had not been awakened by the flood of Evelyn's emanations. In a fit of sudden anger, he pounded the van wall forcefully with a balled fist. "Teddy Aspic," he cried, knowing it was useless, "do you hear me? Do you understand? If so, say so. Then I'll let you out of there. And only then, you bastard. Come on, speak up."

The words, spoken in Old Order English, had no effect on Aspic's latter day successor. Jack turned angrily from the van. He told Tovarish to keep the van rocking until he returned again. Jack then rejoined Hamster's Shoe and Shoe's principal assistant, and the three men set off together down the slope. They walked in a northeasterly direction.

It was now late afternoon. The sun struggled against thick layerings of dust overhead — a pale, ghostly, foggy shining. The horizon lay like a black ring around the world. Unpredictable wind gusts moved across the land ahead like giant, invisible fists; dust clouds boiled up under their impact. The psychotron lay somewhere beyond the dust.

Walking in single file behind the monks, Jack saw the economic side of Plutonium now — a few miserable fields ringed by water channels, a few head of cattle, a swarm of wretched-looking mutants in the distance harvesting mutagrain under the eyes of a whip-toting man who didn't seem to be a plutojack. All this to Jack's left. On his right five men worked on a kind of kiln. They melted metal and cast it in crude molds of clay; they minted the short rods that served for money these days. They also looked like hired hands. Plutojacks had time only for worship.

Soon all this would pass away, Jack thought, and it was about time it did. Aspic's idea had been fraudulent. He had looked too far ahead; he had not seen the future as it would really be, an empty and crazy world whose least problem would be nuclear waste.

Down in Plutonium's caverns, Jack had seen the coming of the end. Lava had entered nearly all the articaverns. He had walked up to his ankles in grey dust — a mixture of ashes and bones. All plutojacks were carried to the caverns when their "union" with Godbod approached; recent skeletons had lain amidst hot, boiling vats whose shielding had been removed the better to broadcast Its ineffable perfume. Choking fumes had filled those once bright cavities to such an extent that torches lit outside flickered and sputtered inside for lack of oxygen. It had been hellishly hot in there although, as Hamster's Shoe had put it, "the fire has been sleeping lately — maybe because you were on your way." But Godbod's emissary, as Jack knew, could do nothing to arrest the process under way.

The entire region underwent constant geological change — giving the lie to all those astute planners who had once picked the Shashtuk lands precisely because they appeared so stable geologically. Geology was no more a constant than anything else — unless all this steam and smoke was nothing but some kind of trick by that old Indian up there.

The trip to the psychotron consumed an hour, not because the distance was great but because Shoe led by a circuitous route. They had entered the volcanically active zone again and had to skirt large, ash-covered ponds, fiercely hissing barriers of steam, and rough terrain covered by giant boulders.

Jack knew that they had arrived when he glimpsed huge mounds of ashes up ahead. They resembled dunes. He had seen these piles through spirit eyes each time he had been sucked into the psychotron. Hamster's Shoe and his assistant advanced reluctantly now, and although Jack walked behind them, he saw that they were wringing their hands. The monks clambered up the first layer of ash and stopped. Shoe bowed to Jack, then pointed.

From this raised vantage point, Jack could see the psychotron ahead. It lay deep inside a hole. He left the monks and moved to the lip of this peculiar crater. There stood the familiar, hexagonal building. Baskets turned on its roofs. Jack shivered.

The land had risen around the building so that even the baskets lay below the hole's edge. Dust would have covered this construct decades ago; but that had been prevented. Jack saw grey, thin, mole-like mutants; they worked in a narrow space along the building's sides and on its roof. A monstrously huge stump-walker stood on the roof as supervisor; the stumper wobbled from one side to the other, peering at the mutants; the latter scraped dust into wooden buckets, pulled buckets up to the natural grade of the land on the end of ropes, and built yet more long dunes on the opposite side of the hole.

Puzzled by all this, Jack returned to Hamster's Shoe. "What has happened here?" he asked, hoping for a meaningful reply. "Why are you afraid?"

Shoe wrung his hands. "We can't go near. It's filthy, filthy." He spat to demonstrate his disgust.

Jack had to agree. The place *was* filthy, and in more ways than one; nevertheless, the plutojacks' aversion was illogical: a breeder reactor had to operate beneath the hexagonal structure; else the baskets would have stopped their turning long ago. To find out more, Jack had to take a risk.

"The perfume is fine. Godbod breeds Godbod down below. I can feel it."

Shoe immediately bowed, twice in a row."The perfume is fine, Magic Jack. It's the filthy hum."

Hum? Jack neither felt nor heard a hum. "If you can't go near the place, why don't you let it be covered up? Why have these mutants working?"

Shoe rolled his eyes. "Someday . . . The perfume is fine here, Magic Jack, but we can't approach the place now owing to the hum. But someday . . ."

"That someday will be soon," Jack assured him, sounding resolute, determined. "I know how to stop that hum once and for all, and then this perfume will be yours as well. And the caverns of the psychotron will be your worship halls."

Shoe bowed to signify his deference, agreement, or simply his amazement at Jack's statement. His companion threw back his head and barked.

"Wait for me here," Jack said. "I'll go down and inspect the place."

Shoe kneaded his hands and rolled his eyes. "You know best, Magic Jack, but . . . the hum drives people mad."

"I'll be all right. Wait for me here."

A long ladder gave access to the hole. Jack went down carefully. His submachineguns were in the way. He didn't want to fall and break his neck, not next to this damned construct.

Soft, fluffy ash rose as he jumped off the ladder at the bottom of the hole. He headed for the entrance. Could the mere vibration of Golden Age machinery repell the monks from a spot presumably so rich in that ineffable perfume?

The mutants' families used the building's lobby as their quarters. The odor of bodies met Jack like a wall when he opened the door; he squinted involuntarily in harsh electric light. Muta-chids and Henriettas scurried at the sight of him and tried to hide behind shabby, filthy Old Order furniture.

Jack crossed the room and entered a long, dark, curving corridor. He tried light switches along the way, but here the lights were out or the bulbs had been stripped to light the lobby. He groped forward. Dust covered floors and walls thickly near the lobby but thinned out as he left the point of his entry. He listened intently as he advanced. Machinery hummed somewhere, very faintly, so faintly that he could barely hear it; the monks could hardly object to *that*! What then?

At last he reached a light switch that worked. In harsh light he saw a stairway. He moved on, up the stairs.

Eventually he reached a large, circular room. A column in the center supported the roof; consoles and television screens stood on one side and an odd wall of glass, cut into many, many cubicles rose to his left. Most of the lamps behind the milky ceiling had burned out, and the glass wall lay in relative darkness. Tiny, flickering lights in some of the cubicles caught Jack's attention; he drew nearer. And then he felt a peculiar something . . . a presence, an awareness of profound disgust.

The feeling had a mild and distant character, like the first signs of an impending toothache. But as Jack stopped before one of the cubicles and peered close to see the tiny fire fish behind the glass, his disgust grew to a powerful nausea, and he understood what he was seeing in a flash, with shock! The luminous fiber in that boxed of fused silicate — it was a captured soul. And to that soul Jack's face had the aspect of a giant continent.

Heat passed through Jack, an instant fever. He had yet to eat this day. The liquor he had taken in Plutonium seemed to turn to bile or acid. His breath stank. Sweat tickled his sides.

The hum, he thought. He stood for a moment; then he turned and ran out of the room; he didn't bother to put the lights out, unconcerned with anything except escape. Like a powerful distillate, his years of spirit capture came back to him now in one powerful pulse.

He stumbled down the stairs. He crashed against a door post; he reeled down the corridor bouncing against walls; he tried to move with utmost speed, but his body was disordered and disjointed. Just before he reached the door to the mutant-filled lobby, he had to stop. He vomited against a wall in two, three spasms. Spittle trailed from his mouth. He spat; he wiped his mouth.

With an intense effort at self-control, Jack drew himself together. Appearing as if unaffected by his stay inside the psychotron, he emerged again into the open air. Fluffy ashes dusted under his feet.

He stood for a moment, trying to recover. He saw no one to either left or right, but he felt observed nevertheless. He turned around, looked up, and then he saw the stump-walker up on the roof. The creature had moved to the roof's edge, leaned forward slightly, and was looking at Jack. Jack averted his eyes from the massive mutant's curious gaze. He walked to the ladder, feeling weak in limb. Then, slowly and carefully, he climbed out of the hole.

Hamster's Shoe and his assistant awaited Jack. They peered toward him curiously. Jack guessed that his ordeal would not go unnoticed and decided not to pretend. He nodded several times to Hamster's Shoe.

"It's as you say," he called, approaching. "The hum is terrible." He arrived and stopped. "I have a plan to fix that hum once and for all. I'll tell you about it on the way back. But now, let's get away from here."

He looked back once more and noticed that the stump-walker had moved again. The walker stood-sat and still gazed at Jack.

After they had scrambled off the dunes of ash, Jack turned to Hamster's Shoe. "Those mutants have to go," he said. "I want them out of this valley." Shoe bowed to acknowledge this order.

36.
The Fire Mutant

The caravan moved to the psychotron on the following day; the exercise consumed several hours. It was dark again when the tent had been raised at the new site and Jack, inside the tent, laid a rough drawing on a table. Candles on the corners of the table illuminated the sketch of a huge wooden tower. Tovarish was present; so was Hamster's Shoe in company of a number of "managers."

"This is the Tower of Babel," Jack announced, sure that no one understood what Babel meant; the joke was entirely between Me, Myself, and I.

Jack then explained the sketch; for a number of hours after that, the men discussed the actions needed to carry out the work Jack deemed essential for purifying the psychotron.

Later that evening he approached Evelyn's van once more. It had been placed some distance from the camp itself so that Evelyn's emanations would not interfere with the work. Jack carried a whip. He placed himself the length of a whiplash from the vehicle. Then he began to crack his whip, his feet apart, as during a magic show. He continued until his arm grew numb and he was drenched in sweat. Then, discouraged — he would have been angry if he had not been so tired — he withdrew into his own van. Fenwick had still not awakened.

Fenwick, in fact, was neither awake nor asleep. He lay in a corner of the van, curled up in a fetal posture, in a torpor. Five days had passed since he had been locked into the van during the hurricane. He had eaten nothing in that time. Evelyn ate muta-shoots thrown into the vehicle throught a narrow, high placed slit. A few kernels of muta-grain fell in with the shoots each day. Fenwick gathered and chewed these grains; they gave very little nourishment, and he was badly weakened. Had it not been for a skin of water someone had thrust in to him two days ago, he might have died.

Evelyn's emanations no longer aroused him sexually. Many strange sex acts with the rabbit now lay in his past; the acts had added to his present state of degradation. Evelyn had fought his mad attacks. Her organ had refused his penetration. She had scratched and bitten him; her bites had begun to fester on his neck and shoulders; but at least his lusts had burned themselves out at last.

Evelyn's telepathics continued to work on his mind, and he was almost always in a state of confusion. Images moved in his head in random order. He had lost the distinction between reality and Hip No Tism. The scenes he saw caused strong emotions; in response, his body manufactured hormones; all this activity further strained him.

Tonight he fell asleep at last, dropping into deeper and deeper slumbers the more Evelyn herself relaxed.

He dreamt about food and a little pudgy man who said that his name was Godbod.

Morning brought a period of brief lucidity. Evelyn still slept, the only time when Fenwick was entirely himself. Rest had restored a little of his waning strength. As always when he managed to shake off his confusion, he crawled to the spot where Evelyn's fodder fell into the van. He gathered kernels and chewed the dry, dusty grain. He washed it down with a mouthful of tepid water from his skin. Then he sought out each small crack between the sturdy boards of his prison and tried to orient himself again.

The van had moved; now they were near the psychotron. Fenwick recognized the ash dunes from an earlier visit to this spot. Through one crack he glimpsed parts of the camp — the back of a van and a line strung somewhere. Clothing dried on the line. Silence lay over the camp. Through another crack he saw movement, but it turned out to be a mutant pack moving toward the east. A gigantic stumper rode in the center perched on a donkey's back.

Fenwick crawled across the van toward yet another crack. He paused in the middle; he had heard a sound. Then some heavy object — a club, a spade, a rock — banged harshly against the van. Evelyn awoke in terror, and Fenwick swooned again into a confusion that deepened as the banging continued and intensified.

In such an alternation of confusion and brief periods of lucidity, several days passed. Fenwick grew weaker day by day. At times he was vaguely aware that some sort of structure was being built. Plutojacks filled the camp with noise by day; mutants wove ropes from mounds of wetted mutagrass; the dull hollow sound of logs being handled reached Fenwick; and through one crack he saw the edge of some kind of platform.

At first he felt an interest in all this activity, but later he grew dull and uncaring. Jack continued his terror tactics. No day passed without a series of attacks on Evelyn's peace of mind and hence Fenwick's sanity.

One evening Fenwick lay in a state of near-alertness, and in that state he wondered dully what would happen next. Something was sure to happen. The day had been too still. Magic Jack planned some new horror — not that Fenwick cared. He didn't give a damn; only his diminished body still clung to the hope of escape.

Inevitably, something began to happen. Fenwick knew it first when Evelyn began to spread her cloying Hip No Tism. Then he heard it himself — a hushed, furtive activity outside the van; something rustled; mutants whispered. The sound advanced and soon issued directly through the floor boards. Mutants had crawled under the van and set something in place.

By now Evelyn had begun to emote with strength, and Fenwick had slipped away into unconsciousness. He remained unaware of the smoke that began to pour into the van through every crack until it began to choke him. Fenwick then started up, coughing and gagging. Evelyn's greenish phosphorescence lit the van. Fenwick knew himself in danger now — real danger rather than a vision. He was choking to death; his lungs were bursting. He roused himself to a last, desperate effort to save his life.

Evelyn was at the van's opposite end; she hopped up and down in a peculiar way, and Fenwick immediately understood the reason why. She tried to reach her feeding slit, a source of fresh air.

Starved and weakened though he was, Fenwick found new strength. He stumped through dense smoke and grabbed Evelyn by the neck. Using her as he might have used a tree or a rope, he climbed up on her back. From that precarious position, he threw himself forward and caught the bottom of the slit with a desperate, clawing motion. A wrench, a scramble with feet against the wall, and his mouth had reached the slit.

Evelyn fought to reach the air. She crashed repeatedly against the wall and Fenwick as she hopped high into the air. He held on only because a semblance of paralysis had stiffened his fingers into steel.

Fenwick experienced visions more vividly than ever before, but these were familiar to him already; he paid no attention to them. His body trembled more and more as excruciating pain lamed his arms. He no longer felt his fingers. He gasped for air with a rattling sound, over and over again. Then came another heavy impact from the fear-crazed rabbit, and this time Fenwick's strength gave out; he dropped down into the dense smoke and knew that he would die.

Something then interrupted the continuity of his awareness. He found himself inside a vision, not sure how he had gotten there. The vision differed from the others in one important respect; he was *in* it; he didn't merely *see* it.

He flew through the air, high in the sky, by night. He was a carry crow. A deep, palpable darkness surrounded him, almost a soft darkness. Stars shone in that darkness like diamonds. Yet, despite the darkness, a giant sun blazed ahead of him. The sun had the face of a huge mutant, an ancient, leathery walker. The stump-walker smiled. Fenwick flew toward the burning mutant; he was afraid, but not of the giant. A vast expanse of blood-red Ice lay beneath him. Ice dragons with tremendously long, luminous necks tried to reach and swallow him. The mutant winked an eye, as if to encourage Fenwick, and Fenwick heard words in his head.

"Nonetheless, I promise you. You shall see Old New York."

The words echoed, reverberated, and repeated.

"Nonetheless, I promise you. You shall see Old New York."

Once more the fire mutant winked. Then the vision flipped away as if it had been on a piece of paper.

Fenwick was back again, back in his body, back in the van. But the situation had changed.

He heard the sizzle of water hitting flames. The van door stood open. Evelyn had evidently bolted from the still smokey space. Lights revealed the shape of a man peering in through the opening. He looked like Magic Jack.

"Do you remember, Teddy? Are you awake?"

The voice was Jack's. Fenwick felt like laughing. He wanted to answer his tormentor, but his tongue was so thick that he couldn't make a sound. "Nonetheless," Fenwick wanted to say, "nonetheless, I shall see Old New York." When a beam of light shot out of Jack's hand and searched the van until it found Fenwick slumped against the wall beneath the fodder slit, Fenwich grinned at Magic Jack, sure of his ultimate liberation.

37.
Jehovah's Voice

Babel was finished the following day; it was a crude, massive construct towering up into a dark, leaden sky. Grooved logs held together at the joints by tightly wound mutagrass twine formed the tower. Though it had the coloration of seasoned bone, it looked like the Eiffel Tower just a little the way it rose up from a wide base and tapered toward the tip. Babel stood above the psychotron. It rested on the edge of the crater in whose depths baskets still turned.

Jack stood near the tower's base in the afternoon when three plutojacks high above him lashed the last of the logs in place. Plutojacks assembled all around the crater greeted the event with a cheer. The tower was a minor masterpiece for this day and age. Building it with plutojacks had seemed the most improbable of ventures; building it with plutojacks and on this site had seemed impossible. Nevertheless, the work was done; the difficulties had been overcome. Jack had conquered the abbot's fears and objections with promises of Godbod more abundant; then Hamster's Shoe had done the rest.

So Babel stood. Whitish-yellow against a sooty sky, it exuded an odor of fresh wood. Plutojacks now carried Templar toward the platform. Others already clambered up like the skeletons of monkeys. They carried coils of silvery rope. Soon the hoisting would begin; then everything would be ready for the psychotron's destruction. Even if Templar didn't explode, the weight of the missile alone would crush the damnable machinery. All set. All ready. Yet Jack felt despondent.

He watched the proceedings, but his mind rode in a single groove. He couldn't banish from his thoughts the vision of Fenwick's face as he had seen it the night before in the bright circle of his precious flashlight's beam — a thin, long, wasted face covered with wounds shaped like moons; an expression of madness had marked Fenwick's face, a ghoulish grin, but no trace of Aspic's presence. The tower didn't matter if Fenwick just stayed Fenwick.

Jack didn't wait to see Templar hoisted. He saddled his horse and rode off into the valley to be alone. When he returned late that evening, he had still not lifted his spirits. Without a word to anyone, without so much as a glance at Templar who hung in the tower in a harness of leather, he crawled away into his van.

Inside he lit candles on either side of his mirror and sat down heavily. He looked at himself, momentarily frightened by the dead, mask-like appearance of his ashen face. The last few days had sorely tried him. The roots of his depression lay in his failure to win the battle for Aspic's soul; failure prompted him to seek for causes now.

He spent hours in the van, occasionally muttering to himself. He argued with his many selves; he paced the van from time to time; at one point he went out to urinate; but most of the time he sat. He tried to understand this latest of his lives.

Atlantis had been a good beginning, especially in the Age of Dust. Old Order fires still glimmered in Atlantis waiting only for a favorable wind before they flared up into the "restoration" of which this era never tired of dreaming. Filled with memories of the Golden Age and many remembered skills, Jack might have lead Atlantis into a new age; but he had blown that chance. As for love ... JoAnn the Ursula ... ? He had spoiled that ripening relationship before it could begin.

Since then ...? He had become a perverted madman, a good-for-nothing, a sadistic wanderer, a freakshow impresario. Since joining up with Fenwick, he had lived inside a questionable myth.

Jack pondered these events; he turned, mulled, and observed them. The more he stirred the muck, the more his life as Magic Jack appeared to him like a series of blunders.

Some time after midnight, his mind ran down; he sat before his mirror cold, clear, and almost thoughtless, and his icy contemplation resolved itself into a certainty. Then panic set in. It came to him that despite his memories of other lives, despite his time in Paradise, despite the vast cultural and geological changes that the Holocaustic War had wrought, he had just relived his Jack Clark life all over again with a few small modifications.

"I don't have a karmic mission," he said out loud, addressing his mirror image. "All that stuff about Chief Walk-on-air was just a bunch of crap."

Not long after that thought struck him, he rode out of the camp whipping his pony like a man possessed. He carried only a small sack filled with a few tins of precious Golden Age food. He wanted to get out of this dreadful valley; it had occurred to him forcefully that he had wasted his life and, in a fit of madness lasting better than two years, had brought himself to the point of death for — nothing; for the past. Great shivers passed over him as he rode. It seemed to him that if he didn't rush away — to life, to Atlantis, perhaps to JoAnn the Ursula — the past he had so assiduously cultivated, the ghostly multitude of his recent sins — would reach out and pull him back.

His panic increased when, still quite close to his abandoned camp, he felt the wind rising and heard distant thunder. That goddamned, arbitrary wind began to blow now with peculiar purpose. It drove clouds of dust before it; it tore through the valley in separate thrusts; where it passed steam plumes were swept out of existence.

Two hurricanes in rapid succession in the same region of the world suggested heavenly foul play to Jack; moments before he had abandoned his faith in Chief Walk-on-air's agency on earth, but now he couldn't rid himself of the thought that this storm — its very presence, much less the suddenness with which it had begun — was ominous. Frightened out of his wits, teeth chattering, he tried to assure himself. He argued that Chief Walk-on-air was giving him a send-off. That explained the coming storm and why it came from behind. It pushed him *out*; it didn't try to hold him back. His pony already resisted; Jack lashed it unmercifully and forced it to move forward, snaking between luminous lakes of fire.

He had arrived close to the edge of the Volcano Ring when the storm hit with full force. Thunder and lightning filled the valley with light and sound. The rain came first as driving needles of ice, then in a torrent. He lost control of the animal; it reared up at one point, whinnying in terror, and Jack fell, rolled on steaming ground. He tried to rise, but the wind knocked him down; he ended up in a kneeling position, facing east toward the volcanoes.

Water fell now in such stupendous masses that Jack

could see nothing ahead. In the midst of the shattering electrical discharges and pummelled by the mad-dog wind, he couldn't think clearly. Half-kneeling, half-crouching, he waited for the storm to abate, oblivious to the danger he was in. Torrents of water seeped, trickled, and gurgled down; they collected underground and pressures built down below as water came in contact with lava. Jack couldn't see the jets of steam whistling up sharply all around him to relieve the subterranean pressure. He felt the trembling of the ground, but he thought it was the consequence of thunder.

The volcanoes errupted in unison. Vast plumes of steam, lava, ash, and rock shot out into the air above him; a dreadful sound accompanied this geological event, a rending sound, a roar. Fire filled the sky; it formed a wall in front of him, blocking his way out of this hell. Moments later giant boulders began to fall around him in such numbers that, following an instinctive urge for self-preservation, he crawled backwards as fast as he could move, away from the site of this bombardment.

Later he wandered for hours, disoriented, drenched, and etched by flying dust. His camp was out there in the darkness, but he couldn't see it and had no idea in which direction he should walk. The storm abated finally. Its roar receded. The sky turned brilliant with stars and the impeccable sliver of a waning moon. Jack then looked about. In the far distance he saw an odd reflection. He judged it to be Templar high up in that marvellous Tower of Babel which had somehow withstood the hurricane.

Jack set out toward that gleam. The sun was rising by the time he arrived. He was ready this time to finish what he had begun.

38.
The Execution

Jack walked toward the ashen dunes in the early morning light. He marvelled that the Tower of Babel still stood, had not been toppled. Templar's skin up there caught and reflected the unobstructed sun. For Jack this was just one more piece of evidence that he walked the earth by Chief Walk-on-air's sufferance and, will-ye nill-ye, was the Chief's emissary to Plutonium. Chief Walk-on-air had blocked his path with fire. He had preserved the tower. The bone-white structure stood as if untouched, waiting to release its load.

The storm had dealt more harshly with the balance of the camp, and Jack saw more and more of the damage as he approached. The show tent had been blown away; the wreckage of wagons littered the landscape; his own van still stood, but Evelyn's colorful abode lay on its side.

The people he had left behind him were also

scattered. His crewmen wandered aimlessly amidst the wreckage; they sought their personal belongings. Only Tovarish seemed concerned with ordinary chores; the foreman squatted by a pile of soggy bark and tried to start a fire, but that task had little chance of succeeding this morning. Jack saw no mutants, but the plutojacks were still about. They stood in small clumps, facing west. Jack stopped to look in that direction and saw what drew their gaze. Plutonium had disappeared; the hill where but a day ago the eggshaped pods had stood had turned into a volcano; a thick column of steam rose from the hill, and above it hovered a gigantic canopy of cloud.

Jack advanced into the area, picking his way among huge, oily puddles. He came abreast the first group of plutojacks and saw that these cadaverous men were crying. Huge tears ran down their hollow cheeks. Odd sobs issued from their sunken chests. They mourned Plutonium and had no eyes for Jack. Jack searched for Hamster's Shoe but didn't see the abbot anywhere, and when he asked for the "general manager," the plutojacks either disregarded him or simply shook their heads. At last Jack came upon a clump of managers; he repeated his question.

"Hamster's Shoe is dead," said the youngest of the men. Then he rolled his eyes.

"Dead?"

The monk nodded. "He died during the storm. A rock crushed his skull." The monk gestured. "We've laid him over there."

Dead... Jack recalled a prophecy of many, many years ago. He, Jack, would be the last general manager around here. The end was clearly near; it had to be. Hamster's Shoe had vacated the post that Jack must now assume. But if old Charlie had just died — again — could Jack be far behind?

Jack mounted a dune in front of the plutojacks. The

rising sun was in his eyes, and he saw the brothers imperfectly now, as through a golden haze.

"My friends," he called. Then again, in a louder voice, "My friends... By now you must have learned... Hamster's Shoe is dead. He died during the storm."

The plutojacks rolled their eyes. They already knew; they probably linked the two events — the passing of Plutonium and their leader's perpetual union.

"I share your sadness... I haven't known him long, but Hamster's Shoe had become a friend. He led you ably, brothers. We shall cherish his memory. His calls on the telephone, his tireless calls — they have brought the prophet among you. And the promise of Godbod more abundant. For that alone we shall never forget him; his name shall live so long as there remains a body such as ours, devoted to the everlasting worship of Godbod's ineffable perfume."

Some of the brothers threw back their heads and barked. Tovarish and his crewmen had drawn close; they stood toward the back of this assembly and formed their own distinct clump.

"Hamster's Shoe is dead, my friends; the fire has swept away Plutonium. But remember this. The old must pass away so that the new can be born. You have lost your caverns and your homes, but remember this: a new time awaits you. Godbod cares deeply for Its servants. The tower stands. The hurricane could not destroy it. It is like a finger pointing to the future, a new era. It will be a time of glory for all of us, my friends, but only if we reach out for it boldly; only if we can forget what's past and turn our eyes towards tomorrow."

Jack paused. He couldn't tell whether the brothers were listening or not. "Look behind you," he called to them. "Look up at the prophet. There's your future." A few of the brothers turned around and looked up at

Templar; a few of them barked. "All of us want Godbod. None of us likes the psychotron's hum. Today is Godbod's day. With Its help I will destroy the hum. The prophet will break open, and the purest essence of Godbod will spill out. But I cannot help you unless you help yourselves. Turn around, my friends. Gather around the tower as you were gathered yesterday; then our ceremonies can start."

A circular platform had been built around the psychotron's crater, a kind of stage. The tower's structure rose up from it at an angle. Steps led to the platform from the dune. Jack passed through the mass of the monks and mounted those steps. He stopped in front of an X-shaped cross erected on the stage. Loose leather straps had been fastened to the four extremities of it; they waited for Fenwick's wrists and ankles.

"Brothers," Jack called again. "My friends. Fellow plutojacks. Here is where you should be facing. Here is where you must assemble. Turn around. Turn around and come over here."

He continued in this manner for a few minutes longer. Little by little the plutojacks heeded his cajoling invitations. They came and settled down in tight groups on patches of dry ash; puddles separated them. The rising sun reddened their bony, skeletal faces.

Jack had no idea what you had to say to plunge the brothers into tranceful worship, but one of the managers grasped the situation; he shouted some thing — to Jack it sounded like a bark — and instantly the brothers froze into that peculiar still attitude Jack had now observed for several days.

He left the platform and approached Tovarish. "The mutants. Have they run away? What happened?"

Tovarish shook his head. His clothing was still wet, like everyone else's. Beads of rain gleamed in his bushy red beard.

"It was a madhouse around here, as you know. I didn't see them when the sun rose. I thought they were with you."

"No. Well, it doesn't matter. Let's go and raise up Evelyn's van. And have someone find some rope. I'm taking Fenwick out of there."

Evelyn's van had been toppled during the night in such a manner that it now lay on its door. Jack approached the vehicle with some anxiety, wondering if Fenwick might have escaped; Evelyn's emanations soon reassured him. She was still inside, and if she was, so would he be.

Tovarish and his men arrived a moment later, and the van was soon righted again. Jack no longer had the key. He found a large rock nearby — courtesy of the storm. He held it above his head in both hands and brought it down upon the lock. Evelyn sent out a pulse, causing visions to dance. Jack lifted the rock again. On his third attempt, the lock opened; Jack dropped the rock, and swung open the door. A rank smell issued from within.

"Fenwick," Jack called. "Come on out of there." He listened, heard nothing, and repeated his call. Silence.

Then Jack heard a shuffling sound, and Fenwick appeared in the van's opening, eyes squinting. He looked dreadful. Always a thin man, now he appeared as wasted and emaciated as the plutojacks. His Hell's Angels jacket hung about his body loosely. His golden watches had slipped down his arm and clustered around one of his wrists. Moon-shaped festering wounds disfigured his face and neck. His pants were smeared with blood.

And he was grinning. Jack couldn't tell what the grin signified — be it the idiocy of a mind deranged or the insolent bravado of a man who refused to be cowed by misfortune. The squinting eyes denied Jack access to the real person behind those slits. But Jack knew nonetheless that he still faced Fenwick. Aspic had not been aroused.

"You don't remember anything — do you?" He felt the anger of impotence. Fenwick just grinned. "All right." Jack turned to Tovarish. "Tie his hands. And tie a rope around his neck." He turned to Fenwick, impelled by a sudden inspiration. "You are about to pay a visit — to your own handiwork. Maybe that'll wake you up."

Tovarish moved forward and, taking his cue from Jack's harsh tone, he grabbed Fenwick roughly by an arm, jerked. Fenwick had been weakened to such an extent that his knees buckled when he hit the ground. He fell forward and caught himself on his hands.

Tovarish straddled Fenwick's back. He pulled up on his victim's arms to tie them, and Fenwick fell forward, face against soggy ash.

Jack watched all this in a peculiar state of mind. Evelyn had moved; her lurking, ghostly form hovered in the murk beyond the door, and she broadcast tentative telepathic messages directed at Jack. "Kill *me*," she seemed to say. "Kill *me!*" — as if she could read Jack's intentions toward Fenwick. She managed to conjure up in Jack's awareness scenes of that day in Washington when she had gone to bed with Aspic.

Those were helpful memories just now. Jack wanted to hate Fenwick; but his anger was only partially genuine. He felt pity for the wretch; and pity was the wrong emotion for what Jack now intended.

Tovarish drew Fenwick to his feet. He fashioned a noose, slipped it over Fenwick's neck, and handed the rope to Jack.

"All right, Fenwick," Jack said gruffly; "come along." Then he led Fenwick toward the tower. He felt like a butcher leading a lamb.

Fenwick followed meekly enough, but he didn't think himself a lamb. He had stopped grinning, but inwardly he felt confident despite his bonds, despite his weakness. With every step he took, the rabbit's sickening Hip No Tism receded. The clarity of mind he had gained since the night of the fire grew stronger. He knew that he would be all right. The vision of the fire mutant remained sharp in his memory. Now, walking behind Jack, he peered at the scene around him, already seeking some opportunity to escape.

He saw the wreckage of the camp, many shiny puddles, a mass of plutojacks, the tower.

The tower made an impression. Fenwick had never seen a construct quite like it; his squinting gaze moved up, up, up along the network of lashed logs. He saw the Needle hanging up there, pointing down, and wondered what that might mean.

But Fenwick had no time to ponder that question. They arrived beside the construct. Fenwick saw the psychotron through a screen of logs for a moment, then Jack jerked his rope, Fenwick choked, lost his balance, and fell on his knees.

"See that down there? See those radar dishes? That, good buddy, is your handiwork."

Radar dishes? Fenwick didn't understand the word.

"Nothing will bring you back, will it?" Jack's face was so close to Fenwick's that Fenwick felt the heat of the magician's breath. "Maybe this will," Jack said. He jerked on the rope again and pointed. "Go on. Crawl through there and slide down."

It had been days since Fenwick had last tried to speak. His tongue was thick and his mouth very dry. He gathered spittle and moistened his tongue.

"What is all this?" he croaked hoarsely. "What do you want with me."

"Crawl! *Crawl!*" The rope wrenched; Fenwick became unbalanced and fell to his side. "Son of a bitch!" Jack yelled, sounding beside himself. He disappeared from view. Then Fenwick felt a brutal kick; he lurched forward between two logs, tumbled down a steep slope, and landed face-down in an accumulation of water. He turned, coughing and spitting. He saw Jack descending by way of a ladder, and the thought came to him that Magic Jack was mad, was crazy. It made sense that he should be. All those years living with that awful rabbit...

Now came a series of actions that Fenwick saw as further evidence of Jack's insanity. Jack dragged Fenwick into the building and, once inside, from room to room. In each room he spoke to Fenwick in a language Fenwick couldn't understand. Jack also changed. He grew more and more excited; his face lost its color in proportion to the shining of his eyes; his features grew distorted, as if by pain. Then his body began to bend in the center as if an invisible blade had torn his guts, and at one point he dropped Fenwick's rope and threw up against a wall.

They arrived at last into a humming cavern somewhere deep underground. The air smelled strange, and it was very hot, so hot that Fenwick felt faint. Jack had grown rougher and rougher. Fenwick had fallen several times. Jack had kicked, pushed, and dragged him. They had been up and down a lot of stairs. Fenwick's strength was ebbing; strong doubts assailed him now.

Witch doctors were common in the mountains of Colorado, and Fenwick had heard many stories about their uncanny powers. It had come to him little by little that Jack might be one of these — powerful and yet also demented, capable of sending visions that could fool a man. And this madman took him for another.

Magic Jack is crazy, he thought. And it occurred to him that that vision of the blazing sun might have been a dream...whereas this place...Fenwick had seen all this before many, many times under the sway of Hip No Tism.

Jack faced Fenwick at the moment. He ranted and

raved incomprehensibly; he gestured, pointed, waved his arms. Fenwick swayed uncertainly. Then Jack dropped his arms and seemed to slump. He stood for a moment, then advanced. "Did you understand?" Fenwick understood the question at least. "Answer me, damn you!"

Fenwick felt dizzy — very hot, confused, and dizzy. The room began to turn in a circle.

The rope jerked harshly.

"Look at it. Look at the damn thing and tell me what you called it. Come on, the name of it. Spit it out. Try, damn you. You made it; you should recognize it. *Look at it.*"

Fenwick looked up and squinted past rising blood at a ball of fire turning inside a thing that resembled a huge drinking horn.

"See it? Before the day is over, Fenwick, you'll be in there. That's right. You'll be one of those little flames because you'll be dead. Dead. Little screw-worms will come and bite you. And when they do, remember who it was that told you all this. Remember me. Remember the name — Jack Clark. Jack Clark."

"You're crazy," Fenwick croaked. "You're mad." His ears sang; he swayed. Before he fainted, he heard the magician's crazy laughter.

Tovarish went down into the hole with instructions to drag Fenwick back up and to tie the sweeper to the cross. Jack stood for a moment near the crater's edge; his face was greenish in cast and his hands trembled. Walking uncertainly, he went toward his van to fetch the machette. He left the van door open so that he would have light. The finely honed cutting tool lay beneath his cot; he pulled it out and removed the oily rags he had used to protect its edge. He was about to leave again when a weakness forced him to sit down. The tour through Aspic's devilish construct had worn him out.

Soon it will be over. He calculated the time. He had to give Fenwick at least six hours in the psychotron. Half that time should be sufficient to capture and to load Fenwick's spirit with spirouettes, but Jack wanted to be doubly sure. He had six hours of life left — assuming that Templar was lethal and would explode — and Jack had no doubt that the missile would go. Chief Walk-on-air would settle for no less. He had made his meaning plain to Jack during the night. Jack would not escape this valley except as a ghost.

His mind told him to move, but his body sat as if it had been rooted to the flimsy cot, and Jack realized that he didn't want to do it. He could face his own death, but killing Fenwick was quite another thing. Yet he *had* to do it. He had been given the sign. In an attempt to force himself into action, he retrieved one of his submachineguns from beneath the cot. He had meant to slaughter Fenwick in the manner of a primitive priest, but in the end it would be easier... Still weak in the knees, he walked toward the tower again.

Fenwick already hung on the cross, spread-eagled for the sacrifice. Tovarish squatted by his feet; he fastened one of Fenwick's ankles. He had left the platform by the time Jack arrived and mounted the steps.

Jack stopped in front of Fenwick, one hand at rest on the gun slung by a strap from his shoulder, the other dangling with the machette loosely in his grasp. He forced himself to look at the crucified sweeper. Fenwick stared at him through slits. Fenwick was no longer grinning; he had lost all color; his mouth worked in anticipation of speech. But before he could bring forth whatever it was he meant to say, Jack had turned from him abruptly.

Jack couldn't do it, and in a great perplexity he turned to the brotherhood, feeling very alone. He needed help. *Dammit all,* he thought, *Fenwick looks so damn much like an innocent victim.* He had to have support in this; his was a social act, not a private deed, not something that could be decided just between the three of them — Me, Myself, and I. *One* other person at the least had to be involved and had to *know*. And if that man could not be Aspic, it had to be someone else.

Jack looked out over the plutojacks. "Brothers," he cried to them, "listen to me. Look at the man tied up behind me. He is your enemy." The brothers peered up at Jack and obviously failed to grasp his meaning. Jack tried again. "This man — he is the one who made the psychotron, he is the one who made the filthy hum all of us hate." The plutojacks groaned, but only because Jack mentioned the psychotron. They looked at Fenwick on his mockery of a crucifix beneath that mockery of the Tower of Babel, and their skeletal faces expressed puzzlement. How could this scrawny sweeper have constructed something back in the Golden Age?

Jack tried again. "I know it's hard to understand a thing like this," he cried, "but you must believe me. Long ago, long before any of us were born, in another body, this man..." The words died out. Jack's fists clenched. His eyes jerked about. He simply had to make them understand, but how...? Then he had his answer, and it had come to him because his eyes had passed over Evelyn's distant van. Fenwick had resisted Evelyn's emanations, but all these bony wretches...

"Tovarish," he yelled. He waved an arm vigorously. He crouched down and whispered to his foreman; when Tovarish lumbered off, he rose again.

He waited, swaying back and forth, the machette across his front; he held it in both hands. The sun blazed from the east, rising now. The plutojacks sat; most of them had gone back into a worshipful trance.

Presently Tovarish appeared again from behind Evelyn's van; he led the rabbit by her chain and carried Jack's coiled whip in one hand. Evelyn, of course, was terrified. She saw the whip, the scene was strange, the plutojacks reminded her of an audience, and the platform resembled a stage. She emoted in anticipation of the whipping she thought would come, and her telepathics had an immediate effect upon the monks.

Jack watched that reaction. The brothers stirred out of their trance, those nearest the rabbit first and the others in sequence as Evelyn advanced. Her emanations enfolded more and more plutojacks, and as she moved, they moaned, barked, and wrung their hands.

Tovarish steered a course toward the rear of the assembly. Only a few of the brothers turned to follow Evelyn with their eyes; the rest were much too preoccupied with events proceeding inside them. On the way Tovarish beckoned to the half-wit crewman. The man came forward and took the end of Evelyn's chain. Then Tovarish began the whipping.

Immediately, there was silence; only the whip cracked. Evelyn's chain rattled as she tried to bolt, and the half-wit cursed loudly as he tried to control the animal even as his mind, like that of everyone else, swam in a mad confusion of scenes.

Jack experienced Evelyn's cloying touch but disregarded it. He leaned forward, tense with expectation. His head moved back and forth as he observed the monks. Would *they* awaken? For the moment they sat as if entranced. Many had rolled their eyes to such an extent that only the white of their eyeballs could be seen. A few had swooned or thrown themselves flat on their backs. Tense moments passed as the whip cracked, cracked, cracked; then Evelyn's frantic hops and leaps tore the chain out of the half-wit's hands; Tovarish slumped in confusion or fatigue while the half-wit simply stood and made no attempt to recapture Evelyn.

A few of the plutojacks opened their eyes — here one, there one. Then more and more eyes stared up at Jack, and he knew that he had created a receptive audience. He waited until most of the monks had awakened before he spoke.

"Now you understand me, don't you? Now you know what I was talking about. The psychotron has lost its mystery, hasn't it? Well, friends, let me tell you all about the psychotron and how it came about; and how this man here—" the machette flashed in the sun as Jack pointed at Fenwick "— has caused your sufferings and mine."

An awful awareness stared back at Jack from hundreds of pairs of cold, icy, immortal eyes. He had succeeded in arousing the brothers' memories. They no longer barked or wrung their hands; they merely stared.

"In the beginning," Jack called to them, "there was a consultant named Teddy Aspic..." Then he went on from there, telling the story of the psychotron as he knew it or could reconstruct it.

. . .

Fenwick hung on his cross behind Jack, and terrors passed over his mind. He had lost his certainties; the world had become enchanted. Through squinting lids he saw the plutojacks seated before the tower, and now by some magic incomprehensible to Fenwick, Jack had transformed them all. All of them had Jack's awful eyes, his dreadful, evil, penetrating stare. And from time to time they turned their death-skulls in Fenwick's direction and stared cold hatred at him — as if he had done them untold harm.

He tried to listen to Jack's story. He heard and understood it in snatches. Some words and phrases eluded his comprehension, but Fenwick knew that Jack spoke of the Golden Age and this man Teddy Aspic. He spoke with growing vehemence and volume. Fenwick heard his passions mounting, rising. Jack worked himself into a frenzy, and the brothers were responding; their faces mirrored horror, hatred — and

Fenwick knew that he would die as soon as Jack's long tale was done.

He began to struggle against his bonds, snatching out for hope. Nevertheless, I promise you ... It *had* to be the truth and not some maddening illusion. Fenwick felt a greed for life, life, life. He wanted to live, to roam, to search the earth's face for hidden treasure. He wanted to lope over the endless Ice; he wanted freedom; he wanted the simple joy of motion, of food, drink, and the companionship of men. He didn't want to die for nothing, for some magician's feverish dream!

The bonds held tightly. His wrist grew raw with the effort to escape. His weak body tensed more and more as he heard the end approaching. He heard it in the rising pitch of the magician's voice. Jack's voice rose, trembled, broke. The monks were shouting now, waving their fists. "Kill," they yelled, "kill, kill, kill." The sun blinded with brightness. Carry crows circled. And then it came. Jack whirled around — his face a mask of rage, his mouth wide open. The machette gleamed silver as it flashed through the air.

Fenwick let go. He opened his eyes in animal terror and he screamed; he screamed again; and again. And yet again. He didn't see Jack, he didn't feel a thing. He was beside himself with fear.

Jack stood in front of Fenwick, machette still raised. He had stopped the blade just before it had reached Fenwick's left wrist. He stood stunned. He stared into Fenwick's wide-open and terrified eyes. The scream reverberated ... through the hallways of his mind, the hallways of his mind ... Incongruous though it was, he remembered now a snippet of Golden Age song.

Behind Jack the plutojacks yelled in a ragged, random chorus; they demanded Fenwick's death. Jack could not oblige them. He dropped his machette to the floor and turned. The monks had risen and advanced toward the platform now; they shouted and shook their fists, their skeletal frames tense, crouched, in motion. They resembled a huge pack of coyotes. Angry. Hungry for blood.

"You don't understand," Jack called, but his voice was lost in noise. The plutojacks advanced. "Back," he shouted. "Stay back; don't come any nearer." He ran forward and jabbed the first of several plutojacks clambering up the steps using the barrel of his submachine gun. The monk fell backward and carried several others with him. "Tovarish," Jack yelled, his voice signalling panic, "get me two horses. And you too, you and the others — get ready to ride. See this?" he shouted, now addressing the plutojacks and brandishing his weapon. "You recognize this, don't you? It's a gun and it really works. Don't make me demonstrate it. But any man who interfere will die — and go right back to the psychotron."

The plutojacks understood. They retreated slowly from the platform.

Using his retrieved machette, eyes warily on the plutojacks who, friends and allies moments before, had become the enemy, Jack cut through Fenwick's bonds. "Can you walk?" he asked the sweeper. Fenwick nodded. His eyes had disappeared again into a squint. "Come along, then," Jack said, and he led the way off the platform.

He eased past the plutojacks, observing them vigilantly and pointing his barrel toward them at all times. "Don't follow," Jack called, reaching the edge of the assembly. "Don't any of you try a thing." One of the managers stepped forward. "Back!" Jack yelled.

The monk stood his ground. "Why?" he asked. "Why didn't you finish it. You started it. Why didn't you go through with it?"

"You wouldn't understand."

"Try me," the monk said. "I understand a lot more now than ever before. You're Jack Clark, aren't you?

And you should know me, too. I used to be Ray Pisciotta, of the Perpetual *Gazette*."

Jack didn't answer. He moved on, walking backward. He had no stomach for reminiscing now about all that, about the past, least of all with these skeletons. He had one urge only, an overwhelming urge to disengage, to disengage ...

The plutojacks receded; only their icy gaze lingered over Jack and Fenwick. They emanated a deadly awareness. *Immortals, all of them. I repaid them poorly for their help* ...

Tovarish and the crewmen waited in a cluster holding the reins of saddled ponies. Their eyes were cloudy with puzzlement and expectation. Little wonder. The last few days had been a nightmare of incomprehensible events. Jack stopped before them, suddenly affected. Most of these men had served him for two years, Tovarish from the very start — Tovarish who was a cosmic mate from way back, on his own career of repentance. But Jack had to disengage; it was time to say good-bye.

"We will have to part for a short while," he said. "Something has happened to the brothers, and I don't think we'll be safe here. I want you all to go to Cactus. I'll follow you there. We'll meet again and start all over."

"What about the caravan?" Tovarish asked.

"Never mind the caravan. We'll start a new one."

"And Evelyn?"

"I'll take care of Evelyn. But go on, men. Don't waste time. I'll see you all in Cactus in a couple of weeks."

Tovarish looked up at the tower; Templar gleamed up there, a brightness in the sun. "What about the talking Needle?"

"The Needle stays behind," Jack said. Then he went on, urgently, impatiently. "Move, men. Move. It's dangerous to be here. Get up on those ponies and get the hell *out* of here!" The men complied. "In Cactus," Jack called after them. "I'll see you all in Cactus."

Disengage, he thought.

They were near the wreckage of one of the wagons, and Fenwick knelt next to a shattered barrel. He stuffed himself with salted beef; he chewed in a frenzy; shivers passed over his emaciated frame. Jack also shivered. *Disengage.* He waited until Tovarish and the crewmen had gotten well away. Then he called Fenwick.

Fenwick looked up, squinting, chewing. Morsels of salt and meat clung to his dark, unshaven face.

"We're leaving," Jack said. "Get up on that horse."

Fenwick grabbed another handful of meat. Then he rose and staggered unsteadily toward the nearest of two waiting ponies. He tried to mount the animal, but his full hands and weakness prevented it. Jack moved in; he shoved the sweeper up. Then he took the reins of Fenwick's pony, mounted himself, and rode off in a southerly direction, circling the tower on the side opposite from the one where the icy, immortal skeletons still waited.

Before Jack passed through the first curtain of brilliant steam plumes along his chosen path, he stopped, turned in his saddle, and looked back. The tower; the plutojacks . . . And there was Evelyn. She stood off by herself, a huge, white, furry apparition. She hadn't followed him this time. She knew where she had to stay to meet her death.

39.
The Nest

Days had passed now since Jack had released Fenwick on the other side of the Volcano Ring and the sweeper had rushed off, furiously lashing his pony with a naked hand. Since that time Jack had wandered. Pristine prairie surrounded him now, once more an ocean of swaying, silvery mutagrass. Herds upon herds of heavy, brown-black, antlered cattle formed huge, dusty islands in the dark, gloomy distance. The sun was now behind him, sinking toward the west, a pale lamp in a very dusty sky.

Days had passed — three, four, five. Jack didn't know. He still wandered, trying still to disengage, but he couldn't do it quite. The past haunted him even now. It was not too bad by day, but by night he saw Fenwick's eyes, Fenwick's naked and wide-open eyes, Fenwick's eyes as he had seen them for a moment only on that platform in Plutonium. In that moment he had known the truth about himself, about Fenwick, about his own misguided quest. He had arrested his murderous blow. He had tried to undo it all, but it hadn't worked. Something still clung to him. Something was still not right.

Should he have returned? Should he have gone back to die? Had he dealt fairly with Evelyn? Did he owe the rabbit something that had yet to be repaid? And Templar? Did he owe it to Templar to kill that machine? Would he remain forever in the plutojacks' karmic debt . . . for awakening them to immortality?

I had eyes and I saw not, Jack thought. *I had ears, yet I heard not.*

In the end, though, he had seen and heard the truth. Dr. Mahler's eyes had looked out at him from Fenwick's emaciated face, and beneath the terror of those eyes, Jack had glimpsed the steely glint of Fenwick's immortal spirit. And he had known as in a flash that that spirit would endure no matter what Jack did to capture, torture, or to kill the body in which at present it was housed. And then, holding those naked eyes in his own gaze for the fraction of a second, Jack had known clearly the enormity of his own illusions. All eyes looked like that. Fenwick's eyes, his own eyes, the plutojacks' icy eyes, the eyes of animals and men — they were but windows to a single brilliant light. They refracted, clouded, and obscured that light, but in the end their luminosity came from a single source.

I knew it all along, Jack thought. *I knew it better than any man before me ever knew it. I had been up there; I had come back. I remembered everything I had ever done — crimes and benefactions both. I was no stranger to the Law. And even so I deceived myself.*

He thought about it once again. He had pondered all this now for days — knowledge and will, the power of self-deception, the magnetic pull of self.

I blamed it on Chief Walk-on-air, he thought, recalling his rationalizations. *I made myself God's agent . . .*

as if that Fire up above were partial to one man against another... I wanted vengeance, not the Chief, and by God, I nearly had it. Just in the nick of time...

Jack's pony moved slowly, its head bobbing up and down. Jack listened to the hissing sound of mutagrass moving beneath the breeze. Carry crows noised somewhere up ahead. *Watch and wait*, Jack told himself. That dull unease deep in his guts would disappear sooner or later. Then at last he would know what to do.

As the eastern horizon darkened, Jack saw far off what looked like a column of smoke. He felt a pulse of elation, then a touch of wariness. He was alone in empty prairie, in the center of a badlands. Days ago, disgusted with his past, he had flung his submachine gun into the grass. He was naked and vulnerable now.

Nonetheless he nudged his pony until the animal fell into an easy trot. Smoke meant fire, fire meant people, and Jack needed company now, the nearness and support of others, even if they were total strangers. He longed for the knowledge that he was a member of humanity despite the madness of his recent life and the string of his recent sins.

Nearly an hour passed before he came upon the fire. He couldn't see it, even from close up. The mutagrass reached very high here, and the fire burned behind a rise. He nudged his pony forward, and the beast scrambled up the elevation.

A moment later Jack stopped; sudden fright beat a drum in his throat. Down below him lay a mutant nest, a huge circular expanse of trampled grass and partially cleared land. Twenty or thirty mutants gathered around the fire and, just as frightened now as Jack, scurried in all directions with little screams, flutings and whistles. They disappeared into circular tunnels formed beneath the grass. Only one creature remained by the fire — a stump-walker of huge dimensions, ancient and leathery.

Jack had seen stumpers before but none quite so huge and old as this one — or maybe one. This creature looked faintly familiar. The walker who had looked at Jack from the psychotron's roof . . . ?

The old man sat or stood on thick, elephantine stumps, his upper thighs; they finished in thick, leathery "soles." His torso was huge and powerful and muscles rippled beneath the dirty, open jacket he wore over his chest. His arms hung down, thick as branches. His fists pressed into the nest's flooring, supporting the walker's weight. He looked like a squatting gorilla.

"Come down here," the stumper called. The voice rumbled deeply, as from a volcanic depth. Jack hesitated. He was afraid. "Don't be afraid," the stumper called.

Afraid? Jack felt stung. He got off his pony and clambered down into the nest. No mutant would ever call him a coward.

He had just stepped into the nest when the mutant moved; he wobbled toward Jack with surprising speed and agility. Reaching Jack, he held out a massive hand. "Welcome," he rumbled.

Jack took the hand after a moment's hesitation. He peered down into the old man's face. The face was human and so was the creature — save only for the brutally foreshortened legs, absurdly well-developed arms. The skull was massive. Light blue eyes danced with bright, alert, youthful light and intelligence in a dark, leathery, fissured face. The walker's face had the look of dried-out clay, but his eyes shone with timeless . . . merriment?

The stump-walker now waddled backwards, to the fire. He called out in a loud, leathery voice. Mutants left their tunnels slowly — beemen with bony reticulations in place of nose and mouth, twitching colorfrees, cackling birdfems, and finally, rump first, ready to squirt effluvium at the least notice of danger, a couple of sleek Henriettas with glistening fur.

Once more Jack felt fear. He recognized most of these mutants. They had been part of Fenwick's train, had carried Templar, had rocked Evelyn's van. He saw that they recognized him too. He glanced back toward his pony. The beast stood on the rise, head bent, seeking young muta-shoots.

"Don't be afraid," rumbled the stumper. "Cakes," he ordered. And in a moment a birdfem advanced. She knelt before Jack and held up a plate woven of flat mutagrass strands. Her feathers trembled slightly. Three honey-drenched biscuits lay on the plate.

"Sit down, my friend," the walker said.

Jack sat down; he felt ill at ease and avoided all those staring mutant eyes. He had wanted company, but not *mutant* company! He would eat quickly and be on his way — if they would let him go.

The unleavened biscuits had a dry, dusty taste, but the honey had the mingled flavor of a thousand herbs. It stuck to his fingers. He licked his fingers carefully once the biscuits were done; then he wiped his hands on the pants of his suit.

Now what? He looked up at last and saw the mutant eyes . . . faceted bee-eyes, jerky colorfree eyes, beady birdfem eyes, languid Henrietta eyes. Then he spied Co-Cheese among the rest, and a sense of menace caught him. Co-Cheese grinned. His face was changing colors.

They've poisoned the honey, Jack thought with a rush. He looked down at the ground; he searched his body for signs of pain, drowsiness . . .

Then a very low rumbling sound made Jack look at the walker. The stumper's face had turned into a thousand wrinkles. A vast amusement rocked his massive trunk. The stumper chuckled. His laughter bubbled, higher and higher, until he roared. Then, in a set of motions that were pure gorilla, he pounded his chest. Jack's peripheral vision told him that the others were withdrawing to the outer edge of the nest. He was left alone with the laughing, gurgling walker by the fire.

Abruptly the stumper stopped. His face fell back into its usual folds, but the bright blue eyes, looking at Jack, continued to smile. "Don't you recognize me, Magic Jack?"

Jack stared at the walker. He stared into the dancing, liquid eyes. Then he covered his face. "It can't be," he mumbled. "It's too much."

The stumper started laughing again; he pounded his chest and danced a wobbly dance around the fire.

"But Chief," Jack said finally, looking at the stumper, "how come you're now a mutant?"

"Can't you guess?" The ancient face was grinning. "Divinity is like water. It seeks the lowest places. Ah, Magic Jack — you are as dense as ever. You're a hopeless case. I don't know what to do with you. I coddle you in Paradise, I hold you to my bosom for a century, I burn you clean, I scour your spirit — and no sooner do I drop you down than you're off on your little trip again. And now you ask me why I am a mutant. Dense, dense, dense."

"My trip is over. I let him go." Jack shivered. Was this still some sort of illusion? Was this still part of the myth he had left behind — God as the smelly mutant in a stinking mutant nest . . . "Chief," he said, "why did you let me do it? Why didn't you just stop me?"

Blue eyes peered at Jack across the fire. "You ought to know that. You're powerful, you're free. You are a spirit. You're the master of your own fate."

"But," Jack cried, "you *made* me. You're my creator."

The stumper laughed. He pounded his chest gorilla fashion and danced a little on his stumps.

"Oh, Jack! How dense, how proud, how vain you are. You think that God is here before you, sitting on His stumps? The world is greater than you think, the spiral coils farther than you can imagine. Can you shake hands with a hurricane? Isn't that the question? Can you embrace a mountain? Can you put the ocean in a cup? Can you catch the sun inside a net? The question goes something like that. And the answer is that you can't do any of these things, Magic Jack — you're not *that* magical."

"If you're not God — who are you?"

"I just work here," the stumper cried. His own statement amused him. He fell into a gurgling, chortling laughter. "I just work here," he cried again, laughed again, and pounded his chest.

The mutant's behavior exasperated and humiliated Jack; the old man teased him — and to what end? He waited until the Chief had settled down again.

"Chief," he said, "don't treat me like you did the last time — when I was Clark. Answer my questions. I want to know the truth."

The stumper wobbled to the fire's edge. He planted his fists, leaned forward, and peered at Jack with an obviously mock-serious expression on his ancient features.

"Shoot, pardner," he rumbled.

Jack had to laugh. He couldn't help himself. The mutant made an awfully comic picture.

"Now!" the stumper rumbled. "That's a lot better. A *lot* better. Did you know? You haven't laughed in years. You're bunched up like a living, walking, talking, breathing *cramp!* You're a dreadful creature, Jack. So fanatical, so compulsive, so mean, so intense. How can you live like that? No wonder you drift through nightmares; no wonder you're a mess. Laugh. Let go. To hell with all your questions. *Be* something. Be *joyful.*"

Now the stumper threw his heavy body up into the air. He came to rest on his massive arms. He moved his stumps in a peculiar way. The next moment he began to roll around the fire, turning cartwheels. His laughter rumbled as he moved, head-over-stumps, around and round and round.

The spectacle was not so much funny as grotesque. Nonetheless, Jack was infested. He had to laugh. It was as if the mutant's bubbling, chortling, rumbling, roaring laughter had a physical, tactile quality — as if the laughter entered Jack and caused an irresistible tickling in his stomach. And once Jack had started, he couldn't stop. The laughter was a storm, a flood. It came in shocks, in waves. It shook him as with inner tremors. Tears came. His stomach hurt. He pounded the ground; he could barely breathe . . .

Slowly his laughter subsided. Still chuckling with the residues of mirth, he wiped his eyes, he took a deep breath. His body felt light. Once more he took in breath, exhaled. He felt elated, liberated.

The stumper had stopped his antics. His arms filled with a thick pile of mutaroot, he wobbled to the fire and threw the dark, shiny, resinous fuel on the reddish coals. A crackling sound came first; then the roots took flame. Bright sparks danced up from the flame tips. It had become completely dark.

The Chief settled down across the fire. He smiled at Jack. His eyes were very blue, and sparks danced in their depth.

"So, Magic Jack . . ."

Jack didn't answer. For the moment he had nothing to say. They sat thus in silence, and Jack could not help but remember the ancient past when he had sat, much like this, enjoying the silence, enjoying the peace. Only one thing still nagged him mildly.

"Chief," he said, after a while, "did I do the right thing, back there?"

"In Plutonium?"

"Yes."

"Are you still back there? I thought that that was all behind you now."

"It is," Jack said. "But there is still Templar, Evelyn, and all those plutojacks."

"They're not your business."

"But they *are*," Jack insisted. "If I hadn't killed Dr. Mahler, if I hadn't approved that contract, if I had left the rabbit alone, if I had stayed with JoAnn the Ursula, then those people — "

"Uh, uh, uh . . ." rumbled the Chief, and he waved a finger. "You're starting it again. I just loosened you a little, and now you're tightening again. Let go. Relax. Forget."

"If you say so, Chief . . ." Jack sat for a moment. "If you're not God," he said, "who are you? You never did answer me."

"You can't help scratching, can you?" the stumper said. "What else? Like you, like all the rest of us — I serve . . . Let's call it the Cosmic Flower. Ever unfolding, ever evolving, ever changing, ever blooming, ever fruitful, every youthful, Ancient Beauty."

"But you're *not* like all the rest . . ."

"Oh, pretty much," the mutant said. "A little brighter in the Void, a little lower on earth. But all the same, really — if you compare me to that one out there, the Ancient Mystery."

"So there is one above you."

The stumper chuckled. "'Always. Didn't anybody ever tell you, boy? The world is infinite."

Silence. The flames burned lower now. The outer rind of mutaroot had been consumed; the flames blazed blue, eating the resinous core. Jack heard the mutants moving about. They whispered in tunnels and hollows. They waited for the guest to leave before they could emerge again for the evening meal.

Perhaps I should move on, Jack thought. *The Chief is right. I have nothing more to do here in this region. I did what I did. The rest is up to him — or to that Ancient One he serves.*

But where to go? Back to Atlantis, obviously. Maybe she still waited for him — JoAnn the Ursula. The thought of her warmed him. It seemed possible now. The world seemed ordered once again. Laughter had swept away the past. Chief Walk-on-air had shown himself. Jack felt pardoned and cleansed. He had done the right thing after all. Let go and forget . . .

"Chief," he said, "I think I'll go. I'll go back to Atlantis."

That very moment the night turned into day. The flash lasted but a moment, yet it blinded Jack. He ducked involuntarily. He raised his hands to shield his eyes. *Templar. Son-of-a-bitch!* The plutojacks had dropped the bomb! Then, just before the sound of a tremendous explosion came, followed by a shock wave that carried him away, end to end, flying through the mutagrass, he heard the Chief's rumbling voice.

"You did it, boy. You did it. Good-bye, God bless!" Then came a snatch of rumbled laughter. It was drowned out by the roar of the explosion.

EPILOG
Minstrel and Princess

Many, many years rolled by. Two generations came and went, a third was growing old.

The world had changed. West of the Mississippi and south of the Ice, cultural growth sprouted as the population grew and the climate improved. City states had risen where once villages had smoked. Their leaders fought for caravan business in jealous competition. Where once there had been nothing, prosperous villages now steamed. Water had become abundant. The mutagrass was in retreat, pushed ever back by human cultivation. The sky had lost much of its dust. Days of blue were common. The sun blazed in sharp glory as if the long decades of darkness had intensified its power.

Rumors had it that the longed-for Restoration had begun far in the east. Old New York had risen from the Ice again, and travellers told fantastic tales of buildings reaching to the sky. The people in the West marvelled at these stories, but they were much too busy for anything else. They were building their own life, and life was better now, much better.

. . .

In the spring of a certain year, a young man left his home in the Colorado Rockies. He kissed his mother and embraced his father. He was heading out into the world to make his fortune and to find the princess of his dreams, he said. No one doubted that he would.

His family and the people of his village followed him out, way out, past the final cultivation. Many sobbed and wiped their eyes when at last he walked on by himself, a round hat on his head, a stick over his shoulder, a bundle hanging from his stick.

The village of Boulder had never raised a man as popular, as skilled, as kindly as Jacob Hunt. He was tall and slender with a pair of jet-black, dancing eyes. He could play every instrument and he sang as sweetly as a god. He alone could read and write in Boulder, arts he had taught himself. He had a knack with tools and instruments. He could do sums and reckonings without a beadboard, in his head, fast as lightning. And by nights he entertained the people in Boulder's tavern with his tales.

People said that Jacob Hunt had more imagination in the tip of his little finger than most others had in the head. He invented marvellous stories about the Golden Age, speaking always as if he had lived in that mist-shrouded time. He also had stories about the Age of Dust, strange accounts of magic and of sorcery. He told of souls possessed by love of enchanted rocks, of women who'd been turned into giant rabbits, of mutants who knew the future and the past and turned into crows to fly through the air.

Jacob would be missed. No one thought that he would return. He had the makings of a very rich merchant, a bold explorer, or a minstrel of renown.

Jacob Hunt followed the caravan routes, moving south and east. Once out of the region of his home, he began to call himself Minstrel Jack. He earned his living singing songs, telling tales, and by the reading and writing of letters. He never lacked coin. Young girls fell in love with him by droves, but he escaped them ever and always saying that a certain princess waited for him somewhere. To her he would be true.

Toward the end of spring, in a little town called Bennett, after his singing as he sometimes did about that princess of his dreams, an older man, another traveller, said to him with admiration: "I know just the princess you might be looking for, Jack. She'd be just the right one for you."

"Who's that, who's that?" people asked.

"Zeronica, of course," the traveller said.

People smiled and nodded, hearing the name.

"Who is this Zeronica?" Minstrel Jack wanted to know.

"She's the daughter of One-Eyed Eugene, of Phoenix," the man said.

"Phoenix, did you say?" Jack pushed up his tall, round hat with a ringed index finger. His black eyes gleamed. "Tell more about the sweet Zeronica."

People vied with one another to tell him all they knew.

The only child of One-Eyed Eugene, the president of Phoenix, they said. Beautiful. A kindly person. Loved the people. Much wooed. Suitors came from all over the country, but she refused to marry anyone. ("A true princess," Jack murmured. "Just like in the fairy tale.") She had no time to marry, the people said. She was always working in her schools. Schools? Yes, the people said. They explained the meaning of the word to Minstrel Jack. "Ah," he said. "Schools just like they used to have, back in the Golden Age." Yes, the people said. Then they went on to tell Jack about Zeronica's hospital, a place where the sick were healed and women came to be delivered in their hour. They told Jack about Doc Templeton, the old man Zeronica had found. Blind as a bat. But he could heal people by the touch of a hand. Nothing more. Just the touch of his hand. And he knew the future, too, and told people's fortunes. And because of her — and One-Eyed Eugene who let her have her way — Phoenix was the finest city this side of Old New York.

"Whoa, whoa, whoa," cried the traveller who had introduced this subject in the first place. He held up his hands to command all to silence. He looked at Minstrel Jack. "Phoenix is a nice enough place," he said, "but not everything is perfect. Not everybody likes Zeronica's ways. It takes a lot of metal to pay for those schools and hospitals, for one thing. The merchants have to pay it, and they don't like it. They're not saying anything. Not now. Eugene is old and sick, but they still remember the way he used to rule."

"The whip and the machette," someone said.

"You bet," the traveller said. "And a little fire thrown in for good measure. He still has his army, too. The man who runs it is another Eugene, if you ask me. He still has hopes of marrying Zeronica, but if she persists in refusing, there will be trouble in Phoenix after the old man kicks off."

"Sounds like my kind of tangle," Minstrel Jack murmured under his breath. "My kind of plot." Aloud he said, "Who is this man who wants to marry her? What is his name? Where does he come from?"

The people talked all at once, full of eagerness to inform him.

Henry Cappo was his name. A ruthless soldier. Ambitious. No one knew where he came from. Not true, not true, cried someone. He came from the east. He came from Old New York. That's just a story. No, someone cried, I heard that for a fact. They forced him out of Old New York for murdering his father or the president. I've heard that too, someone else said. It's still just a rumor, a third one cried. Be still, Jim, a fourth said, let a body talk.

"I've met Henry Cappo once," the traveller said. The people subsided. "He is a tough bird, all right. And there may be something to that rumor about Old New York. Cappo talks with a kind of lilt I've never heard in these parts. And he *is* ambitious. He likes to talk about an Empire of the West reaching from Phoenix all the way back to the California badlands."

"You people wouldn't like that very much, would you?" the minstrel asked, looking around.

"No, sir, Minstrel Jack," someone said. "We've never been under anybody's yoke. Bennett ain't no city, but it's all ours now. If Henry Cappo had his way, we'd be paying taxes."

Jack turned to the traveller. "What about Doc Templeton? What does he say about the future. If he tells fortunes, he ought to know."

"Doc Templeton? He says that he sees Phoenix burning. But Phoenix will rise from the ashes."

"Well put," the minstrel said, smiling.

The minstrel came to the edge of Phoenix two or three months later, not a day too soon, not a day too late. He also knew a thing or two about the future even though he'd never told a single fortune.

The city stood up on a hill, a mass of gently domed roofs held in tightly by a high, forbidding, but severely damaged wall. A host encircled Phoenix. Siege-machines stood ready at three points. Part of Phoenix smoldered, sending a thick smoke-column into the sky. Old men, women, and children hid behind parapets and towers on the wall defending the city against attack. Not a day too soon. Phoenix was on the verge of falling.

Minstrel Jack spent part of a night in the company of soldiers guarding one of the approaches to the city. He sang bawdy songs for them and made them laugh. In exchange, they told him what had happened.

Old Man Eugene had died not long ago. Henry Cappo and a portion of his army had been out of the city hunting a group of bandits. Eugene's will and testament had been read before the Senate. The old man had named his daughter as his successor to the presidency in the will. The Senate had thereupon split into two groups — those loyal to Zeronica and those who planned to side with Cappo. The latter gathered portions of the army and rode off to join their chief west of the city. By the time Cappo marched up before the walls, Zeronica had organized defenses. The siege had lasted for a month, now, and it was going against her. The people inside the walls were starving. The end was near.

Jack slipped away late that night. He passed carefully through the host of besiegers and approached the city wall at a sheltered spot. Tossing rocks until he roused one of the exhausted defenders, he called up a message.

"Tell Doc Templeton that Minstrel Jack has come to Phoenix and wants to be lifted up by rope. Tell Templeton that we are friends going back, way back, to Plutonium."

A little later he clambered up by a rope held above him by three men. A whispy, blind old man waited for him down below in the torch-lit circle of a tower room. A child stood near, Templeton's eyes.

"So you have come," Templeton said; he touched Jack with his fingertips, his arms extended.

"Here I am, to the rescue," Jack said. "I see that you're still blind."

They spoke in a tongue incomprehensible to the child and the other citizens of Phoenix present in the room.

"Still blind," Templeton said. "Or blind again. My work is better done in darkness. Some people see better that way. And you? I can feel your presence. You have become much milder, much brighter. You're not the Jack I used to know."

The minstrel laughed. "Not much dross left in my metal," he said. "I'm turning into a mythical figure little by little, inhabiting pure fairy tales. The ugly frog you knew once upon a time awaits only . . . "

"The kiss of a princess," Templeton said.

"Yes. The kiss of a princess. How is she, my Zeronica?"

"Troubled," Templeton said. "Unlike the two of us, she has no sense of the future. And she does not recall the past."

"Perhaps that's just as well," Jack said. "Tell me. Is Henry Cappo who I think he is?"

"Aspic? Fenwick? Yes, he is."

"Does he really come from Old New York?"

"Yes. Fenwick succeeded in those days. Did you know that? He found the city. He dug up a part of it. He died there. He has lived a few life-times there since, in midst of his discovery. Most recently he is one Henry Cappo, a grandee of New York, in exile."

"I had guessed as much," Jack said. "Which way is he headed now? Down again? I mean in the ways of karma."

Templeton sighed. "Poor Henry. Something still drives him. He seems bent on excess. He rides another wave of ambition. He was a mad scientist once upon a time. These days he has become a conqueror."

"They say that you see the future clearly," Jack said. "I see it vaguely. Not much dross left in my metal, but there is still a little too much for clarity. What is likely to happen to our Henry if I should succeed in driving him off?"

Templeton stood for a moment, his blind eyes searching the murk of possibility.

"Europe must be rediscovered," he said at last. "I have a vision of sailships out at sea fighting storms, eastward bound. Henry Cappo might be their admiral. But I can't be sure. You speak of dross. A little dross obscures me too — else I would see with mortal eyes."

They stood for a moment in silence.

"It's good to see you," Jack said at last. "It's a little lonely, living as a demigod. It might be fun to sit and speculate with you about the nature of the world."

"This one or the one to come?" Templeton asked.

"The one to come, of course." Silence. "I'd really like to see her now," Jack said. "Is that possible?"

"She is asleep," Templeton said. "Let's go to the presidential pod. I'll wake her up and try to prepare her a little. Then you can come in and talk to her."

"Will she fall in love with me?"

Templeton smiled. "Maybe yes and maybe no. No prophet should ever presume to predict the movement of the female heart." He turned and held out an arm so that the child who had brought him hither might lead him away again.

. . .

Minstrel Jack entered a chamber some time later to meet Zeronica. Candles burned on stands around the room, their light amplified by mirrors. Doc Templeton sat on a chair, the child, his eyes, close by his elbow.

Zeronica lounged comfortably in an armchair next to a table filled with the implements of her presidential trade — papers, books, maps, and architectural drawings of Phoenix's defenses. She had been roused from sleep and sat enfolded in a long cloth, worn in the fashion of a gown, in lieu of a robe. Regal in her disregard of decorum, she wore no shoes but presented to the minstrel a full view of white calves and small feet — in this day and age a very bold display by someone of her rank.

Jack bowed before her.

She was beautiful rather than pretty, and presently she seemed careworn and fatigued. She faced him with her defenses up, mask upon comely mask, eyes challenging, head straight, chin up, shoulders back, breasts forward.

"Templeton tells me that you are a friend of his and have an urgent request."

Minstrel Jack bowed again. The manners of this age had evolved to the medieval.

"Yes, Zeronica. With your permission, I would like to save the city from its enemies."

She looked at him. Half puzzled, half amused.

"And how would you propose to go about that?"

He smiled back at her, his dark eyes sparkling. "I would walk into Henry Cappo's headquarters and cause him to lift the siege by the magic of my song."

"The magic of your song," she said, eyebrow lifted. "Do you think that song alone will tame Henry Cappo?"

"I can't be sure, Zeronica, but my song has great power."

"Templeton," she said, "is this man serious?"

"He is," Templeton said. "And he may well succeed."

"By song," she said. She mused about that. She looked up at him. "Surely there is some price for such a . . . a magical service. What is the price. It may be too high."

"If all goes well," the minstrel said, "you won't perceive that you are paying anything."

She blushed a fiery red, no doubt because of the way he smiled.

"I assure you," the minstrel hastened to add, "nothing is demanded except what you may yourself ardently desire."

She blushed an even deeper red, and Jack guessed the cause of that embarrassment as well. Something deep within her recognized him. Hidden memories of crimes and pleasures stirred her heart and loins. She was so young and passionate and he stood before her radiantly free and young himself — his glistening eyes and raven hair, his slender form, erect yet deferential, and she experienced contrary emotions: her city under siege; her city smoking from incendiary tar-wrapped, flaming missiles; siege machines erect and ready to pierce her walls; her people starving, decimated by fierce encounters at wall breaches — yet here she sat facing a random stranger who stirred her deeply with a twinkle of his eyes and the mere tilt of his head.

"My wish," the minstrel said, "is merely that you permit me to woo you fairly. And should I find favor in your eyes — to be your consort."

"Consort," she said.

"Nothing more," he said.

"You do not seek the presidency, then — by marriage? As the price for delivering us? By song?" She uttered the last phrase with a scornful intonation.

"I don't want to share your power or your title," he said. "Government is no longer one of my predilections."

"What is?" she asked. "If you become my consort — " she blushed again " — what would be your work?"

"I'd sing and tell my stories," Jack said. "I'd help you to make Phoenix rich and famous. If my voice can banish Henry Cappo, it could also attract to your doors the richest caravans, the most talented men and women of the western world. We would build libraries, protect the search for truth, foster the arts and sciences. Phoenix would soon begin to shine, a veritable western star, a center of restoration, a magnet for all excellence."

"Tell me that I'm dreaming, Templeton," Zeronica said.

"You're dreaming," the old man said.

She smiled. She stirred in the wrap she wore over the simple cotton smock in which she had been sleeping — on a bed the minstrel saw partly revealed by a half-drawn curtain. Her naked toes moved, curled, uncurled — an intimate signal from the new young body her spirit had captured?

"Seriously," she said to Jack. "What do you propose to do?"

"Appoint me your emissary," he said, "and I'll negotiate with Cappo. I'll try to get him to withdraw. If I am successful, I ask only that you permit me to entertain you for an evening with songs and stories of the past."

"Templeton," she said, "what will he do?"

"I don't know, Zeronica," Templeton said, "but I know that Minstrel Jack knows Henry Cappo. There is much between these men. Jack might well succeed."

She peered at the minstrel. Her toes curled, uncurled.

"Have *we* ever met?" she asked.

"Yes and no," he said. "Perhaps I can tell you our stories tomorrow in the evening."

He moved across the littered field of battle under a white flag at misty dawn.

The soldiers made way for him. They formed the borders of an avenue pointed toward a tent where Henry Cappo already waited, one hand at his hip, one booted foot a step out before the other, a hat with a tall feather stuck in its band a-slant across his hair. He was a dark, powerful commander with a short-cropped, black beard.

"Who are you?" he asked harshly as Jack stopped before him. He towered over the slender minstrel. "I don't negotiate with underlings."

"I have full powers," Jack said. "If you will be kind enough to invite me into your tent, I will give you a demonstration."

"Demonstration?" Henry Cappo frowned. "All right," he said, gesturing to his retinue, "let's go on in."

"Pardon me," the minstrel said, "but I must talk to you alone."

"Alone?"

"Alone. It'll be better that way. I must reveal secrets meant for your ears alone." Henry Cappo hesitated. "Surely I'm no threat to you," Jack said. "I'm even willing to give up this." He thrust the shaft of his white flag into the hands of one of Cappo's officers.

"All right," Cappo said. Inside the tent he turned to Jack, his arms folded across his chest. "I know you from somewhere, don't I? What's your name?"

"My name is Minstrel Jack. You've never met me before — not in this life."

"In this life?" Cappo echoed, smiling uneasily. "What's that supposed to mean?"

"It means that we have met before — in other lives, in other times."

"Cut out the mystical crap," Cappo said. "Get to the point."

"I am asking you to lift the siege and leave the territory of Phoenix with all of your men and your dependents."

Cappo laughed. "Just like that? You walk in here..." He laughed again, he shook his head. "What are you? Some kind of clown?"

"I'm just a simple minstrel who asks that you lift the siege."

"Why should I?"

"Because I ask it. And because you're in my debt."

"*Me?* In *your* debt?"

"Yes," Jack said. He looked around in the tent. "Allow me," he said. "I can express myself much better in song."

"Well, I'll be damned," Cappo said, shaking his head. "This is getting better and better. Now he's going to sing to me."

"If you don't mind," Jack said. He stepped to the side and picked up a guitar that lay amidst cushions.

He began to tune the instrument. "I call it the ballad of Talisman's Fenwick," he said. "Listen to the ballad, general; listen to the end." He twanged a string, tightening it bit by bit. "If you still want to conquer Phoenix after my song is done, so be it."

"I'll be damned," Henry Cappo said. "This is the damndest surrender *I've* ever negotiated."

"Just listen," the minstrel said. And he began to pick out chords.

The officers and men outside the tent heard a faint twanging of music from inside the tent. Then a sweetly lilting voice began to sing a strangely wailing, mournful, troubling melody in an odd and foreign tongue, very faintly, very faintly. They looked at one another in some puzzlement. A moment later they heard Cappo cursing. The music stopped. The emissary from the city said something. The song resumed.

Later traditions of the City of Phoenix carried many versions of the events that followed, but all had a common element. By some magic of strings and voice and foreign or goetic words, the slender minstrel threw an enchantment over the doughty general of the besiegers.

One version of the story had it that the rhythm of the strummed strings threw Henry Cappo into a writhing, groaning, foaming fit, his eyes bulging from his head, his nose and ears a-spouting blood. Screaming in terror, he tore through the side of the tent and ran right off the horizon.

According to another version, the music sickened the commander so that he burst from the tent, bent over, vomiting black bile and white frogs. He threw himself across his horse and rode away like one possessed.

Yet another version of the story, the most improbable, claimed that the minstrel's faint, low singing—

the gentle pluck of fingertips on gut — grew louder and louder and louder and more and more and more insistent. The singing filled the tent, spilled from the tent, and rose up to heaven like the wailing of an ice dragon wounded to the death. Louder and louder, harsher, and harsher, sharper and sharper — until the walls of Phoenix itself began to shake and quiver and Zeronica herself, roused from troubled slumbers, rose from her bed and rushed to the wall to see. Then she saw beneath her the besieging army in full flight. Men fled madly in all directions abandoning their gear and weaponry. They ran for their dear lives, hands pressed to ear to hold out that crazy coyote melody, until no one stood about below the walls of Phoenix. Then Minstrel Jack stepped from the commander's tent, his hand about the neck of his guitar. Feet close together, he bowed deeply before Zeronica who stood high above him, flanked by archers, next to a tower athwart the city wall.

It was thus. Or perhaps some other way. The story fades into legend. But be assured of one thing. They lived happily ever after. And after . . . and after . . . and after . . .